"Warm and charming, with a uniquely vulnerable and affecting hero, *This Wandering Heart* moves with insight and grace. Janine Rosche's writing hits all the right notes about family, fidelity, and faith."

—Jo Goodman, *USA Today* bestselling
author of *A Touch of Forever*

"Janine Rosche's debut novel sparkles with romance, reconciliation, and deep emotions. I thoroughly enjoyed traveling to beautiful settings, exploring the ties that bind us to our family, and experiencing the hero and heroine's second chance at love. . . . A delightful beginning for a talented author!"

—Becky Wade, Christy Award–winning
author of *Sweet on You*

"A tender look at how the wounds of the past impact the present. It delves into spiritual aspects of forgiveness, second chances, and refocusing our priorities on a God-centered view instead of a fear-centered view. The dialogue is fun, the growth is sweet, and the hero . . . well, he's just absolutely wonderful. This story is reminiscent of Becky Wade's *My Stubborn Heart,* with a heroine who needs a lot of help, hope, and love to get her sights turned in the right direction. What a fun story."

—Pepper Basham, author of the Mitchell's Crossroads
series and *My Heart Belongs in the Blue Ridge*

"With her emotionally rewarding debut, Janine Rosche sets herself apart as one to watch. Lush imagery, relatable characters, and a spot-on balance of humor and heartache come together to create a romance that speaks to the wanderer in us all—and the part of us that wants nothing more than a place to call home. *This Wandering Heart* is a must-read for anyone who believes love is the greatest adventure of all. Highly recommended!"

—Bethany Turner, award-winning author of *Wooing Cadie McCaffrey* and *Hadley Beckett's Next Dish*

THIS
WANDERING
HEART

JOVE
New York

A JOVE BOOK
Published by Berkley
An imprint of Penguin Random House LLC
penguinrandomhouse.com

Copyright © 2020 by Janine Rosche

A JOVE BOOK, BERKLEY, and the BERKLEY & B colophon
are registered trademarks of Penguin Random House LLC.

ISBN: 9780593100509

First Edition: May 2020

Printed in the United States of America
1 3 5 7 9 10 8 6 4 2

Cover art by Chris Cocozza
Book design by George Towne

*To every person whose eyes instinctively seek
the horizon, whose fingers automatically
trace lines on a map, and whose heart forever
longs to go and to know more: may your
wanderings be weird, wild, and wonderful.*

*To my children: wherever your road leads,
I pray you always recognize home.*

ACKNOWLEDGMENTS

Four years ago, I determined to pen a story that had lived in my hand for far too long. In a move I do not recommend to anyone, I sent that rough first draft to a group of amazingly supportive friends and family. Despite the fact that I didn't know how to string words together or where to place commas, they read that story. Their nudging and kind words paved the way to this novel, so thank you.

From there, Christina Tarabochia took the time to teach me that while conjunctions are not the enemy, steamy kisses that take place in libraries are suspect. Without your magic, I'd still be gerunding, and my career would have stalled at daydreaming in libraries.

Carol Moncado, thank you for your plotting help and constant encouragement. You're truly a gem. Lindsey Brackett, your advice to this new writer has saved me time and again. Deborah Raney, your ACFW critique gave me the courage to tame Robbie and Keira's story into what it is today. Tina Radcliffe, your sweet, uplifting spirit is an example of everything right in this industry. Pepper Basham, a timely coffee with you in Asheville meant the world to me. And your books gave me an education on how to write good-and-not-so-proper kiss scenes (see above: library kisses).

I'd like to thank my writing group, my Quotidians, for your support and friendship. Rejection and success both taste better with you all near. They both also taste like nachos, but I'm not complaining.

To my dear friends, who took the time to read this book on a short deadline to help me bring these characters to life, I appreciate you: Tracey, Shana, and BJ. Thanks to my critique partner, Stephanie, for your time and ideas.

Thank you to my lovely agent, Tamela Hancock Murray, whose friendship and wisdom made this book possible. My team at Berkley and Penguin Random House is a dream, and I appreciate your partnership and expertise. Oh, and I'd like to thank the door to the NYC office that I couldn't figure out how to open; you keep me humble. To my editor, Grace House: thank you for believing in me!

So many people lent their expertise on different subject matters for this book: Cara Putman, Alexa Hirschfeld, Kelsey Anderson, Janette Foreman, Angela Ruth Strong, Megan Logue, and Karen Barnett. Any mistakes that were made were my own!

Thank you to the Toledo Books and Queso Club. Your enthusiasm for my books, romance, and queso dip keeps me going on this journey!

To Riley Callahan, Michael Hosea, Charlie Lionheart, James Alexander Malcolm Mackenzie Fraser, and yes, even you Ty Porter: your fictional heroism is the stuff of legend. You and the authors who created you inspire me. Denise Hunter, Becky Wade, Bethany Turner, Melissa Tagg, Joanne Bischof, Cara Putman, Courtney Walsh, and Susan May Warren, you are all beautiful, kind, and gracious women whom I admire greatly. And to Francine Rivers and Diana Gabaldon: I can never hope to meet you, but you are the reason I write!

Lindsey Allen, thanks for encouraging me to keep speaking and writing when all the rest of the world would love for me to pipe down. I've cherished your friendship, laughter, and fellowship over the years. P.S. Can I have your mom's brownie recipe?

Thank you to my brothers (Bob, Dave, James, Michael, and Daryl) and sisters (Leanne, Raelyn, Kim, Cathy, and Dani) who gave me a love for creating stories in front of the Barbie house, in cardboard box forts, inside homemade haunted houses, and on road trips. Okay, some of those were lies that you told, and I believed because I was the youngest and really gullible. But it still made for fun times. Piranhas in Grandma's lake? That was a good one.

I'd like to thank my kids, William, Braden, Jonathan, and Corynn for putting up with a lost-in-thought mom for years, then cheering loudest when I got my contract. I love you all! To my Jonathan, who is the hardest working kid I've ever known despite the added challenge dyslexia brings to every written word. You are a brilliant builder and a master storyteller. And your honest and kind heart is admirable.

My husband, George, has been the picture of patience, faithfulness, and grace through the years. He has put up with skipped dinners, unfolded laundry, conference bills, research trips, and so much huckleberry—all without complaints. I love you.

To my father, who shared with me his love of traveling, writing, and Montana: I wish you were here to see this. And to my mother, who has carried on for nearly five years without the love of her life, I'm so proud of you for all you've accomplished, and Dad would be proud of you, too. I love you.

Finally, to the God of runaways, wanderers, and the banished: you see me no matter how far away from home I find myself. Thank you for your ever-present love, your all-sufficient grace, and the gift of story. I pray I have been, and continue to be, a good steward of it.

AUTHOR'S NOTE

West Yellowstone, Montana, has kept a piece of my heart since I first visited decades ago. If you live there, I hope you can see my desire to honor your home through my words. While some details have been changed for the purpose of the story line, my prayer is that this series accurately represents the strength, kindness, and beauty that exists down Canyon Street, up Hwy 191, and along the banks of the Madison River. To the people who reside in Jackson Hole, Rapid City, Twin Falls, Lake Tahoe, and Southern California: I'm sure I messed up details of your lovely cities, towns, and landmarks. If I made any mistakes, let me know, and I will gladly come visit to do more research!

CHAPTER ONE

Ever since she was seventeen, Keira Knudsen's internal compass needle had failed to point north. For a high school geography teacher and avid traveler, this little fact was inconvenient at best and infuriating at worst. Today, it was the latter.

"Keira, will you marry me?"

The collective gasp from the crowd whooshed like a breeze rushing up from a canyon floor. One girl let out an "aww." Another squealed. Then it was quiet, save the classical melody wafting from the stringed quartet she'd seen near the pines moments ago.

What was meant to be a simple—and private—dinner had turned into a surprise gathering in the park, where she'd been paraded past half the West Yellowstone, Montana, townsfolk and beneath the picnic shelter. Now this.

Keira glanced down into the deep-brown eyes of the man kneeling before her.

John. Kind, responsible, and loving John. She wanted to say yes. She wanted to cry. That's what the girls in movies do. Clap a hand over their mouths, while their eyes fill with tears. But Keira hadn't cried since she was seven years old. Smiles were only slightly less rare.

John. *Everything you need in a husband.*

Rather than freeing her voice to exclaim *yes*, her father's words seemed to wrap around her throat, strangling every sound.

A murmuring cut through Canon in D. Her lungs captured the breath that had eluded her for at least thirty seconds. A bead of sweat dripped down her chest, darkening her dress. If only John had asked her in private.

The glow from the Edison lights strung overhead nearly blinded her. Only by squinting could she see the crowd around them, frozen. Her parents were closest. Her father met her eyes and nodded once, hard and stern. As always, her mother stood by his side, the light long since faded from her eyes.

Then she saw *him*. Smack-dab in the front row. Robbie Matthews wore blue jeans and a plaid shirt. His head bowed low, so only the top of his backward baseball cap showed. But it was him all right.

Keira's knees threatened to buckle. She placed one hand on John's shoulder to steady herself and wrapped her other arm around her stomach.

Against his chest, Robbie held his sleeping daughter. What was he doing here? He'd never have come if he'd known this would be a proposal. Probably wouldn't have come if he knew this had anything to do with her at all. Sharing a small town wasn't easy, but they'd mostly managed to avoid each other, thanks to Keira's reclusive life. Only three run-ins in five years. Three painful run-ins that had stirred up memories she'd gone to great lengths to smother.

Slowly, he lifted his face. From this distance, she couldn't read those sea-greens of his. Last summer at the Madison River Trout Festival, they'd brimmed with hurt and glinted with anger, as if he had any right to play the victim. Robbie shifted his weight forward, and the butterflies in Keira's stomach may as well have burst through her skin. But then he turned his back on her and parted the crowd, the red curls of his daughter's hair bouncing with each step. Soon, the darkness swallowed him. The only evidence of his presence was the scrape of that old, rusted compass needle across Keira's scarred heart as it followed him into the night.

Robbie Matthews leaned into the fridge, but the cold air couldn't touch the heat he felt in his face and neck. Even undoing another two buttons of his shirt wasn't enough. *It's your fault, bud. You had your chance, and you blew it.*

He perused the shelves for the strongest drink he had. After all, what's a pity party without something hard and cold to pour down a throat? Hmm. Milk, apple juice, or soda? He grabbed the neck of the green two-liter, then spun the top until it clattered onto the wood floor. He sucked down a gulp like a real man. After the 7UP slid past the walnut-sized lump in his throat, he poured the rest down the drain. It was cold but flat as stagnant water. He'd gotten it for Anabelle's upset tummy. When was that? Two weeks ago?

He grabbed a glass and poured himself some milk, then heaped a spoonful of Anabelle's chocolate powder in. Oh, why not? It'd been a long day. He added another and stirred it until it was the color of Keira's hair. Not all of her hair. Just the locks hidden from the sun that spilled from the nape of her neck, down over her shoulders. Unlike the dyed-blond waves on top, the darker, natural ones beneath had always felt like silk. Not that he'd been anywhere near those locks for years. And he'd certainly not had permission to run his fingers through them.

He yanked off his baseball cap and pitched it across the

room, knocking Anabelle's pink hair ribbon organizer onto the floor.

"Great." He set the glass on the coffee table and bent down to pick up the twelve dozen or so rainbow hair ties, sparkly pink nail polish, and Princess Patty Cake eye shadow. Flipping open the lid of the organizer, he caught his reflection in the mirror. When had he gotten so old and weathered?

You are every bit Young Redford. She'd said it a lot in their five years together. And she always kissed him afterward. He looked like Old Redford now, though. Way older than his twenty-seven years. Who did she tell John he looked like? One of those Ken dolls of his sister's that he used to torture? And not the cool Ken dolls, but the ones that looked like they would hang a new-car-scented air freshener in their minivan, all while wearing a pastel tie and Dockers that were two inches too short.

Gravel shuffled beneath shoes on the driveway in front of his cabin, and he froze. Quick, light footsteps climbed the steps, followed by a soft rap on the door.

Robbie jumped up, leaped over the glittery mess of elastics, and yanked open the door without taking a single breath.

Not Keira. Instead, he was met with a mane of wild red hair and a pair of green eyes that matched his own. With all her weight on the heels of her boots, all it would take was a finger poke and his sister, Ryann, would topple backward.

"Hey, Ryann."

"You okay?"

Well, I accidentally crashed my ex-girlfriend's proposal. How do you think I'm doing? What a fool he was, giving in to his curiosity to join the gathering crowd in the park. So what if he recognized half the cars? He hadn't been invited. After the movie let out, he should've taken Anabelle straight home.

"Right as the river." Robbie quirked his smile, to which

Ryann rolled her eyes in true big-sister fashion. Who was he kidding? She knew him too well.

Ryann stared hard at him now. "She said no, Robbie. She turned John's proposal down."

Something sparked within his chest. No? After dating the guy for . . . what? Two years? She said no? Ryann had to be wrong. Theirs was a teasing relationship, even now as adults, but she wouldn't pull this trick.

"She said no. Right there in front of everyone." A hint of hope flashed in her eyes. "I mean, she did it with grace. Lifted him off his knee and whispered in his ear for the longest, most uncomfortable minute in Montana history. Then he turned to us all and thanked us for coming."

Well, that's good, I guess. John Garfield was a nice guy. Principal at the local high school where Keira taught geography. Robbie had never heard an ugly word about him. And from what he'd seen around town, he'd treated Keira like a precious jewel. Almost as good as Robbie had. Which made this turn of events even more surprising. She had no reason to say no.

Unless . . .

"I'm here to babysit. But you may want to button your shirt a bit, Hasselhoff, and maybe wipe off that purple eye shadow."

Robbie jerked a hand to his eyelid. He thought he'd washed off all that gunk Anabelle put on him long before he'd left the house earlier.

"Kidding. But seriously, button the shirt. That's gross."

Any other time he'd love to banter with his sis, but his head felt like a moose had climbed in and made a den. "Whoa, back up. Why are you going to babysit again?"

"So that you can go get Keira. Don't act like you haven't been praying about this ever since you first heard about them dating."

Robbie blocked her entry. "Nah. I think I'll turn in." He tugged at his collar. "Too tired to even button my shirt. Good night." He eased the door closed on his sister's confused face.

No, Keira wouldn't be looking for him. Not after what he'd done to her. He wasn't exactly keen on another go-round with her, either. He'd like to keep his heart in one piece for the time being, even if it had other ideas.

Oh, Keira. If only missing you was the worst of my concerns . . .

He returned to the kitchen counter, where the long business envelope stared at him. Vivian hadn't even had the nerve to use a return address or write her name. But the handwriting was a dead ringer for the signature on Anabelle's birth certificate. As he lifted it closer to the light, the pink ink glittered. *Anabelle Matthews c/o Robbie Matthews.* Care of. Two words had never been truer. Robbie sucked in a shaky breath. What could she possibly have to say? He knifed through the envelope's seal. A sheet of puppy stickers slid out and landed on the Formica. No note. No *I'm sorry.*

He should be happy. After nearly four years with no contact, this was something. And a little girl needed her mother. Even a mother like Vivian.

Still, he couldn't shake the feeling slithering inside him. For Anabelle's sake, he needed to be smart. And that certainly wasn't his strongest trait.

Ping.

Robbie slid his phone out of his back pocket. A notification read: *Kat Wanderfull posted a pic.* Clicking on the box, the Momentso app opened. The square photograph showed a midnight-blue sky dotted with hundreds of stars, some brighter than others.

The caption read:

Just me and a trillion stars #infinite #Prov356 #loneli-
nessisntforthefaintofheart

Robbie typed out a comment as MRCustom. A generic
name, sure. But he'd only joined the app to get ideas on
custom home projects from fellow builders. Plus, he'd never
intended to use it for actual conversations. If he had, he
might've come up with a better profile picture than a stack
of river stones.

MRCUSTOM: Who better to trust with your heart than
the Creator of those stars?

KAT WANDERFULL: @MRCustom, I can always count
on you to say the right thing at the right time.

Robbie stared at her comment and the empty box below
it, begging for a reply.

"Daddy?" Above him, Anabelle, in her pink nightgown,
clung to the railing of the spiral staircase. Her lip quivered,
and tears glistened on her flushed cheeks. "I had a bad
dream."

Robbie raced up the steps. When he reached Anabelle,
he swaddled her in his arms. Her shuddering breaths soaked
through his flannel shirt. "You're safe, Kitty Kat. Daddy's
here." And he always would be.

CHAPTER TWO

"Ladies, let's keep the whispering to a minimum." Keira focused on the big clock on the wall. The school day was nearly over. Then she'd be free. For a couple days, at least.

On Friday afternoons, electricity always hummed beneath Keira's skin. With only two weeks before the end of the school year, that hum buzzed at a higher frequency and included an occasional shock with each thought of her upcoming summer. Wide-open spaces, fresh air, sunshine, and a whole lot of solitude were precisely what she craved.

Especially after this week. She didn't need to ask what the girls were whispering about. The geography teacher turned down the principal's proposal in front of the whole town? Gossip galore.

So far the rumors weren't even original but stolen from some classic teen movies. That she'd only dated him on a bet. That he'd paid her to date him to make him more popular with the students. But her personal favorite? That she was the result of a weird science experiment where Principal Garfield brought a Barbie doll to life.

The truth was way more interesting. Of course, her students would never know it. No one would.

"Ms. Knudsen, they're talking about the way that construction worker looks in jeans. It's offensive to hear girls talking about men in such vulgar ways. May I go see the counselor?" Gabe asked from the back row.

Keira placed a hand on her hip and rocked to the side. "Gabe, you have four minutes until the final bell. Ladies, please remember the school code about respect for others."

Peyton squared her shoulders to her classmate. "You're jealous because no one is talking about the way *you* look in jeans."

"Just 'cause you haven't said anything doesn't mean you haven't noticed, princess." Gabe leaned back in his chair and put his hands behind his head.

Peyton waved him off. "Ms. Knudsen, didn't you, like, almost marry the guy doing the teachers' lounge remodel? Robbie Matthews?"

Keira's throat seized. She turned away from the other gaped-mouth students. Even a swig from her water bottle didn't help. In fact, she nearly choked on it. "Last time I checked, this was Geography class. Not Ancient History."

The classroom's stale warmth was nearly intolerable. Keira lifted her ponytail off her neck. She should have brought the box fan from her apartment to combat this old building's terrible air circulation. Yes, that was the problem. Poor circulation. Not what's-his-face. "Just a reminder that your Wonders of the World paper is due next Friday. Any questions on the rubric?"

Minutes later, when the bell rang, Keira was right on her students' heels out the door. All that stood between her and the open road was grabbing some photocopies for Monday's class. She paused outside the office door.

John's voice carried through the open doorway. He was talking to Sheila, the administrative assistant, about prom details for tomorrow night. Keira and John were supposed to attend together as chaperones before he went and ruined it all by proposing.

She scurried past the doorway. The copy room linked to both the office and the teachers' lounge. Rather than John's moping puppy-dog eyes, she'd risk glares from her fellow teachers, most of whom clearly took his side and questioned her sanity. Could she blame them? John Garfield was a sweetheart, and he deserved to be with someone who thought of him when the nights turned cold.

A gaggle of giggling girls stood outside the door of the teachers' lounge, staring in.

"Excuse me, ladies." Keira sneaked past them. Inside the lounge, she was assaulted with the smell of new construction, a cloud of drywall dust, and the sight of the most handsome man she'd ever kissed. He was standing on a ladder near two sections of drywall that had been mudded together. He wore a plain white T-shirt and jeans. And, well . . . the girls in class hadn't been wrong.

From behind her, the whispering continued, followed by the unmistakable shutter sound of a cell phone camera snapping a picture.

Keira spun to face them. "Have a good weekend." She dismissed them with a nod. Maybe she was wrong, but it sounded as if one of them said, "Get him, Ms. Knudsen." Inside, Keira's nerves were dancing beneath her skin. Outside, she smoothed her ponytail between her thumb and forefinger.

Robbie stared straight ahead at the drywall seam, but his arms, tanned and muscular, paused.

Keira hurried to the copy room and pulled a sealed manila envelope with the print order tab taped to it from her mailbox. After shoving it into her satchel, careful not to crush her road atlas, she steeled herself. She owed him nothing. Not a glance. Not a word. Ancient history, like she'd explained earlier. After she stepped around the door-frame, she met his eyes, and suddenly every thought melted like butter on hotcakes.

Robbie, still atop the ladder, had turned sideways. His steady gaze held hers. She could count the number of times they'd shared a look since their breakup five years before. This was why. Those eyes of his didn't speak pain—they preached a whole sermon on the subject. "Keira." The sound of his voice snaked inside her and coiled around her backbone. Unwelcome, but not unpleasant.

"Hey, Robbie." Her own voice was sharp, her attempt at sounding casual failing. Sickened by the effect he still had on her, she clenched her fist around the strap on her satchel. Had she not matured at all since he'd first spoken to her in that hallway so long ago? Yes, he was still good-looking—maybe even more so. She'd seen him around town, too, and he clearly hadn't lost his charm. Only last month, he'd been flirting with the new waitress at Ollie's right next to the table she shared with John.

Silly John. Why did he have to hire *this* man to do *this* job? "I heard you'd been contracted to do the remodel. Couldn't you have waited a couple more weeks until summer?"

"I had some time, so I thought I'd get started. Plus, I've got plans this summer."

"Kind of inconvenient for the teachers, isn't it? Doesn't seem too smart." Her own words tasted bitter. She still knew how to hurt him most easily. Leave it to her to take aim at his biggest insecurity.

He shrugged. "Maybe not. But if it were up to my scheduling, this would've been done last fall." He jerked his head toward the office. "Your boyfriend strung me along for months."

"Yeah, well, not everyone acts on their every impulse." As the hurt rippled across his brow, the sourness in her stomach raged into full-blown nausea. Insecurity #2? Check. She swiveled on her heels then headed to the door, needing to flee. Before she got sick. Before she weakened. Before she apologized. After all, *he'd* betrayed *her*.

"Same old Keira. Dropping grenades and running away before you can see the damage you've done."

She swung around and stomped straight to his ladder, stretching herself to her full height. "What's that mean?"

Robbie grinned. Some guys did all they could to quell a girl's emotions. Not Robbie. He'd always loved getting reactions out of her. Said he loved seeing her come alive. He shook his head. "Nothing. It's over."

"Only for one of us, apparently. I've moved on."

Returning his focus to his work, he picked up a sanding block and scrubbed the plastered seam. "I saw that on Saturday. Why break one heart when you can break them all?"

His words cut straight through. Keira should have fled when she'd had the chance. She should leave now. But no. He didn't get to play the victim.

Keira narrowed her eyes at him and stepped closer. "Didn't your dad teach you to look at someone when you insult them?"

Robbie let the sanding block fall. It hit the floor with a clap, and a cloud of dust mushroomed outward. He descended the ladder, each clanging footstep jolting her heart, yet she stood her ground. The way he loomed over her once his boots hit the tile should have been intimidating. A good nine inches taller, and shoulders as wide as a school bus, he was a force, to be sure. He could snap her like a twig if he wanted. But the only thing equal to his strength was his gentleness. His cologne, bold and oaken, mixed with the dust. It peppered her nose and warmed her like a steamy bath.

In their time apart, his face, now glistening with sweat, had matured nicely, broadening across his jaw. Shallow wrinkles etched the corner of his eyes. His scar, the one he'd earned in a college fight defending her, was barely noticeable on his cheekbone. Auburn hair, usually streaked with tinges of blond, now held a dusting from the plaster. Some strands had fallen over his forehead, catching his eyelashes. Her fingers itched to brush them free. Standing this close to him, it wasn't the only way her flesh was tempted to betray her will.

Based on the way he studied her mouth, she had a feeling he battled the same temptation.

"Like I said, it's over." Robbie stepped past her, lifting his hands in the air so as not to brush against her.

"Afraid I'll bite?" she asked.

He snickered. Bending down, Robbie palmed a thermos and lifted it to his side.

"What's so funny?"

With his shirt, he dusted off the lid, and a sprinkle of particles descended like snow. "Nothing. Nothing at all." He popped open the top and poured a stream of water into his mouth. An endless stream. His Adam's apple bobbed again and again. Yet, she stood, waiting. Always waiting for Robbie Matthews. Wasn't that the story of her life? Enough was enough. With a huff, she stalked toward the door until fingers gripped her wrist, stopping her feet and her breath.

"Keira, wait." Robbie, still holding the thermos in his other hand, wiped a stream of water from his chin on his shoulder, like a little kid. This time, his eyes were wide, vulnerable.

At that moment, her heart quaked and the shell she'd built around it splintered. But a hairline crack. Easily fixable. Like a drywall seam. Tape it, mud it, and sand it down. It'd be good as new. All she had to do was pull away from his grasp.

His hand, covered with mud and dust, contrasted against her silky, periwinkle sleeve. He loosened his grip slightly, exposing her bracelet, which slid down over her wristbone. He thumbed the braided leather cord. Fluorescent light glinted off the silver infinity symbol.

Robbie blinked hard. "Keira, I'm—"

Knock-knock-knock. "Ms. Knudsen, may I see you in my office?"

Tearing her eyes from Robbie's, she found John in the doorway, his jaw set. Even though they hadn't spoken since Saturday's debacle, she'd heard him through the intercom every morning and afternoon.

"Of course." Keira slid her wrist out of Robbie's grip and pretended she couldn't still feel his touch warming her skin. Unwelcome, but not unpleasant.

R obbie moved the ladder to the next seam that needed sanding, this time on the opposite side of the room. After patting the sanding block on his jeans, he pressed it against the dried mud. Up and down, he scrubbed the wall until his bicep burned with the fury of a Yellowstone hot spring.

Why had he accepted this job? It was hard enough to be in this school where he'd constantly been reminded that he couldn't measure up. At least not inside the classroom. Put him on the football field, and he was the hero. More than that, this was where his memories of her began. He pushed even harder against the sanding block until the pressure propelled it out of his grip.

Leaning against the ladder, he caught his breath, which was no easy feat. His lungs struggled to get enough oxygen, and he couldn't blame the dust.

"I miss you, Keira." Through the vent on the ceiling, John Garfield's voice resonated.

Robbie climbed another step and cocked his ear to the sound.

"I miss you, too." Keira didn't sound convincing.

"It was foolish of me—making a scene like that. I shouldn't have put you on the spot. I'm sorry."

From his back pocket, Robbie's phone buzzed. Whoever it was could wait.

"John, please don't apologize. It's just . . . we talked about this. I'm not ready for marriage yet. There's more I want to see, do, explore."

"Yeah, yeah, yeah." His voice took on some gravel. "I get it. I made a mistake—rushing you like that. Guess I figured if the mood was right, you might reconsider."

Silence. Again, Robbie's phone vibrated.

"It's not about the mood." Keira's voice was soft now. Had she moved closer to John? Robbie prayed she hadn't. "It's not even about us. At least I don't think it is. It's me. I want marriage, kids, the whole thing. I do. One day."

A third time, his phone signaled a text. After digging it out of his pocket, he laid it on top of the ladder and opened the text messages.

RYANN: Don't be too late. I have dinner plans.

RYANN: Want me to whip up some mac and cheese for Anabelle's dinner?

RYANN: Btw, I had an interesting conversation with Hallie about you. Someone has a crush. And don't act like you haven't noticed how pretty she is. I've seen you hanging out at Ollie's more often when she's working.

Robbie thumbed a quick response.

ROBBIE: Not my focus. Anabelle's my focus.

RYANN: Think about it. If you aren't going to make a
play for Keira, you should give Hallie a chance. You
deserve to be happy.

He climbed one step higher until his ear was nearly flat
against the grate.

"Could I take you out to dinner tonight?" John's voice
had lost its edge.

"I can't. After what happened Saturday, I went ahead
and scheduled a trip. I need to get away. I'm supposed to hit
the road by five."

"Can't you skip this one?" A pause. "Sorry, I get it."

Stay strong. Don't give in.

"John." The irritation in Keira's tone could be heard
through the vent. "How about Monday instead?"

Ugh. She'd given in.

"It's a date," John said.

Robbie's heart sank three ladder rungs.

"Keira, I love you."

The silence that followed John's words delivered the
sweet taste of satisfaction. It didn't last long, though. Robbie
descended the ladder, feeling sick. He knew the sound of two
people kissing, even when eavesdropping through an air
vent. After cleaning up the area and setting his tools in the
corner, he grabbed his jacket off the chair, his lunch bag, and
his water bottle. Back at it tomorrow, bright and early.

"Robbie?"

He swung around so quickly, he nearly toppled a saw-
horse.

Keira stood outside the doorframe. She peeked back
into the office then padded into the lounge. Her eyes darted
about. "Earlier, about the remodel . . . I wasn't saying you
aren't smart. You know I think you're intelligent and capable and all those things, right?"

Robbie waited until she lifted her eyes to his, then nodded. "I know."

"Good. Not sure I'd get any sleep this weekend if I didn't remind you of that. Probably means nothing to you—"

"It actually means a lot."

She nodded, then she was gone. Again.

Robbie turned off the lights in the lounge and shut the door. Down the empty hallway, he headed past the gymnasium and the display showcasing his glory days. Next to his senior football photo, the front page of the *Gallatin Courant* was framed. The article was titled "West Yellowstone All-Star Makes History." Beneath the title was a black-and-white picture of him after the state championship game. Keira fit perfectly in his arms then, even with his pads on. It was the only high school game of his she'd ever seen. She'd snuck out to watch, and she'd paid dearly for it. Even now, he shuddered at the memory.

Through the double glass doors, Keira and John stood by her car door. She was in John's arms now. Had been for two years. Probably would be for sixty or seventy more.

Robbie rolled his shoulder backward twice, then forward once. But it was no use. That old ache of his tugged at the left side of his chest, beneath the muscle. The one he'd first felt the day she left him without so much as a goodbye.

As he watched them, he slid his phone from his pocket and thumbed a text.

Hey Ry. Can you send me Hallie's number?

CHAPTER THREE

Kat Wanderfull was a great woman. Brave enough to walk straight into a dark cavern. Hopeful enough to set her eyes on the mountaintops. Yet, gentle enough to glide through a field of wildflowers without harming them.

Countless stories had poured in through the years of the inspiration others had found in her adventures. She'd helped women—old and young, abused and ignored—find their voice, their courage, their dreams. It was her gift, this ability to see beauty in places others had merely passed by. The moss growing between cracks in the sidewalk or flowers in the desert. And in the case of red rock canyons and endless oceans, she could see past the grandiose and bring focus to the most basic of miracles—that the same God who made these wonders knit each of us together, intricately, lovingly, and purposefully.

And he didn't intend for us to live as slaves. Not to our pasts. Not to our sins. Not to our fear.

Keira envied her. Perhaps that was why Keira had created Kat Wanderfull in the first place. While she taught others about the great big world, Kat held it in the palm of her hand.

She closed her road atlas, mindful of the hundred colorful bookmarks and spiral coils. She'd already had it rebound once before. Those two days it had been at the print shop had felt as if she'd loaned out her right arm to a toddler with a habit of throwing things in the toilet. Not that she needed the book to know where she was going. The highways were so familiar to her, she sometimes wondered if she hadn't drawn them herself on God's map of the Pacific Northwest. Rather, it was the memories those blue, red, and gray lines stirred that helped her sleep at night. She tucked the atlas carefully into her satchel. The rest of her bags and supplies were already loaded in the 4Runner. This trip down to Jackson Hole, Wyoming, would be an easy one. Which was good, because this week had been tough. This whole year, actually.

Although she loved teaching, deep in her heart she felt God calling her to something else. Keira pulled her laptop nearer, opened the latest e-mail from EndeavHerMore.com, the female-run, female-focused travel website that had been sponsoring her trips for the past three years. Dora, her contact, was like a big sister. She skimmed Dora's words again. *Dear Kat . . .*

The theme song to a new episode of *Traveling Light* caught Keira's attention halfway through the e-mail. She locked her eyes on the television screen as if she hadn't seen the gorgeous montage of old-world architecture, vast beaches, and natural wonders hundreds of times before. After the show's title sequence faded to black, a pair of designer boots appeared, gracefully strolling along a cobblestone street. The Rue des Rosiers? Probably not. The show visited Paris's Le Marais neighborhood in season fourteen, and this episode looked new. Panning upward, the camera displayed the petite form of Margot Jorgensen, still as beautiful today as she'd been on the show's premiere.

Margot splayed out her arms to welcome the viewers. "Today, I am in Europe's second-oldest capital city . . ."

Lisbon. It has to be Lisbon.

"You guessed it," Margot said. "Lisbon, Portugal. Right now, I'm standing on the Rua da Bica de Duarte Belo. With its distinctive multicolored buildings and flower-covered balconies, it's easy to see why this is Lisbon's most photographed street. You can also see that the street isn't exactly flat. But don't worry if you forgot your hiking shoes. You can always hop a ride on one of the classic 1930s yellow trams. Here comes one now!"

John hated Margot's picture-perfect persona. And no matter where the episode was set, he had something to say about the locale that dampened Keira's mood. If he were here, he'd probably knock the cleanliness of the Portuguese café or mention the increasing incidence of crime.

Keira slid open the drawer of the side table and retrieved a stack of tiny, arrow-shaped Post-its. On the top one, she wrote *Lisbon.* The city's name even sounded seductive. She peeled off the note, crossed the room, and placed it on the wall-sized laminated world map. Hundreds of arrows in a rainbow of colors littered it. So many places to see. Too few weekends in a year. She sighed and slinked back to her couch.

Margot's final stop was at a small artisan shop specializing in alpaca-blend textiles. The shopkeeper wrapped a gray-and-white scarf around the host's neck and sent her on her way with a blessing.

Outside, Margot smiled. "My thanks to the city of Lisbon for your delectable food, exhilarating adventure, and warm hospitality. Until next time, I'm Margot Jorgensen, and this is *Traveling Light.* Remember, you've only got so many heartbeats. Use them well." The host climbed aboard a tram, then turned back to the camera and blew a kiss.

The show's tagline rattled around in Keira's brain. Kat

Wanderfull would not waste a single heartbeat. And she would not let anything get in the way of her dreams. Not a needy boyfriend. Not an overbearing father. Not even a handsome man's smile. She moved to shut her laptop, but once again, the words of the e-mail from Dora caught her focus.

Dear Kat, Great news. Constance Fleck reviewed the travel vlog we sent. The Adventure Channel is very interested in you. So interested they've offered to sponsor several of your stops in June. This is big, Kat. You're on your way. Can't wait to say I knew you when!

It was 4:59. Time to go.

After double-checking that the next episode of *Traveling Light* was recording, Keira switched off the television. She packed up her computer and stuffed it in her satchel, next to her atlas. After she grabbed her knit scarf from the coat rack, she stood before the mirror. It took work to wrap the scarf in the Portuguese style, but she eventually secured it. With an approving nod, she said, "Until next time, I'm Kat Wanderfull, and this is *Traveling Light*. You've only got so many heartbeats. Use them well."

CHAPTER FOUR

"Who dared to wake me from my slumber?" The troll snarled when he spoke, and curiously, he had a touch of an English accent, despite being one of those well-known, highly feared Montanan trolls. With his hunched back and dragging leg, he prowled the bank of the Madison River. He came upon a picnic table with two plates. One of them still held a quarter of a sandwich. He sniffed it. "Peanut butter and jelly. Disgusting. I only like peanut butter and unicorn sandwiches!"

A snicker alerted him to the trunk of a towering lodgepole pine. The trunk itself was only ten inches wide. On either side of it, the curls of a child poked out. Beneath that, shoulders donned puffy purple sleeves. Princess Patty Cake. His greatest nemesis.

His stagger turned to a gallop until he neared the tree, spooking the princess from her hiding place. But he was faster and stronger. He scooped her up and carried her to the picnic table. Her struggle, while valiant, was in vain. "Your tickle attack won't work on me, Patty Cake, my dear. I'll only set you free if you answer my questions. First, can you count to ten?"

She recited her numbers one through ten, skipping seven. They'd have to work on that.

"Can you spell your name?"

"A-N-A-B-E-L-L-E."

"What's our phone number?"

She listed the digits.

Hmm. What else does a mighty princess need to know? "What do you do if you get lost in the woods?"

"Find a river. When Trixie the unicorn got lost, Princess Patty Cake found him by the river."

"But in real life, you stay in one spot and let *me* find *you*. You are too brave for your own good."

"That's no fun, Daddy." She pouted.

"You know what is fun? Eating two more bites of your sandwich."

She scrunched her nose.

Robbie mimicked her expression. The sun, when it ducked behind the mountain a few minutes ago, had taken the day's warmth with it. He felt Anabelle's bare arms. Her skin was freezing, signaling that his time as a troll was over for the day. "How about this? As soon as you take two bites, we can start our movie night. I can't wait to see what other terrible ideas that princess is going to put in your head."

Hey, hon. The cowboy at the bar sent this drink over to you." The waitress nodded to the man ten yards away, then set the tall glass of foamy ale on the table next to Keira's laptop.

Handsomeness-in-a-white-Stetson tipped his hat to her, summoning warmth to her cheeks. She nodded her thanks but realized her mistake when he gathered his jacket and drink and stepped in her direction. "Um, please tell him thank you, but I don't drink . . . and that I have a boyfriend."

The waitress retrieved the drink and glanced back at him, which paused his progress toward Keira's table. "You sure? That's a Marlboro Man if I've ever seen one."

"Yes, ma'am." Keira forced her eyes back to her computer screen, only sneaking a quick glance at cowboy-come-lately after he'd returned to the bar. He tossed down some bills, then shrugged into his worn leather jacket and made his way to the front door. The man reached for the handle but stopped, waiting. Finally, he turned back to her, placed his hat over his heart, and bowed.

Keira blinked hard, then focused on her photo-editing program. When she looked up again, he was gone. *Good. Take your alpha maleness elsewhere, buddy. I've got my hands full.*

Her fingers stretched over her mouse pad. With a slight movement, she dragged her cursor to the Momentso icon. After she clicked it, the app's tagline spread across the page's header.

A MOMENT SO _____, IT MUST BE SHARED.

In the blank space after *so*, words appeared and disappeared quickly, one after the other. *Perfect, enchanting, hilarious, hopeful* . . . Below the header, her home page flooded the screen. The grid of recent photographs, all meticulously staged, filtered, and cropped, caused her pride to swell. These new pictures would be gorgeous. Her notifications blazed red. No doubt she had a couple hundred comments on her photos to skim. There was predictability to this game.

Sometimes she wondered if she should've gotten a sociology degree instead of a teaching one. Her strength as a social media influencer was her understanding of people. She knew which category of pictures garnered the most engagement and which hashtags reached the targeted audience. She would get more likes if she posted earlier in the morning when her followers were waiting in line for their skinny vanilla lattes with almond milk. However, a pretty picture posted in the evening with a more thought-provoking caption garnered more comments. There was something about the midnight hour closing in that brought out honesty and vulnerability in her followers. They became real to her.

Keira dipped her fork in the Italian dressing cup, then stabbed the last pieces of lettuce and slice of cucumber, leaving the pile of croutons, shredded cheese, and bacon bits on the salad plate. She chewed the bite and washed it down with her ice water. Still, her belly panged. She pinched a crouton between her fingers and raised it to her mouth. Nah, better not.

The door to the bar swung open. Laughter preceded the woman through the doorway. Cheerful and doe-eyed, the girl looked a few years younger than Keira but close enough that they might be friends. If Keira *had* friends.

A man wearing head-to-toe Patagonia trailed her, their hands locked in the space between them. Keira pictured the girl surrounded by a halo of sunlight, looking back over her shoulder and reaching toward the camera with their handhold in the foreground. That'd be a sweet picture.

The hostess led them to the table in front of Keira.

The girl pulled the beanie off her boyfriend's head and scrubbed his hair. Considering the way he gazed at her, she could probably shave his whole head and tattoo Daffy Duck on it, and he'd still be in love.

"Where are you folks from?" the waitress asked.

"Fort Collins," they answered in unison, then laughed.

"Just passing through?"

"Yep. We're headed up to Yellowstone tomorrow. Glacier after that." The man nodded to his date. "We graduated from Colorado State. Seeing every national park is on her bucket list. She's letting me tag along."

"You're aren't a tagalong." She stroked his hand and gave him an exasperated look.

"Admit it. If I couldn't have come, you'd have made the trek by yourself."

Attagirl. Keira loved to see young women choose a dream and chase after it. After all, it was her whole brand.

"Just because I could do this by myself doesn't mean I want to." She beamed at him.

The laptop screen went black, and Keira hastened to awaken it, nearly knocking over her water in the process.

After the couple placed their order, the woman excused herself to the bathroom. The man watched her disappear, then reached into the front pocket of his backpack. His intake of breath was loud enough for Keira to hear. When his hand reemerged, it held a ring box. With a flick of his thumb, the lid cracked open. The neon lights from the bar turned the stone into a kaleidoscope of color. Even more brilliant was the man's smile.

He caught her staring at the ring. A tilt of the box gave her a better view. "I'm asking her tomorrow at sunrise."

"Congratulations. Where are you planning to do it?"

The man's eyes darted back to the bathroom door. He flipped the lid of the box closed and hid it in his backpack. "I was thinking the Mormon Row barns. Is that a good place?"

"It's gorgeous, but you might not have much privacy. Schwabacher Landing would be nice. You'd have to hike a bit, but it's worth it."

"Really? Thanks!"

The girl practically skipped back to the table. Keira felt a stirring inside. Excitement for them combined with nervousness for the boy preparing to ask the biggest question of his life. Maybe there was a touch of jealousy.

Keira packed up her laptop. Per usual, her meal was on the house. All it took was the promise of a check-in or a flattering picture of either the restaurant, the food, or a drink. She'd already posted an angled shot of the musician on the patio beneath the restaurant's sign. Still, she slipped a note to her waitress, along with a couple of twenty-dollar bills, and nodded to the couple. The waitress winked, then paired the money with a ticket she pulled from her apron pocket.

As Keira slung her bag over her shoulder and stood, the girl checked her phone. She hit her boyfriend's arm. "No way. Guess who checked in at this restaurant an hour ago? Kat Wanderfull!"

"Who?"

"You know, that travel blogger I follow on Momentso. She was *here*. I wonder if she still is."

Keira slinked across the room and out the door before the girl could glimpse her face.

O n her bed, beneath the pile of stuffed animals, Anabelle finally dozed off. It only took fifteen lullabies or so. Robbie brushed a curl off her warm cheek.

Lord, protect her from cold, fear, and harm. Give me wisdom to be a good father. Let me be enough for her.

He slid off her mattress. Careful to avoid the loudest-creaking floorboards, Robbie ducked out of the room and descended the stairs. On his way past the coffee table in the family room, he grabbed the bowl of popcorn and empty chocolate milk cups from his movie night with Anabelle. He washed them out by hand and placed them upside down on the drying rack.

More than ever, his cabin felt cold and empty.

In the movie, Princess Patty Cake didn't have a mother. She seemed to turn out fine. Then again, King Hubert was the smartest man in the land. Every decision he made was wise. Maybe in the sequel, the king would go on a date with a woman—maybe a waitress like Hallie? Maybe he would walk her to the door afterward. Perhaps he would even kiss her. But would he marry her?

Why shouldn't he take a chance on Hallie? She seemed cool. No drama. No history. She was not Keira. And unlike Kat Wanderfull, she was real.

That's it. Time to move on, once and for all. He searched for Hallie's number in his contacts.

"Hello?" she said, in that cheerful way of hers.

"Hey, Hallie? It's Robbie Matthews. My sister gave me your number. I hope that's okay."

She laughed. "It's more than okay. How are you?"

"I'm good. You?"

"I finally saw a bear in the park. Some friends and I went kayaking on Yellowstone Lake, and he was hanging out on the shore like a beach bum. So adorable."

Robbie pulled the phone away from his ear. He wasn't used to loud talkers. "Cool. Hey, I was wondering if you'd like to go on a date with me?" After an enthusiastic yes—did Hallie do *anything* without enthusiasm?—they made plans to go out after he finished the teachers' lounge remodel. For him, it would be a celebration. Proof that he could be in Keira's presence and come out with an in-tact heart.

Then, with a tap of the red circle on his phone, Robbie ended the call and sealed his fate. He was officially dating again. Robbie could certainly imagine hugging and kissing Hallie. She was easy on the eyes, and her breath always smelled like cherries for some reason. He'd been a good kisser once. At least that's what he'd been told. And he liked kissing . . . a lot. But that had fallen off the list of priorities after Anabelle came along. So why wasn't he more excited?

To his right, Anabelle's Fisher-Price globe sat on the bookshelf. He spun the earth on its axis. *Where in the world is Kat Wanderfull tonight?*

On his phone, he pressed the bright-yellow icon with the cursive *M*. A star twinkled new activity by her name. A picture showed a large tent beneath the dark-blue sky of twilight's end. The canvas doors pulled back to reveal a queen-size wrought iron bed under a matching chandelier. Below, a caption read:

Into the great wide open #glamping #JacksonHole

Robbie found her location on the globe quickly. He knew the location well. So close Robbie could practically walk there. He tapped the comment bar and typed out a reply.

MRCUSTOM: Big fan of Tom's?

A few minutes later he lay in his bed, humming the Tom Petty and the Heartbreakers song. It had been the first song of every road trip he and Keira had taken in college. He could still see her feet sticking out the window, propped up on the side mirror. Could still feel her leaning back against his chest and her hair whipping around his face as he drove.

His phone pinged, and a glow surrounded the bedside table. He tilted the screen toward him. The mailbox icon flashed, indicating a new message. He clicked it.

KAT WANDERFULL: The biggest. I know every song, every line.

A green circle shone on her avatar. She was online right now. Waiting for his response? He let the swell of breath fill his lungs and push out every thought of Keira.

MRCUSTOM: In all our conversations, how have we never talked about this before? Let me guess. Your favorite song is "Here Comes My Girl."

KAT WANDERFULL: How'd you know?
MRCUSTOM: Lucky guess. Did you see my message
    earlier?

She sent him a pic. That was a first. She'd never sent one just to him. Plus, this one was more casual. Less staged. Not the kind she'd share as Kat Wanderfull. The photo was taken as she sat on the bed, apparently, facing the footboard. She held a copy of *The Lion, the Witch and the Wardrobe* on her lap. Past that, small, socked feet crossed casually atop the blank. Man, she even had cute feet.

KAT WANDERFULL: I did. And I wholeheartedly
    disagree. Aslan would NOT have been a more
    powerful Christ figure if he were a skunk. No one
    likes skunks. They avoid them. They don't want
    to get sprayed.
MRCUSTOM: But not many liked Jesus, either. They
    avoided him, too. And those who knew him were
    changed because of it. Like they had a new scent to
    them that others didn't like. Just sayin'.
KAT WANDERFULL: But there was also something
    attractive about Jesus. Maybe not in appearance,
    but in spirit. Lions are more attractive than skunks.
MRCUSTOM: We're back to this again? You certainly
    have a type, don't you? The alpha male. Let me
    guess. If you have a boyfriend, I bet he looks like
    John Cena.

Robbie cringed. *Nice one, Robbie. I'm sure that won't creep her out at all.* There was no response.

Three dots appeared to indicate she was typing. That was good.

They disappeared. That was bad.

MRCUSTOM: Sory. I crossed a line.

He cursed.

MRCUSTOM: *Sorry

Nothing. So not only was he a creep, but he also couldn't spell a simple word like *sorry* without waiting for autocorrect to catch his mistakes.

Robbie tossed his phone onto the vacant spot on his bed. He pictured Kat using her slender fingers to block him from contacting her. She'd flip her curls over her shoulder, then rub her hands over her makeup-free face with the perfect naturally pink lips and sparkling eyes. Not that he'd ever seen her face. Her pics—at least the ones that showed her—were always distant and partial or masked somehow. As if she was hiding something. What he could see from pictures was she was slim, with long blond hair that either curled down her back, twisted into an updo-thing, or was braided. She had a bohemian style of dress most of the time. Flowing blouses and long skirts that gave her pictures a dreamy quality.

She reminded him of Keira . . .

Except Keira was a high school teacher. She didn't have the money to travel. And most of the time when Kat checked in at Niagara Falls, the Everglades, or Mesa Verde, Keira was stuck in her classroom. Lastly, unless she'd finally grown into the nickname he'd given her, Keira was way too timid to travel by herself the way Kat did.

Still, sometimes he pictured Keira's face on Kat Wanderfull. The face he'd first fallen in love with at seventeen years old, free of the makeup she caked on now. He sunk his head in his pillow and pressed the heels of his hands into his eye sockets.

Ping.
Robbie sighed in relief and found his phone in the sheets.

KAT WANDERFULL: It's okay. My boyfriend is a great
    man. Just not necessarily like Aslan. Speaking of, I
    owe him a call. I should go.

There it was. She had a boyfriend. A great man, huh?
Robbie hoped so. If Kat Wanderfull had to be with someone, he thanked God it was with someone full of integrity
and goodness. Like John Garfield.
Another chime interrupted his thoughts.

KAT WANDERFULL: Oh, btw, I'm reading *Of Mice and
    Men* next. I'm curious to hear your thoughts on
    that one.

He considered a response. *How about a comic book instead? Or the instruction manual for a new power tool?* He
could handle that. Not these old books, though. He could
hardly read them in school when he had help. His thumbs
tapped a response.
A fool. That's what he was, agreeing to read yet another
book this woman—this stranger—presented to him. And for
what? To send her back to her boyfriend after a message or two?
Robbie set his phone on his nightstand. He was tired.
Almost too tired to pray, but he did anyway.
*Lord, thank you for keeping my Anabelle safe today.
Thanks for your grace and forgiveness when I do stupid
stuff. And God, one day, if it's your will and all, could you
make me into one of those great men?*

CHAPTER FIVE

※

For Keira, each school day toward the end of May dragged slower than a spoon through cafeteria mashed potatoes. The week and a half since she'd returned from Jackson Hole had felt like a lifetime, but this sun-drenched late afternoon was proof. Summer was near.

While an old George Strait tune played over its speakers, Keira's SUV rounded a bend. She drew in a lengthy breath. In college, Robbie used to joke that the Madison River had a unique scent to it. A mixture of pine, huckleberry, and all-American male. Even now, her lips kicked up into a smile. His plan worked. Whenever she was on this side of town and smelled the river, she thought of him and the many kisses they'd shared along the bank.

Easing her foot on the brake, she slowed her 4Runner. The worn sign for River's Edge Resort straddled white, orange, and purple wildflowers. She turned onto the familiar gravel road. Fourteen rustic cabins of varying sizes stood off to the left. Straight ahead, a red wooden building with a tin roof doubled as a café and fly shop. To the right, the entire Matthews family lived in cabins.

During her college summers, she'd occupied one of the

two small cabins flanking the edge of the property. A newer, more sophisticated cabin split the distance between the family cabins. Robbie couldn't have built that beauty, could he? She had avoided the teachers' lounge lately, so she was unsure of the quality of his work. Was that the cabin he shared with his daughter?

At a loss, she idled the car. In no scenario would she risk knocking on the wrong cabin door. Instead, she put her SUV in park next to the café and cut the engine. After grabbing the book she'd borrowed from Ryann off the dash, she stepped down out of the vehicle. The river, which ran along the south edge of the resort, roared its welcome. Mountains cradled the majestic Madison beneath skies of brilliant blue. This place was the best Montana had to offer.

A quick scan of the property came up fruitless. No one was outside. No campers, either. Rumors around town warned of trouble for the resort. She hoped not. The Matthewses were good people. The kind that treated strangers like friends and friends like family. Her shoes padded softly on the pebbles. As she passed the ice chest, the first notes of a John Mellencamp song wafted past her ears.

Keira peered through the window. What she saw paralyzed her. The café was filled with several members of the Matthews family and then some. Ryann stood by her father's side, her arm playfully draped around his shoulder. The two had always been close. Shirley, Robbie's mom, carried a large casserole dish to the table. Her movement, just as Keira remembered, was accompanied by a smile.

Pink and purple crepe-paper streamers draped across the ceiling, ending in bouquets of matching balloons. Keira's lungs twisted. May 27. This day four years ago had been one of the hardest days of her life. How had she forgotten?

A squeal from inside the café brought her back to the present. Robbie, holding his daughter in his arms, spun into her view. For a moment, she worried she'd be seen, but Robbie only had eyes for his daughter. Slowing the motion, he moved into a two-step. His lips seemed to sing along to the song. Poor girl. Robbie couldn't find the right note if it came with a map and was marked with a big red *X*. But Anabelle looked at her daddy as if he was the greatest singer in all the world.

Suddenly, Robbie stilled, then turned as if somehow alerted to her presence. When his eyes landed on Keira, the glimmer of softness she'd seen in the teachers' lounge was gone. She felt like an elk caught in a wolf's sight. In his arms the little girl wriggled and kicked her legs until he lowered her to the ground. She scampered off to her grandpa.

When he heaved open the door, the bells fixed to the top clanged loud enough to echo in Keira's bones. When he shoved the door closed behind him, the front windows shook. His head remained down until after the bells finally quieted.

An old urge to run reared inside her. Angry men shout. Angry men throw things. Angry men cause pain. She took a step back.

Her movement yanked his chin up. She realized now that she'd been wrong about that look in his eye. Robbie wasn't angry but worried. He wasn't the wolf. She was.

"Why are you here?" he asked.

Keira held out the book. "I wanted to return this to Ryann. I borrowed it last month, and I'm trying to clear things out of my apartment. I didn't mean to interrupt. I forgot it's your daughter's birthday."

The café's door burst open. Anabelle, clinging to the doorknob, nearly tumbled onto the porch. Her giggly squeal was kind of magical. Chuck Matthews followed his granddaughter outside, heading straight for Keira.

"The prodigal daughter returns." As his broad arms wrapped her in a bear hug, the smell of his cigars, faintly sweet, played tricks on her. Suddenly, she was eighteen again and given a shelter over her head. "How are you, darlin'? We sure have missed you around here."

Hello. I'm doing fine. Even simple words lodged in Keira's throat. The more complex words pooled in her stomach. *I've missed you. This feels like home. I'm sorry for leaving.* Of course, the only response she could muster was to embrace her surrogate father back. With the way the Madison River Canyon seemed to spin, she needed to.

Chuck released her. Too soon. But even before she opened her eyes, someone else took his place. She knew immediately from the softness against her breast, the warmth that soaked through her dress and into her skin, and the scent of rose perfume that it was Shirley who held her now. A delicate hand smoothed Keira's hair at the back of her head.

"Sweetheart, welcome home."

The sentiment gentled Keira's soul. The embrace might have lasted only a few seconds or several minutes. Keira didn't know. It was as if the structure of time broke into a thousand pieces at the Matthewses' resort and got washed down river. This was no exception.

"It's good to see you. My, my, you're as pretty as ever," Shirley said. Wrinkles, more than Keira remembered, surrounded the woman's tear-filled eyes. The past few years hadn't exactly been easy on this family. Internally, Keira cringed, knowing she had only added to their pain.

Something wrapped around her leg and giggled. Keira looked down. The mop of red curls tilted back, and a wide, pudgy-faced smile greeted her.

"Hi," Keira choked out.

Chuck de-suctioned Anabelle from Keira's leg and held her in his arms. "Have you met Princess Anabelle of River's Edge?"

The name pierced her heart. *Anabelle.* "Yes. Once." A serendipitous—scratch that . . . an unfortunate run-in at last year's trout festival had brought Robbie and Keira closer than they'd been in years. "She won't remember, though."

"That hug said otherwise. Annie, do you remember Keira?" Chuck asked.

Anabelle nodded sheepishly, pulling closer to his neck. Her hair would be classified as more strawberry than Robbie's auburn. But those pale-green eyes were exactly like his. She looked nothing like the Vivian Keira remembered from college. All Robbie.

She glanced back to where he'd stood. Where had he gone? Guilt twinged her heart. If he was worried about Keira hurting his family, how hard must it have been to watch his mother, his father, and even his child welcome her with open arms? This was his refuge. She'd have been better off mailing the book back to Ryann. "I came to bring Ryann her book. I should go now."

Shirley took a quick inventory of Keira. "You're skinny as a whip, sweetheart. Come inside. We've cooked up a great meal. And we're having a party. You don't want to miss that, do you?"

Heat rose in Keira's cheeks. She grabbed Shirley's hand and looked deep into her eyes. Theirs was a bond not quickly forgotten. Considering the way a tear spilled down Shirley's cheek, Keira guessed she felt the same way. "But Robbie."

Even Shirley's smallest smiles held enough compassion to fill the whole state of Montana twice over. "Don't you worry about him. He's a big boy."

She should leave. Flee far from this place. But she didn't want to. So, in what could only be explained by pure, utter selfishness, Keira allowed Shirley to usher her inside.

The café was timeless with its aged oak and pine. The smell of one hundred years' worth of good meals steamed into the walls, which wrapped around Keira like a soft quilt. Not much had changed in the past five years. The same old cashier's desk, hostess stand, and cases upon cases of fly-fishing gear in the fly shop to her right remained.

Ryann met her with a hug. "It's good to see you here." The sleeveless shirt Ryann wore highlighted the scars that laced both of her forearms. Rumors had circulated for years about the origin of them. It was public knowledge that she'd gotten them on her twenty-first birthday, the night of her husband's gruesome death. Most lacked the courage to ask about them and were content to believe the rumors. Keira knew the truth. Her husband, Tyler, had locked himself in their bedroom with a handgun, and Ryann had hacked down the door with her bare hands. As her scars attested, flesh was no match for shards of wood. Likewise, her efforts to save him couldn't combat the severe depression that had stolen his will to live.

But Ryann didn't let the tragedy, scars, or rumors get in her way. She was confident, faith filled, and fierce.

Another familiar face greeted her.

"Hi, Thomas," she said to a good-looking man with dark, wavy hair that fell to his shoulders. He'd been friends with Robbie for as long as Keira could remember. She held out a hand, and he accepted it warmly in his. "It's been a while."

"Yes, it has. Nice to see you."

Mrs. Matthews scooped into the casserole dish. When she lifted the spoon, creamy strands of golden, gooey cheese stretched a full foot before she slapped it on a plate.

Nope. Definitely not part of her diet.

She took the open seat next to Thomas. Robbie re-emerged from the kitchen. He eyed the empty chair on her left. Rather than sitting in it, he nudged Ryann. The whole family chair-hopped, filling the seats around Keira. Robbie settled across the table as far from her as he could be without eating in the kitchen itself.

While they ate, she and Thomas spoke easily. More than

once, she caught Robbie serving Thomas a glare so icy it could freeze the sun. Each time, Thomas would bow his head and focus on his food, until a new, seemingly safe topic arose from the group. A half hour later, once Keira had sufficiently pushed the macaroni and cheese around her plate, she stood to clear her dish.

"I'll take that for you." Thomas stole the plate from her hands and added it to a large stack he was gathering. Then he pushed his way through the swinging kitchen doors, with Robbie hot on his heels.

Was he jealous? Something flitted inside her. Probably the two bites of mac and cheese. She couldn't remember the last time she'd had pasta, let alone pasta that fat laden. Her digestive system was surely in full freak-out mode.

A few minutes later, Robbie reemerged. Perhaps it was the poor lighting, but his face looked red. He planted his feet on the linoleum and crossed his arms. Feeling the full weight of Robbie's stare on her, Keira slipped her purse strap onto her shoulder. No need to make this more awkward than it already was.

Keira excused herself from the group and joined Anabelle at the back of the café to say goodbye. A dollhouse towered over Anabelle. Carefully crafted entirely from wood, it had intricate detailing inside and out. A masterpiece. Keira couldn't stop her fingers from gliding down the walls.

"Daddy made it for me." Anabelle sank to her knees and pushed a shoebox to the toe of Keira's sandals.

She bent down, tucking her feet beneath her on the cool floor. Keira took one of the small wooden figures from the box. On the smooth, natural-wood sphere, someone had inked a smiley face with green eyes. Orange lines squiggled down the back of the head. The cylinder body was painted pink.

"That's me." Anabelle took the figure from Keira and placed it on a bed in the room with floral wallpaper.

Robbie appeared, kneeling between them. He handed Anabelle another figure, one with a gray beard.

Keira caught his eye. "This is beautiful. A little girl's dream."

He shrugged but said nothing. He and Anabelle set up all the figures in the house. They were all there. The entire Matthews family. All smiling. All together.

Keira rubbed a hand over her heart.

"Daddy, where did Princess Patty Cake's mommy go?" Anabelle sat her figurine and Robbie's on the couch in the dollhouse's family room, careful not to let them roll off. The wooden dolls leaned against each other.

Robbie brushed a curl out of Anabelle's eyes. "I don't know, Kitty Kat. They've never said."

A lump lodged in Keira's throat. She'd have backed away from the conversation, but Robbie blocked her way to the main dining room. Somehow, crawling under the adjacent table and chairs didn't seem like the most inconspicuous way to excuse herself.

Then Anabelle's big, innocent eyes fell on hers. "My mommy loved me so much, she grew me in her tummy. Then she gave me to Daddy and went on a big, big 'venture. She sees oceans and deserts and rainbow waterfalls."

This was more than Keira's heart could handle. Her stomach wasn't feeling too hot, either. All she could picture was the Momentso post she'd shared five weeks ago of Hanging Lake in Colorado, and how a cascade of colors shimmered across it. A rainbow waterfall.

Robbie shifted uneasily. "Ready for cake and your other presents?"

With a *"Yesssss!"* Anabelle jumped off the floor and dashed to the big table.

Keira expected him to offer his hand and help her up. He did not. Just stared at her until she stood, dusting off her dress.

"I should head out."

He didn't argue. Chuck, however, did. Not with words, but with two hands on her shoulders. It was the same way her own father used to hold her in place. But Chuck's hands were soft and steadying, not threatening at all. They sent waves of peace through her, not fear. Slowly, with his encouragement, she turned her back to the front door and faced the dining room.

Ryann handed her a sliver of cake. Vanilla with buttercream frosting and fresh huckleberry filling that Keira couldn't turn down. At least not a small bite. The only thing sweeter was watching Anabelle open her presents. Her face lit up with such joy that Keira dearly wished she had something to give her. Kids loved opening presents.

Not that she'd experienced that in her home. There was the yearly Christmas gift from the counselor. A small stuffed animal or a night-light. Things that helped her feel safe when the dark closed in. It wasn't until she'd moved in with the Matthewses that she'd ever received a birthday present.

A flurry of wrapping paper later, Anabelle held up a Barbie doll with blond hair and a turquoise dress. "I'm going to name this one Keira." Immediately, she carried the doll to the dollhouse and placed her in the family room.

Minutes later, after a series of goodbyes that included way too many comments like *Don't be a stranger* and *Our home is your home*, Keira rushed to her car. After wrenching the door open, she flung her purse onto the seat, then uncoiled her scarf from her neck. Still, breath didn't come. She steadied herself against the car.

"Don't go."

She didn't need to look over her shoulder to know who stood behind her. Robbie's voice was as familiar as the Montana sky to her. How good would it feel to sink back against his chest as if all the hurts and betrayals hadn't happened? Yet they had. She stared over the top of the car to where wildflowers were beginning to shield themselves for the chilly night ahead.

"Don't go. Not yet. There's something I need to ask you. Something I need to know."

Here it comes. *Why did you leave?* It was the question in his eyes every second she was around him. She'd tried and failed to answer that question herself many times. What would she say now?

"Are you all right?"

That's what made him chase her out here? She exhaled her deep breath slowly. No need to show her hand now. "I'm fine. Just tired after a long day of teaching."

"I meant after everything that happened with John. You guys have been dating for a long time. Couldn't have been easy to turn down his proposal."

Nope, not easy. And it had only gotten more awkward ever since. Maybe because she wasn't sure what she was trying to save. Yes, a part of her loved John. But when she'd been with Robbie, her whole heart, soul, and mind had loved him more than she thought was possible. He'd been the very air she breathed. Leaving him had been devastating. As tonight proved, its consequences were still rippling.

She shuffled her feet on the gravel in a slow circle until her pedicured, sandaled toes met his worn work boots. She took in the faded blue of his jeans, up past the ridiculously large Montanan belt buckle to the fitted green T-shirt with a smudge of pink frosting dried on his left pectoral muscle. His neck, always clean-shaven and totally kissable, was thick beneath his chiseled jaw. Up to his perfect, full lips. Oh, those lips, which could not only say the perfect words to make a woman feel honored and cherished . . . but the touch and taste of them? Mesmerizing.

She let the shiver up her spine chase that memory away

before finding his eyes, which still lingered on her mouth. A dreamy expression flickered across his face. If she had to guess, he found his way to the same memory, but he set up a picnic there.

"Are you two still together?"

"I don't really know. He treats me well. He's got a good future ahead of him." She leaned her hip against the car's doorframe.

"I bet he's your parents' dream come true." Shoving his hands in his pockets, he rocked back and forth on the soles of his boots. Toe to heel, heel to toe. "You've reconciled with them, I see."

She shrugged, feeling the lump return to her throat. "They're the only family I've got."

"Not true." He looked back over his shoulder at the café.

A little smile broke through her mask despite her efforts.

"Ah, there it is. I knew I could still make you smile."

She needed to leave. Now. After climbing in the car and putting the door between them, she pulled a U-turn, a cloud of dust encircling him as she drove away.

Gripping and regripping the steering wheel, she steadied her breath. She stopped at the sign and waited.

A sports car slowed as it neared the River's Edge drive. The driver had chestnut hair, cut bluntly at the shoulder. She turned to Keira, and her brown eyes widened.

It couldn't be. Could it?

The woman pulled onto the drive, her Mercedes barely missing Keira's 4Runner.

Keira twisted as much as her seat would allow.

Then Vivian, Anabelle's mother, climbed out of the car and greeted Robbie with a hug.

CHAPTER SIX

"V iv." The rest of her name caught in his throat. If her presence had surprised him, her hug might as well have knocked him dead.

"Robbie." Vivian pulled back. Turning her toes inward, she balanced between coy and anxious. She bent her finger backward from her wrist the same way she had in college while she flirted with him when Keira wasn't around. And sometimes when she was.

He coughed, hoping to clear his throat, but not so loud to alert attention. He didn't want the last hour of Anabelle's birthday devoted to explaining who the brunette was to his daughter.

"I figured I'd stop by and see how you two were doing. Was that Keira I passed?" She looked back at the road, where the 4Runner had finally driven off. Why did Robbie wish that it remained? And after all these years on his own, why on earth did he suddenly feel so alone without Keira by his side?

"You thought you'd stop by?" Robbie took several breaths, but with each one, his collar got hotter. "After almost four years."

"I'm still her mother, Robbie. It's my right to know how my little girl is doing." A coldness in her eyes chilled Robbie. Vivian wasn't a good person to have on your bad side. She could manipulate the best of them.

Ignoring the glare, Robbie swept his gaze across the Mercedes. It was a newer model. Someone had paid a pretty penny for it. Considering Vivian had the work ethic of a sloth, he doubted it was her. She was dressed nicely, in a pair of slacks and a sleeveless blouse. Even her hair looked rich. It was shinier. She hadn't exactly come from money. Then he caught sight of the ring.

The rock was big. Large enough to signal airplanes from here. She must've seen him gawking, because she held up her hand.

"I did it. I got married. Can you believe it? His name is Eric. He and his brother own the law firm Cartwright and Cartwright in Bozeman."

Robbie had seen their commercials. Ambulance chasers, he'd heard them called. No wonder Eric could afford that ring. "Congratulations." He tried showing some emotion, but nothing came.

Vivian looked over Robbie's shoulder. "I always think of her on her birthday."

That's it? Only on her birthday?

"Can I see her?"

"Vivian, we need to talk about this. She's a little girl. I can't spring this on her. If you want a relationship—"

"It's not like that. I don't have to talk to her. I only want to see her. For a minute. Come on, Robbie, I drove more than an hour to get here."

A hundred flares blazed inside him. He paced a few steps. "You just want to see her?"

"Yes, that's it."

It seemed innocent enough. "Okay, I'll have my sister bring her outside by the river. You can watch her from the café. Wait a minute, okay?"

Robbie snuck into the café, making sure to silence the clanging bells on the door. One day he'd rip them out altogether. He found Ryann in the kitchen. "I need your help, Ry. Vivian's here."

Ryann's eyes went dead. She lowered her head like a bull ready to charge a matador. "Where is she? I have a few things I'd like to say to her."

"Not the time, sis. She wants to see Annie. Not meet her, just get a glimpse. Will you take Anabelle and everyone else out by the river? Please? I'm hoping if we go along with this, it will all blow over."

"Yeah, blow over like a tornado," she scoffed.

Robbie tried a smile. None came.

"I'm only going along with this so it doesn't ruin Anabelle's birthday." She sighed and put a hand on her brother's back. "You okay?"

"I will be."

Ryann kissed his cheek, then drew back. "These women will be the death of you if you aren't careful. You know that, don't you?"

He scrubbed a hand over his jaw. "Yes, yes, I do."

Robbie found Vivian on the phone. She quickly cut the call. "Are we good?"

"Yeah. Come in the café with me." He led her in then switched off the fluorescents, so only the blue light of evening washed in through the windows. Back by the dollhouse, they stood, looking out over the Madison River. On the bank, Anabelle twirled, with the occasional flash of a firefly sparking nearby.

Vivian gasped. Her manicured nails covered her mouth. "She's beautiful, Robbie." Her eyes glossed over, and he could see Anabelle's dancing reflection in them. "But she . . . she doesn't look like me at all."

Robbie's anger took a back seat to an overwhelming pity. Vivian's selfishness had made her miss so much of their daughter's life. What a fool she'd been.

"Does she still cry a lot?"

"Uh, no. She grew out of that a few months after you . . ." Finishing that sentence might turn this a different direction. Which one, Robbie wasn't sure, but he knew he was too exhausted to deal with it today.

Vivian was back. That alone was enough to undo him.

But also watching his family slaughter the fattened calf for Keira? Witnessing Thomas flirting with Keira throughout dinner? Thomas knew better. Keira was out-of-bounds.

With a hand, Robbie massaged the back of his neck, remembering how Keira's nearness still affected him. *Lord, help me.* The way his skin warmed around her? It was as if he'd been buried in an avalanche for five years and she was a fire in a hearth. And that dress she wore should be outlawed.

He couldn't erase the image of her and Anabelle sitting by the dollhouse. Keira had been so good with her. For the thousandth time, Robbie had the thought that Anabelle should have been hers. Then again, maybe she still would have left. Just like Vivian. At least he knew his type: the leaving kind.

Vivian watched another couple of minutes in silence. The longer she stayed, the faster Robbie's heart raced. What was happening behind those glassy eyes of hers? Finally, after releasing a breath so deep she must have pulled it from her feet, she dug a hand in her purse. It reappeared holding a small gift, decked in silver paper and tied with a perfect pink ribbon. She placed it on the table next to the dollhouse. "Could you give this to her? I don't care who you say it's from."

Robbie forced a smile. He could promise that much. Maybe in the span of time since Vivian had been gone, she'd cast off her cunning ways. Anabelle could grow up knowing both her parents. She could have two families to shower her with love, working together to give her the best upbringing a kid could have.

Vivian's head tilted a touch. The corner of her precisely painted lips crept up.

Then again, maybe not.

Later that night, Robbie went on Momentso to see if Wanderfull was online.

KAT WANDERFULL: I kind of picture you living in your parents' basement, eating whole cans of Pringles and looking like Jabba the Hutt.

MRCUSTOM: LOL. I do love Pringles, but I live down the road from my parents. If they had a basement, I'd consider it.

KAT WANDERFULL: You must be close to your parents if you're willing to live down the road from them.

MRCUSTOM: Yeah. Not sure what I did to deserve them. Family's a big part of my life. You?

KAT WANDERFULL: No family. Just me.

MRCUSTOM: I'm sorry.

KAT WANDERFULL: Why? I'm not. It gives me the freedom to live however I want, go wherever I please. The open road, the big sky, the miles of pines . . . that's my family.

MRCUSTOM: It doesn't bother you? Not having a place to call home?

KAT WANDERFULL: Home is a dirty word for some of us.

MRCUSTOM: What about holidays? Where do you go? Who do you spend them with?

KAT WANDERFULL: Anywhere I want and no one. Not anymore. As a child, I had enough scolding around the Thanksgiving table and getting punished on Christmas morning. All for crying that I didn't get a present.

MRCUSTOM: Man . . . if I was in the same room right now, I'd wipe the Pringles crumbs off my hands and give you a hug. How does that boyfriend of yours fit into all that? He can't possibly be okay with your lifestyle.

KAT WANDERFULL: What are you getting at?

MRCUSTOM: Just saying that if you were mine, I'd want to be around you. I'd want to see you in those fields of wildflowers. Sink my feet into the lake, next to yours. Stand beneath the waterfall with you. And I'd give you a stack of Christmas presents so tall, it'd put the Eiffel Tower to shame.

KAT WANDERFULL: How old are you?

MRCUSTOM: 27. Why?

KAT WANDERFULL: Because your notions of love, while sweet, are unrealistic. Anyone with experience should know better.

MRCUSTOM: Or maybe I have enough experience to know what love should look like. I won't settle for anything less.

KAT WANDERFULL: I hate to say it, but if that's your philosophy, you better get used to being eaten alive.

MRCUSTOM: I'm not concerned. Who'd want to mess with Jabba the Hutt?

CHAPTER SEVEN

❧

"You must think I'm the dumbest man on the planet." John wiped his mouth, then tossed his balled napkin on the table at Stella's. "I don't understand why you've kept this from me. For two years, Keira. Two years. And then you finally tell me right before you leave on a long trip?"

"I didn't tell you because you're always complaining about how dumb social media is. How everyone on there is a fraud, trying to be someone they're not."

"You've certainly proven my point, haven't you? All this time, I thought you were going on these trips to find yourself—"

"I have—"

"Instead, you've been building this SimCity life for yourself. Let me ask . . . do you open yourself up to your virtual friends?"

Guilt swelled in Keira's chest cavity. Should she tell John about MRCustom? *Well, honey, there's a man who has become my dearest friend, and we counsel each other through life's trials. But, oh yeah, I don't know his real name.*

A vein in John's forehead pulsed. "Do any of them know the real you? Keira?" He held up a hand, not that she had planned to say anything. "Or is Kat the real you, and I've latched on to this character you've created?"

"They're both me, John."

"Nope, I don't know this woman." John waved a dismissal at her phone, still displaying her Kat Wanderfull profile picture. "I know Keira—the local geography teacher. Keira—the girl who likes keeping a man around in case she ever decides she's ready to settle down—"

"John, stop."

"Keira—the girl who's scared to death to take a risk. Keira—the girl who's afraid to be alone even if she won't admit it."

"Stop, please."

"Keira—the little mouse—"

She slammed her palm on the table, rattling the silverware and glasses.

At the front of the restaurant, Victor, the restaurant's owner, perked up. He started to make his way across the room. Keira shook her head, and he stopped.

"Enough, John." She smoothed her napkin across her lap. "I haven't intentionally tried to hide this part of myself. Please understand that I do want to be able to give myself to one person fully. But I did that once, and I got burned. Those scars, they changed me."

"I'm not Robbie, though."

No, most definitely you are not. "I know. Look, I came back here with the intention of building a life here—separate from Robbie, but close enough to keep an eye on my mom. You know how my father can be. As far as you and I? I didn't want a relationship. But I met you, and you're good and kind and understanding. You're the only thing that's keeping me here anymore. But I see how miserable I'm making you. You deserve a woman who can give you everything. That's why it's time I make a clean break, from this town, from you—"

"Keira, no. Don't go there. You're being illogical. I have an idea—hear me out. When I'm in this town, I spend way too much time as Principal Garfield and not enough time as John. Keira's John. But hey, I can be fun. I can be spontaneous. You live for adventure. Well . . . so do I."

She gave him a funny look. "Sure, Mr. Irons-his-socks, you're a regular Bear Grylls."

A pout puckered John's mouth. "Give me a chance. Let me join you for this summer Travelganza you have planned."

"Travelganza? Is that a word?"

"I made it up. See? Wild, fun, spontaneous." He patted his chest. "Let me come with you. I know my way around a camera."

That much was true. The school hallways displayed his photographs of the high school students. Pretty good for an amateur. Still, though . . .

"I don't think that's a good idea. Besides, I'm leaving tomorrow night. Don't you have work to do to close out the school year?"

John thought a moment. "I will have some work to do in our downtime. But Gillian can handle some of the face-to-face stuff. That's what vice principals are for, right?" He smiled. "Please, let me join you. I promise to leave my iron at home. Maybe my socks, too."

Sitting back in her chair, Keira shook her head. "I don't believe it. You? Wear sandals without socks? That's not exactly hygienic."

"Okay, perhaps I'll bring a couple of pairs of socks." He kissed her hand. "If you don't enjoy my company, then we'll know it's not meant to be. But promise me something. If you do like having me around, accept my proposal and let's give this marriage thing a shot."

"John, I—"

He pressed two fingers to her lips. Holding her gaze, he

pulled the ring out of his pocket. "I've carried this in my pocket every day since, you know, the last time I asked. Just hoping that you'll realize you can't live without me and beg me to put it on your hand. I'm not expecting you to wear it on your left hand." He took her right hand and slid the ring on her third finger. "Let this be a sign that you haven't completely given up hope. Give me one summer to win you over."

If she could figure out how to open her whole self to him, she would. For all his patience and love, he deserved as much.

Still, blending Keira and Kat wouldn't be easy. Like fire and ice. Oil and vinegar. John and Robbie.

"But if you choose me, really choose me. No more Robbie. Erase the memories. And after you've had your fun this summer, no more Kat Wanderlust, or whatever. Leave those ghosts behind. It's time to grow up and put aside all these silly dreams of yours."

As the clock neared midnight, Robbie tapped out a message on his phone, warding off his exhaustion. It was all catching up to him. Staying up late to read books beyond his comprehension. Chatting with Kat Wanderfull on Momentso. Working like crazy to finish the teachers' lounge remodel in record time. Replaying last night's birthday party again and again. All while trying to plan his date with Hallie tomorrow.

That date. He wasn't in the right headspace for it, but he'd committed. Who knows? Maybe Hallie was the girl he was hoping for.

MRCUSTOM: I think I'm half Lennie and half George. They wanted a simple life at home. So do I. My greatest dream is to meet a girl who'll sit by the fireplace with me, discussing classic novels I barely understand, without having to thumb each sentence onto a tiny screen.

Robbie placed his phone on the coffee table, then lay down on the couch with his basketball-shooting hand stretched toward the ceiling. The Steinbeck novel sprang up through the air, paused about three feet above, then fell back down to his grasp in an un-basketball-like way. If he'd gotten the audiobook instead, he would've had the whole thing finished by now. Not that he didn't like this or other classics. He loved a good story. It sucked him in until he felt as if it was his battle to fight, his girl to save, his kingdom to protect. If only he didn't have to actually *read* the story.

Hey, Kat, sorry it's taking me so long to finish Of Mice and Men, *but I have the reading level of a sixth grader. Not embarrassed at all by that little fact, by the way.*

From where it lay, his phone goaded him to see if she'd responded yet. Anabelle had been asleep for two hours, and there was nothing on television. It was either check the phone obsessively or play book basketball again. When he gave in to another Momentso check, he was rewarded with a new message and a green dot on Kat's avatar.

KAT WANDERFULL: Sounds like a nice dream. And I hope you get that one day, but I need to be clear. If my boyfriend and I want a chance at going the distance, I need to let go of this friendship. Truth is, I talk to you way more deeply than I speak to him. That's not right. I'm so sorry. I didn't mean to lead you on into thinking this could ever be more than a conversation.

Wait. Was she . . . *dumping* him? Maybe Kat and Keira had more in common than he thought.

He put his phone back on the table. Book basketball was

way more fun than this. He tried to spin the book on the tip of his finger. It fell, nearly knocking over his glass of water. Big fail. His phone lit up with her next message.

KAT WANDERFULL: You there?

He groaned and picked up the phone again.

MRCUSTOM: No need to apologize. If he's what you want, I won't stand in your way, I hope he'll make you happy and finally give you the family you deserve.
KAT WANDERFULL: Thanks for understanding.
MRCUSTOM: Before you go, can I ask you a question? It's about the book.
KAT WANDERFULL: Go ahead.

He flipped through the pages of the book, looking for anything he could ask. Anything to keep her with him, even for one more minute. Pathetic. That's what he was. Or lonely. Like Curley's wife.
Aha.

MRCUSTOM: Does Steinbeck ever tell us Curley's wife's name? Confession: I haven't finished it yet. *Hides face in shame.*
KAT WANDERFULL: No shame needed. But, no, we never learn her name.
MRCUSTOM: Why?
KAT WANDERFULL: Her only identity is the one her husband gave her—his wife. Before that, she was probably known as such and such's daughter. To me, she's the most tragic character in American literature. Her life wasn't her own. Neither was her

name. She was on the fast track to self-destruction
because of it.

He pictured Keira in the high school hallway that first
day they spoke. Around town, she was the *Knudsen daughter*. In college, she'd been *Robbie's girlfriend*. Robbie
thought he was helping her, prodding her toward a healthier
identity when he'd nicknamed her Kat.

Kat Knudsen. Not Kat Wanderfull. Same nickname.
Two way different people.

> **KAT WANDERFULL:** Time for my own confession.
>   Sometimes I feel like her. I'm also caught between
>   two names, two identities, both given to me by men.
> **MRCUSTOM:** ?
> **KAT WANDERFULL:** Kat was the nickname given to me by
>   my first boyfriend. I wonder if I'm merely playing the
>   role he gave me years ago. Independent, strong, and
>   passionate Kat. He actually bought me my beloved
>   road atlas, which is more of a diary than anything else.

No. No, no, no, no, no.

> **KAT WANDERFULL:** The other one is written on my birth
>   certificate. That name is meant for the woman who
>   sits quietly, obeys, and accepts pain at the hand of
>   a man. I don't like that name, but I can't escape it.

Lord, I hope you aren't playing a cruel game here.
When her next message came through, he brought the
phone closer to his face, then farther away, but no amount
of squinting could change the letters on his screen.

> **KAT WANDERFULL:** That name is Keira.

CHAPTER EIGHT

⚜

The teachers' lounge was done, and not a moment too soon. The last students had left the building two hours ago with a celebratory yelp that could only be made on the last day of school. Robbie was glad. He couldn't handle seeing Keira again. Not after last night's revelation.

Yeah, he should've known. Perhaps, deep down, he did. How often had he imagined Keira was Kat Wanderfull as they traded messages? Pictured Keira's mouth saying Kat's words? He wanted it to be her. And yet, he didn't.

For the thousandth time that day, Robbie yawned. With sleep eluding him anyway, he'd revisited her old posts into the early morning hours, noticing how streams of the old Keira merged with the new. And what he saw drew him to her the way the Madison River beckoned him on a crisp summer morning.

What did Mom used to say? Don't pet a fret. Of course, that only applied to little concerns. Realizing he was in love with his ex-girlfriend's new persona wasn't a "little concern." He'd not only petted the fret. He trained it, named it, and let it sleep at the foot of his bed. Man, he needed to get away from this place. He had to get through this date with

Hallie tonight, then tomorrow, he and Anabelle would start their drive to California. Sunshine and waves were the prescriptions he needed.

At the far side of the room, Anabelle drew on the wall-sized dry-erase board with a pink Expo marker. She sang the Princess Patty Cake theme song while she created her family portrait. Good thing Keira hadn't made it in the cut of family characters. It was bad enough that she'd rooted her way into his dreams. She had no place in his daughter's. And after last night's weird cyber-breakup, it was clear Keira/Kat didn't want to be there anyway. *Good job, buddy. You've graduated to getting dumped by girls before you even date them.*

"Happy summer." Above the cardboard box she carried, Keira greeted him with a rare smile. The lopsided kind that scrunched her nose and turned her big blue eyes to slits. She called it her ugly smile, but that couldn't be further from the truth.

Tell her.

Robbie's mouth went dry before he could tell the voice inside to simmer down.

"Keira! Keira!" Anabelle skipped toward the door.

Keira set the box in the hallway then welcomed Anabelle into her arms.

"I missed you!" Anabelle's voice was somewhat muffled by Keira's blouse, but Robbie could still make it out.

Keira rested her cheek on the top of Anabelle's tangle of strawberry curls. "I missed you, too."

At that very moment, Robbie's heart exploded and sent shards straight to his brain.

Tell her.

Robbie took a swig from his water bottle.

"Daddy's taking me to California tomorrow." She held up her hand like it was a secret. "I'm gonna swim like a mermaid."

"You, little girl, will be the bravest mermaid in the whole ocean." Keira touched the tip of Anabelle's nose with her fingertip.

Anabelle giggled, then danced her pink cowgirl boots back to her mural.

Keira straightened up, scanning the whole room. "It looks great. The teachers will want to live here. You know, there are a few single gals who work in this school. They'll probably want to reach out to thank you personally."

Robbie scoffed. In general, teachers made his inner eight-year-old squirm. But Keira wasn't like any teacher he'd known. He gripped the broom handle tightly. One last sweep, then he'd be out of here. But, then again, he'd be out of *here*. These chance meetings would be over. Who knows when he'd see Keira again? Suddenly, he wanted this conversation to last as long as possible.

Keira cocked her head, the smallest of smirks twisting her lips. How long had he been gawking at her? The broom slipped from his grip and clattered on the floor.

Anabelle jumped but kept drawing . . . Keira. She'd drawn Keira. In the picture, she wore a blue dress and bridged the gap between him and Anabelle. They held hands, the three of them. He'd never been a smart man. This was proof. He'd let this go too far. A million questions jumbled inside his head. Ones he didn't exactly have permission to ask. Maybe MRCustom could have asked them to Kat Wanderfull. But Robbie could not ask Keira.

Tell her now.

Robbie bristled. *Tell her what, God? Oh, hey, Keira, you know that guy that you dunked in the friendship toilet? That was me. You know that huge secret you've gone to great lengths to hide? I know it.*

Her eyes focused now on Anabelle's drawing. When at last she turned back to him, her teeth had sunk so deep into her lower lip he expected to see blood. She was already upset. May as well finish it off. Nail, meet Coffin.

"Keira, I found out something . . . about you."

"About John and me?" She pinched the ring on her hand. A diamond ring.

Suddenly, the ceiling seemed to bow above him. He expected it to crash down until he noticed that the ring was on her right hand. Not her left. What in the world did that mean?

"What you've heard is true. Robbie, we're going to give it another go."

As her baby blues flickered over him, she shrugged. That was how much she cared about John. A shrug's worth. And Robbie meant even less than that. What a fool he'd been. Kat Wanderfull didn't care about him. Neither did Keira.

"I was packing some stuff, and I found a few things." She returned to the box in the hall, lifted it, and placed it on the new, squeaky-clean countertop. She reached in, retrieving something small that she held in her palm. With the way she stroked it briefly, he expected it to be a mouse. Like that one she'd found in college and named Algernon. Hopefully, whatever she had in her hand this time wouldn't bite him.

She opened her hand. On her palm, the braided leather bracelet—the one he'd seen her wear the first day of the remodel—greeted him like a demon's kiss. It was a souvenir from Yosemite, their first trip together. They'd bought matching ones because, well, they were pathetically in love. *Forever and always*, she used to say dreamily when she'd look at it. Apparently, she had a different definition for those two words than he did.

"I want to give this back to you. I thought maybe Anabelle might like it someday. Do you still have yours?"

"Of course." Sitting in his nightstand's drawer, to be exact.

"Good, you can have matching father-daughter ones.

It'll be cute." Her plastered smile ate through his skin like acid.

"Why are you giving that back to me now?"

"I'm trying to start fresh. Let go of the past."

"I don't want it."

"Neither do I." She set the bracelet on the countertop, then stepped back, placing her hands on her hips. To which, Robbie opened the closest drawer and dropped the bracelet into it. Keira's eyes popped open. She was mad. And he loved it. His cackle echoed off the back wall and came back to him. As far as he knew, he was the only one that had ever gotten Keira to show genuine emotion.

"You're stubborn as ever," she said.

"I know you are but what am I?"

"Immature. Childish. Nerve-racking . . ."

"What about obnoxious?"

"Yes."

"Rotten?"

"Absolutely."

"Breathtakingly handsome?"

Her cheek twitched. "Not at all."

"Really? Remember that part in *Song of Solomon*? Where she calls him a young stag? That's totally me."

"The only animal I'd compare you to is a gorilla. One of the smelly ones."

"Wouldn't you know? Gorilla is my middle name."

"No, it's Charles."

He swung his arm and snapped his fingers. "Can't pull anything over on you. You know me better than anyone."

Muffled voices down the hall stole Keira's attention for a few seconds, giving Robbie the chance to take in the sight of her profile. Still pretty, but her freckles—the ones she'd gained when she'd finally had the freedom to leave the confines of her home and school—were gone, likely covered by the overabundance of makeup she now wore. Man, how he missed those. When the voices faded, she buried her focus back into her box of desk supplies. She paused. "I have something for Anabelle, too."

When she withdrew her hand, it held a green-and-white stuffed turtle. As if she was gazing into its eyes, she stared hard at it, her thumb caressing its cheek. "I bought this for her the day after she was born. I don't know when I was planning on giving it to her. I know she's too old for it now, but—"

"She's not too old." He touched the stuffed animal's back. It was as soft as the first wisps of hair on Anabelle's infant crown. He suddenly had the mind to hold it against his chest, drift his lips over it back and forth, and hum Tom Petty's "Here Comes My Girl." Before he realized it, his thumb was caressing Keira's.

Keira tilted her chin to look up at him. Suddenly, kissing her again didn't seem so terrible. It seemed . . . possible.

"Can I have it?" Anabelle squeezed between them, reaching her hand up to the turtle.

"You sure can, Kitty Kat. Can you tell Keira 'thank you'?" Robbie asked.

Anabelle shook the turtle, sparking a rattling sound. Her mouth opened in a giant smile. She hugged Keira's hips.

A slight quiver wrinkled Keira's chin. "I need to go now." After threading her fingers through the curls one last time, Keira attempted to pull Anabelle off her. When that didn't work, she looked to Robbie, eyes pleading.

"Come here, Annie," he said, lifting her up onto his hip. He stepped back, all the way to the dry-erase board.

Keira slid her arms around the cardboard box. Peering in, she cocked her head to the side. Somewhat frantically, she rummaged through it. Her lips moved in silent questions.

"Everything okay?"

Keira closed her eyes. A few moments later, she exhaled shakily and lifted her lids. "I'm fine. I think I forgot something back in my classroom. Have a, um, great summer, or you know, until I see you again. Bye, Robbie."

Tell her.

He opened his mouth. How he'd say it, he wasn't sure. But he knew he needed to. "Keir—"

"Daddy, can Keira come to the beach with us?"

Robbie kneeled down by Anabelle. He looked back at the place where Keira had stood. She'd already gone. "No, baby, she can't come with us. She's got dreams of her own."

Keira opened the bottom drawer of her desk for the fifth time. Empty. As her throat began to tighten, she shoved the drawer closed. She stood up tall, resting her hands on top of her head. *Breathe in. Breathe out. It's here somewhere.*

"Still no luck?" John asked from the doorway. "I didn't see it in the hallway or my office. I hate to say it, but if your road atlas was here, we would've found it by now. Are you sure you had it with you today?"

"I had it, John. I was planning to add notes at lunch, but I had to help Gillian—"

"Then that's it. I bet you left it at home. You're just now noticing."

"I brought it with me to school. I'm sure of it." Keira gave in to the headache pulsing behind her brow and closed her eyes.

"Can we pick up a new one at the airport tonight?" John asked. "That one was outdated anyway."

Keira slid her hands down over her eyes and nose. So many memories . . . lost. She'd had it in the box with all her remaining classroom supplies and Anabelle's turtle.

John wrenched her hands away from her face. Like a good boyfriend, he pulled her against him, but a hug couldn't soothe the panic rising up her spine. "You said you stopped in the teachers' lounge to talk to the kid. You don't think . . . ?"

"What?" Keira stepped back from the embrace. "Do I think what?"

John buttoned his lips and exhaled through flared nostrils. He peered down his nose at her in that way she despised. When had he adopted her father's mannerisms? "You don't think Matthews would have taken it, do you?"

A vile taste varnished Keira's tongue. Robbie wouldn't. Not the Robbie she used to know. Then again, if she'd learned anything about Robbie since their breakup, it was that she hadn't known him as well as she thought.

B y the time Anabelle's tummy was rumbling, Robbie had finished loading up all the supplies in his truck. He had only one final bag of trash to toss. Anabelle, perched on his shoulders, bounced the turtle atop Robbie's head as he walked around the back of the school.

A figure caught Robbie's eye. John Garfield stood in front of the dumpster. The object in his hand, whatever it was, earned itself a long glare and a headshake by the principal.

Robbie stepped back behind the brick face and lowered Anabelle down to the blacktop. "I think your turtle is sleeping," he whispered. "Let's be super quiet, okay?"

She nodded, cradling the toy in her arms.

Curiosity needled him until he peered around the wall. The blue trash receptacle was marked with rust and who knows what other gunk. John flung open the lid until it paused its arc, perpendicular to the ground. John heaved the object he'd been holding into the bin. He grabbed hold of the receptacle's edge and peered over. John's eyes, which had always appeared to hold kindness and a bit of admiration for Robbie during their talks about the remodel, now darted around. Robbie ducked behind the wall.

Clang! A curse sliced the air. And not one of those mild ones, either. The kind that kicked a movie's rating up to R.

Robbie's attention fell to Anabelle. She didn't seem to hear the word. Instead, she kept humming to her turtle. As Robbie looked back to the dumpster, John yanked his hand out from between the bin's lip and lid. He examined the fingers, shook them out, then scanned the area as if checking one more time for witnesses to whatever misdeed he'd done.

CHAPTER NINE

"Whoa. Back up. Explain who this chick is again. Kat Wandering?" Ryann stole a drink of Robbie's soda. Ollie's Bar and Restaurant was packed this Friday night. He'd known his sister would show up to meet friends. Maybe that was why he'd suggested the place to Hallie, even if she did work there. He could use Ryann's advice.

Robbie blew out a hot breath. "She's a travel blogger and photojournalist. Kat Wanderfull is her username on Momentso."

"A what on the what?" Ryann quirked an ear to him. Like most of the folks in this town, his sister had no use for social media, smartphones, and the tech world as a whole.

"Momentso's a social media app. Try to keep up."

"Believe me, I'm trying. So you have a secret online girlfriend with a gazillion followers who just so happens to share the same nickname with the love of your life, and you only put the two together now?"

"She's not my girlfriend."

"And you caught Keira's lame-o soon-to-be-fiancé throwing out her most prized possession like some Disney villain?"

"Yep."

"So, after doing a classy dumpster dive, you now have the road atlas you gave her years ago, which conveniently has a travel itinerary and her lodging for this weekend pinned to the front cover?" Ryann took a big breath.

"Uh-huh."

"By returning it to Keira, you'd look like a regular Captain America."

"Debatable."

"But you're here on a date with another woman."

"Bingo."

"Why were you on Momentso anyway? You hate social media."

"About a year ago, I reached out to my buddy who owns a custom home-building business in Helena for some ideas on the mantel in my cabin. He told me about some of his new designs on this app. So, I chose some lame username and started checking out his work."

"Go on."

"One of the trending pictures was by this travel blogger named Kat Wanderfull. The name—Kat— made me think of Keira, so I clicked on her profile." Robbie used a napkin to wipe his sister's lipstick from the rim of his soda glass then took a couple of gulps. "Call me desperate, but her pictures kind of mesmerized me. Sucked me in."

"When did the private messaging start?" His sister was relentless.

What was taking Hallie so long anyway? He'd never been in the women's bathroom at Ollie's, but if it was anything like the men's, you wouldn't spend any more time than necessary in it. "A couple of months ago, she posted a Bible verse. We kind of started talking then. Nothing personal or anything. It's innocent."

Hallie appeared next to him. "What's innocent?" She draped an arm over Robbie's shoulder, and he felt his muscles turn rigid at her touch. She withdrew her hand, wading through the awkwardness to her spot around the small table.

Robbie gripped the seat of his stool. "What took you so long?"

"Ew," Ryann said, with a puckered expression. "Don't ask a girl why she was in the bathroom for a long time."

With a wave of her hand, Hallie giggled. "It's fine. Both dispensers were out of soap. I know tonight's my night off, but I couldn't help myself. Dirty hands gross me out."

The jukebox blared a Garth Brooks tune, and someone in the larger-than-normal crowd sang along, never quite finding the right note. Robbie searched his mind for anything he could say. He and Hallie had covered all their common interests in the twenty-minute drive over here. Even then, his mind was a mess. When she told him she was from Phoenix, he couldn't think of a single thing to say. All he knew about Arizona was the way the sun had turned Kat Wanderfull's hair to pure gold when she'd posted from there. When Hallie told him she'd gone to school in Portland, he could only think of how he'd kissed Keira at Salt & Straw over ice cream on that spring break trip. Her lips had tasted like snickerdoodle, forever changing his appreciation of cinnamon. But Hallie didn't want to hear that.

What was wrong with him? Hallie was beautiful. And man, did she have a great smile. One that he didn't have to work too hard to see. Yet, he'd felt nothing.

Ryann nudged Robbie. "Why don't you come sit with my friends and me? So far, Thomas is the only one here. Nick and Jessi are on their way," Ryann said.

Hallie, who had been staring into her drink, perked up. "Thomas? I don't think I've met him."

That's one way out of this. Robbie grabbed his glass and extended his other elbow to Hallie. She accepted. "Thomas is the safety director at the River Canyon Dam. He's been my best friend since we were kids. For the life of me, I don't know why he isn't married. He's the kind of guy you can always depend on, you know? Plus, he has a reputation for being a hero around these parts." Robbie took a peek at Hallie. Was this as obvious of a sales pitch as it seemed?

"Is that him?"

He followed Hallie's gaze to the man sitting alone at the end of a long table. "Yep. That's Thomas." She didn't respond. But he thought he heard her emit a noise from her throat—the same noise Keira used to make when Robbie would kiss her good night.

Robbie nudged Hallie forward. "Thomas, this is Hallie." Thomas stood. "I'm honored, ma'am."

"Ma'am? I'm only twenty-four. Call me Hallie." Their handshake looked less formal and more third date.

This may be easier than he thought. Robbie pulled out the chair between his and Thomas's, which Hallie quickly accepted. Ryann took the seat at the head of the table, next to Robbie.

Before the waiter finished taking their order, Hallie and Thomas were already knee-deep in family backgrounds. The two conversed easily. The way Robbie and Keira spoke in the past. The way he and Kat spoke in their messages.

Forty-five long minutes later, Robbie's thoughts raced faster than ever.

Nick, another friend who'd shown up with his girlfriend, Jessi, took a bite of a quesadilla. They'd moved to town a year ago to run her uncle's souvenir shop on Canyon Street. "I heard you . . . and Anabelle . . . are taking off on a trip," he said between chews.

"Yeah, we are. I wanted to take her to California. Maybe that Royal Village theme park. You know how she's crazy about Princess Patty Cake? I think she'll love it."

"When are you leaving?" Jessi asked.

"Tomorrow." A piercing giggle yanked Robbie's attention toward Hallie. Apparently, she thought Thomas was hilarious. Did she touch Thomas's hair? Yep, the girl was in love. Or at least serious like. And definitely *not* with Robbie, thank goodness.

"So . . . what's the plan, brother?" Ryann whispered. "Since your date is tanking, are you going to take that atlas back to Keira?"

"Head to South Dakota instead of taking my daughter to meet her favorite princess? Sounds brilliant." Robbie tilted back his glass.

"Robbie, California will be there all summer."

The first few chords of an old Tim McGraw song played. Wes Crenshaw, a local mechanic, beat all the other guys in Ollie's to Ryann's side. "Care to dance?"

"I'd love to. Give me one sec," she said. Her cold hand on the back of Robbie's neck made him jump. "We weren't raised to be cowards. You need to do this."

"Ry, I don't *need* her in my life."

"But what if she *needs* you in hers?" She tousled his hair, then allowed Wes to lead her to the dance floor, joining a half dozen other couples in a two-step.

Hallie sighed.

Why had he thought this date was a good idea again? "Hallie—"

"Robbie, can I talk to you? Alone?" she asked.

"Yeah, of course."

Hallie grasped his hand and led him away from the table. She took a deep breath. "Um, you're a really nice guy. And, like, gorgeous."

"But you want to get to know Thomas better?"

"Kinda." She bit her lip. "No hard feelings?"

"No way. Thomas is a good guy." Robbie pulled her into a side hug. "Wait here." He made his way back to his friend.

When he got there, Robbie wrenched his face into something that was meant to be a scowl and pounded a fist on the table. "How dare you!"

Nope. Couldn't keep a straight face to save his life as Thomas shrunk back.

Robbie palmed Thomas's shoulder. "Kidding. Hallie likes you, man. Go dance with her."

"What?" Thomas's eyes met Hallie's.

She gestured for Thomas to join her on the dance floor.

Robbie checked the time on his phone. Just after eight. "Drive her home, okay? I have something I need to do."

CHAPTER TEN

❧

In the hotel room mirror, a thick swath of mauve lipstick spread across Keira's bottom lip. The simple movement took effort since her arms felt as if someone had filled them with sand as she slept. The word *slept*, of course, was figurative. *Rolled* would be more appropriate. Neither her right side or her left side was comfortable. When she faced the wall, she felt the lumpiness of her final message with MR-Custom beneath her shoulder. A turn to the window shot an ache from her stomach down her legs, where Anabelle had clung before that goodbye yesterday evening. It was as if the distance between Rapid City, South Dakota, and West Yellowstone, Montana, was nothing at all.

Lying on her back only left her vulnerable to the plain white ceiling, which was exactly what she felt like. How could something like a road atlas, when lost, scrape her very soul raw like that? But, honestly, who was she without it?

A knock on the door jolted her hand.

She dropped the tube of lipstick into the sink. After putting the lid back on, she set it in her makeup bag, then dragged the zipper until all her makeup—her paint—was secure inside. She'd need this later for the photo shoot. One last glance in the mirror assured her she'd done enough to cover the circles under her eyes and the blemishes in her skin. Today was a big day, and she needed to look perfect. At long last, her followers would see Kat Wanderfull's face.

In the room's entryway, her hand grasped the handle as a second knock clicked against the door. But not this door. The one to the adjoining room.

Even though she'd brushed her teeth a few minutes ago, a sour taste filled her mouth. She unlatched that door, cracking it to see John's beaming face. Then she was being pushed back as the door swung wide open.

He took in the humdrum decor that likely matched his room exactly. John plopped down on her bed, putting his shoes up on the quilt. "Come sit down."

She didn't have to imagine what he might be thinking. He'd made his desire for her clearly evident last night after they'd arrived at the hotel. It hadn't taken a genius to realize he never intended to use the separate room Dora had booked for him.

"We should go. The predawn light can't be wasted," she said.

Before the clock struck five thirty, the elevator doors opened to the historic hotel's quaint lobby. Pine furnishings, ruby-red walls, and an oversize fireplace with its crackling fire were meant to welcome its guests with warmth. Of course, Keira hadn't felt that when they'd checked in after their flight. She certainly didn't feel it now. Rather, a chill settled in her bones, refusing to be dislodged by something so simple as a cozy tableau.

At the front desk, a man in a heavy workman's coat pleaded with the young female clerk on duty. From the way she smiled at him, she was about to give him whatever he wanted. When she saw Keira and John, her cheeks flushed, and she turned away.

The man who had been leaning on the counter straightened and looked over his shoulder at them.

"Robbie?" His name tumbled out of her mouth.

He began to smile, but after his eyes flickered to John, he pressed his lips together into a tight line. His tentative steps in their direction unleashed either butterflies or hornets in Keira's belly. Time would tell.

Robbie's eyes were bloodshot and weighted. They struggled to keep focus. His face was stubbled, despite almost always sporting a close shave.

"What on earth are you doing here? Did you drive through the night? You look exhausted. Is Anabelle with you? How did you find me?" Keira's words formed a tangled heap on the floor between them. "Seriously, what are you doing here?"

"I need to talk to you . . . alone . . . please."

At her side, John straightened and cleared his throat. "Sorry, Matthews. We're on our way out. Whatever it is will have to wait."

Keira's focus shifted between the two of them. "Make it quick, Robbie. We need to leave. John, why don't you grab us coffee?"

Behind the check-in counter, the attendant watched the unfolding scene with such rapt attention that Keira expected her to pull out a tub of popcorn. Meanwhile, John shuffled his feet. Finally, he stepped away, but not before kissing Keira's cheek.

Keira fought to not shrink away from him. A touch on the other elbow made her jump.

Robbie was leading her in the opposite direction from John. Swooping down to grab the strap of a backpack, he nodded to where Anabelle was sleeping on the couch near the fire. Against her cheek, she held the turtle.

Keira resisted the urge to place a hand on her head. No need to wake her. "What's this all about?"

"There's something I need to tell you. Two things, actually. The first thing is about John."

"Go on."

"I'm not trying to hurt you. I'd never want to cause you pain. Remember that." He pulled the zipper on the hunter-green JanSport bag and retrieved her atlas.

She snatched it from his hand and hugged it to her chest. "Where did you find it?"

Rubbing the back of his neck with one hand, Robbie dropped the bag by his boot. "In the dumpster. At school. After you left."

Strange. The custodians hadn't yet been by her classroom when she'd packed it into her box of belongings yesterday. How had it ended up—?

"John threw it in there. I saw him do it."

In the back corner of the lobby, John was no doubt perfecting his coffee. Two creams, two sugars, with a splash of caramel syrup. Such a man wasn't capable of doing what Robbie was accusing him of. Not a chance. "Why are you doing this?"

"You don't believe me?"

"John's a great man. He wouldn't sink so low. It's not his character."

"I'm not saying it is. I'm not saying anything at all, other than the fact that when I was taking the last bag of trash out last night, I watched him toss something in. When I got there, I climbed up to see what it was. Not sure why. For all I knew, it could've been his lunch. But I had that weird feeling in my gut. Your atlas was there, lying on top of the bags of cafeteria trash. I thought that maybe it was like the bracelet. You were trying to get rid of me, once and for all. But your atlas clearly goes beyond us. I knew you'd never throw that away."

Whispers poured out of the book in her hands then.

Memories of her solo adventures as Kat Wanderfull, but also tender moments shared between her and Robbie. Back when the world was theirs, and he was the only future she dared to envision. Had he read those? If he did, did he think she still felt that way toward him? The back of her eyes stung. She pressed the heel of her free hand to one eye, then the other. *So much for perfect makeup.* "He wouldn't do this to me," she repeated.

"But he did. Maybe he was afraid you would choose that book over him. Maybe he loves you so much that the thought of losing you was enough to drive him mad . . . drive him to do something out of character." He shrugged. "Trust me— you have that effect on men."

John, holding two sleeved coffee cups, crossed the lobby. He slowed when he noticed the book against her chest. "You found it!" He placed the cups on the end table and held out his hand to Robbie. "Honorable thing you did, bringing that all the way out here."

Robbie buried his hands in his coat pockets. "Fess up."

"Fess up? I'm sorry, I'm not sure of what you're speaking, friend."

"I'm not your friend." Robbie's face reddened, except for the scar on his cheek. The one he'd gotten the last time he'd defended her honor, back in college. He'd fight for her. She knew that much. And John, whose only workout consisted of installing new reams of paper into the office copier, would get trounced.

"Excuse us." John pulled Keira by the hand over to the front desk. "What did he tell you?"

"He said you threw this in the trash bin behind the school."

John's pupils grew large. He let out a laugh that was too loud for this time of the morning. "That's ridiculous. Is he saying that he jumped into the dumpster to retrieve it? Who would do that?"

"Robbie would."

"Well, that goes along with everything I know about him, I guess. He's lying. Desperate to get you back, probably, so he made up this ludicrous lie about me. I know how much that book means to you. I'd never do such a thing. I love you too much." His stare settled into her. His fingers wrapped her upper arm.

Back by Anabelle, Robbie sat with his back against the couch. In front of him, he rested his elbows on his knees and laid his forehead on his crossed arms. Would the same man who drove all night, in the opposite direction of California, make up this lie? Only to try to convince her that John had done it because he loved her? No. But then again, Robbie had a track record of stringing her along—keeping her close, but never close enough to commit.

It unleashed a furious pounding in her temples. She rubbed small circles over them.

"Keira? Look at me." When she didn't, his grip on her arm tightened. "I've been nothing but patient with you. Through all your lies and secrets, your teasing. I've let you break my heart over and over. All for it to come down to this?" He sucked in a breath through gritted teeth. "Your father's right. Left on your own, you'll always choose the wrong path. How dare you believe some dumb construction worker over me?"

A furious heat, starting at the place he held her arm, spread to her throat and loosened her tongue. "You said you shut your hand in your car door. What really happened to it, John?"

John's brow furrowed. He spread out his fingers between them. A purplish-red streak spread across the tops of his fingers. The kind of bruise that may be caused by the heavy lid of the school dumpster coming down unexpectedly—something she'd narrowly escaped two weeks ago.

"I believe Robbie. This relationship is over. You should go."

Feigning a look of innocence and hurt, he opened his mouth to speak.

Keira twisted the ring off her finger. She placed it in his bruised hand. "And if you ever call Robbie Matthews dumb again, your heart won't be the only thing I break. Got it, Principal Garfield?"

CHAPTER ELEVEN

The lack of sleep had Robbie feeling fluish. His neck ached. His blood hummed from the endless cups of joe he'd consumed to keep himself awake on the drive. What he wouldn't give for a babysitter and a bed. Neither was in the cards. And the camping cots he'd brought to make this road trip to California affordable didn't count as a bed.

Keira stood a few feet away, hugging herself as she stared out the window at the sunrise. She hadn't so much as shifted her weight.

It was impossible not to hear the last few words of her argument with John. Robbie hadn't noticed he was hurting her until right before he let her go. Darn that ability of hers to hide pain. But the way she'd stood her ground as John tried to control her? Robbie had been so proud. And when she'd defended him, Robbie had half a mind to kiss her.

A new wave of exhaustion rolled over him. He rested his head against Anabelle's pillow. There was no way he could head back out on the road without sleep of some sort. Mentally, he counted the cash in his wallet. He'd have to scrounge money from elsewhere in the vacation budget to get a hotel room. Not this hotel. This place was spendy. What was he thinking about again? Sleep. But not until after No-Principle-Garfield had gotten his stuff and high-tailed it out of here. Sure, the nickname was lame, but Robbie was tired.

The elevator door dinged. The stomps of an angry man-child urged Robbie's eyes open. He didn't look at John. Instead, he watched Keira. She remained facing the window as his footsteps slowed near the door, then stopped. They picked up again until the cool breeze from the automatic door rushed in, then faded as the barrier closed once again.

Finally, John was gone. It was just him, Anabelle, Keira, and the desk clerk. Summoning the remaining strength in his legs, he pushed himself to standing. The few steps to Keira's place at the window were full of terrible, sleep-deprived ideas. He chose the most mild of them all when he placed his hands on her shoulders. She leaned back against his chest.

His eyelids surrendered. The warmth of her body against his was like a mug of . . . something delicious. The heat moved to his hand.

"Come on, sleepyhead. You need a bed."

From what he could see through glazed vision, Anabelle rubbed her eyes with the turtle. When she saw Keira, she shrieked and bounced over to them.

Keira lifted her up, holding Anabelle against her torso.

"I told Daddy I want you to go to the beach with us. We can build sandcastles."

"Is that so? First things first. Your daddy's tired. We're going to let him sleep, and you and I will have a girls' day out. What do you say to that?"

Anabelle wriggled in reply.

A few minutes later, after Keira forced him to eat a package of nasty mini commercial muffins, Keira pulled back the sheets of her bed. She and Anabelle worked together to push Robbie down.

"I'll take Anabelle for the day. You sleep."

"Hold up. There's something else I need to tell you. It's about you. Something I learned the other day." Robbie's head sunk deep into her pillow. It smelled like Keira—her perfume or lotion. Either way, it was heavenly.

"We do have a good deal to talk about. There's time for that later." Keira heaved him more toward the center of the bed, "Goodness you weigh a ton. Sleep tight, you big gorilla."

Anabelle covered him with sheets as soft as the clouds over the Gallatin mountains and kissed his cheek. "Sleep tight, big g'rilla." Her giggle faded into the darkness.

Like a baby bird, Anabelle's mouth rooted around the straw poking out of her cup. When she'd found it, her pretty pink lips closed on the curly plastic tube. The way her whole face—cheeks, jaws, lips—worked to suck up the chocolate milk was fascinating and adorable rolled into a single surge in Keira's heart. The little girl's eyes crossed as she watched the liquid climb up, down, and all around before hitting her mouth. She pulled back and swallowed. When she went back to it, her cheeks puffed out. Bubbles erupted in the cup, making Anabelle dissolve into laughter that proved to be contagious.

Keira rubbed her aching cheeks. She hadn't smiled this much since, well, since Robbie had been a part of her everyday life. In their morning together, Keira had decided that Anabelle was 50 percent Robbie, 40 percent Princess Patty Cake, and 10 percent Tasmanian Devil. Were all kids as full of life as Anabelle? The girl was joy personified.

The only child in a closed-off family, Keira hadn't been

around children much. In fact, she wasn't sure that *she* was ever a child.

"Are you ready to order?" The server, who was a young replica of the restaurant owner, couldn't have been more than seventeen. He was a cutie, especially with those dimples that appeared every time he grinned at Anabelle.

"Anabelle, would you like to tell him what you want?" Keira asked.

The girl slid to the far side of the booth.

"Okay, then. I guess she'll have the peanut butter and jelly. All kids like that, right?"

"Yes, ma'am. Unless they have a peanut allergy."

Dread filled her like wet cement. "Anabelle, are you allergic to peanuts?"

"What's *gallergic* mean?"

"Are there any foods you aren't allowed to eat? Peanuts, um, soy, wheat? I should've asked your daddy." Keira's attention went to the half-empty chocolate milk cup. What if she had a dairy allergy and got sick while in her care? *Sorry I sent your child to the emergency room, Robbie. I had good intentions.* Wait . . . can someone die from a milk allergy?

Anabelle slid beneath the table. Keira cringed. Who knows how long it had been since they cleaned under there? If the allergy didn't get her, the hepatitis would. They'd have to wash their hands before the food arrived.

"I want mac and cheese."

That's right. At her birthday, they'd made her favorite food: mac and cheese. And she'd been drinking chocolate milk. Phew. Next time she watched Anabelle, she'd be more prepared. If there was a next time.

"She'll take the mac and cheese with a side of grapes. But can you slice the grapes in half, please? Maybe quarters instead. Just to be on the safe side. And I'll have a salad with a half portion of grilled chicken."

"What kind of salad dressing? We have ranch, Italian—"

"No dressing."

"Sure thing. I'll bring a coloring page and some crayons." The server peeked beneath the tabletop, gave a short wave to Anabelle, then walked to the kitchen.

Scooting to the edge of her bench seat, Keira contorted her body to look under the table.

Anabelle was perched on her knees on the dirty floor. *Gross.* "You can come back out now. I get shy, too, sometimes. I'm here with you, though, so why don't you come back up?"

Anabelle nodded. Instead of climbing onto her own seat, she scrambled toward Keira. Before she knew it, Keira's arm was tucked around Robbie's daughter. Anabelle curled against her side. On instinct, she held her tight and planted a kiss on top of the little girl's head.

Deep within her chest, a patter tickled her sternum, like the trembling of pebbles on the road during a small earthquake. It should have been unnerving. Instead, Keira took Anabelle's hand in hers.

The waiter approached with the paper and crayons. He pretended to trip, disappearing behind another booth. He popped up like a gymnast at the end of a floor routine.

Anabelle's little body shook in a fit of giggles. She accepted his offering with a polite but quiet "thank you," then set to work, starting with the pink crayon. Left-handed. Like Robbie.

Oh, Robbie. He hadn't responded to her last text stating that she was taking Anabelle out to lunch. One thing about him? When he was awake, he never rested. He worked and played hard. He put his all into every task and every touch. But when he slept, he practically hibernated. Several times in college, his roommates had let her in to rouse him for the early class they shared. Nothing, no amount of prodding or shoving, could stir him. Only a kiss worked. Then, like magic, he'd awaken, and often pull her down beside him while she squealed. He was like Sleeping Beauty. Without the spindle.

She was happy to let him sleep. It was the least she could do to thank him. For what? Saving her atlas? Opening her eyes to the jerk John truly was? Letting her get to know his sweetheart of a daughter? That was all true. But what was she supposed to say when she brought Anabelle back to him in a few hours?

A thank-you didn't convey the whole rainbow of emotion Robbie unleashed in her. Not the vibrant yellows or tranquil blues. And certainly not the reds that bled into the pools of her deepest, most hidden parts. When he'd held her shoulders back at the inn, she'd nearly melted. A vulnerable moment. So what? She wasn't some lonely high school girl who turned to mush at the attention of the star quarterback. Not anymore. She could handle him. And if they did happen to touch in the future, she'd be fine. In fact, a little harmless affection might prove to him that she was a woman who could hold her own against his charm.

"Look, Keira." Anabelle lifted the paper so close to Keira's face, her eyes needed to refocus to make out the two stick figures, one big, one little. All around them, crimson oval-like shapes danced. "I drawed me and you."

The pattering inside Keira's chest grew to a rumble. "That's beautiful. And what are those red things?"

Anabelle's wide green eyes peered up at her. "Those are hearts."

Just like that, a portion of her fortress crumbled. And Keira had no immediate plans to rebuild.

CHAPTER TWELVE

Someone pressed a kiss to Robbie's cheek. And whoever it was had Skittles breath. He grabbed hold of the little body and pulled it onto the sheets beside him. His daughter's laughter rang out, followed by her little voice. "Daddy, you're silly." He snuggled her against his chest and sighed. Between blinks, he made out a gray wall past the edge of the bed.

Where was he? Whose bed was this anyway? And on the wall, why was there a picture of a horse staring down a buffalo? That didn't even make sense. The light from the window reflected off the glass, and a shadow moved across it.

"Sorry to wake you."

Keira. Robbie settled onto one elbow, his stiff neck recalling memories of the nine-hour middle-of-the-night drive and his still-swelled chest cavity echoing that morning's confrontation when she'd trusted him.

And now she stood at the foot of the bed, offering him the kind of cardboard cylinder he'd get at the deli on Canyon Street.

"We brought you soup. Chicken noodle. You still like that, right?" She placed it on the end table on his left. She balanced a plastic-wrapped spoon on its lid, then splayed out three two-packs of crackers in an arc. After disappearing for a few moments, she returned with a plastic cup she must've filled with bathroom sink water. "Sorry, I didn't get you a drink."

"No need to be sorry." He cleared his throat, hoping to get rid of the gravel. Accepting the water, he chugged half of it. "What time is it?"

"Almost four. Anabelle and I had a great day, didn't we?" Keira beamed at the two of them.

That was weird. Keira didn't beam.

"Do you want to tell Daddy what we did?"

Tell Daddy? The way she said that almost made it seem . . . family-like. While Keira's eyes remained glued on Anabelle, Robbie pinched the tender skin beneath his arm. Definitely awake.

"We walked to a store, and Keira bought me a night-light. It has horsies that go round and round on it. I think they're Princess Patty Cake's horsies, because they're brown and pink."

"How nice of her, but she shouldn't have done that."

Keira shook her head. "It wasn't a big deal. She said she's scared of the dark. I told her how I used to be the same way when I was a little girl, and how for Christmas one year, I got a night-light from the school counselor. Mine didn't have horsies, but it helped me not be so scared."

Maybe not *so* scared, but College Keira hadn't grown out of the fear entirely. He'd always had to check every closet, shower curtain, and large cabinet before he bade her good night. And the girl didn't have one night-light; she had one in each room. He eyed her now. Had she changed? Yeah, she was thinner, with longer hair and considerably more makeup. But was she still the girl he'd loved more than life itself? "I'm paying you back."

"No, you won't. It was a gift."

"We saw lots of rocks and buildings and took thirty-seventy pictures. And I had hot chocolate and an apple." Anabelle rose onto her feet, finding her balance on the pillowy mattress and messed quilt. A bounce that began in her legs eventually reached her entire body, until she'd achieve full-blown jumping-on-the-bed status. "Me and Keira ran around a playground, pretending there was a troll chasing us. We ate . . . lunch . . . too."

"It sounds like you had a good day."

Anabelle nodded her head out of rhythm with her body. She stumbled a bit, then went right back to jumping.

Robbie kicked his feet off the bed to allow her more room. He stretched his arms over his head and focused on Keira. "And did you have a good day?"

Though her eyes had been bouncing along with Anabelle's movements, Keira shifted her attention to him. "The best." There was a peace about her. An ease he hadn't seen in their teachers' lounge conversations. Not at the birthday party, even.

"Hey, Kitty Kat, I bet Keira has never jumped on a bed before."

Anabelle stopped her jumps and clapped her hands together. "Jump with me, Keira."

"No way. Grown-ups don't jump on beds."

"Who says?" Robbie inched closer. "There's no rule book anywhere that tells adults they can't jump on the bed."

Shuffling backward, Keira shook her head. "It's in the Bible. I'm sure of it. Second Traditions, chapter four, I believe."

"Stealing my jokes, are you?"

"What in the heavens do you mean? I came up with the Traditions-is-a-book-of-the-Bible joke. Not you."

"You're wrong, darling. I know because I stole it from

my great-grandpa Red." He crept closer. If she kept backing up, she would bump into the mini fridge in five, four, three, two—

"Ouch!"

Robbie saw his chance. He lunged, catching Keira around the legs. When he stood, she bent in half at his shoulder.

She pounded his back. "Put me down, you ape!"

"Is someone tickling me?"

Her fists hit harder. Goodness, was she using her knuckles? Robbie flipped her onto her back at Anabelle's feet.

Keira rolled, taking a tiger's stance, ready to get off the bed.

Robbie met her at the edge. "Oh no, you don't. Not until you jump."

"I won't. I'll break the frame."

"You weigh about two pounds. You won't break the bed. Jump. It'll be the best decision of your life."

Her lips quirked a bit on one side. Feisty. Man, he used to love getting a rise out of her. She'd always come alive around him. The truth was, he longed to see that again. "You want me to jump? Fine, I'll jump." She straightened up, then jostled her knees a bit.

Robbie caught Anabelle's gaze. "That's not jumping. Anabelle, show her."

On command, his daughter bent her knees and sprang as high as her four-year-old body would let her.

"Daddy, your turn."

Robbie hated to disappoint her. Of course, he probably would break the bed. He'd have to be careful. He climbed up, ducking his head to avoid the ceiling, and gripped Anabelle's hand. He reached out for Keira's.

Keira looked down at it as if he had cooties. She backed off the bed and crossed the room, putting the small table and her computer between them. "I have work to do."

* * *

The red embers throbbed, growing brighter each time Keira's blown breath reached them. It was warm here in front of the fireplace as she waited for Robbie and Anabelle to meet her. She should be working on this morning's photos. The change of plans had put her behind schedule. Thankfully, Dora didn't mind. After getting only two days a week out of Keira during the school year, she could handle six and a half days on this first trip rather than seven. As long as the clients were happy, and they were. The one picture she'd posted earlier of a new devotional book propped in front of some flowers in Halley Park already had the title's hashtag trending. According to Dora, the publisher and the author were ecstatic. Easy paycheck. Plus, she got a free book out of the deal. Another picture she'd snapped of the midmorning shadows stretching across the ground would be perfect with some editing, but she couldn't risk Robbie spying her work. Not until they'd had their talk.

She'd wanted to hash it out in the hotel room earlier, but he went and started messing around. Same old Robbie. After that, she'd lost her nerve. Perhaps at dinner she would find it.

Hopefully, Robbie wouldn't react the same way as John had to her secret.

The elevator opened, releasing the clatter of tiny cowgirl boots onto the tile floor. Moments later, small arms wrapped around her neck.

"You look ready for dinner. I love those cowgirl boots."

"We should get you some." Anabelle kicked her foot out, putting the left boot on full display.

"Yes, we should."

Behind them, Robbie rocked back and forth on his heels. He wore his ever-present blue jeans, but instead of a ratty, paint-stained shirt, he wore a fitted black button-up, undone enough to draw her eyes to his chest, but not enough to make him look like the cover model on a steamy romance novel. He'd shaved and gelled his curls back off his forehead. But like Robbie himself, they fought taming. By dessert, they'd be falling to his brow again.

"Anywhere in particular you'd like to go?"

"I made reservations at the place next door."

"Reservations?" He looked down at his clothes.

"You're dressed fine. Trust me." She led them through the doors and out onto the sidewalk.

Anabelle hopped ahead, careful not to touch the cracks, as they headed east toward the Painted Horse.

Robbie caught up to Keira. He matched her stride, keeping to her left. Close, but not enough to risk touching hands or anything. "Are you absolutely sure it's okay that we take that adjoining hotel room? I feel crummy about the whole thing. After sleeping all day, I can drive through the night again. We could still make it to Cali by Monday, probably."

Was Keira acting selfishly with this proposal? He and Anabelle wanted to be California dreaming, not South Dakota touristing. "It was already reserved, and it costs me nothing for you guys to stay there for one night. The hotel was happy to turn it over for you. Besides, don't you think Anabelle needs a bed after sleeping in her car seat last night?"

They passed beneath a streetlight, and shadows sharpened the edges of Robbie's features.

"That sounded judgmental. I didn't mean it to be. We both know I have no place to give parenting advice. I'm sorry."

"Stop with the apologies already! I'm used to people judging my parenting. The curse of the single father, I call it."

"In truth, I want you to stay tonight. I have something I'd like to discuss with you."

"Same here." The cracking of one set of his knuckles set her spine to curling. What was he so nervous about? It wasn't as if he was the one with the big secret.

"We're here." She reached for the main door's handle, but Robbie intervened.

The door, which appeared to be solid mahogany, groaned at having to move. Robbie made it look effortless, of course. "Kitty Kat, this way," he called to Anabelle, who spun around, then frog-jumped through the doorway.

Only the flicker of a pair of sconces lit the entryway. Had she realized this restaurant was so romantic, she wouldn't have accepted this opportunity. The last thing she needed was romance. Especially with Robbie Matthews. Been there, done that, bought the counseling-session package.

Turning in a slow circle, Robbie took a gander at the lobby with its layers of woodwork and halos of candlelight. He sneered at the framed menu on the wall as if it had offended his momma. "What kind of place writes their menu in cursive? And why are there only five things to choose from?" He leaned close to her ear. "Keira, I can't afford this place."

"You don't have to." She patted his arm. "Wait here."

From behind the host's stand, a gentleman nodded. "Reservation name, miss?"

Keira slipped a folder out of her satchel. Pinned inside was the contract Dora had forwarded the week before. "It should be under . . ." A glance back found Robbie sliding his fingers along some woodwork. She fanned the page on the podium for the host to see. ". . . Kat Wanderfull."

"Ah yes. We're all excited to have you visit us this evening. You have two guests with you, correct?"

"Yes. Two." She tucked the folder back into her bag. "You don't happen to have crayons or anything, do you?"

"I'm afraid not. We typically do not cater to children here. Not that they're not welcome, of course."

"I understand."

"Right this way, Miss Wanderfull."

"Call me Kat, please." *Just not in front of that man*, she wanted to add.

But Robbie, holding Anabelle's hand, was already walking this way. His usual swagger was gone. While she wasn't looking, someone must have replaced his spine with an iron poker. "I feel like I should at least be wearing a jacket," he said.

Keira let loose a chuckle, trying to lighten his mood. "The Robbie I used to know wouldn't let some place make him feel like he's not good enough."

"Oh yeah, only a school, a library, a bookstore . . ."

"Stop." Her arm slipped under his, allowing her hand to cradle the crook of his elbow. What *was* she thinking? Nothing at all apparently. Would she always be a slave to her impulses around him?

Robbie didn't seem to mind, though. In fact, he hugged her hand between his arm and his side, as if he didn't want her to let go.

Once they'd all settled into their seats and Keira had assured Robbie three times that he could order whatever their stomachs desired, they gave their requests to the server. For Anabelle, the salmon with a side of croutons and cheese. For Robbie, the New York strip and potato confit. For Keira, the lobster tail sans butter, with steamed broccoli.

After a sip of his iced tea, he turned his focus to Keira. "Please tell me why I ordered seventy dollars' worth of food for me and my four-year-old. And why I'm sleeping in some swanky hotel tonight with toilets that have multiple flush settings? What on earth do you have in that folder of yours? The deed to a diamond mine in Africa?"

"Not quite." She swallowed some water, wishing it contained something stronger. "I haven't been completely forthright with you. With anyone, really."

His eyes sharpened on her. "Go on."

The host appeared behind Robbie, holding a drugstore plastic bag. "The manager sent me to the general store down the block. Your crayons and coloring book, milady." He handed them to Anabelle, whose wide eyes were likely thanks enough. "Pardon the interruption, Miss Wanderfull, er, Kat."

Keira's attention shot to Robbie. He was peering hard at the generic coloring book. Who knew he held so much interest in baby animals? Either he hadn't caught the name, or he didn't care enough to question it.

"How should I begin? Do you know the social media app Momentso?" Probably not. Robbie had been strictly anti–social media in college. He'd tried it once, but as a big football star, he'd been inundated with unsolicited photos and, um, requests—to put it politely—from girls on campus.

He nodded, raised his glass to his lips, then chugged several gulps.

"Shortly after everything happened with us, I joined it. Do you remember Trina from college? She told me I should go on Momentso and share pics from my mission trip. The one—"

"I know the one." Maybe it was the low lighting, but Robbie looked greenish. She shouldn't have gone that far back. Too many soiled memories.

"The pictures gained traction. Suddenly, I had all these followers . . . you know, people who wanted to see what I'd post next." She ran a fingertip over the lip of her water glass. "Soon, companies were offering me free things—clothes, gadgets, phones, books, kayaks . . . you name it, I've been offered it. The only requirement was that I show it in my posts."

She paused. Robbie's gaze bored into her, his thoughts a mystery. "This company called EndeavHerMore specializes in female-led excursions. They encourage women to try new things and pave their own path. That's where I met Dora. She's like a big sister to me. Anyway, she started booking these trips for my online persona, which is . . . you're gonna laugh."

"I won't laugh." Robbie was dead serious. Was he sweating?

"Kat Wanderfull." She buried her face in her hands. Scissoring her fingers, she peeked between them with one eye. "Wanderfull because of the traveling. Get it? It's ridiculous. Making up a fake person and keeping it hidden."

"Not at all. In fact, I need to—"

"I hid it from John, too." Keira released a heavy breath. "I only told him this past week. Shows you how close we were. He was adamant that he join me on this trip. I figured it couldn't hurt to have an extra pair of hands to help with tricky shots. He's kind of an amateur photographer himself. Around the same time, I got word that the Adventure Channel is interested in my work. Like, they think I have a charisma they look for in their shows' hosts."

"That's really cool, Keira."

"They want to see whether my followers respond to not merely the locations, although that's important, but me as well. I've kept myself behind the camera for the most part. Being a high school teacher, I was worried about my students figuring it all out. The Adventure Channel wants me to be more in front of the camera now. For that, I need a colleague. Things as they were, I figured that would be John. But we saw how that went, didn't we?"

"Keira, I need to stop you—"

"This is a lot of time I'll be spending with someone. Your only job would be to take the pictures I tell you to take. That's it. But in that process, you'll get to travel to cool places, stay in amazing hotels and resorts, eat all the New York strip steak and potato confit—" She giggled. Goodness, he had her giggling. "All for free. Also, I'll pay you."

"Anabelle . . ."

"She can come along. We'll work in some fun kid stuff along the way. Maybe after this South Dakota trip, we can make our way to California. All expenses paid while you and Anabelle have the vacation of a lifetime. And you won't ever have to camp in a tent. Unless you want to."

Couldn't he say something . . . anything? Instead of simply staring straight through her?

"Strictly business. We can even write up a contract." She pulled her folder out of the satchel and flipped through it quickly.

Robbie grabbed a roll out of the basket. He gnawed off a large bite. Perhaps chewing aided his decision-making.

Her eyes trailed to his arms. Even through the shirt, his muscles visibly cut across one another. All the food he ate only seemed to stuff those biceps and pectorals. Meanwhile, for Keira, that bite of bread constituted her carb allowance for a week.

"How about this? Let's try it for six days. Worst case, we part ways on Friday and you have enough money to fund your beach trip. Best case, I have someone I can trust to continue this path with me."

Trust may not have been the best choice of words. She'd fully trusted him once. He'd used that to string her along. And when she'd put her foot down, he'd betrayed her completely by getting together with Vivian. Had he grown since then? Maybe. Maybe not. But he had a daughter now—one for whom he was the sole provider. Even if his respect for Keira wasn't enough to allow integrity to bloom, his love for Anabelle was. He wouldn't risk her. Anabelle, also, would help keep things professional between them.

Keira had learned to stand her ground with men. She did a good job keeping John at a distance—too good of a job, in fact. She could do the same for Robbie. No man would stand in the way of her goals. But if she could partner with a man to achieve those goals, all while offering a mutual benefit to him, that was ideal, wasn't it?

Nothing could go wrong.

"Please, Robbie. How will I find someone in such limited time? I was with John for two years before he pulled that stunt of his. I can't handle being betrayed again."

"One week?"

"That's it. We'll see how it goes and decide from there." Keira could play dirty. She knew exactly what looks to give him to make him fold to her wishes.

But her new little friend, scribbling furiously across the table, gave her pause.

She wouldn't play games with Anabelle's heart. "It will be fun, I promise, as long as Anabelle doesn't mind postponing her sandcastle building awhile."

Chapter Thirteen

Keira's empty chair taunted him while he ate. Was he really considering a weeklong road trip with his ex-girlfriend? Well, no one had ever accused him of sanity. Strictly business, she'd said. Of course, it would be. Never mind how his entire body had reacted to her hand resting on his arm. As if the separation had never happened at all. But it had. So sour was the taste in his mouth, this steak wasn't even good. Okay, it was delightful, as were the fancy mashed potatoes. Still, he ate in defiance.

"Look, Daddy, I'm a mermaid." Anabelle was holding her leg straight out. She lifted the skirt of her dress to show the skin of the salmon resting on her knee.

He caught the tail of his guffaw with his hand. Looking around, he was glad no one had seen her comedic talents. "Kitty Kat, we can't play with fish skins in fancy restaurants. We'll get in trouble."

She pouted as he removed the fish skin, then wiped her knee with a napkin.

Keira needed to get back soon or who knows what other crazy ideas Anabelle might try. Over her shoulder, he spied Keira near the bar. After she'd eaten less than ten bites of her food, she'd excused herself to snap some pictures. The bartender started chatting with her. She was grinning . . . with a stranger. Was this part of her Kat Wanderfull persona? Who was he committing to spending a week with? Kat or Keira?

If he didn't accept her offer, someone like that guy might. And he'd probably pretend to be some great man and earn her trust. Then, after a few months or years of stringing her along, she'd discover he'd been misleading her the whole time.

He wasn't so different. He should have told her about MRCustom. These stories never ended well when the guy hid the truth. Except in that Tom Hanks movie every girl loved about the bookstores. That blond chick didn't mind his lie. But Robbie wasn't Tom Hanks. And he was about 90 percent sure that if he admitted he was the guy she'd already dumped the other day, this trip would be over before it began. Then she'd put her future in the hands of someone like Whiskey Jack over there.

That other 10 percent? That wasn't worth getting his hopes up over. Tonight, in the hotel room, he would delete that useless account. She'd never know. Hadn't she cyber-dumped him anyway? She wouldn't even miss him.

Later that night in the dim hotel room, the bright screen of the phone burned Robbie's eyes. Anabelle had finally dozed off. The excitement of the day had taken its toll. By the time they'd returned to the hotel, Anabelle wasn't listening to Robbie anymore. She'd reached full-blown meltdown in the hallway outside their room. Keira was likely regretting her proposal for him and his little velociraptor daughter on this trip already.

His finger hovered above the Momentso icon. *Just erase it. Delete the account. She's right in the next room if you want to talk to her.*

But would she talk to him? Probably not.

The yellow icon flashed.

A new message? He tapped it once, then pressed the envelope in the corner. There was a lag on the hotel's Wi-Fi. It felt like a lifetime before the message appeared.

When he saw Kat's name, his heart leaped so high it might've thunked its head on his collarbone. But, a few words in, that same heart lay down on the ground and started scooping dirt on itself.

> **KAT WANDERFULL:** Dear friend, I owe you an apology.
>
> **KAT WANDERFULL:** I broke up with my boyfriend this morning. I've realized I keep people at arm's length. Everyone I've ever loved has hurt me, so I guess it's my safeguard.
>
> **KAT WANDERFULL:** Do you know why I do this crazy Momentso thing? I was lonely after college. The kind of lonely where the walls bow in on you. I started teaching geography at my old high school, but by every Friday afternoon, the idea of returning to my quiet, dark apartment was too much. I traveled more, taking pictures along the way, and posting about it in case others couldn't travel to see the same sights. Eventually, people started following me. They'd tell me their stories, and it was as if they invited me into their lives, even if only for a moment.
>
> **KAT WANDERFULL:** You invited me in for much more than a moment, and I pushed you away.
>
> **KAT WANDERFULL:** I miss you. Please write back.

Keira missed him. At least a version of him. But learning her why behind this crazy charade wrenched his gut, especially knowing the role he'd played in her loneliness.

Even worse was knowing she trusted MRCustom with her story. Not him.

The green dot on her profile picture called to him. Three dots appeared, telegraphing that she was writing another message to him.

> **KAT WANDERFULL:** If not, I get it. I know what it feels like to be someone's second choice. You deserve better than that. I'm so very sorry.

Second choice? He quickly tapped a message, waited for autocorrect to catch his mistakes, then hit *Send*.

> **MRCUSTOM:** I already forgave you.
> **KAT WANDERFULL:** OH, THANK GOODNESS!
> **MRCUSTOM:** Lol. I refuse to believe you've ever been anyone's second choice.
> **KAT WANDERFULL:** My father chose his anger over me. That was the first eighteen years of my life. Then, for years, my college boyfriend strung me along, waiting for something better to come around. When she did . . . well, she did.

Is that what she thought? No, there was never anyone better than her. She was so first place in his mind that at the Olympics, the national anthem should sing a song about her.

And Keira should blame God for the stringing-along bit. Robbie would have married her in high school. Or right after. Ryann had gotten married a few days after her graduation. He could have, too. If it weren't for the Holy Spirit binding his tongue whenever he considered asking. *Yes, Keira, it was God that didn't want us to marry. Not me.*

But what girl wants to hear that? *You know that thing you want most in the world? Well, God is telling me he doesn't want you to get it.* That would not have helped her whole what-has-God-done-for-me-lately bit.

> **MRCUSTOM:** You aren't second place in my book.
> Why'd you open up to me?
> **KAT WANDERFULL:** Because I need someone to know
> me. Not the me I paint up and pose.
> **MRCUSTOM:** Why me, though?
> **KAT WANDERFULL:** Because you've been there for me,
> without fail.
> **MRCUSTOM:** I'm just a man. I'll fail you sometime.
> **KAT WANDERFULL:** Doubtful.
> **MRCUSTOM:** Isn't there anyone else you can count on?
> **KAT WANDERFULL:** Not without promising them
> something in return. I've got to go for now. I'm glad
> we talked.

Thunder sounded in the distance. He hadn't noticed a storm brewing when he'd looked to the west on the way to dinner. Skies had been clear. Again, a slight rumble. No, that wasn't thunder. The soft rapping was coming from the door adjoining their rooms.

He unlatched it slowly. Anabelle didn't stir at the slide of metal. Before he'd opened the door fully, a white sheet of paper slid in front of his face.

"Your copy of the contract I wrote up," Keira said softly. "Take a look at it and let me know if you want to make changes."

She'd washed her face. Without all the makeup, she looked younger. Less porcelain doll–like. His fingers itched to touch her bare cheek. Her hair, which had been precisely curled by six in the morning, was now put up into a knotted thing on top of her head. Her oversize sweatshirt from their alma mater hung loosely over shorts so tiny he forced his eyes to her stockinged feet. Two hideously ugly alpacas had apparently sacrificed their lives so she could have warm toes.

"Are you texting someone?" Her gaze fell to his phone.

"Nope." He tossed his phone onto his bed, praying it landed screen-side down in the covers.

It did.

He took the contract. The jumble of words below the EndeavHerMore logo assaulted his eyes. He angled the paper to allow the light from Keira's room to illuminate them. Even worse. Was she expecting him to read it now while they stood there? Heat scorched his face.

"There's a lot of useless legal stuff in there. Do you . . . want me to go over it with you?"

"Yeah."

"Come on in."

Anabelle snorted into her pillow.

"I can't leave her alone." He got down to the floor, crossing one leg awkwardly beneath his other. He pressed his back against the doorframe, the trim digging into his spine. He needed her to sit down. From this angle, all he could see were legs. "Can you sit?"

She adjusted to a seated position on the floor much more naturally than he did. Leaning against her wall, her shoulder grazed his back. Holding out the paper between them, he put his fingertip beneath the first word, then the second and the third. The air he was trying to breathe thickened to a syrup.

Her hand curled over his shoulder blade as she angled her body toward him and the contract.

"Read it to me. Go slow."

Keira's beauty was softer without her makeup but not dulled. An intriguing beauty that crept up on him, catching his heart's focus, not his eyes at first. It had been that way for Robbie from the start. For years he'd watched her fade into the background of every classroom and school event. To him, though, she was like one of those optical illusions. If he stared long enough and shifted his focus, he could see the young woman instead of the old woman or the stairs leading up instead of down. And once he saw it differently, he couldn't forget it.

CHAPTER FOURTEEN

Ten Years Earlier

ead it to me. You know the rules." Keira tapped the
Reraser end of her pencil on the table. Robbie didn't
mind that hot-tutor vibe she gave off.

After helping him twice a week all summer, Keira held a
front-row seat to the circus that was his brain. But unlike the
teachers he'd had in school, she didn't pity him or get annoyed
when he, a seventeen-year-old, read at an elementary-student
level. Instead, she helped him. She'd read a book on learning
disabilities and explained he likely had one. She'd explained
that if he did have one, then that didn't mean his brain was
broken—only wired differently. Wired in a way that teaching
strategies developed for the masses didn't reach.

At first, he'd almost stormed out of the town's library,
but she'd grabbed his hand and held it. Now she came to
their sessions armed with see-through colored papers she
placed over top of his book and reading guides to help him
only see the line he was trying to read. She even brought
him a plumbing elbow. The idea was for him to hold it like
a telephone, reading aloud into the one end, then his voice
would come out through the other end and go straight to his
ear. That one he refused. Instead, he had to read everything

out loud to her. He didn't mind, since she sat so close to him when he did.

"Go on. Read it," she repeated. As one of her teaching strategies, he had to write her letters, then practice reading them out loud for fluency or some junk like that.

Write what you think about, she'd said. So, as instructed, each week, he'd slip a folded notebook paper out of his pocket. At first, he wrote about football, fly-fishing, and partying with his friends, but now something else consumed his thoughts.

He stared at the folded note on the flat pine surface as if it were a bomb that would explode if he didn't *Mission: Impossible* this.

"What are you waiting for, silly? I'm dying to hear more about trout and caddis fly larvae." At the corner of her eyes, her skin crinkled.

He'd learned that was her smile. For the longest time, he'd assumed she had crooked teeth or no teeth at all. Why else would she hide her smile away? But when she spoke, he found she had very nice teeth. Which reminded him what he'd written in this note.

"This letter is different."

"Okay. Let's hear it."

"It's personal."

"Good. The best writers use their personal thoughts and feelings to write masterpieces."

"This is no masterpiece."

"How am I supposed to know that if I don't know what it says?" She scooted closer to him.

He followed her gaze to the front desk.

Mrs. Eckels, the woman in charge of the summer tutoring program, headed outside for a smoke break.

Keira's hand curled over his shoulder, sending his nerves into overdrive.

He unfolded the note with trembling fingers. Why was he nervous? He'd fed so many lines to girls in the past. Why was this different? Because it was Keira. And it was true.

"Dear Keira . . ." Robbie blew out a breath.

"You want me to write what I think about. Fine. I think about you." He shook his head, expecting her to remove her hand or scoot away.

She didn't. "Go on."

"When I'm fishing, I think about how your lips move when you say stuff to you. Oh, that should say *me."*

"No editing, remember? Just read what you've written." She sounded winded.

"At football conditioning, I wonder what it would feel like to touch your hair. It's probably soft. When I'm working around the resort, I imagine you putting your hand on my neck." Robbie closed the note.

"You weren't finished." She unfolded it and flattened it with her hand.

Robbie cracked a nervous smile. *"When I lie in bed at night, I picture kissing you. And I hope you want to kiss me, too. Forever and always, your Robbie."* His eyes bored through the paper, through the desktop, to the ground below. He kind of wished he was six feet under in this moment. "I probably used the wrong *your."*

Next to him, she didn't move. He wasn't sure she was even breathing.

Great. He broke her.

Her hand reached for the pencil. She was shaking. On the top of his letter, she wrote, *Follow me.* Then she was gone, walking toward the back of the library.

He could see the back of Mrs. Eckels's head through the front window, a puff of smoke rising above her. Careful not to make any noise, he pushed back his chair and followed Keira's path. He'd lost sight of her. He checked each aisle, each alcove. He was about to check the women's bathroom when he noticed the darkened kids' room. Heading that way, he lifted his shoulders high.

No matter what would happen, he was 150 percent authentic and totally not a coward.

Though the lights were off, he could still make out the cartoon characters on the walls. He remembered coming here for story time as a preschooler. His mom used it as a break since stories were the only thing that kept him sitting still.

Kelli appeared from the shadows, grabbing his hand, then tugging him into a corner of the room.

He'd never seen her eyes wider. Was she scared of him? Or this thing between them?

Slowly, she reached up to her ponytail and untwisted the rubber band that held it off her face. Using her fingers, she combed her chocolate hair down over her shoulder.

His hand didn't wait for his brain, not that any part of him cared much about sound decision-making right now. He touched the tendril closest to her neck. Pure silk. He gentled it between his thumb and forefinger.

Her palm touched his chest first. He inflated it like a balloon. She probably already found him attractive. Most girls did. But she wasn't like most girls. It couldn't hurt to remind her of his muscles. He was suddenly thankful for all those hours in the school's weight room.

Her hand lingered a moment, then slid up over the collar of his shirt, coming to rest on the side of his neck. It was clammy. Had she ever kissed anyone before? Probably not. Her father was a supreme jerk. School and tutoring were the only times she was allowed to leave her house. Plus, no one ever talked to her, except Robbie.

His friend—scratch that—his former friend, Mason, said she wasn't hot enough for homecoming, but he'd probably still show her the bed of his truck. That comment had earned him a black eye and Robbie an extra hour of conditioning.

Lifting onto her toes, she neared. As soft as a whisper, her lips touched his. Closing his eyes, he accepted her kiss politely, all while holding back the cage door to the raging desire inside him.

She drew back. Her lips curled into a smile—the first one of hers he'd ever seen.

The cage door blasted open. Burying his fingers into her hair behind her head and wrapping her waist with his other arm, he pressed her tight against him. He caught the breath she expelled as his mouth covered hers. Her lips were warm and forgiving of his forward behavior. If she wanted this kiss to end, she'd have to be the one to step away. He wouldn't. He couldn't. He'd hold on to her forever, he was sure. Up and over her shoulder, his hand slid, to her upper arm.

She winced.

"Did I hurt you?"

"A little." She moved to kiss him again.

"But I barely touched your arm."

"It's nothing. Just sensitive."

Robbie found a light switch on the desk and flicked it on. He pushed up the sleeve of her shirt. A deep bruise purpled the flesh between her elbow and shoulder.

"Robbie, it's nothing. Let's go back to the table."

He turned her arm. On the back side, stripes marred her otherwise flawless skin. Gently, Robbie positioned his fingers between the marks and aligned his thumb with the bruise in front, mimicking the grip that had harmed the girl he'd fallen in love with one tutoring session at a time.

CHAPTER FIFTEEN

This yawn refused to be stifled. Keira had stayed up way too late helping Robbie with that contract. He was right. They didn't need all the legal mumbo jumbo. One thing she could count on—Robbie Matthews was devoted. At the end of the week, if things went well, he would let this go on and on and on. He should be the one worried she might breach the contract without warning.

She shook out her arms. Nope. *Don't think about that.* This picture was meant to be carefree, not burdened.

Her mind kept going back to the way he'd looked at her when she'd asked him to read the contract out loud. Had he remembered what she'd remembered? Considering how he kept looking at her lips, it seemed so. She should add that to the contract. *Robert Charles Matthews agrees not to stare at Keira Emmaline Knudsen's lips during conversations in close quarters. He shall also refrain from wearing her favorite cologne.* Could she get away with making him cut off his curls? Perhaps a good buzz cut would help with that "strictly business" part.

Who was she kidding? He could still warm her insides with a shaved head and a peg leg.

Focus, Keira. She needed to get a few shots in to make up for yesterday's playdate with Anabelle. One shot, in particular, had her nerves in a fray. What would her followers say when they saw her face for the first time?

If they hated it, she couldn't blame the light, which was perfect. She twirled a curl around her finger and placed it in front of her shoulder next to the others. Keira waited for the cloud of breath to dissipate. A moment later, she held up her camera with the digital screen flipped to stare back at her. Lips parted, she offered the camera the same coy look she used to give Robbie when she wanted a kiss. The orange glow flushed her skin to a perfect tan and enriched her normally blue eyes to a vivid green.

Perfect. Except for that person in the background. Check that—persons, plural.

"Keira!" Anabelle jumped from Robbie's arms and ran to her.

"Hey, sweetie. What are you doing up so early?" Who cared about perfect light when this little girl's arms were around her?

The coffee cup Robbie held out to her made her stomach growl in want. "Do you still like your coffee the same way?"

Did he mean high calorie and fat laden? Not if she wanted to keep fitting into the camera frame. But it would feel warm in her cold hand, so she accepted it.

"I hope we didn't interrupt you. Annie doesn't sleep past six."

"No problem. Just trying to get a quick picture before the sun gets too high."

Robbie set his coffee down on the ground and reached out a hand. "I'll take it for you."

"Um . . ." She glanced down at Anabelle, still hugging her waist. "Okay. I want one, kind of up close . . . with my

face and hair, but off-center. I want the background out of
focus a bit, but I can do that afterward on the computer."

He took the camera and got in position. "Kitty Kat,
come here."

The little girl held tight.

"It's okay. She's short." She reclaimed her coy expression as Robbie flipped the screen.

His smile fell when his eyes focused on the frame.

"What's wrong?"

"Nothing." He swallowed hard. The camera clicked once.
"Hold on." Stepping forward he dragged his pinkie finger
from the outside of her brow, down over her cheekbone to her
jaw. A loose hair?

As the sun's light drove back the shadows, Robbie took
another few pictures. Suddenly, Anabelle's hand reached to
Keira's armpit and tickled her, sending her nerves into a tizzy.

She laughed.

Snap.

"Oh, that last one will look terrible." She tickled the
little girl back, enjoying her tiny giggle. Stepping around
the camera, she pressed the image playback button. Ugh.
Her mouth hung open, and her eyes crinkled at the edges in
the picture. *Not cute.*

She pulled the camera out of his hand. Bending down,
she loaded it into her camera bag.

"I'm done for the morning."

"Good. Take a walk with us to Memorial Park. You can
take more pictures there."

"A walk? It's too early, and it's cold."

"You've gotta embrace the cold, girl. You've gotta get
some meat on your bones. Drink up that coffee creamer."

She wouldn't. But as the steam swirled beneath her nose,
it sure did smell good. Robbie was pretending not to watch

her as they walked. Years ago, she would have drunk this happily. She'd gained weight during college, thanks to two things. Not having a father around to slap food out of her hand. And having a boyfriend who told her ten times a day how beautiful she was, with or without makeup, with or without extra weight. She could guess what he thought when he looked at her now, because she thought it about herself. A few added pounds would make her collarbones stick out less. An additional snack would keep her stomach from twisting on itself.

But as they say, the camera adds ten pounds, and commenters could be mean. She'd seen that in the threads of other social media personalities. If she wanted a traveler's lifestyle, she needed to have someone pay for it. If she wanted someone to pay for it, she needed followers. If she wanted followers, she needed to be the person people wanted to chase after.

Robbie, however, had always accepted her as she was. The only prodding he'd ever done was to encourage her to be her authentic self. Of course, like Curley's wife, she had no self back then. She was Robbie's girlfriend—his *beloved* girlfriend, no doubt, but still his girlfriend. No more, no less.

Kat Wanderfull was her true self. Wasn't she?

Would it be so wrong if Kat enjoyed a few sips of her favorite coffee?

She tilted the cup, letting the sweet, rich drink slide over her tongue and down her throat, flushing her with warmth. The streets of Rapid City were quiet this early Sunday morning. In front of them, Anabelle skipped along the sidewalk. For a moment, Keira let herself imagine a different world, where Anabelle was hers and Robbie might reach for her hand as it swung at her side.

After exploring the park and snagging some photos by Rapid Creek, they returned to the hotel. They settled at a table in a room off the lobby, where a full continental

breakfast awaited them. Robbie and Anabelle looked like a
Scottish laird and lady with all the dishes sitting before
them. As opposed to Keira, who'd filled up on fruit and
unsweetened oatmeal with slivered almonds. She accepted
a bite of scrambled eggs off Robbie's fork. Then stole another when she thought he wasn't looking. The salted butter
coated the roof of her mouth, bringing so much pleasure,
she sank into her seat.

"What's on the docket for today?" he asked, before draining the last sip of orange juice into his mouth.

"It's Sunday. Your day off."

He tilted his head. "Oh, I get days off? Cool. I haven't
even had my first day."

"Wherever I am, I like to attend a local church. Sometimes they're good. Other times they are a bit kooky, but
you know . . . it's still worship. Today, I was hoping to go
see the Chapel in the Hills. It has this old-world architecture. Great for pictures. I bet you'd love its intricate wood
carvings."

"I'm game. And after that?"

"I do my own thing on Sundays." It sounded harsher
than she meant it to. "But it's kind of a drive. Do you think
you could drop me off? All mileage will be reimbursed."

"Sure can."

I'm supposed to drop you off in this shack, pick you up in
four hours, and believe you won't be murdered?" The
small building sat in the middle of rolling hills, nearly two
hours away from their hotel. Various colored tin slats puz-
zled the roof. Its door hung crooked on its hinges, and the
whole thing appeared to have only one window.

"What's *murdered* mean?" Anabelle asked from the
back seat.

Robbie cringed. "Uh, nothing. Pretend I didn't say that, baby."

Keira looped her satchel over her head. "I'll be fine."

"You won't tell me who you're meeting or what you'll be doing for four hours. As far as I know, you're working in a crystal meth lab. Can I walk you in at least? Please?"

"You're cute when you're overprotective." She patted his cheek.

The door of the old truck groaned when she shoved it open.

Oh no, she doesn't. Robbie jumped out of the truck. He ran around the front bumper, impressed with his own quickness, given his size. All that quarterback maneuvering came in handy. Catching up to her before she'd covered half the distance, he grasped her hand. "Wait."

"Robbie, let me go."

"First, tell me why you're here."

Keira scanned the landscape. "To do a small part to fix what others have broken, I guess."

The door of the house swung open. An older man with peppered-gray hair appeared, dressed in head-to-toe denim, broken up only by a leather belt. "Kat Wanderfull?"

Keira twisted her hand from Robbie's to offer a handshake to the man. "That's me."

"Michael Cook. You are?" Angled toward Robbie, the man's hand was calloused and scarred, much like his own. His friendly smile relieved Robbie's fears.

"He's not staying," she said.

Robbie accepted the man's greeting. "Yes, I am. My name's Robbie. I have my daughter, Anabelle, here, too. Whether we wait in the truck or join in the fun is up to Kat." He gave her a pointed look.

"The more, the merrier, as they say." Michael glanced

back to the truck. "We have some toys your daughter can play with inside. She looks about my granddaughter's age. I'll be bringing her by later. Perhaps they can play."

"Anabelle would love that," Robbie said, turning his focus on Keira.

"That's fine, I guess," she said.

Her narrowed eyes tickled Robbie. He did love getting to her. Robbie waved Anabelle over. After hopping out of the vehicle, she used her whole body to shut the door, then ran to the group. Robbie caught her mid-run, swinging her up to his hip, and followed the two inside.

"We got the paint and all the supplies right over there. Of course, I don't expect you to finish everything, but anything you can do would be helpful."

Looking around, Robbie found a makeshift classroom. Mismatched tables and chairs held together with duct tape had been pushed to the center of a large round, stained rug. Several of the walls had been graffitied with slurs so wretched, he was glad Anabelle couldn't read yet. "I brought some bottled water for you. All on the back porch."

Keira lifted her hair up into a ponytail, securing it with an elastic

"Nobody should be by since it's Sunday and all. You have my number if there's anything you need." Michael pulled out a bin of toys for Anabelle and bade goodbye, his truck leaving a cloud of dust behind.

Keira found a screwdriver and began unfastening the light switch from the plaster.

Robbie grabbed another and got started on the outlet covers. "Kat Wanderfull, you're a mystery. Tell me, do your followers know what a do-gooder you are?"

"Are you going to tease me about this, too?"

"I think it's cool. How does it work?"

"I don't want to talk about it."

"Enough with the humility already. You're caught, so spill it."

Keira sighed. "During the school year, I spend Saturday doing the picture thing. I change outfits, hairstyles, and scenery multiple times. Then I schedule check-ins and posts each day of the week. That way, it seems like I've spent a good deal of time in the location."

"Sounds exhausting, but okay."

"It honestly is. Which is why on Sundays, I go to church, like we did earlier. And I find some way to give back. I don't post about it because—"

"Because superheroes don't brag about their work." From where he knelt, he couldn't see her face, but only the stilled screwdriver she held.

"I'm not trying to be a hero or savior of any kind. But traveling around? You see stuff that breaks your heart, like this," she said, pointing the end of the screwdriver toward the graffiti. "The people in these towns welcome me in like I'm family. How can I turn a blind eye if there's something I can do to help them? Even if it's just painting a couple walls."

He rolled the handle of the tool between his fingers. It was the same Craftsman he had in his truck's glovebox. "You're different, Keira. Do you know that? You're brave. Maybe too brave. Have you had anything scary happen to you while you've been traveling on your own?"

"Nothing I couldn't handle."

"Not to harp on it, but you need to be careful coming by yourself to places like this."

"I've managed to survive many years without Robbie the Protector."

"But I'm back, aren't I? For this week at least, I'll be by your side . . . just in case Kat has reached her ninth life."

She played some music from her phone, using a cup as an amplifier. After prying open the brand-new pail of paint, Robbie began cutting in below the ceiling. Keira rolled the flat surfaces. They maneuvered around each other, making surprisingly good progress in the two hours before Michael returned.

"Michael, I run a remodeling business," Robbie said. "If you have some tools around here, I could knock out a few of these repairs for you."

"I might be able to scrounge up a few."

Anabelle took quickly to Michael's granddaughter. The two girls played ring-around-the-rosy outside as Robbie re-hung the door, fixed a stuck window, and repaired some faulty wiring in a light fixture. When he finished, he stepped back inside to find Michael and Keira replacing the last of the tables. The room didn't look good as new, but it was better, nonetheless.

As they drove away, with Anabelle already snoozing in her car seat, Robbie wanted to tell Keira how proud he was. But she had to know already. The sweet smile gracing Keira's face was the best thing he'd seen in South Dakota yet.

CHAPTER SIXTEEN

After grabbing dinner at a sandwich shop, they returned to the hotel. Nestled beneath the quilt, Anabelle wound down by watching a Princess Patty Cake cartoon on the TV at the hotel.

He knocked a rhythm on the door connecting to Keira's room.

When she opened it, she smiled. Her wet hair hung limply over the straps of her tank top. The excess fabric of oversize pants pooled at her feet. She looked comfortable and fresh-faced, with a sprinkling of freckles across her nose and cheeks.

Mercy. Why had he bothered her again? He couldn't remember. "Hey. What are you working on?"

"My shots from this morning. Wanna see?"

"Sure."

"I'll grab my laptop. One second." Keira disappeared, taking her soapy-clean scent with her. When she reappeared, she carried her still-open computer. As she squeezed past him in the doorway, her elbow brushed across his stomach, although she pretended not to notice.

He followed Keira to the desk in his room, where she

placed her laptop. The screen displayed an incredible picture of her with that look. The one he was helpless around.

She sat in the chair in front of the computer and motioned for him to stand over her shoulder. She pulled a leg up, hugging her knee to her chest with one arm, while the hand of the other worked the touch pad. "I could use your opinion. Which filter do you like better?" She toggled between a warmer, more vibrant hue and a cooler, artsier one.

He knew from his time as MRCustom that she preferred the artsy one. "The first one with the orange glow makes your eyes pop more.

Nibbling the nail on her thumb, she focused on each picture, placing them side by side. "I know I'm being silly, but this picture is important. It's the first time I'll show my face to my followers. What if they . . ."

A piece of wet hair on the back of her head looked as if it was caught it some kind of gymnastics move. He smoothed it, letting his fingers trail the length of her locks. When they grazed the fabric of her tank top near her spine, he forced his hand back to the table. "They'll think you're beautiful, Kat. I mean, look at you." His hand stretched over the laptop's built-in touch pad, waiting for permission before he made contact. After a tilt of her chin assured him he wouldn't get bopped for touching her computer, he went to the cascade of pictures from that morning. He clicked on the last one when she'd laughed thanks to Anabelle. "This one's my favorite."

"No way. I look goofy."

"But even your goofy is pretty. And it's more you."

She bumped his hand with hers over the touch pad, going back to the more posed picture from before. "This one is better."

"Sure, if you want your followers kissing their screens."

"What are you talking about?"

"That come-hither look. Every guy who sees that picture is going to want you. Is that what you're going for?"

She scoffed. "They won't."

"Trust me, Keira. I'm a man. Shoot, it makes me want to kiss you right now." He ticked up a brow in her direction.

"Don't you dare. Besides, you don't count. You always had this weird attraction to me, even when others didn't."

"You were always gorgeous. I just noticed before everybody else. Too bad attraction isn't enough to make a relationship last, huh? 'Cause we had that in spades."

"That we did." She looked away from him, quiet for a solid thirty seconds. "Is that what you think? That I'm trying to entice men with these pictures."

"Uh, yeah. Why else would you make that face?"

She enlarged the photo of her coy smile. She looked model pretty, especially with the editing she'd done on it. The small scar on her forehead he used to kiss had been smoothed over. The tiny mole by the corner of her eye had been darkened to look more pronounced. "I'm posting it anyway."

She pulled up Momentso. The mailbox icon flashed, and she paused.

"Hey, you got a message. Who's it from?" Not that he needed to ask. After all, he'd sent it ten minutes ago. Maybe seeing her reaction to MRCustom's message could help him come up with a way to tell her the truth.

"Probably spam. I'll check it later."

"Let's check it now." He reached for the touch pad, and she slapped his hand. "Ow. When did you get so vicious? Do you have some secret boyfriend you don't want me to know about?"

"Maybe I do." Her cheek pulled up, and she smirked. "He's a Nigerian prince who's promising me a big inheritance as long as I give him my bank account info."

"Oh, I had my money on a high-ranking military general who is a single father and likes long walks on the beach."

"He's that, too. The most romantic man in the world."

"More romantic than me? I doubt it."

"I'll give you that. You spoiled me."

"But that wasn't enough, either, was it?" He watched her profile, begging her to look in his direction. If she did, maybe they could lay it all out there. Get to the nitty-gritty of the grenade that had shattered both of them. He tucked a lock of hair behind her ear. "Kat, look at me."

"I should probably go back to my room now. I'm going to post this and turn in for the night. I'll see you in the morning." Stoic couldn't touch the stillness in Keira's face. Whatever she was thinking, she wouldn't tell him. He'd have to wait until she messaged MRCustom.

After rolling her head in a full circle atop her shoulders, Keira reached beneath the thick, loose braid and massaged the back of her neck. Four separate outfits, three hairstyle changes, and scores of photographs over seven hours were tiring. Three straight days of the same thing was downright exhausting.

It didn't help that she'd spent half of her photography time teaching Robbie how to use her cameras. Thankfully, he was a quick learner, and Anabelle had been a good sport, always finding ways to entertain herself. When she'd gotten too bored, Robbie would go into Superdad mode and create a game for her to play. About one hour ago, they'd disappeared over a bluff in search of an evil half troll, half prairie dog out to kidnap Princess Patty Cake in Badlands National Park.

The picture of her face had caused quite the rumble on

Momentso. Not only was it her most liked picture, but it had also received thousands of comments and pushed #whois-KatWanderfull to the list of top ten trending hashtags. The onslaught of new followers had nearly crashed her profile. The pictures she'd posted from Needles Highway in Custer State Park on Monday and Wind Cave National Park yesterday were among her most popular yet. And the Adventure Channel had noticed. Soon, she'd be moving on and up, leaving behind the state and national parks and heading overseas to visit the places of her dreams. She could always keep up with Anabelle through pictures. Surely, she and Robbie had established enough of a friendship to warrant that.

Keira dug the heel of her hand into the aching muscle covering her heart. If it kept doing that, she'd have to either see a doctor or stop imagining saying goodbye to Anabelle. Keira carried her bags to the spot where they'd parked the truck earlier, off the dirt road. She loaded her equipment. Other than some critters, there hadn't been any life in sight the entire shoot.

With the troll hunters off on their adventure, she was alone. There was something to be said for having the world as far as the eye could see to herself. No one to hurt her. No one to fear. No one to get in the way of her dream.

The breeze swirled around her, kicking up the dirt in a dust devil and whipping her skirt around her legs. This was the kind of June day when God was simply showing off. She longed to find a sweet spot in the prairie grass to rest and enjoy the brilliance. But she needed to find the troll hunters and let them know she was finished. Anabelle probably needed a nap. Considering the yawn that escaped her mouth again, Keira may need one also.

Climbing the bluff west of her latest shoot made her calves burn in that "strong is the new pretty" way. Dora and the rest of the EndeavHerMore team would be proud. It probably helped that Robbie had made a grand breakfast in his room's mini kitchen, and she'd eaten more than usual that morning—scrambled eggs, some hash browns, fruit, and even a bite of turkey sausage. He'd become quite the cook since college. Imaginings of lazy Saturday mornings popped into her head. Robbie was a bring-his-wife-breakfast-in-bed type of guy. She could picture him carrying a tray into her bedroom and placing it on her lap. Then leaning down to kiss—

No, Keira. That kind of thinking only led to pain.

About thirty yards away, she found them. They'd unzipped and spread a sleeping bag wide on the grass. Father and daughter lay flat on their backs, pointing up to the sky.

Robbie saw her first. "Hey. All done?"

She gave a quick nod and suppressed the smile he'd tugged out of her too many times already this week.

"Good. Come check out the Cloud Animal Zoo with us. So far, Anabelle has found one of those famous short-necked giraffes and a whale with cow feet."

Anabelle propped herself up on her elbow to face Robbie. "Piggy feet."

"You're right. A whale with piggy feet."

Satisfied with the correction, Anabelle settled onto her back once again and perused the sky.

Robbie still watched Keira. He'd been acting strange the past few days. Quieter. A bit more paranoid, as if every man they encountered was a wolf in human clothing ready to devour Keira. She could understand if he was on Momentso and had seen some of the more perverse comments on the portrait shot, but he wasn't on the app.

He patted the spot on the sleeping bag next to him. She hesitated a moment, then shook off her worry. It wasn't like he was asking her to kiss him. Just lie next to him and his daughter and look at clouds. What could be more innocent than that? The fact that she was drawn to him didn't matter. Not one bit.

She stretched out on the smooth navy material, keeping a narrow strip of space between them. Try as she might to focus on the puffy cloud above, she felt his stare. Giving in, she turned to him.

He grinned. "Hi."

Anabelle peeked up over Robbie's pectoral muscles. "D'you see any animals, Keira?"

"Let me see." She forced her imagination to form shapes when all she really saw was mounds of mashed potatoes and heaps of ice cream. Slowly, as one cloud layer shifted beneath another, she saw two round ears. A face emerged behind a big tummy, maybe with arms and legs tucked in front of it. "Okay, I've got one. It's a mouse."

Robbie squinted his eyes, angling his head in every direction as he tried to find said mouse.

Lifting her arm into the sky, she pointed directly overhead.

"I still don't see it," he said.

She shifted her body until she was practically lying on him. Ignoring his chuckle, she pointed again, placing her face right next to his so they could share perspectives. "Look straight up. Can you see the ears and the little nose?" Her finger traced the air.

"Okay, I can see something, but it isn't a mouse." He grabbed her outstretched hand and moved it in a different pattern. "A mouse would be short with a wide body and a long head. That cloud is tall."

She nudged him, and his brow arched up. Some harmless flirting, that's all this was. "Not a real mouse. Like a cutesy *Tom and Jerry* cartoon mouse." Keira entwined their fingers, and she retraced it.

"Did Tom dismember Jerry? Where are his arms and legs?"

After dropping his hand, she slapped his stomach, making him recoil into the ground and groan. "No, you sicko. He's kind of like this." She rolled onto her back and tucked her knees to her chest and wrapped her arms around them, forming a ball.

"You're terrible at this game, do you know that?" With a playful shove to her shoulder, he rolled her off the sleeping bag.

"If you're so good, you find one."

Accepting her challenge, he extended his arm toward her. "Okay. Come back, and I'll show you a Galápagos tortoise." He winked, and she caved.

She broached their separation and turned, allowing her hip and shoulder to settle into the material. Her chest and stomach rested against his side, and she laid her cheek on his chest. Cradled with his arm snug around her, she allowed herself to relax into an embrace as familiar as a classic novel. *Pride and Prejudice*, perhaps. Instantly recognizable. A dependable mainstay on any given afternoon.

He pointed to a cloud lower on the horizon at the five o'clock position. "Anabelle, do you see that big turtle? With the kinda long neck? That's a Galápagos tortoise. It lives on the Galápagos Islands in the Pacific Ocean, super far away. They're big enough to ride on, and they can live to be more than one hundred and fifty years old."

Keira didn't even have to move her head. She saw the cloud, just as sure as Robbie saw her.

"I see it," Anabelle said. "It looks like my turtle. Wait. Where are his ears? Do those big turtles have ears?"

"We should ask an expert. Do you know whose favorite animal is a Galápagos tortoise?" Robbie's question reverberated through his barreled chest and into her cheek.

"Mine." Keira raised her hand into the air so Anabelle

could see it. "But I've never met a tortoise, so I don't know what his ears are like. If I ever meet one, I'll ask."

"But if he don't have ears, then he won't hear you." Anabelle rolled against Robbie's other side, mirroring Keira's position. She lifted the stuffed toy Keira had given her, placing it on Robbie's stomach between them.

"I'll have to use sign language, I guess."

"I bet turtles are good at reading lips," Robbie chimed in. "As long as you speak slooooowlyyyy."

Suddenly, Keira didn't want this trip to end. If she could hold on to this moment and this feeling forever, she would. She reached into the pocket of her skirt to retrieve her phone. After clicking open the camera app, Keira flipped it to the front selfie camera. With the sun still hidden behind the mouse cloud, the picture of the three of them would be perfect, even if the screen was too dark to see now. Not that she would ever post it. This picture wasn't for Kat. It wasn't for Keira. It was for the real her, whoever that was. "Do you mind?" she asked Robbie as she held it above them.

"Not at all." His breath was soft and warm against her forehead. She wondered as she snapped the picture if he'd brushed a kiss there.

Keira placed the phone on the ground behind her back. She caressed the silky fur of the turtle's leg between her fingers until Anabelle's hand grabbed hers. Keira surrendered to the handhold, and a few minutes later, to the peaceful sleep.

CHAPTER SEVENTEEN

⁊

A giggle tickled Robbie's ears. Anabelle. He tried to open an eye, but it was too bright. Lush warmth pressed against his left side, and he turned into it, nuzzling his nose against hair that smelled like melon. Not Anabelle.

"Robbie."

The way the voice said his name was as soothing as a stream of water on his face after a football game. As soothing as his girlfriend's congratulatory hug after he'd passed for four touchdowns in front of the college recruiter.

"Robbie," she repeated

He wrapped himself around the voice, holding it tight against his chest, unwilling to let it go. At least until fists jabbed the muscles of his abdomen. "Robert Charles Matthews, wake up!"

Mom?

Then he remembered where he'd been—lying on the ground, looking at clouds with Anabelle and Keira in his arms. Oh goodness. Is that who he was smothering in a bear hug right now? Forcing open his lids, he met Keira's eyes. He unspooled his arms and legs from around her. "My bad."

"You guys are sleepyheads." Anabelle sat behind Keira. She was holding something—Keira's phone.

"Annie, did Keira say you can play on her phone?"

The little girl's mouth fell open. She shook her head slowly.

"Baby, you cannot do that. That's Keira's, and it's expensive. Say you're sorry."

Anabelle's lower lip quivered.

Keira, finally able to sit up after being smothered by him, tousled Anabelle's hair. "It's okay. No harm, no foul." She outstretched her hand.

Anabelle placed the phone on it, then popped up to her feet and began twirling.

Rising up to a seated position, Robbie rubbed his neck. "Sorry."

"It's just a phone." Keira waved her hand between them.

"I wasn't talking about that. I think I have a problem."

"I'd say. Other people sleepwalk. You sleepcuddle." Was she blushing?

"Apparently. Not that I ever have women in my bed." He clamped his lips together. *You're making it worse. Cut your losses and leave the conversation.*

"At least I'm not a stranger," Keira said. "It wasn't so long ago that—I mean to say, I still remember . . . ugh. Look, you're not terrible to cuddle with." Smoothing her braid, she looked away. Even above the breeze and Anabelle's singing, he heard Keira's stomach growl.

After pulling his phone out of his pocket, he checked the time. *4:18.* They'd all be ready for dinner soon. But that wasn't what invited the boulder into the pit of his stomach.

Four missed calls from Ryann.

Service here was spotty. Enough to register the missed calls, but not enough to let it ring. He tried calling her back, but the connection was too weak.

Fifteen minutes later, with Keira at the wheel steering

them away from the Badlands, Robbie stared at the bars on his phone, waiting for them to alight, while all kinds of scenarios raced through his mind. Their father wasn't in the best of health. The resort wasn't doing great this summer, and the stress was taking its toll. Could this be about him? Or had something happened to Ryann? She didn't always keep the best company. And, as much as he hated to admit it, his sister was full of secrets she'd never trusted him with. It worried him.

Finally, at the first sign of civilization, the call connected.

"Robbie?" his sister answered quickly.

"It's me. We had no cell service. What's up?"

"It's Vivian. She called the office and left a message. She's coming over Saturday and wants to spend time with Anabelle."

"Oh." Robbie stared through the windshield. More clouds had filled the sky. Beams of sunlight shone through. The kind, according to his mother, that angels used to come down to earth. Proof that God watched out for his children. Everything would be fine. Anabelle should know her mother. It could only bring more good than harm. Wasn't that the saying? "Isn't that what I've wanted? For her to be around? And we'll be back Friday night. It'll be fine."

"Will it?" There was an edge to Ryann's voice. "She sounded . . . insistent. Like, remember on that double date with Thomas and me when we were playing cards, and she kept telling me how she always finds a way to win at everything?"

"And then you went and ate all of the chocolate-covered strawberries I got for her birthday?"

Ryann snickered. "I completely forgot about that. No wonder she hates me. But yes, that same night. The way she sounded on the message reminded me of it. Collected. Almost conniving. You know?"

"I do." Robbie had tasted Vivian's contempt enough to burn the taste on his tongue. "Did she leave her number?"

He jotted down the digits on a napkin from the glove box before ending the call.

Keira was quiet, her thoughts, as always, a mystery. In the back, Anabelle sang the wrong words to "Here Comes My Girl." Leaning forward in the passenger seat, he shrugged as the seat belt's edge dug into his neck. No matter how hard he looked, the heavenly beams were gone.

With Anabelle's belly pressed against her shins, Keira held tight to little hands. As she extended her legs, Anabelle squealed, flying like an airplane above her. Keira made engine noises while she swiveled her hips and rocked side to side to mimic some serious fighter jet maneuvering.

Robbie opened the adjoining door.

Keira, lying with her head at the foot of the bed, tilted her chin back. Even upside down, he looked worried after the call he made to Vivian in the other room.

"Daddy, watch me play airplane," Anabelle said, breathlessly.

"That's not how you play airplane."

"Oh yeah? How do you play, Mr. Guy-Who-Knows-Everything?" Keira extended the challenge before she thought better of it.

Soon, Robbie had kicked off his boots, commanded Anabelle to stand to the side, and lain on the bed next to Keira. *Right* next to her . . . on a bed.

Keira rolled off, happy to watch the scene from a standing position several feet away.

He looked at Keira and pulled his knees to his chest. "Climb on."

Anabelle jumped and clapped her hands.

"Nope."

"Chicken." It was less of an insult and more of a dare. He patted his shins. "Think I can't hold you, Knudsen? Do you doubt my strength?" Still lying down, he spread his arms out wide and flexed his biceps.

Definitely strong enough. No doubt about it. He could be one of those Momentso guys who used his girlfriend as a prop, lifting her like a barbell or performing a one-armed push-up with her sitting on his back.

Plunting some of the fabric on her ankle-length skirt in her fists, she climbed on the bed.

Anabelle grinned, scrunching her facial features in what may have been an attempt at a wink.

"Don't you laugh at me, Anabelle."

The girl balled her hands in front of her and pounded them in a rhythm. "Air. Plane. Air. Plane."

Keira laid her stomach on Robbie's shins, tucking the extra skirt fabric beneath her for modesty's sake. She reached for his hands.

"Put on your helmet," he said in a robot voice.

"What helmet? Have you ever even been on an airplane?" She sought help from Anabelle, who pretended to place a helmet on her head and hook a strap under her chin. Keira rolled her eyes at Robbie. But after he repeated the command, she reenacted Anabelle's motions.

"Buckle seat belt," Robbie commanded.

This time, she obeyed. The sooner this was over with, and she could get away from him, the better.

"Clasp hands."

She interlocked her fingers with his.

He did a countdown from ten before he announced "lift-off." The whole thing was rather un-airplane-like. But then again, there was no game called "space shuttle." Or maybe there was. Keira wasn't exactly the expert on childhood games. All she knew, from her father, was "pour me a scotch," which was way more fun than "if you cry, you get hit."

As if she weighed a feather, he lifted her up parallel to the bed's surface. It was a nice, pleasant ride if she could ignore the strange intimacy of it. But then, Robbie looked to Anabelle. "Should I take her higher?"

"No need to go higher," Keira insisted.

Anabelle's chant changed to "Do. It. Do. It."

"You know what they say about the apple and the tree, right?" Keira said, in a strained voice.

"I'm sorry. I can't hear you. We've lost contact due to the high altitude."

Before she could protest, he straightened his legs until she was nearly upside down. Now she was the one squealing, especially when he started wobbling his legs.

"Uh-oh. Turbulence!"

"Don't you drop me, Robbie Matth—" Her panic caused her arms to give way. She thunked down onto his chest— hard. She couldn't breathe. After a moment, she realized it was because she was laughing. That silent kind that sucks all the air from the room for thirty seconds before it releases in an entirely-too-loud guffaw. It drew out his belly laugh, and she buried her face against his neck.

Anabelle joined the embrace. Something strange bloomed deep within Keira and, despite her efforts to subdue it, forced all her fear and insecurity to the surface of her skin.

Keira rolled away from them both and climbed off the bed. In the mirror, she checked her makeup. It was smeared, but she could fix it.

Anabelle hopped off the bed and ran to the bathroom. "I have to go potty."

Robbie, in the reflection behind Keira, sat on the edge of the bed watching her reapply her lipstick.

"Thanks for keeping her occupied while I called Vivian." Leaning forward, Robbie clasped his hands between his knees. "Saturday afternoon she's coming over, and we're going to have a picnic by the river. Like a regular, old family. But I doubt we'll do any cloud watching."

There was that twinge near her heart again. It was fiercer this time, and she half expected to see an alien burst through her skin above the neckline of her tank top. "Why is she coming over?"

He pushed a hurricane-force wind out of his lungs. "She's her mother. A little girl needs her mother."

"Not one like that. You know what Viv is like. She was determined to come between us our entire relationship. Eventually, she did." She loosened the elastic band securing her braid. "What if that's what she plans to do with Anabelle?"

"I hear your concern. But Vivian has a heart. She does. She wouldn't take Annie away from me." Robbie's gaze met hers in the reflection. "Besides, it wasn't Vivian that got between me and you. I'm not sure what did, but it wasn't her."

From the bathroom, water roared from the faucet. In Anabelle's singsong voice, the alphabet sounded through the door—a trick her dad had taught her, no doubt, to ensure she washed her hands thoroughly.

Then Robbie was there, standing at Keira's back. She didn't need to look in the mirror or over her shoulder. She could feel him just as she could feel an impending rainstorm in the marrow of her bones. When he touched the end of her braid, she closed her eyes. As he unthreaded the sections of hair, releasing the long, loose curls around her face, chills coursed down her spine into the tips of her toes.

In the mirror, his eyes were pained. "We haven't talked about what happens when we go back to Montana on Friday. Annie's loved being around you this week." His arm slid across her collarbone and pulled her back against his chest. "I have, too."

She had enough words in her head to rival *War and Peace*. His warmth and his strength tied them into knots. She didn't dare turn around, lest she give in to the desire to kiss him.

Not a moment too soon, the bathroom door opened. Bounding into the room, Anabelle barreled into their legs. "Family hug!"

From the nightstand, Keira's phone buzzed a rare incoming call.

In the mirror, the look in Robbie's eyes begged her to ignore it, to stay like this.

Within her, claws tore her every which way. The pain was too much. She needed an escape. Stepping away from them, she snatched the phone and answered.

"You are everywhere, girl!" Dora's voice bounced several octaves higher than normal. "Brilliant move."

"What are you talking about?" Keira glanced at Robbie. Oh, the way he looked at her . . . As if he was a sailor lost at sea, and she was dry land.

"That picture you posted today. Sure, it was a bit off-brand, but my, oh my, it has skyrocketed you to a new playing field. Haven't you been keeping up with your notifications?"

"No, I've been busy with other things." Keira opened her laptop and waited for it to awaken.

"Does 'other things' have a brother?"

"Dora, I honestly have no idea what you're talking about." The laptop's home screen lit up. Keira clicked the Momentso icon.

"The hot guy in your picture. Please tell me that's your new assistant. Man, John never stood a chance. Your followers are going nuts over him. The girls love him. The guys? Not so much."

Her profile boasted the newest picture. The one of them cloud watching. It was imperfect. The camera's light shadow covered part of her chin. Still pretty, though. Robbie looked like bronzed perfection with his jawline, made to look even sharper by a shadow. His hair fell just right around his head so that even now, Keira's hand itched to dig her fingers into it.

But one thing arrested her heart most of all. He had, in fact, kissed her crown.

Robbie looked over her shoulder. "I thought you weren't going to post that."

"I didn't." Keira's thoughts jumbled. Dora jabbered on about what she would let the mystery man do to her. It was enough to shock Keira back to the phone call. Dora wasn't exactly a saint. "Dora, I didn't post this."

"You're telling me someone hacked your profile to share a ceiling-busting picture of you and your cute-as-can-be insta-family? Look, I have to go right now, but the Adventure Channel loves this. Don't quote me, but I wouldn't be surprised if you get an offer soon. I've heard that your idol, Margot Jorgensen, is on the outs with the producer of *Traveling Light* again. Rumor has it, they are looking to replace her . . . with you."

During the last few minutes of the conversation, hopes swirled around Keira's brain as if they'd been caught in a blender. After saying goodbye to Dora, she set down the phone.

"What's the time stamp on the picture?" Robbie asked.

She scrolled. "Four forty-one p.m. I was driving, so I couldn't have . . . What if Anabelle uploaded it while we were asleep, and it posted once we got service?"

They turned toward the little rapscallion, who was bouncing on the bed.

"I doubt it. She isn't exactly tech savvy." Robbie looked over his shoulder to where Anabelle had picked up the handset for the hotel room's phone. She slid her finger across the smooth plastic surface of the handle as if she expected it to light up. When it didn't, she replaced the receiver on the base . . . sideways. Robbie glanced back at Keira. "See?"

"But on this phone, all you have to do is hold your finger down on the photo, and it lists apps you could post to. Momentso is the first one that would've popped up." She refreshed the page. The likes and comments on the picture had increased even more. "So much for 'no harm, no foul.' I'll delete it." She clicked the options menu and scrolled the cursor down to *Delete*.

Robbie's hand covered hers. "Hold up a minute. What did Dora say?"

"You mean other than what she'd pay to have seven minutes in a closet with you? She said you've made my whole virtual world implode."

His smug smile was deliciously infuriating.

"Have I ever told you how much you remind me of Gaston from *Beauty and the Beast*?"

He lifted her hair over her shoulder, dragging his fingers down her back until she shivered. "I thought I reminded you of a young Robert Redford."

"Him, too. Anyway, she said this picture is 'ceiling-breaking' and has taken Kat Wanderfull to a new level. She expects Adventure to reach out to me soon."

"Isn't that what you want?"

"Yeah."

"So, don't delete the picture."

"I have to. It's not an honest portrait of who I am."

"It isn't? It's not like you've claimed I'm some royal prince you're engaged to or anything. It's a picture with no caption. Let your followers think what they want. Maybe it will fend off some of those guys who feel you owe them something."

What does he mean by that?

The envelope icon didn't indicate a new message. What would MRCustom think about this? She had to admit his opinion mattered greatly to her.

And yet, so did Robbie's.

CHAPTER EIGHTEEN

Thursday was the kind of day Robbie's old history teacher would have lived for. Not only had they taken a ride on an 1880s steam train through the Black Hills that morning, but they'd headed up to the Old West town of Deadwood around lunchtime. After settling into their lodgings at a supposedly haunted hotel, they'd arrived at the outdoor dinner theater for a western show that was cheesy, kitschy, and altogether perfect, especially when a cowboy led Anabelle up onto the stage.

The only thing better than watching his daughter overcome her shyness in front of the cheering crowd was sharing his pride with Keira. She beamed each time Anabelle mimicked the gunslinger's movements, spinning her pink plastic gun on her finger and saying things like "Reach for the sky, partner."

Other than those aimed at the stage and the stars overhead, the only lights were the lanterns on the long, wood-planked tables. Keira's beauty didn't just shine in the warm light; it shimmered.

Keira sat back on the bench. She settled against Robbie, beneath his arm propped on the backrest.

He wanted to move his hand down to her shoulder and sweep his thumb over the bare skin of her upper arm, but best not to push it. Physical touch was her love language. He was also quite aware that too much too soon would make her run for the Black Hills.

Perhaps an arm on the back of the bench would make it clear she was off-limits to all these cowboys eyeing her. These jokers weren't even real cowboys, but actors. And bad ones, at that. Sure, he'd had to fight guys off her in college a few times, but this felt different. *What's wrong with you, Matthews? It's not like she's your girlfriend or anything.*

He shouldn't have veered into the comment section of her recent Momentso posts. It would have been better for his mental health to walk into a lake of fire. The comments of some of the so-called men on there made his stomach churn. Were they raised in strip clubs? Brothels? They wanted Kat Wanderfull to know how much pleasure she gave them. Their words were disgusting, degrading, and—at least in Robbie's mind—dangerous.

He was probably paranoid. Even after all this time, she felt like a piece of him. He could no sooner see her hurt than sit back and allow a mountain lion to gnaw on his right arm.

One guy, tall and lanky with chaps over his jeans and a button-up shirt his mom likely bought him at the mall, kept looking from his phone to Keira and back again. When she'd posted a selfie an hour earlier using the app's check-in feature, she'd given her location to hundreds of thousands of sickos. What if one decided to try to find her?

After Anabelle's gun toting scared off the train robber, the host fit her with a sheriff sticker. A waitress in full 1800s garb walked Anabelle back to their table. Considering the way she was grinning, she either really liked her job or really liked Robbie. "Thanks for letting us bring your daughter onstage. She did great."

"Yes, she did." He waited for Anabelle to climb onto the bench opposite him, then reached over to her for a high five.

"Is there anything else I can get you?" The waitress flattened her hand against her waist, sliding it across and drawing his attention to her unnatural-looking curves.

"Another iced tea would be great."

Keira held up her mason jar glass with only ice remaining in the bottom. "Can I get more water, please?"

"Sure." The waitress looked Keira up and down, clearly unimpressed. She flashed Robbie a smile. "I'll grab that tea for you."

After she'd walked away, Keira elbowed Robbie's ribs. "She likes you, and she's pretty. You should talk to her."

A cool breeze dipped into the eating area, threatening to steal the paper napkins. A rash of gooseflesh rippled down her arm, and she nestled closer, wedging her arm against his side.

A complete enigma, that's what she was.

"Not my type. I like chicks with forehead scars."

Keira pursed her lips as the flush of pink rose into her cheeks. Another breeze came through as a junkyard band began picking a song onstage. Robbie curved his hand around her arm, sweeping down from the shoulder to the elbow and back until the bumps retreated, then for several minutes after that. "You should've brought a jacket."

"I don't need one. I brought you. You're like a furnace."

Robbie caught the eye of Mr. Tall-and-Lanky as the man held the phone up in their direction. Had he just taken a picture of them?

When the song ended, Keira asked Anabelle if she needed to go to the ladies' room, but she was too busy building a tower with the leftover corn bread to answer.

"I'll be back." Keira stood and shimmied out from between the table and bench.

"Do you want dessert?" She'd been eating a few more bites than normal in recent days. Dessert was far-fetched, but he offered anyway.

She thought a moment. "Why not?" When she batted her eyelashes at him, Robbie may as well have climbed into one of the pinewood coffins the restaurant used as props. He was as good as dead.

The ice cream on top of her chocolate cake was half melted by the time the host of the show introduced the final song of the night. Still, Keira hadn't returned from the restroom. Had she fallen in or something? More importantly, where had the guy with the phone gone?

An eerie fog filled Robbie, like the one that often draped the Madison River Canyon early in the morning.

The waitress leaned against the wall near where the food came out. She looked at him, then the vacant spot at his side. She strutted to him with a tilted smile he may have found attractive once.

Robbie placed his cloth napkin on the table and stood. "Miss, could you keep an eye on my daughter for a moment? I need to check on—"

"Your girlfriend?"

Such a simple question, yet it stumped him for a moment. "Yes. Annie, stay in your seat."

The restrooms were located in the structure bordering the western wall of the dining area. Farther into the opening, the dirt floor surrendered to patio tiles. The hall was dark, with only sconces on the wall next to the men's and women's restrooms, providing a halo of light. Robbie put his hands on the women's room door and was ready to shove it open and call into it, but he heard scuffing noises farther down the hall. He let the sound guide him until he recognized the man's black-shirted back and chaps over jeans. His arms stretched across a doorway. Though Keira was pushing him, he shifted his weight to block her.

Robbie's blood bubbled to the surface of his skin. He sunk his fingers into the man's shoulder and yanked him back.

The man slammed into the wall.

Bits and pieces of something rained down on Robbie's head and shoulders. "Did he hurt you?" Robbie's voice came out in a yell, and Keira shriveled further into the space. He turned his attention to the man, who was straggling down the hall toward the dining room. "Did you hurt her?"

The guy, apparently scared of what Robbie might do, looked back over his shoulder. His foot hooked on the doorframe of the men's bathroom. He sprawled out on the dirt in front of the crowd, then rolled and covered his head.

Robbie stood over the man, volts of electricity radiating through his clenched fists. He was sure that if he touched the guy, he would shock him dead.

The fabric of Keira's skirt breezed against him as she passed. She marched straight to the exit. Didn't bother to hug him for saving her or anything.

The only sound during the drive back to their hotel was Anabelle's soft weeping. Having five men restrain her father so he doesn't attack some college guy making nine dollars an hour can do that to a child. Her cry plunged deep into Keira's chest. It ached, and as far as Keira could tell, the pain could only be soothed with anger at the one who'd turned an uncomfortable moment into a big scene.

While Robbie held Anabelle in his arms, singing to her softly, Keira unlocked the door to his suite and held it open for him. "We need to talk."

"Let me tuck her in first. Take a seat." He nodded to the fancy settee that looked as comfortable as the desk in her classroom.

"I'm fine standing."

"Fair enough."

Ten minutes later he returned to the main room and pulled the bedroom door shut.

"I never asked you to be my bodyguard. That's not why I hired you," she said.

"I didn't think I'd have to be. What was that guy trying to do to you? He kept his voice so low it may as well have been a growl.

"He only wanted a picture."

"Then what?"

Keira clenched her teeth. If she looked straight through Robbie to the curtain behind him, she should be able to dull her eyes enough. He didn't need to know how scared she'd been when the man approached her outside the bathroom and backed her up into that dark corner. Nor the way his filthy words slithered into her ear and coiled around her windpipe, suffocating her voice and draining all the strength from her body.

Robbie scrubbed his hands through his hair. Even the muscles in his neck were strained. As he paced, she expected his boots to shatter the old wood floor like ice over a pond. "Do you have any idea how it feels to see men look at you as if they want to devour you? Or to read the things they say about you on that dumb app?"

"That *dumb app* is paying for the bed your daughter is sleeping in right now. And how do you even know what they're saying? I thought you weren't on Momentso?"

Robbie stammered, his lips tangling over his next words. "Your posts are public, and I did a search. Don't change the subject. Doesn't it bother you what they say about you?"

"Yes, of course it bothers me, but it's part of the job. You don't have to read the comments."

"I wish I never had. They're seared on my brain."

"It shouldn't bother you. I'm not yours to protect. I'm not the weak little girl you dated before."

"You have all these followers salivating over you, and yet you post exactly where you are so they can come find you. That's not brave. It's dangerous. I'm all for the female empowerment that EndeavHerMore stands for, but you need to be realistic about threats."

"It isn't only women that have to worry about harm. I saw the way that waitress was throwing herself at you. I'm surprised she didn't follow you out of there and drag you back to her house."

"That's different. I'm pretty sure I won't be attacked by a woman wearing a gift shop bonnet."

"I can protect myself. If you hadn't come barging in like a rhinoceros, I would have shoved him off me."

"You honestly believe you could've overpowered him? Unlikely. What happens if next time the guy looks like me? You have to be more careful, Keira." He moved closer to her, bending his face toward hers. "Please."

Steadying her breath wasn't so easy with him standing close. Her skin seemed to remember the feel of his embrace beneath the clouds yesterday. The way his shoulder had bumped against hers again and again on the train ride that morning. The warmth of his body at dinner. She cursed the weakness of her flesh. She did not need him. Not his protection. Not his companionship. Certainly not his affection. "I need to go."

"For once in your life, fight. Stop running and fight. I don't care what you do to me or what kind of pain you cause me, but do it here, right in front of me. Don't do it

when you're too far away to see the damage you've done."
His eyes shone pain.

She told herself that running kept her safe. But now, with
his presence awakening her every longing, she wondered
what running might have made her miss out on. Now, more
than ever, she needed to leave.

"I know what you're doing. You're pushing me away because you're afraid. I'm a threat to your world. John? Now,
that guy was safe. He was easy to keep at arm's length,
wasn't he? Then on Momantoo, you form friendships—" He
paused and chewed his bottom lip. "Those people are safe
because they can't see what you aren't willing to show
them. None of them can get through your barricade."

"You don't know me at all."

"Keira, I know the rhythm your heart makes. You know
how? Because I was already inside it when you built the
fortress walls. I can get you to laugh despite a childhood of
pain. I make you feel emotions you tried to bury. That's
what makes me dangerous. I'm right here. You can see me,
hear me, touch me. I make you want more than you've
dared to imagine, don't I?"

He was right. Heaven knows Robbie was right about all
those things. And she hated him for it.

Robbie smirked. "Are we about to fight-kiss?"

Her train of thought came to a screeching halt. "Ficus?
Like the tree?"

"No. *Fight-kiss.*"

"What are you talking about?"

"You know that scene in movies when the man and
woman are yelling at each other and stuff, and then they
kiss? We should do that."

"You've lost it. Why would I kiss you? I'm still angry
at you."

"Because you haven't kissed me in five years. And because your anger might get confused with the passion you feel for me."

No words. She had no words with which to respond to this absurdity. The nerve he had to assume she'd want to kiss him right now.

"Go ahead. Yell in my ear. Slap my face. Then kiss me. And hey, if you want to hit me again afterward, that's okay, too. Just so long as there's a kiss somewhere in there." He grinned and rubbed his hands together.

"Don't do that thing."

"What thing?"

"That thing where you use charm to sweep the big issue under the rug. Don't lessen this."

"I'm not trying to lessen it. I'm trying to . . . uh, *more* it." That smirk again. Couldn't he take anything seriously?

Keira tried to channel all her frustration—and none of her attraction—into her expression.

"What's that?"

"What's what?"

He wagged his finger between her brows. "That cute thing you're doing with your face. Wait. Are you trying to glare at me?"

She turned away from him. "Working together was a mistake. I think we've proved that. We'll drive home tomorrow, I'll pay you for your time, and we'll part ways." She pushed past him and headed to the exit of the suite. Once she was alone, she could think about her next steps She'd find a way not to need him, or anyone, for that matter.

"Come on, Kat. I'll be serious," he said from behind her.

"You don't know how."

"You're running."

Her satchel. Where had she put her satchel? "I'm walking."

"Same thing." As she circled the room, the floor groaning

with each step, he followed her with his eyes. "Will you please stop letting fear rule your life?"

"That's not what I'm doing. Ugh, where is that stupid thing?"

Robbie lifted her bag off the dinette chair nearest to him. He held it out, and she snatched it. "Instead of facing this head-on and working through it, you're taking off. Except instead of just me, this time you're leaving Anabelle, too."

A million words tumbled around in her mouth. No matter what came out, she knew she couldn't look him in the eye when she said it. Instead, she stared at the back of the hotel room door, at the framed map highlighting the emergency escape plan. "Anabelle was never my daughter to leave."

CHAPTER NINETEEN

The next night, Robbie idled the truck in front of Keira's apartment. Why wasn't she getting out? Other than a few short conversations with Anabelle, she'd been silent for the entire nine-hour car trip back home. She hadn't even thanked him for grabbing her a bottle of water and a pack of gum at the gas station. If her goal was to completely shut him out, she'd done so marvelously. She was locked up tighter than a bank vault. He'd tried to turn on some music and crack some jokes, but she stared through the windshield or fiddled on her phone.

Worst was when they'd taken a break for lunch. He and Anabelle grabbed some hamburgers at a travel stop, while Keira had gone to the convenience store to find a cup of fruit to eat. Logging on to Momentso, being sure to avoid all comment threads, he opened a message from her.

> **KAT WANDERFULL:** @MRCustom, I'm sure you've seen that picture of me with that man. I wanted to tell you he means nothing to me. Not that you care. I wouldn't want to lose your friendship. Sometimes it feels like all I have. Talk to you soon.

At least now he knew. He meant nothing to her. Which was great. He could finally move on. Focus on Anabelle. Focus on building a life for the two of them. Keira Knudsen . . . Kat Wanderfull . . . was broken beyond repair. He'd tried to break into her shell. It hadn't worked. So why wasn't she getting out of the truck?

She turned and looked in the back seat where Anabelle was sound asleep.

Keira chewed her lip.

Was that moisture in her eyes? Couldn't be. Keira didn't cry. She was incapable.

She blinked it away. "Anabelle." One word. Her voice cracked between the second and third syllable.

Robbie waited for her to continue.

"That was supposed to be the name for our daughter," Keira said.

"Huh?"

"It was the beginning of freshman year. I was sitting in your dorm room, and we'd finished *not* watching some lame movie. The one part we did pay attention to had this kid in it with a horrible name. We decided that our little girl would be named Anabelle. Don't you remember?"

Vaguely. "Didn't I say something like, 'Our boy would be named Ryan, just to make my sister mad'?"

"Yes, you did. But we'd decided Charles officially. Anabelle, and Charlie, for short." Keira's soft smile slid into a frown.

"I didn't remember. I mean, I must've had it ingrained in my brain somehow. But if I had remembered, I never would have—"

She stopped him with a flinch and a hand up. "That day Anabelle was born was the hardest day of my life. Even harder than when I left you . . . what? Eleven months before? Ryann called me to break the news. When she told me that you'd given our name to the daughter you had with Vivian, I completely fell apart. It was so . . . cold. How little I must have mattered to you. You had everything. I was utterly alone. Keira, the unloved."

Robbie wanted to tell her how wrong she was about not being loved, about his "everything" with Vivian, but Anabelle was stirring. He couldn't risk her hearing the truth.

As quietly as his old truck would allow, Keira opened the door, then stepped out.

Robbie retrieved her bags from the truck bed and carried them to her front door.

She refused to let him carry them any farther.

Right there on the doorstep of her condo, she wrote him a check, nearly shoving it in his pocket when he refused to accept it.

Her bags separated them. The wind was pulling a strand of hair across her cheek and lips.

She didn't smile.

Neither did he.

"You're wrong about my life after you left. How could I have everything if I didn't have you?" He sighed. "Keira, I don't want to say goodbye to you."

Wringing her fingers at her waist, she said nothing for a long minute. Then she grabbed the handle of the biggest suitcase. "The next trip is Tuesday. I'm heading down through Idaho to Nevada, then California. You promised Anabelle that you'd take her to the beach, so . . . I guess I'll pick you up at nine a.m.?"

CHAPTER TWENTY

I wanna catch a great big brown, Daddy. It'll be this big."
Anabelle spread her arms as wide as she could, then
looked back over her shoulder, catching Robbie's eye.

"I think we'd better let the Trout King stay in the river
today, Kitty Kat." Robbie lifted his face to the sky. Clouds
stretched thin across the blue sky. They hardly moved in
the still Saturday afternoon air. As Robbie reclined on the
grass a few yards from the river, he appealed for God's
protection over Anabelle's heart.

"Why *can't* we go fishing?" Anabelle scooted back,
leaning against his chest.

"Because we're going to have a picnic instead. With a
special visitor."

"Keira?" Anabelle's voice burst from her with joy.

"Not Keira." Robbie pressed his lips to the top of Anabelle's head.

"Who?" Her shoulders twisted as she turned to face
him. Full of innocence, her eyes glimmered. She placed her
hands on his cheeks and studied his face.

"Her name is Vivian." He gathered his breath. "She's
your mother."

Anabelle gently pushed against his right cheek, then his left, turning his face back and forth.

"God grew you in Vivian's belly. She's your mom."

"Then she put me in your arms and went on a big 'venture?" When Anabelle squished his cheeks, his lips jutted forward, and she giggled.

"Yes, she went on an adventure, but she missed you. So we're having a picnic with her. You can show her how cute, funny, and smart you are. Would you like that?"

"Can we go fishing?" Anabelle tugged on his earlobes.

"I don't think Vivian likes to fish."

"Maybe someday we can go fishing with Keira." Her hands dropped. She slumped against Robbie's chest, her legs and arms tangled in a knot. Soon her breathing deepened. Her light snore joined in the melody of the river sounds.

Thank you, Lord, for these moments with her. Thank you for giving me the strength to be the daddy she needs. Help Vivian to be the mother she needs.

Twenty minutes later, after his mother had delivered a basket of sandwiches, homemade potato chips, and chocolate chip cookies, Vivian arrived. She walked slowly toward them as if any moment she expected the ground to open and swallow her. The sun reflecting off her stark white blouse seared Robbie's eyes. She wore khaki-colored capris that still had the crease from an iron down the front.

She lowered herself onto the far edge of the blanket. Her legs disappeared, tucked neatly beneath her. Dark, oversize sunglasses covered her eyes. Pursed lips and clasped hands rounded out her untouchable appearance. And yet, the lock of hair that ended in a sharp angle at her chin trembled slightly, and it couldn't be blamed on a breeze.

"Kitty Kat, wake up." Robbie roused her by sweeping a hand down her cheek. "This is Vivian."

Anabelle squirmed. When she caught sight of Vivian, she sat up straighter but kept her hand on Robbie's leg.

"Hi," Vivian said. A simple word, yet it had the sound of a gasp. She fumbled to remove her sunglasses.

Anabelle stared hard for a long time. Finally, she relaxed back against Robbie. "Did you like the rainbow waterfall?"

"What waterfall?" Confusion knit Vivian's brow.

"The one from your big 'venture. Daddy told me all about it." Anabelle rubbed her eyes. "You were gone for a long, long time."

"I know I was." Pain harnessed Vivian's gaze. "That won't happen again. I promise."

CHAPTER TWENTY-ONE

Sitting across the table from Claire Knudsen was like watching a silent film without the accompanying music. Soundlessly, she swirled her spoon in her chamomile, again and again, her focus diving to the depths of the teacup. Once the tea had been sufficiently infused, she scooped out the tea bag, then placed the spoon on the porcelain saucer without even a tap, much less a clink. In contrast to the stark white walls, cabinets, and tile, as well as her mother's pale face and hair, the rich amber liquid seemed out of place. So was the bruised skin peeking out from her mother's sleeve when she lifted the cup for a sip. As if someone had used Technicolor to tinge it for effect.

Keira had to look away. Around her, nothing had changed. Her childhood home was a time capsule of the early 1990s. Her father didn't like change. Or mess. Or noise. Or disobedience. And her mother didn't like to upset him, because here . . . consequences hurt.

"Mama, come with me. I can take care of you out there." Keira waited until her mother had replaced the cup on the saucer, then covered her mother's hand with hers. As gently as if she was detangling Anabelle's curls, she turned her mother's hand over. She pulled back the silk to reveal the splotch on her mother's wrist. "*This* isn't normal outside of these walls."

Lips forming a tight line, her mother remained silent. Always silent.

Like when Keira dropped the pink marker on the rug, and her father pelted the remaining Crayolas at her. Even now, twenty years later, Keira could feel the sting of each one whipping her forearms as she tried to protect herself.

No wonder all the countertops and bookshelves were bare. Everything that could be thrown was either broken or hidden away out of her father's reach.

Keira's thumb traced her mother's wound. She sighed. There was still hope. After all her father's attempts at control, he hadn't completely stripped away her mother's instinct of self-protection.

"I'm heading to California tomorrow, Mama. Remember how we used to talk about the ocean? Or what sand would feel like between our toes? You can feel that for yourself this time. You don't have to take my word for it."

Claire's mouth pursed, forming a heart shape —her smile. A dreamy cast glazed over her eyes. "Wouldn't that be fun?"

"We could rent a convertible and drive down the coast with the sun tanning our face and the sea air whipping our hair into tangles." The giggle that slipped out of Keira's throat surprised her.

Even more surprising? The ceiling didn't cave at the unfamiliar sound in the Knudsen household.

"We could get ice cream cones, Mama. Like when you were a little girl. We can even stop in Twin Falls."

When her mother raised her eyes, they glistened.

"Please, Mama. Come with us."

"Us?"

A light that gave the sun over San Diego a run for its

money bloomed inside Keira's belly. "You always liked Robbie Matthews. He hasn't changed much. Maybe a touch more handsome. He's my assistant, in a way." Her cheeks tightened and warmed. "And his daughter is a sweetheart. Her name is Anabelle, and she's full of joy. I . . ." Keira paused. How could she begin to describe how she felt about Anabelle?

A large insect tapped against the back door's glass a couple of times then flew back to the flower garden her mother meticulously maintained.

"You know how it feels when you see a butterfly flitting around your garden as if it doesn't have a care in the world? And the pride you feel when that butterfly suckles nectar from a flower you've grown? That's how I feel about her."

At the moment her mother placed her hand on Keira's cheek, Keira understood. All the heartache of sticking around this town the past five years was worth it if she could only get her mother to take a chance and leave this prison.

A buzz reverberated through Keira's kitchen chair. It traveled up her spine, paralyzing her lungs. The garage door.

The little color in her mother's face washed away, only to be absorbed by the white tiled floor. "Keira, go." Her voice quaked. "Before he sees you."

Fear for her mother surpassed concern for herself. She found the elusive breath she needed to speak. "Come with me. Please. There's more to life than fear and pain. Let me show you."

After sliding her hand out from under Keira's, her mother pulled down her sleeve and rose from her chair. "You know I can't. My place is here . . . with your father." Her mother's house shoes swished along the ground as she crossed the kitchen and waited by the door.

Kat Wanderfull refused to stand and welcome her father home. She wasn't a child. He had no control over her anymore.

As she stared at the floor, the door opened and banged shut, followed by her father's heavy footsteps and the sound of her mother's commanded *welcome home* kiss.

"You're home early," her mother said. "Keira stopped by to tell me about her recent trip to South Dakota."

"My last meeting got canceled. If I'd have known, I would have postponed the one before that to another day. How nice of her to stop by." His tone chilled her. The footsteps continued. The clack followed by the bending leather. Heel-toe, heel-toe, getting closer until his polished shoes halted next to her chair. "Hello, Little Mouse."

Her muscles petrified. He placed his hands beneath her elbow, then lifted her out of the chair until she was standing. He pinched her chin and tilted her face up. His marble eyes stilled on hers. She shuddered, and he smiled. Not a friendly grin like Chuck Matthews's, or a genuine joy-filled one like Robbie's. A victorious smile.

"Hello, Father."

Satisfied, he released her. "Where's John?" After settling into his armchair, he untied each of his shoes and removed them. Her mother handed him a glass of ice water—he wouldn't start drinking his liquor until after dinner—then she carried his shoes out of sight.

"I'm not sure. We don't see each other anymore."

He scoffed, even as his eyes darkened. "So I heard. And where's the Matthews kid?"

Kid? Not quite. Robbie could pummel her father to bits if he wanted to. Once, in high school, he would have if the police hadn't shown up. "At home, I'd imagine."

"Since you're standing in this house and not traipsing across the country, I trust you've seen the error of your ways. John and I met for lunch this week. His forgiveness knows no bounds."

His forgiveness?

"I'll give him a call and tell him you're here." Her father tapped on his phone screen.

"Don't bother. I'm leaving."

"Before dinner? Why, that'd be silly. I was about to turn on a movie. We'll find one of your favorites. I'll have John come over—"

Keira grabbed her satchel and scurried to the front door.

Her father beat her there. He pressed the door closed. From her earliest memories, his hand was filled with the worst kind of strength—the kind that imprisons and punishes rather than frees and lifts up.

She needed Robbie. After all, he was the only one her father was scared of. Why hadn't she asked him to join her for this visit? He would have, even after the awkwardness of the other day.

With her eyes focused on the door, she caught her faint reflection in the beveled glass. She looked small compared to her father.

Small, but not weak. Not anymore. She had been his Little Mouse long enough.

Swallowing down the fear trying to choke her, she met her father's icy glare. "Move. Your. Hand." Would he grab her, shake her? Throw her against the wall? If he did, she would fight until her blood ran and her bones ached.

But he didn't. He dropped his hand from the door, then stepped back and offered a sick grin, even as the vein above his temple throbbed a quick beat.

All the air in the foyer rushed out the door as she opened it. Stepping through, she took one last glance inside.

When her mother didn't appear, a new type of pain daggered Keira's heart. She pulled the door closed and descended the porch steps, only to hear the latch lock her out. As in one of those dreams, Keira's legs seemed to be stuck in quicksand. Each step was slow and heavy, but she was moving. When she reached her car, she shut herself inside and hit the lock button three times, to be safe. The sound of the ignition brought her peace.

But the feeling was short-lived. Because as she drove away from her parents' house for the last time, she flashed back to that day she'd dropped the marker.

It was a few days before her seventh Christmas. She'd sat on the couch, running the soft plush of her stuffed turtle over the lash marks on her forearms and the welt she felt on her cheek.

On the floor, her mother had kneeled, alternately spraying the carpet with stain remover and scrubbing the tiny ink spot with a rag. Above her, her father loomed, his chest still heaving from the anger possessing him. He looked at Keira, then kicked her mother in the stomach over and over. While her mother lay curled on the floor, straining for breath and moaning in pain, her father came to Keira. Bending close, he whispered, "You caused this."

He wrenched away the stuffed turtle—the one her counselor had given her on the last day before Christmas break—and held it outstretched in his hand. Tears stung the welt beneath her eye.

"Stop crying."

The tears came harder.

"I said, stop crying."

Maybe, she thought, if her father saw her crying, he would say he was sorry and hug her and Mama, like Emily's daddy had when he was late to the school's Christmas program.

But her father was not like Emily's daddy. He took one final look at the stuffed toy, then tossed it in the fireplace. She'd clambered after it, but he'd grabbed her around the waist.

A grotesque rash of charcoaled brown spread over the

green plush until the flames enveloped the toy. The eyes stared at her as they warped and melted. Her friend didn't smell like logs when he burned. His pungent smell stung her nose and coated her mouth, sickening her. But if she got sick, he'd beat her or her mother more, so she swallowed back the bile rising in her throat.

Finally, her father let her go and disappeared into his study.

Keira sat in front of the fire until nothing remained of the turtle, and every tear she might ever cry was burned away by the heat.

Her mother hadn't moved. She'd merely lain on the floor, on top of the stain Keira had caused, until the sky had grown dark.

CHAPTER TWENTY-TWO

Water bottles? Check. Granola Bars? Check. Graham crackers shaped like teddy bears? Check. Tom Petty paused on the first note? Check.

Satisfied, Keira turned off the car's ignition. She took one last look at her road atlas, its pages spread open to show the first stop on their road trip to California. She hadn't told Robbie yet that they weren't heading to some random city. It would give them something to talk about on the drive. She could bundle her recent research with her highest hopes and deepest fears all in one concise, little conversation.

With a sigh, she peeled the yellow Post-it note off the page and held it close. *Sanders General Store. Intersection of Main Avenue and Shoshone Street, Twin Falls, Idaho.* Her lower lip began to quiver, and she caught it between her teeth. Pressing the note to her heart, she squeezed her eyes closed, hoping God understood prayers that words couldn't convey.

After replacing the note on its page, she opened the car door. Despite the June date on the calendar, a chill clung to the earth as if knowing its strength would wane when the sun heaved itself above the mountaintop.

The parking lot at River's Edge Resort's café was nearly empty this Tuesday morning—a bad sign for the business. Keira had parked between two lodgepole pines off to the side. Close as she was, the river had a different sound. Beneath the roar, the water danced over the rocks near the bank, forming a lullaby of sorts. The song kissed her ears. When she turned away from it, the sight of Robbie walking toward her, bag slung over his shoulder, slowed down time.

He smiled, and Keira drew in a gulp of air so big she nearly choked on it. What they say about absence was right. Three days of not seeing him hadn't just made her heart grow fonder. It practically made her heart turn on Michael Bublé and practice writing *Mrs. Keira Matthews* a hundred times in a diary.

"Where's your car?"

"You're looking at it." She did her best Vanna White impression while displaying the new Jeep Grand Cherokee.

"Hold the phone. Did you buy this?"

"Nope. EndeavHerMore has an in with Jeep."

"They just gave this to you?" Robbie dropped his bag on the ground and yanked open the passenger door. He ran his hand over the surfaces like a jockey would over his racehorse.

"I wish. It's more of a short-term lease thing."

"You've got some power in that little body of yours, don't you?"

She shrugged. "Where's Anabelle?"

"Inside with my mom. She wanted my mom to braid her hair."

"Pity. Those curls of hers should never be tamed."

Robbie slipped his hand down Keira's braid. "I think she missed you."

Her heart hummed. "I missed her, too. I hope you don't mind. I reached out to DareBaby, and they sent me their best car seat for road trips."

"We could've used the one from my truck," Robbie said.

"True, but I wouldn't mind having one to keep around in the future. It even has a footrest you can raise for naps. I also made her an activity box for the drive. Plus, I picked up a tablet and loaded it with Princess Patty Cake episodes." She retrieved the tablet from the back seat, awakened it, and showed Robbie.

"Was she the only one you thought about?"

Luckily, he didn't look at her. She'd never been able to control the flush in her cheeks where he was concerned.

"I may have downloaded one or two things for you, too," she said.

He scrolled down the list of episodes. "You didn't."

"I did. Every ridiculous Jackie Chan movie from the nineties and two thousands."

He laid his hand on the side of her neck, opposite the braid, and caressed her jawline with his thumb. "Girl after my own heart. Wait, do you still have a crush on Owen Wilson?"

"Me? No crushes at all."

"Not even one?"

If there were an award for closing distance between two people, he'd win. She wondered how close he might get over these next two weeks as they traveled to the California coast and back. "Maybe one. Just a little one."

When his eyes lit up, the rest of the world went out of focus.

"Robbie." A police officer stood by the Jeep's bumper. Drew Ulrich was a longtime friend of the Matthews family. He wasn't a stranger to these parts, but he carried an unfamiliar air with him. Perhaps it was the way his brow furrowed over his empathetic eyes.

"Hey, Drew. You here for breakfast?" Robbie asked.

"Uh, no. I'm here on official business." He glanced

down at the large manila envelope in his hand. "I'm sorry to do this to you, buddy. But when I saw Vivian come in to get this delivered, I thought it'd be better to come from me." He handed it to Robbie, then shook his head. "I'll go get Ryann."

After Drew headed to the restaurant, Robbie unclasped the fastener and withdrew the papers from the envelope.

The official letterhead and paragraphs deflated Keira's lungs. The title of the document read in big block letters: PARENTING PLAN.

Robbie held it out to her. "A custody agreement? Can you"—he swallowed hard—"read this to me? My mind isn't—"

"Of course." Keira accepted the sheet and held it between them so he could see.

"From the law offices of Cartwright and Cartwright. Vivian Cartwright, the mother of the child, Anabelle Matthews, requests joint custody with Robbie Matthews, the father of the child. She requests sole custody Monday through Friday and every other weekend."

Robbie's breath hitched. Keira placed her free hand on his shoulder blade. She continued to the next line.

"Until the parenting plan is finalized by the district court, Anabelle Matthews must remain in the state of Montana." Fury swirled behind Keira's brow bone, summoning the start of a headache. Who did Vivian think she was to make such demands?

The letter went on for two more paragraphs, providing more specific details about holidays, vacations, and transfers. Behind the cover letter, there was a copy of the Montana parenting plan form Vivian had completed.

Robbie took the handful of papers back. His finger slid beneath the schedule, left to right. He stumbled backward.

His legs hit the bench positioned to look out over the river. He collapsed onto it.

Keira followed, sitting next to him.

His shoulders shook, and she wrapped her arms around them.

"She can't do this." His words were soft. "Keira, she can't do this, right?"

She rested her chin on his collarbone. "I don't know, Robbie. I hope not."

CHAPTER TWENTY-THREE

Inside his cabin's kitchen, Robbie ran the end of his thumbnail down a groove in the table. "Four days a month. I'd only get her four days a month."

Across the room, Keira stared out the window near the fireplace. She'd been fairly quiet since they'd stepped into his cabin. Maybe she was thinking of a way out of this for Robbie. Then again, that was the job of the no-nonsense brunette who was typing on a laptop in the chair opposite him.

"No judge in their right mind would approve this plan. Not if you've had sole custody of the child for four years and the mother has only recently reappeared." Cassie Beck, the youngest lawyer at her firm, had an excellent reputation for protecting children in the field of family law. At least according to Thomas. So far, she seemed to know her stuff.

He'd have to remember to thank Ryann. When his whole life was swirling before his eyes, she'd had the quick thinking to ask Thomas to call his sister.

Luckily for Robbie, Cassie was willing to clear a spot in her schedule to meet with him. Even luckier, she was already on this side of town and could make the house call.

"But what about all that money she has?"

"All money can do is buy a good lawyer."

Exactly. His wallet in his back pocket didn't feel thin but downright nonexistent. Cassie used to have a crush on Robbie, but she certainly hadn't liked him enough to offer her services for free.

"We have twenty-one days to file this response to petition for parenting plan. I'll hold on to it until you get back from California. Make them sweat a little bit. Once we've done that, I'll send a copy to her lawyer." Cassie patted his hand.

"I want this figured out. I don't want to wait two weeks," he said.

She pressed a fist to her lips and blinked hard. Cassie was clearly used to getting her way. She lowered her fist and focused her attention on the papers. "A few days, then. I think your changes are perfectly reasonable. They'd be foolish not to accept them."

"And what happens if they don't?"

"Then we'll try mediation. A neutral party will meet with you and Vivian in hopes of finding common ground. If that doesn't work, there will likely be a preliminary hearing to determine next steps." Cassie withdrew a paper from her briefcase. She slid it across the table to Robbie. "Like I said, this consult was free, but here's my fee schedule."

He stopped breathing while he did the math. She scratched out the first line with her pen. "You know I've always liked you, Robbie. And I hold a great deal of respect for you and your family, so I'm willing to forgo my own income on this case. Still, I have to keep the lights on and pay my assistant. A typical case like this requires around five hours per week, but depending on how long Vivian is willing to drag this out, that could go for a considerable amount of time. Do you have the funds to pay for this?"

He opened his mouth to list all the internal organs he'd be willing to sell, but Keira's voice called out. "Yes, he does."

Robbie looked her way.

Keira stepped closer. "What about him taking Anabelle out of Montana in the interim? Why did that letter from the lawyer say he couldn't?"

"It's not uncommon for exes to try to sabotage my clients' ability to work or form new relationships. She probably demanded he put that into the paperwork—that you couldn't travel out of state with Anabelle. But it has no legal bearing." Cassie looked between the two of them. "I imagine there may be bitterness or jealousy at fault. I'll call Lex Cartwright and inform him that your travel will not be hindered."

"Why would he listen to you?" Robbie asked.

"Because I know things." Cassie's lips curled as she packed her paperwork into her briefcase. "Let's just say his son's 2.3 grade point average wasn't the reason he got into Yale Law."

Robbie walked Cassie to the door. "Thanks for coming out to meet me. If you want a free meal or a fly-fishing lesson—"

"Not necessary. Cases like this are why I went to law school."

After Cassie left, he flattened his hand against the door's knotty pine surface. "This is what I get for helping people out, not charging them for the work I do. I can't afford her."

"But I can." Keira appeared at his side. She held out a check to him.

With one glance, he scoffed. "No way. I won't accept your charity."

"Aren't you stubborn? Willing to give charity, but not accept it in your own time of need. Think of it as an advance. What kind of boss would I be if I didn't look out for my employee?" She flashed that posed smile of hers.

"Some employee. I've already made you late." Robbie breathed deep. Maybe he shouldn't be doing this at all. He could do some odd jobs closer to home. It wouldn't pay as well, but he'd be nearer his family. "Now I'll be bringing all this drama with me."

"Don't say another word about it. Besides, you promised Anabelle a sandcastle. Blame it on my daddy issues, but the thought of you breaking that promise to her . . . Well, we can't have that. Besides, there's something I need to do at our first stop. It's been a long time coming and I need you there, okay?" She pressed the check to his palm. "Take the money."

"Why are you doing this?"

Her fingers slid around his hand, holding it firmly in hers. "Just because we stopped dating didn't mean I stopped caring for you. And just because Anabelle isn't my daughter doesn't mean I don't want what's best for her. You, Robbie, are what's best for her. There's not a doubt in my mind."

The door burst open.

Robbie had to throw up his arm to block it from hitting Keira.

Ryann peeked in. "I'm sorry I couldn't get here sooner. The last table took forever to finish their food. What did Cassie say?"

After he recounted the discussion and counterproposal for the parenting plan, Ryann said a few words about Vivian that would've made their momma blush.

Meanwhile, Keira walked the perimeter of the family room and kitchen. She ran her fingers over the mantel, lifted her eyes to the beams on the ceiling, and tapped on the window looking out over the river.

"What can I do?" Ryann's face had attained the hue of a fire truck. She was fiercely protective of their family. And she held a particular loathing for Vivian.

"Just pray. And *don't* find her address and go to her house."

"No promises," Ryann said.

"We should head out. Best not to delay Keira any more than I already have."

"Robbie, may I use your bathroom?" Keira peeked into the master bedroom.

"Sure." The bathroom had two entries. The first and most convenient for guests was the closed door directly behind her, but he wanted to show off his hard work. "Head into the master, then turn right. You'll see it."

She stepped into his bedroom and paused, looking around.

Fortunately, he'd made his bed and rid the space of dirty laundry that morning. The furniture and decor were definitely fitting for a bachelor, but a bachelor with a sister who had a good eye for interior design. A moment later, Keira was out of sight.

Ryann pounced on the opportunity, a sparkle in her eye replacing the anger from moments ago. "You planning to elope during this two-week trip? You know if you get married without me there, I'll never forgive you."

"It's not like that."

"Do you want it to be? I mean, when Drew sent us out earlier, she had her arms around you. Then, after we'd finished praying as a family, you didn't let go of her hand. We all noticed. And were you guys kissing when I came in?"

"Someone's trying to steal my daughter from me. Kissing is the furthest thing from my mind."

Hands up, Ryann surrendered. "Looks like it's going that way, is all."

Robbie drummed the table. "I don't know. Keira's got me so mixed up."

"You still love her?"

Robbie mashed his lips together.

Ryann laughed. "Yep, you're done."

"It doesn't matter how I feel." He tugged at the front of his shirt. Boy, it was hot. Why hadn't he installed a ceiling fan? "There's too much history. Too much brokenness."

"You sound like the naysayers when Nehemiah set to rebuild the wall around Jerusalem."

"Your point?"

Ryann's big green eyes stared him down. "Well, Nehemiah, ask God to strengthen your hands for the task."

"You don't get it. Even if I can rebuild what we had, it's a matter of time before she leaves me again." Robbie tried to clear his throat. "I don't want to lose Keira. I *cannot* lose Anabelle. What if it's all in vain?"

Ryann's focus dropped to her hands. She thumbed one of the many scars along her wrist. "Even if it is, you won't regret fighting to save the ones you love. Trust me."

Keira glided into the kitchen. "Are we ready to hit the road?"

Robbie stood and swallowed down the last gulp of water—which almost came back up when Ryann jabbed his kidney.

"How 'bout you call once or twice this time? I kind of miss you when you're gone, Slobbie Robbie."

"I'll miss you, too, Cryin' Ryann." He wrapped her in a half headlock, half hug until she patted his arm and cried uncle.

Ryann hugged Keira. Did his sister whisper something to her?

"I'll try. Promise," Keira said.

"Good." Ryann let her go and headed to the front door. "I'm going down to the office to say goodbye to Annie. I don't think Mom's let her go since Drew delivered the papers. Remember, we serve a powerful God, and he loves a good underdog story."

CHAPTER TWENTY-FOUR

𓆸

I have a surprise for you." Keira stood beneath the Jeep's tailgate, shielded from Idaho's searing midafternoon sun. She rummaged through one of her suitcases, no doubt looking for her next ensemble. Her fourth one, even though they'd only been out shooting for five hours. She tossed a couple of items off to the side and closed the bag.

Robbie didn't know who Tumi was or why his name was on all her luggage, but it looked way fancier than his duffel bag he'd had since ninth grade.

"Oh yeah? What's that?" The stone Robbie tossed landed on the chalk square labeled with a three. Like a flamingo, he hiked up one leg in preparation for his turn on the hopscotch grid.

He landed on square one and two, leaped over three, all the while watching Keira comb her long waves into a high ponytail. The sight of her slender neck sent ripples through him. He remembered the many times he'd kissed that soft skin like it was yesterday. In his excitement, he missed box six, and stumbled on boxes seven and eight.

"You did it wrong, Daddy."

"Guess you gotta show me again." Robbie scooped the

stone off the pavement and placed it in Anabelle's hand. Back at the Jeep, he leaned against the rear body panel.

"We're doing one of your favorite things. Before you ask, yes, you can bring Anabelle." The familiar oversize T-shirt Keira slipped over her head had the logo of a fly-fishing guide company on the breast pocket. Beneath the cotton, her arms wrestled like two snakes in a sack.

Robbie looked to where Anabelle was struggling to hurdle square two. Next time, he'd have to draw the grid smaller. When the rustling of clothes ceased, he joined Keira under the tailgate.

It was magic how girls could change clothes without ever showing their skin. Was that a skill they learned in middle school or something? Did mothers teach their daughters how to do that? Robbie hoped not. Add that to the list of things Anabelle could never learn from him.

"Isn't that mine?" he asked.

"I have no idea what you mean." That smile of hers, like always, summoned him closer.

"I must be imagining things because that shirt sure does look familiar." He pointed to a spot in the center, above the breast bone. "See this barbecue sauce stain?" When she glanced down, he flicked her nose.

"Oh goodness. Do your dad jokes never end?"

"Get ready. I hear they'll get worse as I age."

"So when we're touring some castle in Switzerland in sixty years and Anabelle says, 'I'm hungry,' you'll say?"

"Probably 'Where are my teeth?'"

She laughed. Beneath the dingy shirt, she wore a pair of bike shorts.

She looked . . . what was that word? Frumpy. That was it. And he loved the look on her.

Following Keira's request, Anabelle repacked the chalk in the activity box. Robbie grabbed three waters out of the cooler while Keira straightened up the trunk. There was a rhythm to their movements now. Each person did their own task, but the combined effort led to results.

"Follow me," Keira said.

The parking lot only held about a dozen cars, their license plates ranging from almost as many states. The sign on the building read *Gillz Water Sports*.

Awesome.

After the proper waivers were signed and life jackets were fitted, the three of them joined a group out on the Snake River. Keira, by herself, would've made good time to Shoshone Falls. But Robbie and Anabelle, in their tandem kayak, slowed her progress. It was surprisingly hard to paddle with a squirmy four-year-old in front of him. Especially one who kept trying to reach down into the water on one side, nearly capsizing them in the process.

It also didn't help that Robbie couldn't keep his eyes on his own boat. Halfway through the trip, Keira had rolled up the sleeves of the shirt, giving him a clear view of her arms as she worked the oar from one side to the other.

Wonder of wonders.

Finally, they reached their destination. A majestic veil of white water poured over rocks. When the sun caught the spray off the falls, a rainbow shimmered in the air before them.

Anabelle beamed. Perilously, she climbed onto Robbie's lap for a hug and knocked their oar into the water.

"Say cheese." The sun glinted off the phone in Keira's hand.

"Cheddar," Robbie and Anabelle said together.

Keira snapped the pic, replaced her phone in a waterproof bag, then paddled closer. She lugged the oar out of the water and handed it back to Robbie, but not before she gave him and Annie a little splash.

"Paddle fast, Knudsen. If I catch you, you're going over. And I hear there's a leviathan beneath the surface. He likes to eat girls with blond hair who smell like unflavored oatmeal."

"I'll save you, Keira." Anabelle scooped water and flung it at Robbie.

"Hey, I thought you were on my team."

"Girls rule, boys drool." Anabelle grinned and shirked away in case he tried to get her.

Robbie rolled his eyes. He was gonna kill his sister.

Keira was already a dozen yards ahead of him.

He dug his oar deep in the water again and again until his back and biceps burned. He might not catch Keira, but it sure would be fun to try.

When they finally landed their kayaks back at Gillz, Robbie carried Keira into the water and immersed them both—payment for her smack talk about winning their race. Sure, she beat his chest with one fist, but she also tightened her body to his. *Thank you, frigid river water.*

Two hours later, they arrived at their hotel to shower and change for dinner. They stepped foot in a farm-to-table restaurant just as the sun was beginning to set over Twin Falls. Even as Keira took her usual product placement snaps, she seemed out of it. Robbie didn't understand. The day had been perfectly pleasant. He was starting to get the hang of apertures, angles, and ISO. Anabelle had been on her finest behavior, too.

"Everything okay? Has someone else made a nasty comment on a picture?" He hadn't checked, lest he track down the offender and speak his mind.

"Oh, I didn't tell you. I thought a lot about what you said on Thursday after your cowboy brawl. I'm not okay with those comments. I went through as many as I could this weekend and blocked all the users who crossed that line of appropriateness."

"Really? Good for you."

"I'm trying this new thing where I'm not a doormat to anyone. Not even my followers. I gotta stand for something, right? I don't want the girls who look up to me thinking it's okay for a man to mistreat her or abuse her." Her gaze lingered on Anabelle, who had asked for grilled chicken tenders and steamed broccoli, like Keira.

Anabelle, of course, dunked her chicken in a giant vat of ketchup, while Keira ate hers plain.

Keira did accept a roll from the bread basket, eyes rolling back in her head with the first bite.

The *mmm* sound she made almost made Robbie fall off his chair. When he recovered himself, he spoke again. "You didn't answer my question. Is everything okay?"

Her chewing slowed. When she finally swallowed, it looked difficult. After a quick shake of her head, she gave a forced smile. "I'll tell you later. First, I want to enjoy the rest of this roll."

On Keira's suggestion, they took a stroll down Main Avenue after dinner. The town of Twin Falls, Idaho, looked to be straight out of a Hallmark movie. The kind of place where couples probably wore coordinated sweaters in autumn and ice-skated in the town square at Christmastime. On this summer night, the scene was just as quaint. Pairs of folk walked along the streets under the lamplight, holding hands. Children pranced around them, playing hide-and-seek behind trees and benches and sometimes stopping to wave to Anabelle. Yet with every step, Keira's stomach dropped more and more.

"This is a cool town. If I didn't love West Yellowstone

so much, I could see moving here." Robbie's arm swung close to hers.

Any other day, Keira might be consumed with whether he might graze her hand with his. Instead, it was a mere passing thought. "Robbie."

He paused in front of her when he saw she'd stopped.

"Your question at dinner? About if everything is okay? I don't know. But I think I'm about to find out." She motioned to her right. "In there."

Together they stared at the storefront, which seemed to be ripped from the late 1800s. The redbrick face surrounded the yellow light from inside. The front window read *Sanders General Store* in vintage font, also harkening back to the days of the Old West.

Keira's nerves felt as though a preschooler had climbed inside her and was playing hopscotch.

Robbie said something, but she couldn't hear it over the pounding of the heartbeat in her ears.

"There was a reason we came to this town. It wasn't for the waterfalls." Keira nodded to the store. "I've been doing some research about my family history. I was going to tell you, but then everything happened with Vivian." Keira nodded to the store. "Of course, now that I'm here, I don't know if I can go in."

His hand wrapped hers, bringing welcomed comfort. "What can I do for you?"

She narrowed the space between them. "Just stay by my side."

"You got it."

Several seconds passed. Finally, she took a deep breath and led the way into the store. A million different items blurred together. Only one thing took center focus. A gray-haired woman with a welcoming smile.

She stood behind the cash register. "Can I help you?"

Keira couldn't speak.

After a couple moments, Robbie answered, "I think we're just looking."

"If you need anything, my name is Emmaline."

"Thank you . . . Emmaline." Robbie pivoted toward Keira and studied her face. "I think I get it now."

"What if . . ." Endless scenarios scrolled through her mind.

"You'll be okay. And I'll be here for you no matter what."

The corner of Robbie's lips pulled up. They walked to the cash register, then he bent down to Anabelle. "Kitty Kat, you're allowed to choose one of these candies, okay?" Straightening, he glanced at Keira. "That should keep her busy for a while." Then he dropped Keira's hand.

No, don't let me go now!

Instead of backing away, he moved nearer to her, his chest pressing against her trembling arm. His hand settled on the small of her back.

She could do this. "Emmaline Sanders?"

"Yes, that's me."

"Do you have a daughter named Claire?"

"Do you know Claire?"

"She's my mother."

The woman's dainty hand covered her mouth. "Excuse me a moment." She turned and headed quickly toward the rear of the store, then disappeared behind a door.

Robbie tugged Keira close. "This is a big moment for her, too. Give her a minute."

"What if she doesn't believe me, Robbie?"

His lips pressed against her forehead, unmistakable this time. "I think she already does."

After what felt like an eternity, the back door cut an arc into the room. Emmaline reappeared. Behind her, a man with a full head of silver hair and a Mr. Rogers sweater nearly knocked over a display of postcards to get an unobstructed view of Keira. She'd never seen pictures of her mother as a child, but Keira favored her as an adult. How old was her mother when they'd last seen her? Her parents didn't exactly sit around recalling the good ol' days.

The older couple crept toward them as if they expected that at any moment either a choir of angels or a legion of demons might appear.

The man—her grandfather?—tried to speak.

Emmaline reached for her, then seemed to think better of it. "How?"

"I'm the daughter of Joshua and Claire Knudsen. My name is Keira Emmaline Knudsen."

Emmaline Sanders's face crumpled. "How old are you, child?"

"Twenty-seven."

Emmaline faltered, and her husband caught her.

"She should sit," her grandfather said.

Quick-thinking Robbie reached over the counter, balanced the lip of a stool on his fingertips, and lifted it clear over the register. He set it behind Keira's grandmother and helped ease her onto the seat.

"Thank you. This is a good deal to process." The older man stroked Emmaline's hand. "Claire left us twenty . . . twenty-eight years ago. We haven't heard a word since. I apologize. We didn't know about you, Keira."

The words shouldn't have stung. She'd figured as much. Still, the knowledge plunged deep into her core. Why would her parents keep her a secret from these people? "My parents never told me much about you. Just that you lived in Twin Falls a long time ago."

His eyes studied her face, before breaking away to acknowledge Robbie. "And you are?"

Keira cut in. "This is Robbie. He's . . . well, he's my

Robbie. And his daughter, Anabelle." She stepped out of the way, revealing the child who had opened three different types of candies on the floor.

"Annie, no." Robbie kneeled to sweep up the Skittles from the hardwood.

"Don't worry about the candy or the mess. She knows this is a celebration. One a long time in the making, too." Keira's grandfather placed a hand on his heart. "I'm Richard Sanders. Your grandfather. You've no idea how happy we are to meet you, Keira." He took Keira in his arms.

Over his shoulder, Keira watched Emmaline beckon to Robbie.

He hurried to her side then helped her off the stool to join the embrace.

The grandparents who'd only recently discovered she existed held her tight. Suddenly, everything Keira had learned about family mottled the floor alongside the candies.

CHAPTER TWENTY-FIVE

Keira's grandparents lived in an alpine-style house with a two-story wall of windows looking down into Snake River Canyon. With its copper-colored tile floors, aged hickory woodwork, and worn leather couches, the home exuded a warmth that was only surpassed by Richard and Emmaline. They sat on either side of Keira on the couch, sharing stories about their life in Twin Falls. Her mother had been their only child. When she'd run away at seventeen years old, they had only each other.

Emmaline wiped her tears with a tissue. "We did try to connect with Claire over the years. Several times. Your father made it clear we weren't welcome in Claire's life. If we'd known about you, we would have tried harder."

"My father isn't a good man." Picking at her nails, Keira raised her eyes to find Robbie's. "I was raised to believe you had disowned Mama. That you hated her . . . us. It wasn't until I began researching you a few weeks ago that I began questioning that 'truth.' I read about the charitable work you've done here in Twin Falls. You're on the board for the local pregnancy decision center. And you founded a nonprofit to help reconnect estranged teens with their parents? I didn't think people like that would turn me away if I came to Twin Falls."

"Oh, darling, we would never." Emmaline's brow furrowed.

"Most people only see my father as the upstanding citizen and owner of the largest investment firm in Gallatin County. But he . . . hurt my mother and me. I left, but she stayed. I tried to get her to come with me on this trip, but she wouldn't. She's too scared, I think." Keira looked at Emmaline. "You should know. My mother isn't well. Emotionally, I mean. I don't know what she was like as a child, but she's merely a shell now." Keira tried to infuse hope into her smile despite the dread pitting her stomach. "Maybe it doesn't have to stay that way."

Robbie gave her a slight nod. Seated on the love seat across the coffee table from them, he held a pillow on his lap. Anabelle's curls splayed across the embroidered fabric as she slept. *The best is yet to be.* Keira had read the quote on the pillow when they'd first arrived at the Sanderses' home. She had to believe that was true.

Her grandfather grasped her hand. They talked about happier things then. Keira explained her work and her opportunity with the Adventure Channel. Her grandparents were big fans of *Traveling Light*, so the possibility of Keira joining the show set their pride aglow. Robbie bragged about her. She tried to shut him up, but he was nothing if not stubborn. He went on and on about the awards she'd received in high school and college, her Favorite-Teacher reputation, and her businesswoman guile.

"Will you still try to teach if you get the show?" her grandfather asked.

Three sets of eyes bored into Keira. "It wouldn't be possible, I don't think. The reason I pursued teaching in the first place was to show people places they'd never been. To be the one who brought far-off worlds to girls like me who weren't allowed to leave their house except for school. With this show, I can do that on a much grander scale."

"And an inspiration you will be," her grandmother said. "Why don't you all stay with us tonight? We have two guest bedrooms simply begging for some visitors."

"We can't. Our stuff is at the hotel," Keira said.

"I have all you could need. Toothbrushes, extra pajamas—"

Her grandfather cut in. "She lives to host guests. How we've never opened a bed-and-breakfast is beyond me."

"Please stay. We've only begun to get to know each other. We can't say goodbye yet." Emmaline's smoky blues were hard to say no to.

"Anabelle and I need to head back. If she wakes up in a strange room without her blankie or turtle, she'll go WWE, and no one wants that."

"Robbie, do you mind if I sleep here?" It came out strange. As if they were married, and he might miss her in their bed.

The quirk of his lips suggested he'd had the same thought. "Of course not." He hiked Anabelle up against his chest and heaved himself off the couch. After he thanked Emmaline and Richard for the evening and hot tea, Keira met him at the door. She scooped the car key out of her purse and tucked it in his hand. "Thanks for coming here with me."

"There's nowhere I'd rather be than experiencing this with you." Robbie turned, then glanced back. "I'm proud of you, Keira. Seeking them out? It took real guts."

She nodded. "Good night, sweet girl." Her hand moved across Anabelle's back until it found Robbie's arm, taut with the strain of carrying the girl. She let it linger.

"I'll keep my phone on. Just in case they turn out to be alien clowns or something. Sure, they seem sweet . . ."

"But it's the sweet ones you have to watch out for," Keira finished.

"Exactly. But seriously, call me if you need me. Even if just to talk." His gaze held hers longer than necessary. Long enough to bring her lungs to rest.

Her thumb swept across the golden hair and tanned skin on his forearm until she was finally able to pull her hand away and gasp a breath. "Good night, Robbie."

Back in the family room, only Emmaline remained. "Rich went to grab us a snack. We have a new package of cookies from the local bakery. You must try their snickerdoodles."

"Yes, ma'am."

"There are no ma'ams in this house. You may call me Grandmother, or Grandma—whatever you like. Because I do expect you to call me something. Don't you dare disappear from our lives now."

The sunrise filled the canyon with golden hues. Keira had snuck a few pics, but her mission for Twin Falls went beyond Momentso posts.

"Tell me, Keira," her grandmother—Nana, Keira decided—said. "How long has Robbie been in love with you?"

"Excuse me?"

"Inquiring minds want to know. I saw how he looked at you last night. The way he comforted you at the store. I know love when I see it. How long have you known each other?"

"Growing up in a small town like West Yellowstone, you know everyone your age. But he was Mr. Popular, all the way back in kindergarten. I was timid—didn't talk much, didn't have any real friends. In high school, while he was off dating other girls and winning football games, I focused on my grades. My dad told me I wasn't allowed to go to college. His goal for me was to marry someone suitable. Someone like him. If college was my plan, then I'd need a scholarship."

Nana tsked. From the looks of it, they could have funded her college easy peasy. If they'd known she existed.

"Sorry to interrupt. Do you girls need anything?" Her papa carried two blankets. After handing one to his wife, he shook out the second, then placed it over Keira's legs where she sat in the Adirondack chair.

"Join us," Nana said. "Keira is telling me about her and Robbie."

He dipped down into the chair next to Nana. "You do realize he's in love with you, right?"

Keira snickered behind her mug.

"I'm getting to that. One day, after a particularly bad night at home, I failed a trigonometry test. Robbie found me outside the bathroom on the verge of a panic attack. He schmoozed the teacher into letting me retake it." The memory tugged at her cheeks. "For the next two months, he came to eat lunch with me in the English classroom."

Above the far ridge of the canyon, a hawk circled, then swooped down, out of sight.

"That summer, I worked for our public library's tutoring program. Robbie, once again, finagled his way to my table."

"He does seem to be a charmer." When her nana laughed, it was what Keira imagined the spreading of an angel's wings might sound like.

"He certainly is that. But I discovered he had a severe learning disability that the school never diagnosed. He thought he was dumb. That's what he'd been told. Without help, he wouldn't graduate from high school. I learned everything I could about teaching strategies, tips, and tricks to help him. We grew close. Of course, I wasn't allowed to date, so we only ever saw each other at school or tutoring.

"When Robbie discovered what my father was like, he went on a crusade to get me out of that home. It nearly got him thrown in juvenile detention, in fact. But he was willing to deal with the consequences or even lose his chance to play college football to keep me safe. Luckily, that wasn't necessary.

"Together, we headed to Montana State. I got my teaching degree and tutored Robbie so he could keep his scholarship." Keira sighed. "We were great together. At least, that's what I thought."

"What happened, dear?"

"There was nothing in the world I wanted more than to marry him and be his wife. But I realized that Robbie would never marry me. He didn't need me the way I needed him. The moment I realized that—that I'd become my mother, offering herself on a platter to a man—it was as if I was suffocating. Even prayer couldn't open the window to let in fresh air. If I'd been able to find my breath, maybe I would have explained why I was running away, or at least said goodbye."

"That must have been hard."

Keira bit her lip.

The hawk emerged out of the canyon, then flew into the sunrise.

"I joined up with this six-month mission trip my friend was doing. We traveled country to country, serving and ministering to the local people. When it ended, I came home. I'd learned a lot about myself and grown a bit stronger, but most of all, I missed Robbie. I missed my best friend."

While she was swallowing a large gulp from her mug, Nana patted her knee.

"But it was too late. He was living with a girl we'd known in school. She was pregnant with Anabelle." Keira shrugged. "Now here we are, on this crazy whirlwind adventure together."

Rapping his knuckles on the wooden armrest, Papa worked his jaw. After a moment, his forehead wrinkles deepened. "Sounds to me like there are more questions here than answers. What's holding you back from asking them?"

"I've come so far. What if I find out something that sends me tumbling right back to where I used to be?"

Her grandparents exchanged looks. Finally, her grandfather leaned forward in his chair, resting his elbows on his knees. "The girl I see, the one who came here to meet us, isn't scared of a little tumble. If anyone could turn such a thing into an adventure, it'd be you. Also, you said something last night. That you want to show people far-off worlds they could never see for themselves. What if one of the answers you get from Robbie is *your* ticket to a world far beyond anything you could ask or imagine? What then?"

You've got a long road ahead, Robbie," Cassie Beck's voice lacked a touch of her usual confident tone. "Vivian isn't playing around."

If it would have any effect at all, he'd shake the phone and tell her to snap out of it. As his lawyer, she needed to believe Robbie had a case to retain primary custody. They couldn't both see only gloom and doom.

"Vivian rejected my proposed parenting plan outright?"

"You got it."

Vivian likes to win. He shouldn't be surprised. While she'd initially pressed for the extreme schedule that would allow him to only see Anabelle four days a month, he'd opted for a more moderate and logical proposal. Anabelle would be with him Monday through Friday always. For the first month, she would spend twenty-four hours tops each weekend with Vivian. Then, once Anabelle had eased into being away from Robbie for that amount of time, they could bump the schedule to every Saturday and Sunday. Did Robbie like the idea of handing his daughter over to Vivian? No. But the football-sized pit in his stomach told him if he didn't, Vivian would bare her fangs.

"We have a mediation scheduled for two weeks from tomorrow at the courthouse."

"Wait a minute. Will a judge be there for the mediation?" Below the table, his knee bounced.

"Not for the mediation. There's a neutral meeting room we can use. I figured you'd be more comfortable there than the office of Moneybags and Diamonds, Attorneys at Law."

"Absolutely."

"Now, if through mediation there's still no agreed-upon parenting plan, you'll have a preliminary hearing with Judge Rice."

"Who's he?"

"*She* is a tough one. I'll be honest. It would be better to come to an agreement before the hearing. Rice has a history of siding with the mothers in cases like these."

"Vivian has hardly been a mother, though."

"That is exactly what we will have to prove to the court if or when that day comes. It may be ridiculous for me to say, but try to enjoy your vacation. Thomas and I were dragged through a mean custody battle as kids. Two things helped us survive. First was knowing they were fighting over us because they both loved us like crazy. Second? Whenever we were with each parent, they were intentional about spending time with us and building memories because, I think, they feared the other might take us away. So go build memories with your daughter."

"I will." Robbie ended the call and placed the phone on the white plastic table. After peeling off his T-shirt, he piled the fabric on top of the phone for protection from splashes. The sight of Anabelle broke his anxious mood.

In addition to her bathing suit and floatie, which wrapped her chest and arms, she wore her swim goggles upside down.

"You ready for this, little bug?"

Nodding, Anabelle held out her hand.

He took it, holding it tight. "Ready, set, go!"

Together, they ran, jumped, and plunged beneath the surface of the hotel pool.

CHAPTER TWENTY-SIX

Two days with her grandparents wasn't nearly enough to recoup a lifetime of missed visits, phone calls, and holidays. Saying goodbye to them wasn't easy, but Keira had a job to do and a cable channel to impress. Interesting how after being around Nana and Papa's light, her goals seemed dimmer somehow. Sure, they were still there, but they'd lost some sheen. The filter had changed.

Still, an ache burned in her chest as they drove away from her grandparents. It swelled with each mile Robbie put between the Jeep and their home, stifling her ability to take a large enough breath.

That didn't escape his notice, either. While she sat pensively staring out the windshield, he'd give a sidelong glance, ask if the music was too loud, or adjust her vents until she was getting proper airflow. He did not ask if she was okay. The guy knew better.

Keira slid the phone from her bag and logged on to Momentso. Bypassing the notifications, which were getting out of hand, she went to the messages. A dozen unsolicited messages appeared, almost entirely from men. Probably the ones she'd blocked on Saturday. She scrolled until she'd found the latest interaction with MRCustom. It had been two days since they'd spoken. Last night, she was about to write, but a text message from Robbie back at the hotel stole her attention. Instead of MRCustom, she'd found herself engaging in a playful back-and-forth with Robbie.

Robbie, who was making her feel things that scared her.

She couldn't, wouldn't go down that road again. She tapped on the message bar and began her keystrokes.

> **KAT WANDERFULL:** Dear MRCustom, my heart hurts. Remember how I said I have no family? I did something brave. After some research, I found a store owned by my maternal grandparents, whom I'd never met. On Wednesday, I introduced myself to them. They. Were. Wonderful! MR, they invited me to Thanksgiving! But the idea of waiting even that long to see them again brings actual pain. It feels like my chest is caving in. And now I'm regretting ever looking them up. You see, for me

Keira's thumbs stilled above the phone's keyboard. She'd never told him about her past. Not the childhood abuse. Not much about her past relationships, either. She wished she had, because he would need to know it or else he'd think her crazy. And the idea of typing it all out exhausted her. For what? So he could give her advice? Cite Scripture references? That was great and all, but Keira wanted more.

As an old Monkees tune jingled, Robbie's hand reached over the center console. The outside edge of his pinkie finger grazed her wrist. Only for a few seconds, then it was gone. It was his thing that he used to do when they were dating. When a full-on public display of affection might be inappropriate, he'd do this small gesture to remind her he was there, that she could be sure of him.

Keira clicked the *X* on the message.

Are you sure you want to discard this message?

She glanced at Robbie, who was mouthing the lyrics to "I'm a Believer" to her. Her thumb clicked *Yes*, and she replaced the phone in her bag. With a hefty sigh, she leaned her head against the window. If only she could talk to Robbie about the ache growing inside her . . .

The car slowed, veering onto an exit ramp.

"Let's stop and fill up."

While Robbie pumped the gas, Keira took Anabelle to the bathroom. When they'd returned to the car, Robbie was leaning against the passenger door. He watched her walk across the pavement.

To make sure she didn't drop Anabelle's hand? Or to find a breach in her walls? If it was the latter, he didn't need to work too hard. Those walls looked way more like Swiss cheese now, and she wasn't sure how she felt about that.

He didn't move when they neared.

Finally, with Anabelle safely buckled, Keira turned to him. "You want a break from driving?"

Robbie's normal happy-go-lucky nature was nowhere to be found. Without a word, he opened his arms.

Also without a word, she accepted his invitation. The heat from his body blanketed her. With her face buried in his shirt, she picked up the scent of the dryer sheets his family had used since, well, forever. Up and down, his fingertips traced lines on her back. Because he knew she liked it. Robbie knew *her* whether she wanted to admit it or not. There was no need to fill in the details of her past with him, because he'd been right there beside her when much of it occurred.

"Aw, honey," Robbie said. "It's supposed to hurt when you leave the people you love. That means you're doing it right."

"Why, though? It doesn't make sense that the more you love someone, the more pain it causes." She pictured her mother, who, despite the abuse, loved her father too much to leave him. Her grandparents, who'd loved their daughter so much that her absence had caused a twenty-eight-year time of mourning. Then there was the pain of loving and losing Robbie, from which the only escape was to create a new reality where only screen names and avatars mattered. And yet, her fists clutched the back of his shirt tightly enough for her knuckles to sting.

"Because we're far from Eden, I guess. It won't always be that way. At least we can stake our hopes on that." He rubbed his chin over her hair. "Were you telling the truth when you told them you'd call?"

Conviction needled her.

"I think you should," he said. "Just because you can do this thing called life alone doesn't mean you have to."

Thoughts flashed to the young couple in the Jackson Hole restaurant, probably happily engaged by now. Unlike others, she'd never thought Robbie to be dumb. But at this moment, she thought he might be the smartest man she'd ever known.

CHAPTER TWENTY-SEVEN

On the map in Keira's atlas, Lake Tahoe was circled with a heart. In the car, she'd told Robbie about dreams of paddleboarding on the blue-green water and sunbathing on Kings Beach. Of course, neither of them had planned on a line of thunderstorms to roll through. Those two extra days in Twin Falls had thrown off their schedule and ensured she would not be seeing the sun above the lake as she'd hoped.

Although steady rain pelted the windows of the lodge's lobby, she didn't seem to mind. For the last hour, as they sat on the couches surrounding the board game, Keira beamed. Especially when she looked his way.

The lodge was new. A stone fireplace stretched two stories, bypassing rustic wood beams. Pine furnishings and plush upholstery radiated almost as much warmth as the crackling logs beyond the hearth. Images of a similar scene in his cabin on the river sometime in the future teased his mind. A good old family game night. Maybe Anabelle would nod off to sleep, leaving Robbie and Keira alone to enjoy marital bliss.

Too bad *that* would never happen.

"Prince Devin! I got Prince Devin!" Anabelle danced her

carriage-shaped game piece almost all the way back to *Start*. With a completely illogical sense of pride, she plunked the carriage on the square featuring Prince Devin, Princess Patty Cake's egotistical uncle. Why a kids' show featured a chauvinist jerk like him, Robbie would never understand.

"Ooh, I wish I got Prince Devin. He's handsome." Across the coffee table from him, Keira got a distant look on her face. Ugh. Apparently, that was why the show added him.

"I'm, like, right here," Robbie said.

"I mean, he's no Owen Wilson."

Robbie shook his head. "What would you do if I started talking about Lady Audra like that?"

On the lid of the game's box, Lady Audra stood by King Hubert's side. No doubt they were preparing for the two to get married in a future season. As far as cartoon characters go, she was pretty with her long ebony hair and emerald eyes.

Keira eyed the box. "She is beautiful, but I'm not worried. Robbie Matthews, you showed your cards that first day in the West Yellowstone High hallway. You, sir, have a type."

"Chicks with forehead scars."

"Exactly. My turn." Keira picked up a card from the pile. "Double pink. Which means on my next turn, I'll make it to Royal Village."

"Simmer down. You haven't won yet."

The door to the lodge opened. In stepped a man soaked to the bone, holding a jacket over a huddled form beside him. When he removed the coat, he revealed a woman in a sundress cradling a swollen belly.

She looked at her beau and frowned. "You didn't have to do that. I won't melt if I get wet."

"I know, but I didn't want you to hurry, then trip or something. It was slippery out there."

"You're sweet. Baby Layla and I thank you." The woman looked around, taking in the interior of the Grand Lake

Lodge, the finest inn on Lake Tahoe. "You shouldn't have spent our money on this."

"Nothing but the best for my girls." The man placed his hand on his wife's belly and gave her a peck on the lips.

Robbie drew a card. Instead of a character picture or colored squares, there were words. "Take a ride on Rainbow River with any player of your choice." He gave his best villainous laugh, as he tapped the spot on the board significantly farther from the finish marker at Royal Village than where Keira's crown currently sat.

"Don't do it. I'm so close."

"Should I do it, Kitty Kat? Should I force Keira to take a gondola ride with me on the Rainbow River?"

"Yep!" Anabelle said.

"No way. You can ride that gondola by yourself."

"Haven't you seen any movies? Gondolas aren't meant to be ridden by yourself. Then there'd be no one to kiss when you go through the Unicorn Tunnel."

"I think you've watched one too many episodes of this show." Keira locked her hands in a cage around her game piece.

Robbie set to work wrenching her fingers free.

Anabelle hugged Keira's arm.

When that didn't work, he looked at his daughter. "Annie . . . Zerbert."

"What's a zerbert? Is that code for something?" Keira's eyes grew large as Anabelle moved closer. "What are you going to do to me?"

After the world's slowest approach, Anabelle pressed her lips to Keira's cheek and blew a raspberry with all her might.

The noise, combined with Keira's squeal, turned every head in the lodge's main room.

Someone else might've been embarrassed. Not Robbie,

though. This was the moment he'd waited years—scratch that, his whole adult life for. He breathed in the sight like it was oxygen to his soul.

"Fine, fine, fine. I'll take a ride on the Rainbow River with you." Keira pushed her trinket into Robbie's hand. She glowed as Anabelle hugged her neck.

"You guys are the cutest family ever." The pregnant woman settled back into an easy chair nearby.

After an exchange of glances, Keira and Robbie said "thank you" together. "From the looks of it, we may lose that title soon. When's the due date?" Keira asked.

The young woman's sandaled feet, which she had propped on the ottoman, looked swollen. "Five weeks. My husband thought this babymoon thing would be a good idea. But after a few hours in the car, my feet and back are telling me otherwise. It gets worse from here, doesn't it? Was she a summer baby?"

The woman directed her questions to Keira, whose jaw simply hung slack, every blink of hers adding to Robbie's existing boulder of guilt.

"No, she was late May," he said. "Hang in there. Now's when it starts to get exciting. False labor. Eating spicy food to get things going. But the best part? Driving fast to the hospital because you have an excuse."

"Tim will love that, for sure."

The woman's husband kneeled by her side. "They said our room's almost ready. Can I get you anything? Water, ice for your feet, back rub?"

"Some sun?"

"Just say the word, babe. I'll go fight off the clouds like Don Quixote with his sword."

On the table, Robbie's phone buzzed an incoming call. Ryann. "Hey, Ry," he said, reclining against the sofa cushions.

"How's the trip? Mom said you're in Tahoe? Ugh. I'm jealous."

"It's great. Tahoe's nice but rainy."

"You know what Mom says. 'Rain makes flowers grow and . . .'?"

"'Rain makes the time go slow,'" Robbie said.

"Maybe that's what you guys need. How's Annie?"

"Losing horribly in Patty Cake Land."

"She *is* your daughter, loser."

"Brat." Robbie caught Keira's eye and winked. "How's business been?"

"Terrible. The latest review claimed to have seen a mouse in the café."

Gut-wrenching. If he ever discovered who was leaving these fake reviews, he'd smash their computer, smartphone, tablet, typewriter, and anything else they could use to compose a message.

Wait, could it be Vivian? No, probably not. They'd started long before she reappeared.

"If they're offended by a live mouse, they should probably avoid Emil's sausage gravy."

"Oh, ha ha. He's gotten better. Only a few cigarette butts in the eggs."

Robbie silently took his turn in the game. A purple. He moved his token—the king's noble steed—to the next purple square.

The hotel's desk clerk approached the expectant couple. He apologized for the delay and handed the man and woman each a key card. With some help from her man, the soon-to-be mother rose from her seat and gave a small wave to Robbie, Keira, and Anabelle. Together, they crossed the lobby hand in hand.

"But the real reason I called is Vivian again," Ryann said.

"She was here this morning. With two lawyer types and a woman dressed like a sitcom mom. Dad thinks the lady might've been a social worker, but we aren't sure. They were walking around the resort, taking notes and pictures and stuff."

A slideshow of disrepair scrolled through Robbie's mind. Upkeep tasks that he'd not completed over the years while he worked on their cabin. The resort was in rough shape.

And apparently, Vivian, her lawyers, and Carol Brady knew it.

"Did they say anything?"

"Not really. Dad ran them off before I could take a spatula to them. I think he offered them a mouse omelet." Ryann's joke fell flat. "Kidding."

"Thanks for telling me." With Anabelle so close, he had to be careful with his words.

"Remember, you don't have to fight this alone. Me, Mom, Dad. We'll all do what we can to help you."

Anabelle had climbed in Keira's lap and was moving her carriage the length of two white squares. Afterward, Anabelle settled back against Keira's chest, those strawberry curls of hers fanning Keira's eyes and changing their color a bit. Keira's eyes always reminded Robbie of Yellowstone's Sapphire Pool—the deepest part where the blue was the most concentrated. Now he saw the faint tinge of green in them, like the shallow edges.

Those eyes trailed from the game board to Robbie, then over to the expectant parents by the elevator.

The man bent down and kissed the woman's baby bump.

Keira looked away.

The lightning that cut through the sky illuminated the lake and its surroundings. With Anabelle sleeping in the room's bed, Robbie and Keira sat on the balcony's porch chairs. Behind them, the sliding glass door remained partially open so they could hear her if she woke.

Robbie's gaze bored into the darkness. "It wasn't like that for us, you know. Me and Vivian."

Just as when the woman had assumed she was Anabelle's mother, Keira froze. Her tongue stuck to the roof of her mouth. Why hadn't she accepted Robbie's offer of a bottled water?

"You can't force feelings that aren't there. I thought I could. Like if I chose to love her in action, my heart would follow suit. It didn't, though. And she saw through it anyway."

Keira held up a hand. "You don't have to—"

"I want to. I need to." Robbie leaned forward and dug his elbows into the muscle above his knees. "I think if you hear it, you may understand a little bit more about why things went the way they did."

A brilliant flash of lightning lit the sky connecting heaven and earth.

One, two, three, four, five, six—

Thunder cracked.

Look at him. The voice came from somewhere deep within her.

I don't want to, she argued and stood. Keira peered at Robbie, his form contrite. Careful not to scrape the legs on the wood, she moved her chair next to Robbie's and reclaimed her place at his side. "I'm listening."

"After you left, I lost my mind. You can ask Ryann. I was a mess. I slept in your cabin in case you came home in the middle of the night. I didn't know where you were. No one knew. I pictured you getting abused, raped, murdered." Light flashed on his face. "I didn't think you could survive without me protecting you, keeping you safe, holding your hand."

"I didn't exactly give you reason to think I could survive on my own," Keira said.

He laughed a little. "But look at you now. Anyway, after a couple months, I would've done anything to dull the pain. Against Ryann's advice, I went up to Bozeman to hang out with my old teammates. They threw everything at me, thinking they were helping. I was so dumb."

Keira cringed. "Don't say that."

"But I was. I don't even know what I put into my body that night. Then Vivian showed up. I don't remember much else."

Keira buttoned her lips as long as she could. After several moments of his silence, the thoughts burst forth. "With me, you were adamant about keeping those physical boundaries we set, even when I wasn't. Why did you sleep with her?"

"Why did I do anything that night? It felt like an earthquake tore into me, creating this head-to-toe canyon. I was trying to fill it with anything I could find."

Guilt seized her. *You caused this.* It was not the Holy Spirit's voice this time. It was her father's.

She shook her head. "If you don't remember, then how do you know—?"

Robbie stopped her with a look.

Hands in the air, Keira surrendered. "Okay. She's one hundred percent your daughter, no doubt about it."

"But I didn't know about her for a while. After that night, I didn't talk to Vivian. Man, I didn't even call her. What a jerk, huh? But about three months later, she showed up at the resort, looking as if she'd been stampeded by a herd of buffalo or something. When she told me she was pregnant, I've never seen so many tears.

"I just held her. She kept swearing that she hadn't been with anyone else, which I'd figured. Viv was a flirt, but she wasn't one to sleep around, you know? Anyway, she told me her stepfather kicked her out of her house that morning, and she had nowhere else to go. She kept saying, 'I can't do it alone.' Her mom was a single mother for most of Vivian's life, and she'd seen how hard it was."

Pity for Vivian snaked into Keira's heart. She tried to shoo it away, but it didn't listen. She'd never liked the girl, but Keira knew too well what it was like to be alone.

"She was so scared, Keira. All because of my weakness and my self-centeredness. I went over behind the wood pile and got sick. I sobbed, then got sick again."

"Oh, Robbie."

"Afterward, I kind of stumbled back to where she was. From her purse, she pulled out this little pink Bible with her name embossed on the cover. She'd gotten it for her baptism when she was a baby, I think. She placed it in my hands and asked me to show her what God would say. I opened it to Psalm 139."

Keira knew it well. A lump lodged in Keira's throat.

"She kind of sat there for a while, reading it over and over. I prayed and thought of you, and how sad you would be when you heard what I'd done."

The rain fell harder in front of the balcony. Some of the drops came down on an angle and splashed onto the deck, chilling Keira's feet.

She scooted her legs over until they rested against Robbie's denim pant leg.

"Cold?"

"A little."

Robbie removed his hooded sweatshirt and covered Keira's legs with it. "Vivian started going on and on about how she'd been a mistake her whole life . . . to her mother . . . to me. She didn't understand why God would let this happen."

"'Vivian,' I said, 'you are not a mistake. God knit you together, too. You have a purpose in this life, like this baby.' Then I begged her to tell me how to help her." Robbie placed his hand on Keira's sweatshirt-draped knee.

Her heart stuttered.

He traced a circle with his thumb, then shoved himself up out of the chair. His hands grasped the railing, and he lifted his face toward the dark sky. "Then she told me the one thing I could do to convince her to keep the baby. She wanted to be with me. Like, in a relationship. She even said, 'I know you miss Keira. Let me be Keira for you.'"

Another flash of light.

One, two, three—

Thunder.

"I told her it doesn't work like that. She begged me to try." Robbie turned to face Keira. "What could I do? She had no job, no home, no family. And if I said no . . ."

Keira nodded her understanding.

"You'd been gone for more than five months. I didn't know if you'd ever come back. But I had a child who needed me. And I felt a responsibility to help Vivian. I don't know why."

"Because you're a protector. That's who you are at your core."

"A week later we were at the doctor. During the ultrasound, Anabelle's heartbeat flashed real fast. Her tiny body curled on the screen, like a kitten sleeping. For the briefest of moments, I imagined you lying on the table with the wand pressed to your belly. Me, you, and our little Kitty Kat."

Even at a time like that, he'd thought of Keira. A mix of anger, sadness, and joy choked her. She couldn't speak.

"I got a job up in Bozeman, and we moved into a one-bedroom apartment. I wasn't comfortable with it, but my hands were tied. Actually, I was ready to do a shotgun wedding. It was my dad who advised me to wait."

Nausea rolled through her. He'd almost married her?

"It was awful from the start. She was sick constantly. We'd argue. And when we did, she had this list of insults and names she'd call me. Only a few weeks after we moved in, Vivian opened a box of mine and found a framed picture. You know the one of you and me kissing at Yosemite?"

That was her favorite picture of them, too.

"She got this cold look in her eyes. I thought she'd throw it or something. Instead, she handed it back to me real smooth-like. She said that if I ever wanted to hold this baby, then I was not allowed to speak to you or even say your name."

Behind him, gnarled fingers of lightning spread across the darkness as if they were trying to clutch him. The thunder that followed soon after cracked and crumbled loud enough to shake the balcony beneath them and jolt Keira to her feet.

"I didn't want to agree to it. Even though I was still angry that you'd left, I didn't want to let you go. But I had to. This child, without a face, with only a nickname, was mine to protect, no matter what it cost. So when Ryann called the next week to tell you'd come back, I wanted to come to you. If I weren't scared out of my mind about what Vivian might do, I would've."

Keira moved toward him until they were so close that a breeze mingled the loose fabric of her shirt with his. She placed her hand over his heart, feeling its pulse kiss her palm again and again. "Robbie, don't ever apologize for having Anabelle. Or anything you did for her."

Robbie released a breath that warmed her cheek. When he met her gaze, the light and darkness still grappled in his eyes. "I'm certainly paying the price for my sin now, aren't I?"

Keira lay in her room. She wished there were extra blankets. Even under the sheet and duvet, she couldn't get warm enough. She should've hugged him out on his balcony. That would've warmed her up, for sure. But if she'd hugged him, it may have led to more. Was she ready for that?

If she'd had any idea leaving him would send him into such a spiral, she probably wouldn't have left. Of course, she'd convinced herself he didn't love her the way she loved him. Had she been wrong? After all, he still hadn't explained why he didn't want to marry her.

MRCustom could give her advice. He seemed to understand both men and women. She rolled and grabbed the phone off the nightstand. On Momentso, her first photo from Twin Falls posted today, to keep with her new delayed-posting rule. None of her followers would know her exact location in real time anymore. The post was well received.

Snake River Canyon at sunrise. Keira held Anabelle, tummy to tummy, with the little girl's legs crossed around Keira's waist. Because the picture was cropped, only the ends of Anabelle's curly locks showed.

The name MRCustom was missing from her list of incoming messages. Strange. Why hadn't he written? Maybe he hadn't been okay with her assistant's daughter being in the picture. Was he jealous? Hard to say. She searched for his username. A green dot appeared on his profile picture. He was online.

KAT WANDERFULL: Hey!

She fluffed her pillow while she waited for his reply. What was taking him so long? He was a slow typist, but still . . . She glanced at the phone screen. The green dot was gone. And he hadn't replied.

CHAPTER TWENTY-EIGHT

The hands of the clock lingered on each hash mark and number during the volunteering shift he and Keira did in the hospital's pediatric unit. A slow dance of time that Robbie relished, especially after the drive from Tahoe to Southern California. In just two days they'd visited Sequoia National Park, scaled the Sierra Nevadas, and hit the outskirts of Death Valley before hopping on Route 395 to San Bernardino. The drive, filled with singable songs and a Jackie Chan marathon, unleashed the kind of laughter from Keira that Robbie had imagined often in the years they'd been apart. But that same laughter made moments with Keira pass too quickly. He was glad for this change of pace.

Ellen, the nurse assigned to this hospital room, kneeled by the rocking chair. Her hand grazed Robbie's arm. "How's Maxwell doing?"

The baby boy Robbie held against his chest cooed with each exhale. He was featherlight for his eleven weeks of age, hence the feeding tube that disappeared into his tiny nose. *Failure to thrive*, his chart said. "He seems pretty happy. Whatever's in this tube must be good. Got any for me?" Robbie asked.

"You're funny. And very good with him. I wish all volunteers were like you."

"Rocking babies is the easy part. You nurses are the heroes."

On the opposite side of the room, another rocking chair creaked. Keira rose from it slowly.

The little girl in her arms was older. Around four months or so. The baby's fist held tight to a tendril of Keira's hair, even as Keira rocked her back and forth. The gentle motion, the nurse assured earlier, would not incite the seizures that landed Opal a stint in this place.

Summoning all his self-control, Robbie purposed not to watch Keira's swaying hips. Something was definitely wrong with him. Three hours cuddling babies shouldn't be sexy. Keira made it so.

Maxwell squeaked and blew out a warm breath.

"I think I'll walk him a bit." Whenever he'd held Anabelle as a baby, he imagined himself as one of those dancing actors in his mom's old movies. Gene Astaire or Fred Kelly or something. Swoops and glides were better than the jukes and scrambles he was used to. This was no different, except for the tubes and the rolling drip stand, of course. He danced his way to Keira's side. "Hey."

Keira didn't respond. She was locked in a gaze with Baby Opal, whose nickname was unfortunately not Opie or Al, as he had suggested.

"You look good with a baby in your arms. I wish your followers could see this side of you."

Still nothing.

Opal twisted her body to see Robbie. A big, toothless smile spread across her face. At least one of them wasn't mad at him.

"I think Opal's your biggest fan. After me, of course." Robbie nudged her side.

Keira pursed her lips.

Opal mimicked the facial expression.

"Don't be jealous, Keira." He kept his voice low. There was already too much interest in them among the hospital staff already. "You should know by now who has my heart."

Every part of Keira stilled, except for her eyes, which widened to the size of quarters.

Oh no. He hadn't meant to make Keira stop breathing. A swoony sigh? Maybe. A hitch in her breath? Definitely. But she seemed to stop breathing entirely.

Maxwell squirmed. A noise ripped through the room.

"Oh, Max. Some wingman you are. Ellen, diaper change on aisle three."

At least Opal laughed.

Forty-five minutes later, they tossed their scrubs in a laundry bin outside the dressing rooms. They'd stayed thirty minutes past the agreed-upon volunteer time, not that Ellen minded. It gave her the chance to write down her username for a half-dozen social media sites on a paper, which she stuck in Robbie's back pocket while he said goodbye to Maxwell.

Seriously? Flattering, but no thanks.

"Do you think the hospital's KidWatch workers will mind we're running late to pick up Anabelle?" Keira asked.

"Nah. They said we could take our time. Besides, it's probably good for Anabelle to get more time around other kids. Preschool starts this fall."

Keira's steps stuttered. She was out of sorts today. Mom would say she had her knickers in a knot. For the first time, Robbie might actually understand what that phrase even meant. Either she had another surprise set of grandparents or . . .

"You had a tough time saying goodbye to Opie in there."

She rolled her eyes at him. "I wish we could stay longer.

What kind of mom drops her sick baby at a hospital and leaves?"

"Not sure. One who needs to work to pay the medical bills? Did you see all those machines? I bet every beep costs a thousand dollars."

Her forehead wrinkled. "If I had a million dollars, I'd use it to cover lost wages, so parents could be with their babies at the hospital."

Robbie would bet that this was the first time in history that fluorescent lights had a romantic glow to them. He caught her hand on the backswing and threaded his fingers through hers. "You know what, Miss Wanderfull? Your heart is my favorite part of you. Thanks for letting me join you for your Serving Sunday thing—even if we had to postpone it to Wednesday."

"I'm glad you did. Maxwell was a cutie. It's silly, but I kept picturing that he was our little boy, Charlie. You know, the one we'd imagined so long ago?"

"Um, if Charlie is born with skin the color of Maxwell's, we'll have to talk."

She squeezed his hand. "You know what I mean. You're good with babies."

Robbie buttoned his lips a moment, hard enough to burn. He breathed deep. "Did you know I once asked Ryann to raise Anabelle?"

Keira's eyes went wide. "You did?"

He kept walking, tugging Keira along. Outside the hospital doors, there was a line of benches beneath some shade trees.

Robbie led the way to the closest one, and they sat. "As a baby, Anabelle had colic and acid reflux. She cried a lot and puked even more. We tried every formula, but nothing sat right in her tummy. She always seemed to be in pain. One night, when Anabelle was two months old, she wouldn't stop crying. Vivian was holding her and patting her back so hard that Annie couldn't catch a breath. So, I took the baby from her. Vivian lost it. She called me stupid—said God only gave me half a brain."

Keira tsked and twisted her body to face him. She gripped his hand harder between both of hers and held it on her lap. In her eyes, he saw his own pain reflecting back.

"I kept trying to calm her down, but there was no point. Vivian packed a bag, all the while yelling vile things about me and my family. She left that night. Afterward, I struggled to balance it all on my own. One day, I was sitting at Mom and Dad's kitchen table. Ryann was burping Anabelle. The whole three ounces came right back up. Annie started screaming again, but Ryann rocked her, rubbing circles on her back with that baby puke just soaking into her clothes. I said that Anabelle would be better off with her."

"What did Ryann say?"

"You know Ryann." Robbie felt a pull in his cheeks at the memory. "She told me to knock it off. That Anabelle would grow up knowing she had a father who loved her enough to fight her battles alongside her. I quit my job that Monday and moved back to West Yellowstone. Still wasn't easy, but my family was a huge help. After the café closed for the summer, Mom watched her while I began building the cabin."

"Which is breathtaking, by the way."

"You think so?"

Keira nodded. "You're really talented. I could see your stuff pictured in *House Beautiful* or *Wild Montana* magazine. I could make some calls."

"Nah. I don't want the fame. Just enough money to give Anabelle a good life with some time left over at night to be with those I love."

"Robbie, why haven't you started that home-building business you always talked about?"

"You'll make fun of me."

"You know me better than that."

"After I bumbled through the paperwork to launch the LLC, I started thinking about the contracts and stuff that I'd have to write up for clients. It put me in a cold sweat."

"That's why you haven't gone after your dream? Because you're afraid of paperwork? There are people who could help you with that. *I* could help you with that. That is if this digital nomad gig of yours doesn't work out."

"I have no idea what you just said, but okay." Robbie settled back on the bench. It was nice enough here. But mostly because of Keira. The truth was he missed Montana. This life of hers was fun but exhausting. What he wouldn't give to spread out a blanket on the Madison riverbank and dream with Keira on a lazy Sunday afternoon.

"Hey, Robbie?"

"Hmm?" He didn't want to come back to reality yet.

"That night Vivian left . . . did she say anything about me?"

He opened his eyes. After letting go of her hand, he removed his hat and loosened his curls with a tousle. "She was sitting in the car with the engine idling. I was holding Anabelle against my chest and kind of bouncing her a little to soothe her, you know? Vivian rolled down her window and said . . ."

"What?"

"That the bravest thing you ever did was leave me."

Keira crossed her arms over her stomach. "Shows you how much she knows. That wasn't brave. Quite the opposite, in fact."

CHAPTER TWENTY-NINE

✺

The next day's midafternoon sun spilled through the windows of Lady Audra's Tea Shoppe, a small cobblestone house in the center of San Diego's's Royal Village theme park. Steam rose past Keira's nose and eyes until her rounded lips blew a cooling breath on the surface of the tea. The steam swirled and dissipated, leaving a clear view of her perfect face.

Snap.

"Got it." Robbie showed her the phone screen. "Check out how blue your eyes look in this diffused lighting."

"My turn," Anabelle said. Next to Keira, Anabelle held her miniature teacup with steamed milk and whipped cream in front of her mouth. It was the first time she stopped smiling all day. Except for the teacup ride. Not much smiling there.

"Hang on a sec." With his fingertip, he swiped a bit of whipped cream from her cup and dotted her nose with it. He clicked a picture.

In it, her eyes were crossed, staring at the end of her nose in the cutest way.

"Perfect."

"Cute." Keira set the cup on the saucer. "Looks like the

line died down for the ladies' room. I'll be back." Her gaze lingered on Robbie after she stood. She'd been doing that a lot today.

After Keira joined the tail end of the line, Robbie held out the phone for Anabelle to see, but something behind Robbie had grabbed her attention.

"Lady Audra!"

Fold upon fold of glittery pink fabric swept past Robbie. "Hello, sweet girl. What's your name?"

"A-N-A-B-E-L-L-E."

"What a pleasure to meet you. Are you having a happy day here at Royal Village with your"—Lady Audra's eyes fell on Robbie—"your daddy?"

"Mm-hmm. I rode on the flying Pegasusesss, went on the train through Troll Forest, and I almost threw up on your teacup ride."

She lifted a white-gloved hand to her painted lips. "Oh my."

"She was fine," Robbie said. "Just a little green is all."

"How fortunate for her to have a big, strong father to look after her." Splotches of red mottled the skin above the ribbon on her neck. "Wait. How do I know you? Did you go to Kennedy High School?"

"No." He wanted to add, *Neither did you, Lady Audra.* "We're from Montana. I figured you went to Royal Village High." *Stay in character, lady.*

Lady Audra sat in Keira's seat. "Anabelle, I've never been anywhere but Royal Village. Will you tell me about Montana?"

"There's mountains and rivers and bears. When me and Daddy go fishing, he lets me cut the heads off the fish."

"Hey, Annie, let's not talk about that here."

"Lady Audra, do you go fishing with your daddy?" Anabelle asked.

The girl behind the costume smiled sadly. "I don't have a daddy."

"Don't be sad." Anabelle patted Lady Audra's hand. "My mother was gone a long time, but she came back. So I have a mother and a Keira."

"Oh. Who's Keira?"

"She's my best friend. She plays Patty Cake Land and airplane with me and hugs me." Anabelle cupped her hand by Lady Audra's wig. "And I want her to marry my daddy."

The words of her whispered shout carried a peace with them like an old hymn. "It Is Well with My Soul," maybe. Anabelle wanted Keira the same way Robbie wanted Keira.

Okay, maybe not exactly. He chuckled under his breath.

Keira emerged from the restroom. Her Montana State T-shirt and jean shorts didn't hang off her bones quite as much anymore. She was starting to get her muscle back. Her curves, too, though Robbie tried not to notice that.

When her gaze took in Lady Audra sitting in her seat, she looked as if she might go all Jackie Chan on her.

Robbie coughed. "Speaking of, Lady Audra, this is Keira. Keira, Lady Audra."

Lady Audra met Keira's eye. Awareness seemed to dawn. "I believe I'm in your seat. Anabelle, it was lovely to meet you. I sincerely hope you get your wish." Lady Audra stood, then smoothed the folds of her gown. She floated out of Keira's place with the grace that only a lady in the king's court had. Her gaze shifted from Robbie to Keira and back. "That's where I know you from. You're Kat Wanderfull, which makes you her mystery man. I'm a big fan. One day, I want to travel like you two."

Rather than sitting, Keira reached down to Anabelle, who climbed onto Keira's hip as if she'd always been held there. "We're big fans of your show, too." She turned to

Anabelle. "What do you say? Should we go ride some of the bigger rides now? Did you know that when your daddy rides roller coasters, he screams like Princess Patty Cake?"

Robbie held up his hands. "Guilty as charged."

T his, I've been told, is the best spot in the whole park to see the fireworks." Keira peeked into the wishing well. She was tempted to sing down into it to see if her echo would harmonize with her.

Anabelle hopped out of the wagon, nearly catching her foot on her new dress. As part of the experience offered to Kat Wanderfull and friends, Anabelle had enjoyed an appointment at the royal salon to get dolled up like Princess Patty Cake. Afterward, at a meet-and-greet dinner, Anabelle's dream came true when she met the princess and got a picture with her. Robbie's face had never been brighter. Of course, that all ended when Prince Devin noticed Keira and turned on all his charm.

"You sore yet?" she asked Robbie when he lifted Anabelle to peer into the well.

"I have no idea what you mean. Okay, Kitty Kat, that's a long enough look." He set her feet down on the brick path.

She immediately began twirling in the purple ball gown.

Keira moved in front of him. She touched his upper arm and squeezed the muscle.

He grunted.

"Robbie, when was the last time you did that many push-ups? Fess up."

"What was I supposed to do? Prince Arrogant offered up the challenge. Winner gets you? Is he stuck in the sixteenth century or something?"

"Actually, yes, he is."

A sly smile stretched his lips. "I beat him, though."

"And you'll pay for it tomorrow."

"True." His hand slid around her back as he whispered into her ear. "But the prize will be worth it."

Dramatic music blared from the speaker atop the nearest light post.

"The fireworks are starting! The fireworks are starting!" Anabelle bounced here, there, everywhere.

"I think that cotton candy was a bad idea," Keira said.

"I think you're right."

Keira sat on the opposite end of the bench from Robbie, hoping space might give her time to cool down, otherwise . . .

He scooted next to her. "Annie, come sit." He patted the spot on his left.

When the first boom exploded, Anabelle ran to the bench and cuddled under his left arm. Robbie put his right arm around Keira's shoulder. Only Robbie could still smell good after a day of sweating at an amusement park.

The colors splayed across the dark sky in perfect choreography to the Princess Patty Cake theme song.

Robbie watched them with the wonder of a little kid. Twenty-seven years old and he still found joy in fireworks.

One of the many things she loved about him. And heaven help her, she did love him. Despite everything. She burrowed closer.

His eyes dropped from the sky and stared ahead at the wishing well. He set his jaw, then turned to face her. In a seated position, their height difference wasn't as noticeable. Their lips could easily align here with only a slight dip of his chin. His fingers tugged softly on the lock of hair by her ear. He whispered, "Can I kiss you?"

She breathed in a slow drag of the night air. "Please."

His lips pressed against the hinge of her jaw. He placed another kiss, then another, following her jawline and easing closer to her mouth. She closed her eyes, moistened her lips, and turned into the next kiss.

"Ugh," he groaned.

Keira hadn't yet opened her eyes when a bony elbow clipped her ribs, and she made the same sound he'd made.

"Anabelle, honey, try not to jump on Daddy next time." He'd shifted away, making room for the little girl between them, then looked up at the grand firework finale. "She's never eating cotton candy again."

CHAPTER THIRTY

❧

At this time of night, the hallway at Royal Village Resort was quiet. Robbie adjusted Anabelle to the right side of his chest, so he could get the key card from his back pocket.

Keira waited as he swiped the card. They'd hardly talked on the tram ride over. She still had that look on her face, though. The kiss-me one.

"Would you like to come in? There are some unicorn tea packets in here. I'm really hoping they taste more like tea than unicorn, but you never know." Robbie shut his mouth. Dumb joke. Dumber invitation. Still, he pushed the door open farther with his back, giving Keira a path into his room.

Eyes steady on his, Keira stepped through the doorway, grazing a soft hand over his arm in passing. "I'd love a cup of tea. I can get that started while you put her to bed." She lifted her purse strap off her shoulder and let it fall to the floor by the mini fridge. After one last lingering glance at him, she turned her attention to the small coffee maker and row of tea packets.

Robbie's heart pounded so hard he was sure Anabelle would wake up from the beat. After he entered the bedroom, he thought twice. The last thing she'd eaten was that cotton candy. Her hands were still sticky with it. He pictured the sugar rotting her tiny teeth and cringed. "Hey, Kat," he called out softly. "Can you bring me the travel case?" He headed to the suite's master bathroom and waited. Eyeing the light switch, he decided to leave the main light off. The night-light built into the socket would be enough to get the job done without waking his girl up fully. If she did wake up, this night would go a completely different direction than the way it seemed to be headed. Maybe that would be better. Kissing would complicate things. This was supposed to be strictly business, after all.

A hand rested against his back a moment before Keira appeared at his side in the mirror, holding the travel case. *Toothbrush?* she mouthed.

Robbie nodded.

She removed the Princess Patty Cake battery-operated toothbrush. While she placed a pea-sized amount of sparkly toothpaste on the bristles, Robbie settled Anabelle's bottom on the counter, her head still resting against his chest.

Keira moved in close. The length of her body pressed against Robbie's side.

He watched in the mirror as she tentatively raised the toothbrush and placed it in Anabelle's slack mouth. She pushed the *On* button, and the loud vibration startled them all.

Anabelle's eyes popped open, then fluttered shut.

After a minute of toothbrush maneuvering, Keira put the toothbrush down. Gently, she wiped a wet washcloth over Anabelle's droopy lips. She took Anabelle's small hand, washed it with soap and water, then patted it dry.

Robbie shifted his daughter a bit more, giving access to the other hand.

Keira repeated the routine. Once she was done, she leaned in and placed a kiss on Anabelle's cheek.

Robbie's heart tumbled backward. *God, what are you doing here?*

When she withdrew her lips, she tilted her chin up to him.

The soft blue light glinted off her eyes, making it look like . . . No, Keira didn't cry. It wasn't possible. She'd killed that ability long before they'd met. One more self-protective measure in a long line of them.

"I'll go finish the tea." She breathed the words, making him wonder whether he'd heard them or simply felt them through the fabric of his shirt.

He carried Anabelle to the queen bed closest to the bathroom. With one hand, he pulled back the sheets and laid her down.

Immediately, she rolled to her other side and curled into a ball, which made for easy blanket tucking.

He kissed the same cheek Keira had moments ago.

Soft music breezed through the open bedroom door, followed by the clink of metal against porcelain. Tea. Music. Royal Village. Playing family with his daughter and the girl who got away. What good could possibly come from this? His brain told him to lock the door and climb into the other bed. Not even to bother to say good night.

His body, of course, disagreed. He'd never felt such want for a woman. Not that he'd give in to it. He'd learned that lesson. But *his heart* reached for Keira, too. As if there was some invisible rope that tethered them to each other, despite her attempt to sever it.

Even the Holy Spirit inside him seemed to be pushing him to the door. He didn't understand why. Was God in the mood to parade the forbidden fruit in front of him? Let him taste it, then rip it away? Again, he felt the nudge from the Spirit, as if to say, *Go. Talk to her.*

All right, God. I'll throw myself off this cliff. But only because I know you'll catch me. He took one last glance at

Anabelle—an angel with the cutest snoring problem—and headed for the door.

Out in the family room of the suite, only the light above the table was lit, but not brightly. The dimmer switch on the wall was raised only halfway.

Keira swirled her tea with her spoon as she sat. Steam rose from his much manlier coffee mug at the head of the table. Next to it, a small glass bowl held several ice cubes. Then a few white sugar packets and a spoon. All lined up in a row. Neat. Controlled.

Clink. Clink. Clink.

Keira's hand traced a circle in the air above her teacup. She didn't watch Robbie as he took his seat. Instead, her eyes flitted from the amber liquid to the suite's front door and back again.

"Thanks for the mug. You sure you don't want to watch me drink out of a teacup?" He curled his hands around the tea. Bypassing the ice and sugar, he took a sip. It stung his lips. He pressed them tightly together, drawing Keira's gaze from the door to his mouth. "It's not the best unicorn tea I've ever had." He faked a grimace. "You know what the unicorn said when he met his horse cousin?"

Keira shook her head. "Don't do that."

"What?"

"Make a joke. Not now." Keira rested her spoon on the saucer as a new song started. Turning an ear to her phone, from which the music played, she smiled. "You remember this song? From our last night together?"

"I'm sorry, but I don't."

"This was the final song we danced to at Trina's wedding. Did you know that was the last time I danced with someone? John didn't like to dance, so we never did. Isn't that sad? Five years without dancing. It should be a crime."

Robbie's heart, mind, and body wrestled to the upbeat

tune. His chair seemed to develop knobs and spikes that protruded into his back and legs. Sitting soon became unbearable. He rose, towering above her. "Come on. For old times' sake." He led her in a two-step around the room, avoiding the table, chairs, and sofa.

The final bars of the song faded.

Robbie slowed but didn't release her. He couldn't. He knew how it pained to let go of her.

A guitar strummed a slow, folksy tune that Robbie recognized immediately. It was the song that always made him think of her—in the car, in his cabin, at the café. He'd always thrown himself at either the dial or the door before the lyrics could lodge into his brain. But now? With her in his arms? He didn't want the song to end.

She lifted her big eyes. They were full, like always. This time, though, they were full of something that looked like hope.

He opened his mouth to speak. No words came. Only the sound of his own breath leaving his body when her hands slid beneath his arms and around his waist, marvelously dismissing the space between them.

Welcoming her against his chest required no thought. She belonged here, surrounded by his arms. Always had.

With a hand, he combed the strands of hair that trailed down her back. Slowly, they swayed back and forth, making a small circle on their private dance floor and allowing the lyrics to wash over them. Two teenagers growing up to love and build a life together. The song told their story. If things were different, that is. If she hadn't . . .

He pushed away the memory. She was here now. Nothing else mattered. Dipping his head down, his lips grazed the top of her ear. "Kat."

She softened.

Fearing she might melt out of his hands, Robbie cinched

her tighter to himself. Too tight, considering how she exhaled sharp and quick. "Sorry."

"No. It's fine. Don't let me go." She sounded young. Familiar. His Kat. The one he would have died for. The one he'd lived for. She and Anabelle—they were his girls. *His girls.* He could protect them, look after them, keep them forever in his arms.

A pain jolted his chest.

"This is how it could've been. How it should've been. You and me, for our whole lives, dancing like this."

Keira stiffened slightly. "You didn't want this. Not forever."

Robbie pulled back his head, enough to meet her eye. "Yes, Kat. This is what I wanted. Tonight, seeing you laughing and caring for Anabelle. You know . . . sometimes . . ." He shook his head.

"What?" Keira caught his eye line. "Sometimes what?"

Robbie blew out a breath. "Sometimes I wish she was yours. If she were, Anabelle would have a mother. One who loves her and cares for her. And I'd have a partner in this crazy thing."

When had they stopped dancing? When had she pulled his shirt so taut across his ribs? And why did he have to bring this up? After a perfect day, when all seemed to be falling into place.

"I've had that same wish. I love Anabelle." She gripped and regripped the back of his shirt near his belt. "I thought I'd be the one who would carry your child and cradle her. I thought it would be me listening to you sing lullabies to her. This *is* the life I wanted for us."

"Then why did you leave me?"

Her breaths were short now. Robbie loosened his arms around her torso, and she gasped for breath.

"Why did you leave? Kat, I would have spent every moment of my life loving you. Every single moment. I would have done anything for you."

She pushed back from him and crossed her arms. With the light only catching a sliver of her face, he couldn't read her expression. "Anything except marry me."

Robbie's voice caught in his throat, blocked by what felt like a lump of coal.

"Remember the drive home from the wedding?" Keira asked. "You kept asking why I was upset. We'd been together for five years. And sure, you talked about being with me until we were old and gray, but you never talked marriage. After you dropped me off at my cabin, I spent some time praying. I steeled myself and decided I was going to ask why you hadn't proposed." Keira hardly blinked. "I left my cabin to find you. I heard your voice, coming through Ryann's open kitchen window. She asked, 'Don't you want to get married?' Then you said, clear as day, 'I do want to get married, but I am not supposed to marry Keira.'"

Robbie cringed. His own words were like venom in his veins.

"I went back to my cabin, packed all my stuff, and left."

He tried to sit on the arm of the sofa but missed, landing his tailbone on the floor with a thud. No words came when he opened his mouth. *Tell her everything*, the Holy Spirit seemed to say.

"You always told me to be brave. But Robbie Matthews, you aren't so brave yourself. You aren't so loving, either. You used me to get you through high school and college. It was only a matter of time before you ditched me for someone else."

Those had to be her father's words. Not Keira's. She knew better. He couldn't bear to look at her.

"You're wrong," he said.

The music, which had transitioned to an upbeat worship song, cut off. There was rustling in the kitchen, where she'd dropped her purse earlier, followed by footsteps heading toward the door.

"Keira, don't forget. *You* gave up on *me*."

For a moment, the only sound was the hum from the mini fridge. Then the door of the suite creaked open, swept across the floor, thudded, and latched.

Robbie was alone.

CHAPTER THIRTY-ONE

꙰

That night, a storm rolled over the California coast. Keira lay awake listening to the bitter growls of thunder. She'd finally had the nerve to say what she'd buried within for all this time. So why didn't she feel better?

Before breakfast, she headed to the coastline. Though sunrise was slated for a half hour before, the receding storm clouds hit the snooze button on behalf of the beach. She caught a time-lapse video of the moment the sun broke through, spreading its brilliance over the sea.

Anabelle would get her beach day after all.

Her phone buzzed. She imagined—scratch that. She hoped it was Robbie, calling to give the explanation he'd withheld last night.

Instead, Dora's name scrolled on the screen. "Kat, I know it's early out there on the West Coast, but I couldn't wait. You did it!"

"Did what?"

"You landed a guest-hosting gig on *Traveling Light*!"

The ground seemed to swell beneath her and roll like one of the waves, making Keira feel heady. She closed her eyes and waited for it to crest and crash. When it did, she dug her toes into the sand to be sure of reality. "Dora, this is . . ."

"Amazing? Unbelievable? Fabulous? Everything you've been working toward?"

"Yes. It's all those things." She ran a hand down the side of her cheek. "Oh wow. Wow, wow, wow. When?"

"They're about two months into filming season sixteen. Constance said Margot's been finicky. They need someone ready to go the next time she doesn't show up for work. They'll send the contract over today. They'd like to have you join up with them on July seventh. I'll work on clearing the rest of your summer schedule."

"Are you sure the places won't be upset about the cancellations? Some of these locations really need the publicity."

"No worries. I've got someone else to take over your gigs. This girl's only nineteen, but she's already built a good-sized following. She's from Kentucky. And you thought *you* were wide-eyed at the start."

"I know you'll take care of her like you took care of me." Pressure mounted behind Keira's eyes as she spoke. Where would she be without Dora's advice and connections? Not to mention her protection. She'd kept her from making foolish decisions early on. Yes, Dora was a protector. Like Robbie. Now she'd be forging ahead without either one. Was she ready for that?

"But one question they had. How attached to the Kat Wanderfull moniker are you? They think 'Wanderfull' is a bit cheesy. How about Kat Knudsen?"

"Uh . . . I . . ."

"Just think about it. They'll want to Skype with you to discuss logistics and contract terms. I won't be on the call, but if you have any questions, you know how to reach me."

"Thank you, Dora, for all you've done for me."

"This was all you, girl. Your hard work and dedication made this happen. I'm so proud of you."

After ending the call, Keira took a selfie. She hadn't bothered to put on her normal makeup since this morning's shoot wouldn't show her face. Still, she wanted to capture the moment her dream came true. For her and her alone. This was proof. Happiness was something you could chase and catch.

She let out a squeal and stretched her arms overhead, then fell back on the sand. *Thank you, Jesus.*

K eira had barely met his eye since the night before. She didn't seem angry with him. Just distracted. And about as cold as the Pacific Ocean sprawled out beyond the cliffs of Torrey Pines State Natural Reserve. They'd hiked all over the park, finally landing on Yucca Point for the last shot of the night. The only warmth she'd shown at all was just now when she apologized for not joining them at the beach earlier.

"Anabelle understands. Although you did miss some serious sandcastle building. I even gutted a dungeon for Prince Devin to live in." Robbie's joke didn't land with Keira, though. Over the last few hours they'd spent together, she'd made it evident that he was her assistant and nothing more. The only clearer sign would be if a pod of dolphins spelled out *In Your Dreams* across the blue water below. The mental image threatened to pull the corners of Robbie's lips into a smile despite the disappointment turning his stomach.

At least she hadn't reached out to MRCustom last night. Even in the days leading up to that disaster, her messages had been short, infrequent, and friendly. Just friendly. Maybe hope wasn't lost . . . yet. "Are you ever going to tell me what you were doing all day?"

"I had a couple of Skype meetings. And some paperwork—" She paused her movements, then scrunched her eyes closed. "I guess I'll have to tell you sometime. I submitted my resignation to John. I won't return to teaching this fall because, well, I landed *Traveling Light.* I signed the contract today. I start July seventh."

A glory not his own washed over him. Within four seconds his arms bound her waist. He lifted her in the air and twirled her in a circle.

Her silence, though, cued the return of reality. Twenty-four hours ago, this would have been an acceptable, even modest way to congratulate her. Now it was not.

Her hands pressed against his chest, and he set her feet back on the dirt. "I'm really proud of you, Kat. I knew you could do it. How are we going to celebrate?" Robbie checked on Anabelle.

She was a huddled glob of sunscreen, sand, and cracker crumbs as she snoozed on the blanket a couple yards away.

"Anabelle may appear partied out, but it's nothing a little sugar won't fix," Robbie said.

Keira's dead-eyed expression didn't match the rosy flush of her cheeks that had appeared after he'd hugged her. She smoothed out her shirt. "These pictures are enough. It's almost time for sundown. Let's do this." She grabbed a folded hunk of fabric from her bag, despite already looking perfect in her shorts and knitted tank top. After eating somewhat normally these past two weeks, she looked healthy. With the sun setting, her skin glowed amber. Beauty had nothing on her.

He blew out a breath and shook out his hands. Gawking at her would only get him in more trouble. He'd messed up enough as is. This picture, he knew, was a big deal to her. A sketch of it was not taped but glued to the inside cover of her atlas. Without having to ask, he understood it was why she'd come to California in the first place. Torrey Pines was the perfect place to do it, too.

Keira didn't look back. She stepped to the edge of one of the many cliffs at the park.

In the distance, the ocean spread from right to left, north to south. Occasionally, a distant swell reached up to the falling sun, inviting it to take a dip.

From this angle, Robbie couldn't tell how close she stood to the drop-off. His heart drummed violently against his sternum. The breeze was light, but what if a rogue wind knocked her off-balance? Somehow, he couldn't imagine she'd take the suggestion to move back well. *God, protect her when I can't.* The prayer would have to suffice.

She faced the ocean, releasing the folds of the fabric. A veil of what looked like silk boasted blocks of color set against black outlines. Grabbing two corners, she spread the scarf across her shoulders. The fabric draped down to her calves. Backlit by the sun, sections of it appeared sheer. The sunlight took on different hues of the scarf as it shone through each colored section. Keira's dark body formed the center line. The breeze ruffled the scarf, and it roiled like a flag on a pole.

For a moment, Robbie's fingers, like the rest of him, froze. It took effort to click the button on the DSLR camera. Once he was able, he snapped many pictures, praying that one would catch the fabric perfectly. His eyes blurred. He'd have to trust that the lens could capture what his eyes no longer could.

"Did you get it? Please say you did," she said over her shoulder.

"Think so." Fortunately, his sleeve served as a good tissue to wipe his eyes. Stinking Matthews tears. When he'd finally regained his sight, he found her staring at him. She'd wrapped the shawl thing around herself. For warmth or comfort, he wasn't sure.

"Can I see?"

He unhooked the camera from the tripod stand and carried it to her. He'd been right. She was too close to the edge. Didn't whole houses fall off cliffs in California? He didn't want to take the chance. By placing a hand on her hip, he tried to inch her back to safety. Just a bit.

She resisted. In fact, by pushing back against his palm, she was actually torquing her body weight toward the cliff.

"You're making me nervous, kid."

"I'm fine."

"Please? Just a step or two?"

Although her eyes remained cool as steel, she relaxed her body, then shimmied her feet a respectable trout-length closer to solid ground. It would have to do.

Hesitantly, he removed his hand from the waistband of her jean shorts.

Keira uncocooned a hand to block the glare on the small camera screen.

They both leaned in close to see as Robbie clicked back over the series of pictures. Like a flip-book, the scarf came to life, blowing in the breeze with stilted motion.

Her lips parted. "They're beautiful. It's exactly what I wanted it to look like . . . like a butterfly." Her head began to turn toward his but stopped. Any more and her forehead would graze his chin. "Thank you. We can go now." Her voice sounded almost robotic.

"And miss this sunset?" He nodded his chin to the horizon.

As timidly as Anabelle had earlier, the sun dipped its toe in the ocean. Of course, it didn't squeal like she had. It certainly didn't sizzle the way he'd once seen in a cartoon. Rather, its light spread across the water, concentrating in a cone-like shape, narrower where the sun appeared to touch the horizon and widening as it spread toward them—too pretty not to capture.

After he clicked one more picture, he turned off the camera and placed it carefully on a patch of grass near their feet. A brief glance proved Anabelle was still safely asleep ten yards away.

Tell her everything.

Robbie wanted to blast the voice. Telling her the truth would gut her, leaving her heart and maybe even her soul to spill down over the cliffside. Instead, he focused on Keira. The blue in her eyes had been overwhelmed by coppery reds and splashed with glints of gold.

July seventh, she'd said. And then half of his heart would be lost forever.

Tell her, the voice repeated.

"Okay," Robbie said.

"Okay, what?"

"You want to know why I wouldn't marry you? This is why."

Her brows knit together, but she didn't look at him. Instead she stared even harder at the sun, and Robbie was sure she'd go blind if he didn't get this out quickly.

"Growing up, I saw you live beneath your father's thumb. I saw how he sheltered you to the point of suffocation. How he hurt you and kept you trapped. No matter what I tried— and you know I tried—I was helpless to stop it.

"But then when we went away to college, you had the chance to be free. For the first time in your life you could live how you wanted. And it was so fun, seeing you start to discover yourself. You got that job working at the ice cream shop. I'll never forget the look on your face when you got your first paycheck, and there was no one to take it away from you."

Keira chewed her lip. But she was listening—not fleeing—so he continued.

"I loved seeing you come alive. I knew, from the moment you kissed me in the library, that I never wanted to spend a day without you by my side. Yet as college went on, these little warning flags appeared. The first time you highlighted your hair, you kept asking me if you looked okay and if I liked it. Which I did, of course, but I'd have liked you with skunk hair. You kept trying to cook for me and clean up my apartment for me. I'd ask you what movie you wanted to go see, and you'd choose some car-racing movie because you knew I'd enjoy it."

Robbie saw the way her shoulders rose higher and fell deeper with each of her breaths. "At first, I thought you were selfless and thoughtful. Then I realized how scared you were. Scared that one day I'd leave you . . . by yourself. I know I didn't help. I liked playing the knight in shining armor to your damsel in distress. I wanted to wrap myself around you like this scarf, and I would have if that's what God wanted me to do."

Here came the hard part.

"Kat, I begged God to let me marry you. It may be silly, waiting for God's blessing. Maybe I needed that because I couldn't ask your earthly father for your hand. But each time, God told me no. If I was honest with myself, I knew why.

"I told God for the longest time that I wouldn't propose to you, but selfishly, I refused to let you go. I needed you too much—and not because of the tutoring or helping with reading and stuff. I needed you to bring color to my world and breath to my lungs. You started shutting down. I was so scared that I'd lose you. My prayers were answered, but not in the way I wanted. At graduation, he told me that it was time to let you go. You know, in that voice you feel right in the middle of your rib cage that's as loud as a freight train to you but silent to everyone else? It was that one. I told him I loved you more than my own life. He said he loved you more. It's the only time in my life I've cursed at God. Then I asked my mom for my great-grandmother Mary's diamond ring, and she, of course, said yes. It's platinum with this art deco design from the thirties. You would've loved it."

"Sounds beautiful." Her eyes had softened by the time she looked his direction.

A lightbulb clicked. "Kat, where's your atlas?"

"In my satchel. Why?"

Anabelle was using Keira's satchel as a pillow. Inwardly, he groaned. He left Keira's side. With the care of a surgeon, he lifted Anabelle's head, removed the atlas from the satchel, and replaced the mop of curls. Making his way back to the cliff's edge, he flipped open to Alaska's page. He pointed to a blue star on Mt. McKinley, its name since changed to Denali.

"I drew this star. You remember me saying that I had a surprise trip planned for us? We were going to fly into Fairbanks and drive to Denali National Park. I knew you'd always wanted to see Alaska." Robbie sighed. "Kat, I was going to propose."

"You were?"

Robbie nodded. "But we had that fight after Trina's wedding. I went to Ryann for advice. Yes, I did say that I was not supposed to marry you. If you had stuck around, you would have heard me explain that I'd decided to throw up a fist at God and marry you anyway. Call me stubborn, but I was sure that if there was ever a time to be disobedient to his will, this was it."

"I was happy being your girlfriend. I knew I'd be happy as your wife. Why wouldn't God want me to be happy?"

"Because *this* is what God wanted for you."

"That I would be a digital nomad?"

"One day, you'll have to explain to me what that is. But yes and no. If I'd married you back then, it would have been like putting a butterfly in a cage before it ever had the chance to fly. And Keira, look at you. You were meant to fly."

She angled herself to him. She was so close that the loose wisps of her hair, raised by the breeze, tickled his cheek.

"It was selfish and wrong, but I would've rather kept you in a gilded cage than risk your flying away from me."

She stepped forward.

Her nearness weakened him. He was at her mercy. With a pinch, he would crumble. With a nudge, he'd be shark bait at the bottom of the cliff.

Instead, she placed a hand on his neck. Her thumb grazed his jaw, and the silk she held caught on his stubble. "Marrying you could never have been a cage. After all, without you, I never would have noticed I even had wings. I am who I am because you loved me once."

"Once?"

The sun was gone. When it sank below the horizon, it must have sucked the air from between them, as her chest now grazed his ribs. She was still so petite, but no longer fragile. Which was a good thing, because as his hand slid around her waist, his self-control was swan-diving over the edge.

"I'm sorry for running away that day." She searched his eyes. "I don't want to run anymore. I won't. From now on, any problems we have, I'll deal with them head-on. I promise."

He tightened his embrace, pulling her flush against him and lifting her onto her toes. Her breath escaped with a small squeak. "I've been waiting five long years to kiss you again, and I don't want to wait anymore."

"Me neither."

She touched her lips to his. It was sweet and soft. Gentle

as a raindrop that fell on his skin and lingered a moment. A sharp contrast to the raging river racing through his veins. A river that threatened to spill over the banks.

"Robbie . . ."

The whisper of his name on her lips broke the dam. He leaned into her and captured her mouth with his, pouring years of unquenched desire and long-held love into the kiss. Her lips moved between his with such familiarity it was hard to believe they'd ever been separated at all. If it were up to him, they'd never be separated again.

Her body softened against him in the most marvelous way. He had a feeling the moments she showed vulnerability or weakness would be few and far between. When they appeared, he'd move heaven and earth if that was what she needed or wanted.

She buried her hands in his hair, tugging his curls a bit. Not enough to be painful. But enough so that her strength, in addition to the hunger he tasted in her kiss, proved to Robbie that she was not the same girl who'd left him back then.

Robbie opened his eyes in time to see the breeze capture the shawl. He reached for it, but the effort was in vain.

Her wings fluttered out over the canyon, flitting back and forth in the waning daylight, eventually dropping and disappearing into the surf below.

CHAPTER THIRTY-TWO

❧

Robbie closed the door to the bedroom, careful not to make a sound, even if he was in the hurry of his life. He spied Keira waiting for him on the couch. Keira Knudsen. On his couch. Wanting to make out with him. He leaped over the back of the sofa—*thank you, football*. After landing on the cushion, he scooched toward her on the far end. Her velvet lips on his zapped all of his strength. Still in a crouch, he thought he may collapse on her. He could imagine the headline: "Montana Man Crushes Girlfriend During Kiss."

Girlfriend. Is that what she was?

Behind him, the door clicked. He settled back on his heels and drew in a breath. "What do you need, Annie?"

"Daddy, I'm thirsty."

Robbie sighed. "One glass of water coming right up." He hopped off the couch and scampered, his mom would say, to the kitchen. While he grabbed a glass out of the cupboard and filled it with room-temperature water from the tap, Anabelle cuddled next to Keira in his spot.

Great, you're jealous of your own daughter now.

Taking the seat on Anabelle's left, and eyeing the gorgeous woman on Anabelle's right, he handed the water over. She sipped the water about one milliliter at a time. So slow Robbie thought evaporation might be a quicker way to empty the glass.

Above Anabelle's head, Keira gazed at him.

With a lifted hand, Robbie acted as if he was going to tilt the glass higher.

Keira pursed away a laugh.

He really wished she hadn't. Boy, did he love to hear her laugh.

Thirty or so slurps later, Anabelle exhaled an "ahhh." She handed him the empty glass, then hugged him, wiping her water mustache on his sleeve in the process. Little stinker. After giving Keira another hug, she made her way back to bed.

"Shut the door, please," Robbie asked.

Anabelle watched them through the crack until the crack was no more.

Robbie listened for the sound of the bedsprings. Once he heard them, he returned his eyes to Keira. "I thought she'd never finish."

"Why did you fill the glass all the way to the top?"

Robbie didn't have to move closer. She came to him. And the way she took the lead with her lips and dug her fingers in his hair proved he wasn't the only one glad the distance between them was gone.

Sometime later, Robbie's breath warmed her neck and tickled her ear. "I love you, Kat. Have I told you that?"

"Only after every kiss."

"I can't help it. I spent way too much time *not* telling you. Do you mind hearing it? I can stop."

"Don't you dare."

He reclined back against the pile of throw pillows and pulled her on top of him. When Robbie Matthews kissed, he didn't only use his lips, although those would be enough. He used his hands, his arms, his chest. Even now, with her hand pressed between his back and the pillows, his vertebrae undulated between her fingertips and the muscles worked against her palm. She'd never get tired of it. The way he led her in a dance from sweet kisses that plucked her heartstrings to passionate ones that, well, plucked everything else.

While she waited for her heart to settle back to a healthy pace, she rested her forehead against his.

"Daddy?"

Robbie groaned. "Yes, Anabelle?"

"I had to go potty. I'm all done."

Robbie pinched his eyes closed. "Thanks for letting me know. Go back to bed now."

They waited for the door to shut. When it did, Keira pulled her lips into a smirk. "Like I said, you shouldn't have filled the glass all the way to the top."

Robbie brushed her hair back. "You know, this is what my life is now. A series of happy interruptions, one right after another. And I wouldn't trade it for the world."

"Okay . . ."

"I want you to know what you're getting yourself into. With me. With us." There was almost a sadness in his eyes.

Did he honestly think Anabelle and her needs were a deal breaker or something? "Robbie Matthews, listen to me. I love you . . . still . . . always." She kissed his cheek. "And I love Anabelle, too. I'm not sure I could love her more if she were my own daughter. The two of you are the happiest interruption I could ever imagine."

KAT WANDERFULL: Hey, @MRCustom. I'm glad you aren't online right now. It's so much easier to be

cowardly when I know you won't respond
immediately. Not that you'd know. Cowardly
is my thing, not yours.

KAT WANDERFULL: Listen, you know my assistant? The
one I said meant nothing to me. The truth is, I love
him. I've loved him since we were seventeen. If
there is such a thing as a soul mate, Robbie is
mine. I have no doubts about that now. I was fooling
myself before. Finally, we are in a place where we
make sense, and I couldn't be happier.

KAT WANDERFULL: Please hear me when I say that I
value your friendship very much. You've been the
listening ear and the giver of advice this past year.
Thank you, MR. I really do hope you find your own
soul mate. Take care, and God bless.

CHAPTER THIRTY-THREE

On the tablet's screen, Princess Patty Cake stomped on the dragon's toe. "I may be small, but I'm also mighty!"

The dragon roared in pain, shooting animated fire into the sky, but he also dropped the net that had trapped Trixie, the princess's unicorn.

Trixie shook off the net and waited for Patty Cake to climb on before racing back to Royal Village, where King Hubert and Lady Audra awaited them.

Anabelle clapped as the credits on the movie scrolled.

"But what about the evil troll? Aren't they going to put him in jail or something?" Keira asked Anabelle. "Whatever happened to the squirrel family? And why were the squirrels and dragon able to talk, but Trixie only neighs?"

"I dunno." Anabelle shrugged. On the tablet, she slid her finger backward on the progress bar, restarting the movie at the beginning. "Let's watch it again."

"Nope," Robbie said from the driver's seat. "Once is more than enough."

"I don't know. I think I could watch Prince Devin again," Keira said.

In the rearview mirror, Robbie's green eyes narrowed.

Suddenly, a sting traveled from the tip of her middle toe down to her heel.

"Ouch!" On instinct, she pulled her knees back toward her chest. If she'd thought her toes might play victim to Robbie's pinches, she never would've propped her feet up on the center console near the Jeep's control panel. "Annie, I think your daddy is jealous."

"What's *jealutz* mean?"

Robbie reached back between the seats. His massive hand gripped Keira's ankle and placed her right foot back on the vinyl. Her left foot followed. Soon, his thumb had resumed its graze over the top of it.

Sure, it wasn't the most romantic form of affection, but it was something. The past four days, as they meandered along highways and national parks in California, Arizona, New Mexico, and Utah, Keira and Robbie had only let go of each other to sleep, shower, and use the restroom. While public displays of affection with John had always made Keira cringe, they came naturally with Robbie.

Anabelle didn't seem to mind, but she had begged Keira to watch this movie with her on the last leg of their journey. How could she say no?

"Jealous is what a guy might feel when his girlfriend has a crush on an arrogant cartoon character," he said. In the mirror, his eyes stared straight ahead, concentrating on the stretch of road taking them back into Montana.

"Girlfriend, huh?"

"You think I'd caress the stinky foot of a girl who wasn't my girlfriend?"

"I adamantly disagree with you," Keira said.

His brows furrowed in the mirror. "So, you're not my girlfriend?"

"Of course I am." Keira turned off the tablet and returned it to its pouch. "But I do *not* have stinky feet."

"Daddy has stinky feet," Anabelle said.

"I know he does. See? Anabelle knows what's up."

Robbie mumbled something under his breath.

"What was that you said?" ·

"I said Prince Devin is the one with stinky feet."

She couldn't see his mouth, but his eyes crinkled a bit. He ran his fingertips over her ankle bone.

Keira met Anabelle's gaze. "Jealutz," they said in unison. Giggling filled the back of the car.

Wayne, is it? Look, you're probably the seventh customer service person I've spoken to in the past week. Help me understand why I can't erase my profile again." Robbie would wear a path in his family room if this didn't get cleared up soon. He leaned over his computer on the corner desk. His Momentso account still showed the latest conversation between MRCustom and Kat Wanderfull.

"I told you, Mr. Custom, you can suspend your account, but you cannot erase it. Your profile will still be available to search, but it will be marked inactive."

"First of all, it's M-R-Custom to you. Second, I don't want it anymore. I want to erase it entirely."

"Our account settings are designed so that when you decide to return to active status on Momensto, it will be easy."

"Okay, fine. Suspend my account, then."

"This will take between twenty-four and forty-eight hours to take effect."

Robbie groaned. "Are you kidding me?" He reminded himself that Wayne probably hated his job as much as Robbie hated the way Wayne did his job. "Whatever. Thanks for your help, Wayne."

After declining the opportunity to take a satisfaction

survey, he ended the call. *No offense to Wayne, but Momentso, you do not want to hear my thoughts on your customer service right now.*

He stared at the final message she'd sent the night of their photo shoot at Torrey Pines State Natural Reserve overlooking the ocean. After their kissing session in his suite. After they'd exchanged *I love you*s. After they'd restarted their relationship at eighty miles an hour.

When he'd read the message the following morning, he couldn't wipe the smile off his face. For five minutes, he had determined to be honest. But no matter how he practiced that honesty, he came across like a grade A jerk.

Keira, hey, remember when you hated me and turned to this guy for comfort? Poured out your heart? Told him things you never told anyone? That was me. My bad.

Instead, he'd kept it short and sweet.

MRCUSTOM: He clearly loves you as much as you love him. Probably more. Who wouldn't? God bless you both.

Immediately after pressing *Send*, he'd begun the process of trying to hide any possible link to the online persona. Now, a week later, he still hadn't had any luck. And she had called herself a coward?

A rap on the door sharpened his breath. "Honey, I'm here."

"Come on in, Mom."

His mother donned her normal attire—slacks and a light sweater, even though the temps in Montana hit eighty today. But she was always cold. It was her children who were hot-blooded. She set her purse on the kitchen table and slipped off her boots. When she caught sight of Robbie, she did that mom head-tilt thing, and her eyes got misty. "Honey, you look ruggedly handsome."

"Thanks, Mom. It's kind of weird you added *ruggedly*, but all right. You been watching Hallmark again?" He greeted her with the hug he knew was coming anyway.

"It's less drama than what you and your sister bring home with you. Where are you taking Keira on your date?"

"Just to Ollie's."

"Robert Charles, you take her someplace nicer than Ollie's. That place smells like a bear's rear end."

"Mom, how do you know— You know what? Never mind. We're going to Ollie's because it's where the whole town hangs out. And if it isn't a problem with you, I'd like to show off the prettiest girl in town . . . aside from you, of course."

She patted his cheek. "You keep lying like that and they won't let you in church tomorrow. Now where is my baby girl?"

"She's up in her room playing with her dolls. Oh, can you give her a bath? She took a dive in the river earlier when we were fishing." His chest squeezed. Robbie gripped the rungs on the back of the kitchen chair. "Vivian is coming to get her in the morning."

"I don't know why you're simply handing your baby over to her. Especially after how nasty she got during yesterday's mediation." Tears spilled past her lower lashes. She looked around for something to catch them.

After a quick yank of a napkin from the overstuffed holder, Robbie handed it to her.

She dashed away the droplets.

The other fifty or so napkins fanned out across the table and the floor.

"Robbie to the rescue," she said with a sniffle.

"The meeting wasn't as bad as you're imagining it. We sat down with the mediator, he asked some questions to both of us, and Vivian shot laser beams out of her eyes."

Robbie quirked a smile for his mom to see. "So, we didn't come to an agreement. No big deal."

"You have a court hearing. That's a big deal, son."

"Just preliminary. Besides, I'm confident that any judge in this state will side with me. And in the meantime, I'm hoping that if Vivian sees my willingness to be flexible, she'll change her mind about what she's asking. I want her to share custody, Mom. I want Anabelle to know her mother. I just want her to know me, too." He put his arms around his mom and held her as she wept. "It'll turn out fine."

It was the first time he'd ever lied to his mother. He wasn't confident at all. The mediation meeting had shaken him up. Enough that he'd pushed for Vivian to take Anabelle for a full day. If Vivian won, he didn't want Anabelle spending all that time at a place she didn't know, surrounded by strangers.

Robbie's own tears burned his lids. He didn't dare lift them and let the tears show, or he and his mom would end up watching Hallmark over a package of Oreos all night, and he'd miss his date.

"Oh no, I blubbered all over your shirt." She grabbed a napkin and wiped his shoulder.

"Mom, no worries. I heard somewhere that wearing a mama's tears makes a man more attractive anyway."

CHAPTER THIRTY-FOUR

A haze surrounded the lights in Ollie's Bar and Restaurant despite the place being smoke-free for decades. It wasn't too busy yet, but the sign outside said a local band was playing later. It would pick up for sure. Typically, Keira would have shied away from such an event, but Robbie missed his friends. And considering the puffed-out chest he sported, he also wanted to show her off. She didn't mind one bit. Besides, she hadn't told Robbie about her phone call with Nana and Papa the other day or her decision. The moment he stepped foot in her apartment and saw all the moving boxes, well, out of the bag that cat would fly.

Robbie led her toward a series of tables lining the front windows. Officer Drew, his wife, Evie, and another couple, Nick and Jessi, joined the group. They all glanced up when Keira and Robbie approached.

"You're late, *Robbie*." Ryann said his name with an accusatory inflection.

"We were busy making out, *Ryann*," he retorted.

The group laughed.

One person clapped, although Keira couldn't tell who because she'd buried her blazing cheeks against Robbie's back.

Thankfully, a server interrupted the catcalls with everyone's food, giving Keira and Robbie the chance to find their seats. At the head of the table, Ryann shoved her plate of greasy fries and chicken tenders toward them in an offering.

The thought turned Keira's stomach. Yes, she'd been eating more in the past couple of weeks. Her tightening waistband was proof. But she wasn't ready for Ryann's diet. Of course, she also didn't run five miles a day like Ryann. No wonder the girl could eat junk and keep her figure.

Across the table, Thomas sat next to the waitress Robbie had flirted with once in this exact restaurant. "Keira, this is my girlfriend, Hallie," he said.

Crisis averted.

"Hiya!" Hallie said. "We've been following your journey out to Cali. You're adorable."

It was meant as a compliment, Keira told herself. Maybe it was the pang of jealousy that twisted it sideways in her head. But before her mind could linger on the fact that Robbie had once found Hallie attractive, his pinkie traced ovals on her hand beneath the table. And the way he was looking at her now brushed away any worries. Robbie Matthews only had eyes for one girl.

"Thank you. It was a remarkable trip," Keira said.

"Congrats on landing that Adventure show. Has that always been your dream?" In this light, Thomas's brown eyes had an amber hue to them. They steadied on Keira.

"Uh, yeah. Ever since I allowed myself to dream, anyway. I was told I'm learning the ropes at first. I won't get camera time."

"Just wait till they see your light in person. Pictures don't capture that. They'll fall in love with you and put you center stage." Robbie flashed his smile in her direction. "And we'll finally get to go to Denali. Maybe make good on those plans we once had."

Butterflies swirled in her belly, making it difficult to concentrate on the conversation as it moved to a new topic. Thomas shared about some stress at his job. As the safety director at the River Canyon Dam, he was working to implement a better warning system for when water levels rose on the river. A necessary but tricky task, considering the seismic activity in the region. Only sixty years ago a major earthquake caused the top half of a mountain to slide off its base, blocking the Madison River and flooding the canyon. Stories of the Hebgen Lake earthquake had kept Keira awake more than once when she lived on the river during her college summers.

Keira finished off her grilled chicken sandwich and carrot sticks. She had no food in her apartment nor any plans to go grocery shopping, either. Even if she did, she couldn't get to her fridge with all the moving boxes piled up. Her stomach soured. Every time she'd tried to tell Robbie about her plans to move her belongings to Twin Falls, she'd chickened out.

Onstage, the band opened with a cover of an Aerosmith song. The crowd had grown thick. Hallie and Thomas had to scoot closer to the table to avoid being knocked in the head by patrons swaying drunkenly to the beat.

"We're going to slow it down now. Guys, grab your girl before someone else does and come on out to the dance floor," the lead singer said. The twangy opening of "Meet Me in Montana" played. The old song was a favorite of Joe's, the owner of Ollie's. He had a rule. When the duet played in his bar, every woman must be asked to dance. Those first few bars also caused a stir in the crowd, along with a few eye rolls.

"Would you like to dance with me, Kat?" Robbie took her hand.

"Always."

"Ryann? Do me the honor?" The voice was loud and deep.

Behind Ryann's shoulder, Stuart Ashcroft, the town's real estate mogul, held out his hand. He was no Robbie, for sure, but he was quite handsome in that Bradley Cooper way. He commanded each room he entered, maybe because he could buy the building and everyone in it with the cash he had in his pocket. Women, especially out-of-towners, were entranced by him. But the only one he wanted was Ryann. Never mind the fact that she used to be married to his little brother.

"No, thanks." Ryann buried her nose in her glass and drained the remainder of it. Fortunately, it was soda.

Based on the redness in Stuart's cheeks and his history, he'd drunk all the remaining alcohol in the bar anyway. He placed his hand on Ryann's shoulder, directly over her thick scar. "Come on, babe. I haven't seen you in forever. We've got business to discuss."

"Take your hand off my sister, Stuart." Robbie's eyes had darkened when he spoke.

"Robbie, don't you have enough worries of your own?" Stuart asked.

His question sent a quiver down Keira's spine. Not only did Stuart have money, but he also had power and connections. One of those connections was Keira's father. Several more of those connections were in the same courthouse where Robbie would be fighting for custody.

Ryann's cheek twitched, then lifted to a smile. "I'd love to dance." She accepted Stuart's hand and allowed him to lead her to the dance floor.

An ashen look swept over Robbie's face. His palm grew clammy against hers.

"Your sister is strong enough to handle a man like that," Keira said, as she hugged his arm.

"I hope so."

* * *

"Would you like to come in?" Keira breathed the invitation against his lips, making it sound more suggestive than she'd intended.

Her porch light cast a biting glow over Robbie's wry smile, making him appear even more mischievous than usual.

"Not for that." She placed her hands against his chest and gave a small shove. "You've never seen my apartment, is all."

"Yeah, I'll come in for a bit."

Keira fumbled with her keys in the lock. Most likely due to Robbie's lips on the side of her neck, which inhibited any and all concentration. She elbowed him in the ribs. "What will my neighbors say?"

"Probably, 'Lucky guy.'"

Once the lock turned, she paused. She couldn't pretend her racing heartbeat was merely from his kisses. At least not entirely. How would he react to what he saw inside?

"What are you waiting for? You're acting like you have some weird collection or something. Wait. Let me guess. Creepy dolls. No, too obvious. Um, you have all your baby teeth on display. Or . . . you have the baby teeth of *other people* on display. That's it, isn't it? You have another secret identity as the Tooth Fairy, don't you?"

"Not quite. I don't want you to do that thing you do."

"Okay, I'll bite. What thing?"

"Where you assume this has to do with us, okay? It doesn't."

Robbie's grin faltered, then reappeared. "You're making me nervous."

Over her shoulder, Keira attempted a reassuring smile, then turned the handle and opened the door. With a flick of the switch, the light illuminated the stacks of cardboard boxes. Her walls were mostly bare, with spots of white Spackle dotting old nail holes and awaiting a touch-up of paint. The one thing she'd yet to pack was her world map.

But Robbie wasn't looking at that or the boxes labeled *Kitchen*, *Bedroom*, or *Books*. His eyes focused on hers.

"There's no sense paying for an apartment I don't need. I spoke to Nana and Papa." She paused. It was still strange to refer to grandparents at all. "They're going to let me store my stuff at their place in Twin Falls. I don't have much. I'm kind of a minimalist."

Robbie's mind seemed to work a frantic pace behind those sea-greens of his. "But filming will only last, what? Three months?"

"Yeah. Afterward, I thought I'd spend some time with them when we wrap. I want to get to know them more. We've talked about trying to get Mama to come stay as well. Even hatched a little plan to get her away from my father. I'd appreciate your help—after the hearing, of course."

"What about—?" He buttoned his lips. Next to him, the flaps of a box yet to be scaled rested at awkward angles. He peered inside, then retrieved her copy of *The Lion, the Witch and the Wardrobe* and thumbed through it.

"You, Anabelle, and I will be together during most of the filming. You'll probably be sick of me by then anyway."

"Never." Robbie replaced the book in the box. "I'm glad you're going to spend that time with them. We'll have our whole lives to spend together."

"Promise?"

"Promise."

Keira's breath stalled when Robbie came to her, only to resume when he bypassed her and headed for the map.

"So the geography teacher has a wall-sized world map in her home? You're such a nerd, Knudsen."

"Hey, I wear my nerd hat with flair."

"Yeah, you do." Robbie's gaze panned the pastel countries marked with thick black font.

Each one was either partially or mostly covered by her arrow-shaped sticky notes.

"Are these all the places you want to visit?"

"Mm-hmm." Keira stood next to him. She slid her fingertips along the bottom edge of the wall hanging. Ever since Robbie gifted her that atlas for her eighteenth birthday, maps held a romantic quality. No matter where she was on earth, she could trace a path to anywhere she wanted to go. It merely took trust in the cartographer's hand and a whole lot of courage.

"Denali's on here." He tapped on the Alaskan national park near the top of the map, where a red arrow pointed. "Just think. Soon, we'll be standing right here."

She felt that awful grin of hers contort her face. The blue star from her atlas flashed in her mind. He'd once planned to propose there. Within her, hope surged.

Robbie gently pulled her hand away from her face. "Don't you dare hide your smile. You earned it."

CHAPTER THIRTY-FIVE

The inside of Vivian's Mercedes was so fancy Robbie began looking for the tray of caviar and a button that turned the whole car into a hot tub. At least ten cows had died to provide its leather. Man, this stuff may be alligator, knowing Vivian's taste for the exotic. And it was immaculate.

"Where do you put all your fishing tackle?"

Vivian's face remained plastered in her usual *I'm-better-than-you* expression. For someone who'd spent years giggling after every word he said, she certainly didn't find him funny now. In fact, she hated his sense of humor. Cracking a joke was the quickest way to get her to leave a room. Of course, right now, he wasn't in a rush to run her off. When she went, she'd be taking precious cargo with her.

"Where is her car seat?" Robbie saw only a backless booster.

"What do you mean? I have a booster. She's four."

"But she's still less than forty pounds. A car seat with a five-point harness is still the safest."

"Are you calling me a bad driver?" Vivian's eyes pinched together.

"No, I'm saying that she needs to be in a car seat still."
Robbie put a hand on her shoulder. "It's okay. You didn't
know. I'll get mine out of the truck."

Vivian glared at his hand. Everything had changed since
she'd demanded custody. At mediation, she'd been downright
mean. Was he making a colossal mistake letting Vivian
spend the day with Anabelle away from him? His family and
friends sure thought so. If it weren't for the niggling Robbie
felt in his heart to narrow the gap between Annie and Viv, he
might agree.

"Sorry." He removed his hand. "I'll get the seat." Inside
his truck, he unfastened the belt securing the car seat in
place. Underneath, he found a year's worth of fruit snacks,
Goldfish crackers, and . . . were those raisins or bug car-
casses? Gross. As he pulled the car seat out, crumbs along
with tiny toys and sections of broken crayons sprinkled the
gravel. He shook it, feeling Vivian's stare burn into his back
and flood up his neck into his face. She'd been MIA for four
years, and yet he was the one feeling like a terrible parent.
Score one point for Vivian.

He carried it to her car. She had those fancy clips meant
specifically for car seats. As he fumbled with the latches, a
Cheerio fell on the floor mat. When he finished, he scooped
up the old Cheerio.

"We're going back to our house. Eric has his girls this
weekend. Then we may go shopping or get mani-pedis."

"What are those?"

The café door opened. Ryann led Anabelle by the hand
toward them.

"Girlie things. Belle needs a female role model. Your
sister hardly counts."

Fury swirled in his belly. Ryann was a thousand times
the woman Vivian was. "Her name is Anabelle. Or Annie.
Not Belle. That's not even her favorite princess."

"Why? Because Belle can read?"

Lord help me. "Princess Patty Cake is her favorite. She got a good night's sleep, so she should be in a good mood for you. She'll eat anything, but macaroni and cheese is her favorite."

Anabelle slowed her steps when she spied the open door of the car.

Ryann bent down and spoke to her.

It did no good. Anabelle shook her head, taking a backward step.

"What's wrong? I thought she liked me." Vivian's brows pinched. She worked her jaw until her dimple appeared on the side of her chin. "I thought about buying her a teddy bear. There was this pretty pink one at a boutique on Main Street. Perhaps if I had—"

"She does like you, Viv. Or at least she will. No teddy bear required. I'll go talk to her." Robbie kneeled, welcoming Anabelle into an embrace.

"I don't wanna go," Anabelle said.

He stroked her hair. "I know, Kitty Kat, I know. Remember how much fun we had on the picnic with Vivian? Now you get to go to Vivian's house and play with some big girls. After dinner she'll bring you right back here to me."

Pulling back to see her face was a mistake. Her lower lip jutted out, and her chin trembled. Pools of tears formed. The kind that Vivian had mocked Robbie for during their so-called relationship.

Even now, Robbie blinked back his own tears. "How about this? Tonight, we'll turn on a movie, and I'll let you put barrettes in my hair and makeup on my face."

"I'm scared."

"You don't have to be. Vivian loves you."

"And that's why she grew me in her belly and gave me to you?"

"Yes, baby." Robbie used his sleeve to dry Anabelle's cheeks. "Now, be a big girl and say hi to Vivian."

"Do I have to hug her?"

"Only if you want to."

Vivian dropped her hands from her hips when Anabelle approached, letting them fall to her sides. She didn't ask for a hug.

Anabelle didn't offer. They exchanged hellos, and Anabelle climbed into her familiar, stained, gunk-covered car seat.

Robbie leaned over, helping her arms through the car seat's straps. Once she was safely buckled, Robbie kissed her. "I love you, Kitty Kat."

"I love you, Daddy."

Ryann clung to Robbie's arm as the car drove out of sight.

An ache the size of Yellowstone consumed him. This would only be a few hours. Still, when he met his sister's eye, he couldn't smile. "There goes my girl."

We'll be filming at Denali's new Fifth Summit Lodge for about a week. After that, we'll be heading to Brussels. Can you believe it? Me and Anabelle in Europe." Robbie speared another bite of steak with his fork. He'd almost skipped the Matthewses' Sunday family dinner. With Anabelle spending the entire day at Vivian's, the word *family* didn't seem appropriate. Leave it to his mother to extend an invitation to Keira, so he had to attend. Although he hated to admit it, his father's home cooking was enough to rouse him from the cuddled heap he'd been in all day worrying about his baby girl.

His mother cleared her throat, but she couldn't remove the concern she wore on her brow. "When will you come back?"

"After Brussels, we head to Egypt and Morocco. Then, I think we'll come home for a week. That way Anabelle can spend time with Vivian, and I can get some projects done around here. I'm sorry I haven't been around—"

"And then?" Ryann asked.

"And then Annie and I will catch up to them, wherever Keira is." He put the bite of peppery meat in his mouth, savoring it a moment before his first chew.

"Who's paying for all this?" Ryann perched her elbows on the table.

"The Adventure Channel will cover most of his costs." Keira caught Robbie's eye. "Plus, he'll get paid to be my assistant . . . as long as the coffee doesn't get cold." Her joke fell flat, and she squirmed in her seat.

Robbie washed down the steak with a drag of milk. Over the glass, he read the room. Sometimes his ability to gauge everyone's thoughts and emotions was a gift. Now? Not so much. "What's that look?" he asked Ryann.

"What look?"

"The one you gave Dad."

"I'm not allowed to look at Dad?" Ryann asked.

"Not if you're going to send him silent messages. Say them out loud if they're so important," Robbie said.

"I'll tell you later when we're alone."

"Tell me now. Keira's going to hear it anyway."

His mother rested her hand on Ryann's red mane, flattening it at least two inches. "Take it out to the river, you two. You may come back in once it's been resolved."

Robbie's inner ten-year-old kicked, shoved furniture, and garbled foul words. In reality, Robbie's outer twenty-seven-year-old coolly kissed Keira's cheek, then stood, even taking the time to push his chair in before following Ryann out to the riverbank behind the café. Born only sixteen months apart, he and Ryann had spent a lot of time out here as kids and teens, sorting out their sibling squabbles. The theory, he'd always assumed, was that the river swept the anger downstream, leaving only the root of the issue exposed. Robbie came to that conclusion after he'd thrown Ryann's favorite Barbie in the current mid-fight and watched it float away. Robbie bit away a grin at the memory.

Unlike that day, Ryann wasn't angry now. Just concerned. "I think you're heading toward heartbreak."

His face warmed despite the cool evening air. He shoved his hands in his pockets. "You're wrong."

"Am I? In a few days, you have a court hearing to discuss custody of your daughter. Your focus should be on proving how great a father you are, not planning all these globe-trotting adventures with your girlfriend."

"This is my job. It's how I make money. How I provide for Anabelle."

"Is that why you're forcing this?" The wind whipped some curls across Ryann's face. She tried to smooth them back into place, but they had a mind of their own. She pulled an elastic from her wrist and twisted it around her hair. "You can make money around here."

"Not enough."

"Okay, then stop giving away your services for free. Charge people for your labor, not only the materials. You have a sweet heart, Robbie, but maybe if you were a bit less generous, you could have already started your business—"

"This isn't about my financial well-being."

"No, it's about the life you want. Quit pretending that life is a jet-setting, Momentso-posting, never-see-your-family one. I know you."

Robbie had half a mind to dive beneath the ripples and not take a breath until he got to Quake Lake. "Weren't you the one telling me to go after her? I did. I got her back. I'm happy, so lay off."

"Yeah, I was. Back when she was traveling to neighboring states and nearby landmarks. But Belgium? Morocco? How is this supposed to work during a custody dispute?"

"I love her, Ryann. I won't lose her again."

"Why not? She's made it perfectly clear she's too wrapped up in her own dreams to consider yours."

"I don't even know what you're talking about. What dream do I have?"

"The one of a quiet life on the river with your family."

"Can't you see? Without her, that dream doesn't exist."

"How are you going to feel if you lose Anabelle because you're so desperate to keep a hold on Keira?"

A mayfly danced in front of his face. With a swat, he knocked it to the ground.

It hit a rock. Its wings fluttered but no longer flew. Instead, it moved about in a panicked circle on the stone surface.

"That won't happen," he said.

"It might. And if she actually loved you—"

"You don't think she loves me?"

Ryann lifted her chin as if she were looking for words to fall from the mountaintops. "I know she loves you, but she's trying to love herself, too. That chick Margot—the one she idolizes?—she's been filming that show for, like, fifteen years or something. Is that what Keira's hoping for?" Ryann rolled her eyes. "Are you willing to spend that long chasing Miss Wanderfull, or whatever her name is? That won't be healthy for you or Anabelle."

The river roared in Robbie's ears, louder with each heartbeat. "Since when did you become the expert on healthy relationships?"

Oof. He stared ahead, feeling about the size of a huckleberry on the far bank. His Sunday dinner threatened to make a reappearance. Any second Ryann would wallop him, pound him with her fists, or throw a stone at his head like when they were kids. And he deserved it. He'd even let her call him dumb if it would right this.

Yet, she said nothing. Did nothing. Just stood in the periphery of his vision. His words dulled the whole landscape to an ugly sepia tone. Robbie wouldn't be surprised if their river stopped moving or dried up altogether.

The memory of Ryann lying in that hospital bed seven years ago assaulted him. She had been bandaged neck to fingertips, with swollen eyes and chapped cheeks from her endless crying. She would have faced off against the devil himself to save her husband. Tyler didn't give her a chance to.

Finally, he humbled himself and turned to Ryann.

Her jaw was hardened. Her glare, a striking emerald color thanks to the flush blazing her face, zeroed in on him. "Take it back."

Robbie sucked in a breath and moved toward her.

She stepped away. "Take it back, Robbie, or I'll—"

He pulled her into an embrace.

Her body was granite, though. Except her lungs, which drew and expelled air frantically.

"Sis, I'm sorry. That wasn't fair to say. I'm a colossal jerk."

Thirty seconds must have passed before her breathing slowed and her muscles thawed. When they had, she adjusted until her chin rested on his shoulder. "True."

"Will you forgive me?"

"I guess."

He angled back to see her face. "I look up to you, Ryann. You taught me to fight for what I want. For Keira. For Anabelle. And at the end of the day, if I can get this to all work out, I'll have you and God to thank for it. Come on. Let's go inside. Mom made those lemon-huckleberry bars we love for dessert."

"I call the middle piece. You owe me that. It's penance."

"Deal." He gave her a playful shove toward the café.

Inside the windows, Keira was watching him. When she gave a little wave, he returned the gesture. It would all work out. It had to. He drew in one more deep breath of river air, then walked back to the Anabelle-less family dinner and Keira's side. On the way, he stepped over the stone where the mayfly lay still.

CHAPTER THIRTY-SIX

Four days later, Robbie felt only twelve inches tall inside the Gallatin County courtroom. Vivian and her team of black-suited lawyers looked like giants. If this were the movie *Space Jam*, they'd be the Monstars, and he'd be Porky Pig. At least he had the Michael Jordan of lawyers next to him for this preliminary hearing.

Cassie, at only five feet six inches, was the fiercest person in the room. And she was on his team. Behind him, in the first row, Keira, Ryann, and his parents sat together with the promise to be in prayer. Thomas had taken off work to babysit Anabelle this morning, so Robbie's whole family could be there in support.

"You look like an elk in a wolf den. Lift up your shoulders and loosen up. Nothing will be decided today." Cassie opened the file with his last name on it. "It's just a preliminary hearing to see where we go from here. But there's good news. We don't have to worry about Judge Rice. The case got reassigned this morning."

"To who?"

"Judge Keller."

Robbie gripped the table's edge. Even that wasn't enough to steady him as he felt the world shift.

"What's wrong?" Cassie asked.

"Judge Keller and I . . . we have a history."

"What kind of history?"

"A bad one."

Cassie's gaze drilled into him, and her mouth opened before someone stood at the front, and she clamped it shut.

"Please rise. The Honorable Judge Keller is presiding."

He almost felt the oxygen leave the room as his family let out a collective gasp behind him. They knew. A tremor shook Robbie's shoulders.

Then a strong hand beneath Robbie's elbow nudged him upward. He stole a peck behind him to find his father's reassuring grip.

"Please be seated." Judge Keller hadn't aged since Robbie was in high school. However, his black robe was statelier than the pajamas he'd worn that fateful night. "Good morning. This hearing is for the court to set a schedule for the contested petition for parenting plan for one Anabelle Matthews, age four. Looks like the petition was filed June ninth by Vivian Cartwright. An answer to the petition was filed by . . ." The judge's eyes stared above the rim of his glasses. ". . . Robert Matthews."

Ice chilled Robbie's veins.

"Since there is no consent on this case after mediation, it will proceed to a final hearing. Each of you may present evidence and witnesses on that date. You may testify if you want to do so. As your judge, at the end of the hearing, I will decide the matter of custody and the visitation petition involving the child." He went on to explain more of the specifics for the final hearing in regard to evidence and the questioning of witnesses.

"Your Honor," Lex Cartwright, the tallest of Vivian's

lawyers, began, "my client has concerns for the child's welfare with Mr. Matthews while this matter is pending."

The weight of the accusation bore down on Robbie's shoulders.

Behind him, a noise banged against the bench. Probably Ryann's fist, if he had to guess.

"Is it your belief that the child is in immediate danger?"

"Not immediate, no. My client is concerned that the child will be traveling out of state with Mr. Matthews. There are no guarantees they will return."

Cassie stood. "Your Honor, the travel is required for Mr. Matthews's job." She described the nature of the television show and its upcoming travel schedule. When Vivian's lawyer tried to interrupt, Cassie effectively shut him down with a reminder that it was Robbie who had parented the girl after her mother abandoned the child, and he had a history of looking out for Anabelle's best interest. She went on to explain Robbie's dedication to providing for his daughter's current and future well-being.

The judge tapped the side of his thumb on the desk. "I'll allow the travel during the interim, but I would like for Mr. Matthews to submit those travel plans to the court."

"My client also has concern over the condition of the Matthewses' family property, as well as its proximity to the Madison River."

"Mr. Matthews, does your family still own River's Edge?"

"Yes, sir."

"Can your daughter swim?"

"Very well for her age."

He looked over the rim of his glasses. "And I trust she understands the dangers of the river?"

"She does."

"The court orders a child custody evaluation to be performed on both Robert Matthews and Vivian Cartwright prior to the next hearing, which will be scheduled on October eighth of this year."

Not so bad. *Traveling Light*'s filming was set to wrap up right around that time.

"Court is adjourned." Judge Keller pushed back his chair and stood. "And Mr. Matthews, I suggest avoiding brickyards in the interim."

So what? A social worker comes to your home, and you schmooze her a bit. She'll see you're a nice guy and a capable father." Cassie crossed her arms. "My concern is the history you have with Keller. Spill it."

In the hallway of the courthouse, the plastered wall cooled Robbie's back. He thunked his head against it and closed his eyes. "I was eighteen. My girlfriend, Keira, was living in an abusive home. Mostly verbal stuff, but occasionally her father would beat her and her mother up. The thing is . . . her father is Joshua Knudsen."

"Oy."

"Right. I was trying to get her out of there. But every time I tried, he was there with the so-called law on his side. My parents helped me file a complaint against her father. Judge Keller threw it out, claiming there wasn't enough hard evidence of abuse."

"That doesn't sound so bad."

Robbie coughed. "Then I went to his home and threw a brick through his front window."

"Oh, Robbie." Cassie rubbed her dark brow. "He obviously knew it was you. How were you caught?"

"I wasn't caught. I went up his steps and sat on his porch swing. His dog was barking. His daughter was crying. Of course, his wife was going nuts. I just sat there and waited. Finally, he came out in his flannel pajamas.

"I told him that Knudsen would kill Keira one day if he didn't act. I told him about her bruises and the way she flinched at loud noises. I explained how her food was monitored and withheld based on her behavior. I told him about how after she'd snuck out to see my big game, he'd hurt her so badly that no one saw her for eight days."

"What'd Judge Keller do?"

"Nothing." Robbie scraped his fingers through his hair, which had already fallen back onto his forehead despite his attempts to gel it in place. "I sat there on his swing, sobbing like a kid, and he did absolutely nothing. The police showed up, arrested me, took me to jail."

"Why didn't I know this?" Cassie's voice took on a shrill quality.

"Because Keller dropped the charges. I paid for the replacement window. Actually, installed it myself, with my dad's help. I probably should've thanked him. If the charges hadn't been dropped, I would've lost my football scholarship. Call it grace or whatever. Of course, I didn't see it. Keira still had to live in that home for another month."

"And then?"

"Keira's father had a change of heart." Robbie sneered. If the man *had* a heart at all. "He allowed Keira to leave home on her eighteenth birthday, about a month before graduation. She came and lived with my family instead."

Down the hall, his parents and sister still welcomed Keira as one of their own. They formed a half circle, waiting for him to finish speaking to Cassie.

Cassie adjusted the briefcase's strap on her shoulder. "I'll see about getting a new presiding judge. But it's unlikely. Let's hope he's still got some grace left for you. Do me a favor. Lie low and don't get yourself into any trouble. Got it?"

CHAPTER THIRTY-SEVEN

❧

Y ou ready for this?" Robbie asked Keira. His eyes studied her face.

"I have to be." She opened the door of his truck and
stepped onto the pavement in front of her family's property.
After her last visit, she wouldn't be surprised if her father
had rigged the street with IEDs or something.

Papa pulled his Lincoln within a few yards of the truck's
bumper. If she was a bundle of nerves, then he and Nana
were a freight load of them. That morning, while Keira and
Robbie loaded up the U-Haul with her belongings, they'd
been eerily quiet.

Keira held hands with her grandparents as they walked
down the driveway.

Her father's sedan was nowhere to be seen. As long as
Keira could remember, he'd spent the Fourth of July at an
annual charity golf tournament up in Bozeman. Ironic that
the money went to supporting victims of domestic violence.

The four of them climbed the porch steps. Nana was
looking even more frail than she had upon discovering she
had a granddaughter. Keira and Papa flanked her, watching
for any sign of a stumble or faint.

Robbie signaled for them to stand back, while he stepped toward the door. "Just in case." He pressed the doorbell.

Inside the house, the Westminster chimes echoed. No one answered.

"Where could she be? She never leaves the house." Panic chilled Keira's flesh. What if she was hurt? What if she couldn't come to the door?

The doorbell chimed once more.

Nothing.

Except for the faint sound of a squeaky faucet.

Keira caught Robbie's eye. "The garden."

The group descended the steps and plodded around the side of the house. In the middle of the garden, Keira's mother held the sprayer over a rosebush. She seemed thinner. And paler, despite the July sun.

"Claire," Papa said on a breath.

Nana whimpered, leaning against Robbie.

Her mother angled her face toward the sound. At the sight of them, she dropped the garden hose, leaving the water to spray across the paving stones. She ran to them. Her mother *ran*, then embraced Nana.

Together, they dropped onto the ground, Robbie cushioning their fall. Papa joined them on the ground. Keira couldn't help but laugh. If only Anabelle were here, then all the people she loved would be in this heap of arms, legs, and tears. Funny. After all the beautiful places she'd seen as Kat Wanderfull, this was the moment she wanted to capture the most.

"What are you doing here?" her mother asked.

Nana sniffled. "Keira found us in Twin Falls three weeks ago. We spent a few days with her. You've raised a wonderful daughter, Claire. We love her."

"So do we. She has Joshua's courage—"

"Mama," Keira cut in. She threaded her fingers through her mother's hair, blond with only the slightest of gray roots. Soon, Father would make her color them. That is if their plan didn't work. "About Father. He's not a good man."

Behind her, a throat cleared. "Now, now. Is that any way to speak about the man who raised you?" Her father's voice could melt obsidian back into lava.

Fear choked her.

"You kept Claire and Keira from us far too long, Joshua." Papa stood tall and unafraid as he faced her father.

"You were the ones who cut off the relationship with her. I was the one who took care of her when you tossed her out."

"Not true, Claire. We never wanted you to leave. We tried. Over and over again, we tried to see you, but he didn't let us. We've always loved you," Papa said.

Nana stroked her daughter's face. "And we're worried about you."

"Perhaps you should worry about this granddaughter of yours, with her manipulations and schemes. My Little Mouse has been good-for-nothing since the day she was born. I should've set a trap when I had the chance."

Robbie was in his face then. Her father had two inches on Robbie, but there weren't many men in town that could match Robbie in strength. Certainly not her father. "You have no right to speak about her like that," he growled. "You weren't a father to her. All you are is a fist. From this point on, if you want to take a shot at Keira, you'll have to get through me."

"You talk a lot for a kid with so much to lose. But then again, you never were a smart one." Father's voice remained steady. Calculated. Baiting. "You and your family are a stain on this town. And not one that can easily be bleached. No, I think one day someone will have to cut the stain out entirely. This community would be better off with nary a Matthews in sight."

The image of Anabelle flitted through Keira's head. She jumped to her feet, pressing herself in the narrow space between the two men, facing Robbie. She nudged him back, shooting him a warning glance. Her father had an impressive ability to make good on threats.

"Come away with us, Claire. There's no pain in our home. Only peace," Papa said.

Everyone was standing now. Her mother, with her arms crossed over her chest, trembled.

Father moved to the back door of the house only five yards away from them. "Claire, inside now. As for the rest of you, I want you off my property immediately. I'm calling the police."

"No need." Officer Drew, in uniform, rounded the side of the house. He approached casually with his hands on his belt, inches from his gun. "Robbie thought there might be trouble. Time for you all to leave." He placed himself between her father and the rest of them.

Nana held out her hand. "Let's go home, Clairey."

Keira's mother stayed still.

"Mama, you said I got my courage from Father. That's not true," Keira said. "He's the one who's afraid. Look at him. He knows he's losing control of us. I've learned that courage isn't something we're born with. It's a choice. Please come with us."

A flicker danced in her mother's eyes.

Father in heaven, move in her heart.

Several seconds passed, then her mother lifted her chin higher than Keira had ever seen before. "Goodbye, Joshua."

Her father couldn't have looked more shocked if a lightning bolt struck him.

"Mrs. Knudsen, is there anything you need from inside?" Robbie asked.

She thought a moment, then looked her husband dead in the eye. "There's nothing I want here."

Keira's father took a menacing step toward her mother, but Drew blocked his path.

"You must let her go." Drew pressed a button on his radio, pinned on his shoulder. "Request for backup."

A string of curses sailed from her father's mouth, many of them targeting Keira's mother. Vile names that could snap twigs. When she kept walking, he spewed a promise to have her replaced by nightfall.

Robbie and Keira followed her mother and grandparents to the front of the house and out to the street. Robbie gripped her hand but kept watch over his shoulder. Ever her protector. Even when she told herself she didn't need one, it was comforting to know he was there. This time for her family, as well.

But she couldn't dislodge the look of fury in her father's eyes as they left. One day, she knew, he'd take his revenge. On whom was anyone's guess. But as they drove away from the Knudsen property once and for all, Keira prayed it wouldn't be Robbie or his family.

CHAPTER THIRTY-EIGHT

❦

The July skies above Denali were the bluest Keira had ever seen. In all the travel shows, Alaska promised white-mountain majesty and unencumbered exhilaration. Over the past two days of filming, it had delivered both. However, Keira did not expect it to feel quite so lonely.

Soon. They'll be here soon. Leaving Robbie and Anabelle behind to move Mama and all Keira's possessions to Twin Falls five days ago wasn't easy. Mama's transition to Nana and Papa's home had been rough. There were moments when Keira wondered if Mama's grief over her abuser might actually kill her, as she lay in bed, shrouded in sorrow. In those times, Keira had wanted the respite of Robbie's arms. With his plane scheduled to arrive any minute, she could almost feel that embrace already. Then, with his new job as her assistant on set, she'd have his comfort (and Anabelle's joy) on standby whenever they were needed.

Isaac, one of the *Traveling Light* production assistants, sat in the Escalade they'd rented from the Fairbanks airport. The driver-side door was propped open, and he'd reclined the seat back. He was an easygoing guy with a full beard, one typical of her millennial peers, and a penchant for gas station snack food, though Keira didn't know where he put it. He was slim as a lodgepole pine. So far, he was the one who'd gone out of his way to make her feel the most comfortable. Everyone else pretended not to notice her. High school all over again.

"More Than a Feeling" hummed on the car's radio.

"Kat, what kind of music do you like?"

Standing near the front wheel well, Keira rechecked the skies. Nothing. "I'm pretty eclectic. My favorites are Tom Petty, George Strait, Casting Crowns. But this is fine."

"Pooh. You're a lot easier than Hurricane Margot. You don't ask for much."

From what Keira had witnessed during filming, Margot's off-camera persona was nowhere near as sunny as the show portrayed her. There was a reason the crew had given her the nickname. "I'm just happy to be here."

"That'll wear off soon enough." His laugh was the life-of-the-party kind. "Hey, don't be put off if people don't take a liking to you right away. We're all walking on eggshells around Margot right now. She likes to make heads roll when people cross her, so most don't."

"What does that have to do with me?"

"You're the new and improved model. People are afraid if they welcome you, Margot will get them fired."

"Oh." Keira toed a pebble with her boot. "Why are you nice to me?"

"Because everyone needs at least one friend. Especially in this industry."

"Thanks, Isaac."

His focus lingered on her a moment too long.

The faint hum of the Cessna cut through the air.

"That should be them." She clapped her hands together. The Alaskan air soothed her soul. Or maybe it was the fact that her arms would surround Anabelle and Robbie soon. Her feet danced.

"How long's it been since you've seen your boyfriend?" Isaac asked.

"Five days."

"Only five days? You guys must be serious. It may be silly, but I was hoping . . ."

The plane's engine grew too loud to hear anything else. A few minutes later, the plane landed safely and taxied to a stop a few dozen yards away.

Thomas, in the pilot's seat, nodded to her. After completing the installation of the dam's new alarm system, he'd planned to spend a week in Fairbanks with friends. He offered to fly Robbie and Anabelle to meet up with her and the crew in Denali.

She mouthed a *thank you* to him, and he nodded in reply.

The door hinged, and Robbie dropped down onto the runway. He lifted Anabelle out of the plane. Robbie held her back, and her legs looked like a cartoon character's spinning in a circle and not making headway. Once he checked the coast was clear, Robbie let her go.

She ran to Keira. "Mommy Kat!"

Keira's heart nearly burst. She accepted the little girl into her arms. "Anabelle, I missed you." Peering above the strawberry curls, she eyed Robbie as he strolled toward her. In all of creation, man never looked so good.

Anabelle stepped back, clearing the path to Robbie. "Hug Daddy. Hug Daddy."

"Yes, ma'am." Keira ran to him, and he beamed. Dozens of movie scenes flashed across her memory. Lovers reuniting. Should she jump in his arms and allow him to spin her around? How about the desperate action-movie kiss? Or the slowed approach with a timely line of witty dialogue? In the end, she went with the black-and-white movie reunion. He leaned over her, and she tilted her head back, welcoming his lips on hers. But this wasn't exactly the innocent kiss from a Frank Capra film. She suddenly understood how a kiss could make someone weak in the knees.

"That's a long hug, Daddy."

"Can't help it. I missed Keira."

"Mommy Kat," Anabelle repeated.

"Mommy Kat?" Keira asked Robbie.

"Vivian asked Anabelle to call her 'Mommy.' She refused. But she did start referring to you this way. I guess it's her way of getting her voice heard. Do you mind? I can tell her to—"

"I love it. And I love you."

"I love you back." He drew her into another kiss. This one had the makings to last even longer, except that Anabelle was knocking on Keira's leg as if it were a door.

"Yes, Kitty Kat?"

Anabelle held up her hands.

Who could resist that? Keira hefted her onto her hip then returned her focus to Robbie. "How did the meeting with the social worker go yesterday?"

"The meeting itself went well. I could tell she loved the cabin. She had this checklist she went through. I'm glad I was a stickler for safety when I built it. She didn't even seem to mind the property." He pushed his hair back off his forehead. "Until the alarm from the dam went off."

Keira gasped.

"Remember how Thomas said they were making adjustments? One of those adjustments set off the alarm. We'd been warned, so we weren't worried. Of course, we followed protocol and evacuated all the guests to higher ground until we got the all clear. But, you know . . ."

"The damage was done?"

He shrugged.

"We'll just have to pray that much harder."

"I like your attitude. How's your mom adjusting?"

"The drive to Twin Falls was rough. There were moments I thought she might open the door of the car and throw herself out. Over the next two days, she cried a lot and struggled to get out of bed. But the night before I flew up here, we played a game of Scrabble, and she laughed. Actually laughed. It gave me hope. I'm looking forward to spending some time there in October with them."

"Did they get the home security system installed just in case?"

"Yes, they did. Top-of-the-line."

"Good. Tell me about your first two days of filming."

Keira worked to not let her smile falter. What to say? "Uh, it was okay, I guess. So far it's a lot of standing around and watching. But I'm learning the ropes about how television works. I'm hoping they'll let me hold the boom mic one day."

"You'll get there." He hugged her tight. "It'll all fall into place. It already is. You? In Alaska, working for the Adventure Channel? What could go wrong?"

Keira clung to Anabelle's waist as they crouched behind the boulder. Beneath the scarf, the ever-present sun was dim, and the smell of cut grass, baby lotion, and danger tickled Keira's nose.

"Who dares cross my bridge?" The voice was too husky to be human. It must be the troll Princess Patty Cake had spoken of.

Anabelle started to creep out from behind the rock.

"Don't go!"

"But I'm brave."

"Then we'll go together." Keira yanked down the scarf. Anabelle flinched from the light but grasped Keira's hand.

"Ready . . ."

". . . set . . ."

". . . go!" Keira popped upright and began to run across the clearing. Beside her, the girl laughed. It wasn't long until the monstrous footfalls trimmed the distance to her heels. Anabelle dropped Keira's hand and cut right. Traitor.

But the troll kept after Keira no matter how fast she tried to run. He unleashed a yawp so barbaric it curdled her blood. She was a goner.

Arms seized her waist, lifting her off the ground. His chest heaved against her back. The world around her spun. Mountains, woods, valley, resort, mountains again. Once it stilled, she felt the troll's hot breath behind her ear. Then his lips. Mercy, why had she hidden again?

"My queen. You're mine forever." The laugh that followed was more of a brutish grunt than anything else.

"Come get me now, Daddy Troll." Anabelle made a silly face in their direction.

"I saw you cross my bridge, Princess Patty Cake. Now you must pay." Robbie released Keira and launched himself toward Anabelle, who took off toward the forest. He caught her before she reached the tree line. "Now I shall make a princess stew."

Behind Keira, a cacophony of voices sounded. The production team. Most of them anyway. Margot was nowhere to be seen.

Isaac, who'd been holding the door for the group as they exited the lodge, trailed them now. When he saw Keira, he smiled, then jogged over to her. "We're grabbing drinks at the lodge down the road. Elk's Snout or something."

"Elk's Peak, you mean?" On the flight up to Alaska,

Keira had studied the area's history, geography, and commerce. If she got the chance to appear on camera, she'd be prepared.

"That's it." His gray eyes had a twinkle to them when he laughed.

"Thank you for the invitation. Robbie and Anabelle and I are going to stay and eat here, I think."

"You sure? It'd be a great time to hang out with the crew, let them get to know you. Robbie could come along."

A couple of dozen yards away, Robbie gave a sidelong glance. He held Anabelle's hands and allowed her to walk her feet up his jean-clad legs, then kick off his stomach to flip herself backward.

"Not this time."

"Cool. I'll see you tomorrow, then."

"See ya."

Isaac jogged to catch up with the group. Markus, another twentysomething, gave him a shove, knocking Isaac into Therese, the hair and makeup artist.

With Anabelle slung over his shoulder, Robbie neared. "If you want to go with them—"

"I don't." She brushed a hair off her face. "Besides, I've always wanted to try princess stew." She took hold of Anabelle's arm and pretended to nibble, all to the girl's shrill delight.

Twenty minutes later, Keira, Robbie, and Anabelle stepped through the arched doorway where the smell of braised beef awakened Keira's carnivorous appetite. The restaurant was nestled in the northwest corner of the lodge. It was small and expensive, but the atmosphere, with its gaslit lanterns and rustic wood, couldn't be beaten.

Keira, out of habit, snapped some pics for Momentso. Her followers would want to see this. Plus, it would give a teaser for what lay in store for Kat Wanderfull. Soon, she hoped to get the go-ahead to announce the big news about *Traveling Light*. Not that they'd ever see her on there. Three days of shooting and Keira had yet to see the front of the camera.

The hostess sat them at a table by the windows that overlooked the clearing where trolls were known to chase queens and princesses. Past that, the grass gave way to pine-needled floors and the open air became crowded with trees, wild animals, and maybe a yeti or two. Then the Great One, Denali. It only took standing in its shadow to understand humility.

As Robbie settled Anabelle into her seat, Keira glanced at a neighboring table. Her arms and legs seemed to have turned to stone.

Only the touch of Robbie's hand was enough to bring her flesh back to life.

"You okay?"

"It's Angela Woodward."

"Who's that?" Robbie's face swung toward the table next to theirs. "Whoa. Isn't that Teddy Woodward?"

She nodded.

"It's fine. There's, like, zero percent chance we're embarrassing ourselves right now, gawking at them."

The couple glanced up from their plates and looked at Keira and Robbie.

Robbie shifted his weight. "Okay, maybe, like, ten percent."

Angela, Keira's favorite photographer of all time, had a friendly face that was framed with long, thick locks, so close to the color of cinnamon, Keira wondered if she smelled like Christmas. Seated across the table from her, her husband, Teddy, remained as handsome today as he was when he'd first begun starring in films forty years ago. Keira couldn't remember how many Oscars he'd won, but it was enough to seal him in Hollywood history forever.

"Honey, I think they may want a picture with you." Angela touched her husband's arm.

Swabbing a napkin against his mouth, he nodded. He rose from his chair and stretched out his hand to them.

Robbie, who didn't typically get starstruck, accepted the handshake, nearly ripping the man's arm out of his socket. "I used to play with your action figure."

Seeing Robbie's awkwardness bubble up and over gave permission for Keira to throw caution to the wind herself. She lunged ahead, past Teddy, straight to Angela. "Ms. Woodward, I'm thrilled to meet you."

"Me?"

"Your book, *Life in Quotidian*, has been my favorite as long as I can remember. The way you paired your spectacular nature photography with prose has always inspired me."

"That old book? It's been out of print for decades. You don't look old enough to have read it."

"It was in our high school library. I would check it out each week. One day, they gifted it to me. I still have it." Keira touched her cheek. If it grew any hotter, she'd combust. "I am—er, um, was a photojournalist. I've been trying to emulate your style, but I don't even come close to capturing nature the way you do."

"Bless your heart. You've made my year. People only ever recognize that old fuddy-duddy."

"Eh, he's all right," Keira joked, waving him off.

"What's your name, dear?"

"Kat Wande—Kat Knudsen, I mean."

"Were you about to say Kat Wanderfull?"

"You've heard of me?"

"Our granddaughter, Lana, adores you. She follows you on . . . Teddy, what's that app called?"

"Beats me."

"Momentso." Keira tilted her head. "I'm guessing your daughter is between sixteen and twenty-eight? That seems to be my main demographic."

"Fifteen going on thirty," Teddy said.

"I'll say. You are such a good role model for her, especially compared to some of the other folks on social media. I love how your faith and values show through your posts. Thank you for that."

"You're welcome. That's a big reason why I do it. Or did it. I have a new job now."

"Wait a moment. Are you with *Traveling Light*?" Angela asked.

"I am."

"Oh, I bet Margot is shaking in her boots over you!" Teddy chuckled.

Angela swatted Teddy's arm. "Margot has never been scared a day in her life. The bigger concern is . . . has she been nice to you?"

"She hasn't *not* been nice." The truth was she hadn't been anything to Keira. The woman hadn't even acknowledged Keira's presence on set. "Oh, this is my assistant, Robbie."

"We were watching you all play out there. You sure he isn't more than your assistant?" Teddy eyed them in that grandfatherly way.

"He's my boyfriend, too. That's his daughter, Anabelle."

"She's a doll."

"Thanks." Robbie grinned.

"Would you all like to join us? I'm sure they wouldn't mind us pulling the tables together. I'd love to talk shop with Keira."

* * *

Wood-grilled salmon. Our salmon is ethically sourced from Prince William Sound and brushed with our Fifth Summit brown sugar bourbon glaze,'" Robbie read the menu in his best Teddy Woodward impression, and Keira's heart swooned.

"That's one of the better impressions of me I've heard." Teddy Woodward had a unique and distinguished voice, rich and smooth. Over the years, he'd lent that voice to documentaries, commercials, and movie narration. The sound of it immediately inspired trust and confidence.

Robbie rubbed the back of his neck. "You know, on dates in high school, I used that impression to win over the mothers."

"That smile of yours likely helped. You know who he looks like, Teddy?" Angela asked.

"Don't say Redford. I've been compared to that man my whole career."

"There are worse folks." Angela winked at her husband.

Teddy waved the waitress over to request a platter of their finest desserts. Afterward, he turned the focus back on Keira. "Kat, has television been your dream for long?"

"Not television, but traveling, yes. My childhood wasn't the best. It was Robbie who showed me that just because the world is big doesn't mean it has to be feared. Now I want to see and experience as much as I can. It sounds cheesy, I know."

Angela laughed. "Not at all. What about you, Robbie? What do you hope for out of life?"

"For me, if I could wake up next to this beauty every morning, catch some trout on the river, and be a good daddy to Anabelle"—Robbie glanced down at Keira's stomach—"and maybe a couple more, that's my dream. Honestly, I'd be happy spending my whole life on one square mile."

"I hate to be the bearer of bad news, but those don't exactly align," Angela said.

Robbie's smile fell. "I guess that's what faith is for. God wove a thread of adventure in Keira's heart when he first knit her together. Who am I to stand in the way of God's calling for her life?" His eyes flickered to Anabelle, scribbling in a coloring book. "As for me, I'd sacrifice almost anything for Keira. Even that one square mile."

Emotions swirled in Keira's heart. Good ones. And bad ones. Was she doing the right thing, stealing him away to be by her side? Did that mean she was in love? Or selfish?

"Where's home for you?" Teddy asked.

"My family owns a fly-fishing resort on the Madison River in Montana."

"No kidding." Teddy's voice shook the timbers. "No wonder you'd be happy never leaving that place. Angela and I are headed that way next month. We're looking at property for a cabin."

"If you need a builder, Robbie is extremely talented. He built a cabin for himself and Anabelle, and it's a marvel. I keep telling him he should start a business building luxury cabins in the Yellowstone area."

"I'd like to see your ideas," Teddy said.

While Teddy and Robbie launched into a side conversation about fly-fishing on the Madison, Keira turned her focus to Angela. "Do you still take photos?"

"Only for myself and our family. Not for a career."

"Is that hard for you?"

Angela thought a moment. "Sometimes. But I don't regret it. You know, back in the eighties, I was at the height of my photography career. My book sales had taken off. This was back when Adventure wasn't a channel but a magazine. They offered me a gig traveling the world to take pictures for them."

"I had no idea."

"I said no. I was pregnant with our son. Our daughter was only eighteen months old. And I knew how much I'd be sacrificing to leave. Our marriage was stable and likely could've handled the separation, but I actually enjoyed life with Teddy. I could have lived without my love by my side. I just didn't want to."

Keira bristled. This woman, this stranger, didn't know Keira's history or her future. Who did she think she was?

"Kat, I only tell you this for one reason. Your story isn't my story. And it isn't Margot's or anyone else's, either. But life is full of difficult choices. There may come a time where you have to choose your path. And you'll have many voices directing that choice. But if you lift it up to the Lord, he'll tell you which choice is best for you."

"God doesn't speak to me like that."

"Maybe you aren't listening for the right sound." Angela squeezed Keira's hand. "He speaks in whispers when all the world is loud. Just remember—mountains, oceans, prairies? They may give beauty to our eyes and depth to our experience, but it is God who gives peace to our soul. Don't lose sight of him and don't forget where or with whom your home is."

CHAPTER THIRTY-NINE

I'm being paranoid, right?" Robbie's nerves were on edge this morning for many reasons. Not even a reassuring smile from Keira could settle them.

"Parents hire babysitters all the time," Keira said. "You didn't freak out when we left her at the hospital's KidWatch."

"Yeah, but that place was licensed by the state of California. I met Willa three days ago. And she's never looked up from her phone long enough to tell me anything about herself."

"She's an intern on this show. I'm sure she's responsible enough. And it's only for a few hours. Besides, would you really want Annie to walk on a glacier with us?"

"Good point." It had broken his heart to leave Anabelle behind, knowing how much she wanted to see the "glaitser," as she called it. But she was his daughter, after all. Her gumption surpassed her common sense too often for her own good.

Besides, he was nervous enough as is. For the hundredth time since he'd left the hotel room, he slid his hand over the left front pocket of his jeans. With his fingertip, he traced the ring's circle and vintage diamond. Still tucked away, waiting for the right moment.

Isaac strode through the front door of Denali Grand Tours. He looked around until his beady eyes pinned on Keira.

She angled her shoulders to the man. "Hey, Isaac. How responsible is Willa?"

He held up his hand flat and rocked it back and forth. "Eh."

Robbie groaned. "That does not make me feel better. I should head back to the lodge."

"Kat, big news. It's showtime." Isaac grinned. "You'll be interviewing a park ranger up on the glacier for a clip."

Keira gripped Robbie's hand hard enough to hurt. "Really? But what about Margot?"

"She's not here. I guess she wanted to see Kodiak or something and took off. Phil's had enough."

Outside in the sun, Phil, the producer, paced. The helicopters had been scheduled to take off thirty minutes ago, and Margot was hours away.

With the same fervor she'd used to squeeze his hand, she now choked Robbie's neck in an enthusiastic embrace. "Anabelle will be fine. You can't leave me now. After all, you *are* my assistant."

Therese broke them up, squeezing in front of Robbie to start on Keira's makeup. She highlighted and bronzed, brushed and sprayed Keira's face until she looked like a porcelain doll. Thanks to Keira's own styling that morning, her hair only needed to be placed around her face. A new Patagonia coat arrived next.

Keira shrugged into it.

Robbie stood by with nothing to do. Some assistant he was. "Can I get you anything?"

"All I need is prayer." She grinned at him.

With a hand in his pocket, Robbie blew out a shaky breath. She'd say yes . . . if he got the chance to ask her up there on the glacier. What better place to ask her to marry him than on top of the world, which was how he felt when he was with her.

But first, she had a job to do.

When it was time to load, Robbie made one last call to Willa. Apparently, Anabelle had thrown a fit about not getting to go up on the mountain with them, even telling Willa that she could run up the mountain to join Robbie and Keira. It had taken a Princess Patty Cake video to settle her down. But Anabelle was fine now. They'd eaten lunch and would be heading outside to play in a few minutes.

Keira was whisked away by Isaac, a guy who appeared to get his fashion advice from Jeff Goldblum's character in *Jurassic Park*. He held her hand as she boarded the plane with Phil and the pudgy camera guy. Dusty, maybe.

Robbie got corralled onto the third plane with the other intern, the lighting girl, and a guy whose entire job seemed to be writing on a tablet all day. The seats weren't comfortable, and it quickly became apparent that someone didn't believe in deodorant.

On the ride up, he could have marveled at the sights through the window. Instead, he prayed for the Lord to put his hand on Keira today.

Once they arrived on the glacier, production went into high gear. Microphones and light kits clashed with the otherwise natural landscape. Keira, in all her glory, stood before the camera with the national park ranger. While the cameras rolled, they bantered back and forth, discussing the age and depth of the glacier. With her questions and responses, Keira seemed to be best friends with the guy, knowledgeable while still flirting with the camera. It was masterful.

"And that's a wrap!" Phil called. "Excellent way to introduce Keira to our viewers. They'll love her. Now, go rest up, because tomorrow we head to Brussels, with stopovers in both Seattle and Frankfurt. We'll have to see if Margot decides to join us." He approached Keira and spoke to her.

She nodded and brought a hand to her mouth.

Boy, Robbie wished she'd stop covering up her smile. At least she was happy. All her dreams were coming true, except one.

Again, he felt for the ring.

This wasn't ideal. There were too many people. Maybe if he waited, they'd all head back to the helicoptors, and he and Keira could be alone.

For the first time in nearly two hours of filming, she looked in Robbie's direction, and they locked eyes.

"Do you ever feel like you're watching history being made?" Isaac asked Robbie, nodding to Keira. He was kneeling on the ice, looping the length of audio cable in his hand. "She's a natural. I've only been working in television for about ten years, but I'd say she's got quite a career ahead of her. It's cool that you're so encouraging of it."

"If you saw where she came from, you'd understand."

"I hope you're hanging on to her tight." Isaac hooked his arm through the wound cable and set it on his shoulder before clapping Robbie on the back. "Because she's about to soar."

Isaac's words, or perhaps the look of adoration on the guy's face whenever he looked at Keira, clenched Robbie's stomach like a vice grip.

The time had come.

Robbie jogged to Keira, still standing on the vast Yanert Ice Field.

"How was I?"

He bear-hugged her. "I've never been prouder of you."

"Thanks, Robbie."

The crew was still milling about.

Except for Isaac, who was watching them. No, this was not ideal, but Robbie had missed his chance once before. He wouldn't do it again.

"Kat, I've wanted to do this for so long." Robbie raised her gloved left hand to his lips. He kissed each knuckle, then held his lips a moment longer on the spot where his ring would soon rest. Slowly, he tugged each finger of the glove, until the entire thing yielded.

Her bare hand trembled slightly. Her cheeks, tinged pink from the cold despite Therese's constant reapplication of powder, made her eyes appear as blue as the sky above.

"My love for you is as wide as—"

"Hey, guys, sorry to interrupt." Even the sound of the glacier breaking in half couldn't be as irritating as Isaac's voice at that moment. "I need to get some things straight as Adventure Channel announces the new staffing. For liability reasons, we need to make sure no one on our payroll has any skeletons in the closet that the gossip rags will latch on to. Kat, you have your blog and Momentso account as Kat Wanderfull. That's it, right?"

"Yeah, that's all. Isaac, can you give us a minute, please? We're in the middle of something."

"Almost done. Robbie, you said you aren't on social media."

Robbie felt the rumble of a tremor in his legs. He gave a small nod.

"We did a search, and you're linked to an inactive Momentso profile. There's no problem with it. You kept it clean. Hardly posted at all. It was under the name, uh, MR—"

Robbie silenced him with a raised hand.

Confusion warped Keira's features.

He should have told her long ago.

Understanding turned her confusion to sadness. In her eyes, Keira's dream of love shattered, leaving shards of glass to rain down on their joined hands.

He didn't dare let go.

Her breaths grew heavy. Finally, she opened her mouth to speak. "MRCustom?"

Robbie nodded. "Madison River Custom Homes. The name of the business I had planned to start."

Isaac backed away, but Keira did not. She had promised Robbie she wouldn't flee.

Robbie almost wished she had. Seeing her back as she fled would be easier than watching the pain of betrayal rippling across her face. Her lips struggled to pair sound with their movement. Finally, after a long minute of silence, she asked one question. "Why?"

"I didn't know it was you. Not when we were talking about books or your goals in life. I fell in love with you when I thought you were a stranger. It wasn't until you told me about your two names, Kat and Keira, that I realized the truth. When I brought your atlas to you, I planned to tell you. But you were still bleeding from John's betrayal. I couldn't deepen the wound."

"Why not after that?"

"You were looking for any excuse to run from me. After seeing you with Annie. After seeing you paint that school in South Dakota, holding babies in California. After falling for you all over again, I couldn't tell you." He caressed her cheek. He trailed his hand to the locks spilling over her shoulder from the nape of her neck. They were as soft as the first day they'd kissed in the library.

Keira's eyes fluttered closed.

It would be okay. She'd forgive him. "Kat, I'm sorry. So sorry. I was wrong to hide it from you once I knew. Forgive me. I love you too much to lose you."

"A simple apology can't fix this. I told him things."

"Those are things you'd tell me now, aren't they?"

"But not then. He was my friend. You were not. How could you betray me like that?" Keira's words pierced the flesh around his heart. Her eyes narrowed to slits. "You aren't much better than John. Maybe my father was right about you all along."

The world became void of sound, save a ringing in his ear. His hand dropped to his side. He stumbled back a step, expecting, hoping a crevasse would swallow him whole.

Someone caught his arm, keeping him upright. Producer Phil.

"Matthews, we need to get you back to the lodge. It's your daughter. She's gone missing."

CHAPTER FORTY

❧

I don't know what happened. She was running around the clearing pretending a troll was chasing her or something. I looked down at my phone. Next thing I knew, she was gone. I called to her, but she didn't answer," Willa said, wiping her nose with a tissue. "I think she might've been trying to find you guys."

Robbie couldn't look at her. He never should've left Anabelle. He needed to think. Make a plan. His mind, though, had turned to mush the moment he'd learned his daughter was missing.

"How long ago was this?" Keira asked.

"About two hours. The lodge already called the Denali Rescue Team. Then they sent out some guys on ATVs to look for her. So far they haven't found anything." Willa's red-rimmed eyes spilled more tears down her cheeks. "Oh, I hope an animal didn't get her."

The image was too much. Robbie's stomach heaved. He bent over behind a shrub and got sick. Afterward, when he opened his eyes, the scenery warped. Robbie was falling backward. His body thudded against the ground, and pain shot from his tailbone up his spine.

He sensed movement around him as he lay on his back, looking at the spinning clouds. What he wouldn't give for a ray of light to appear. If ever he needed the help of angels, this was it. *Lord, I need you. Anabelle needs you. Protect her from cold, fear, and harm. Please.*

A shadow loomed above him.

His eyes finally focused on Keira's face.

She rolled him a bit and withdrew his phone from his back pocket. She handled it carefully. Had he crushed it just now? Not that it mattered. Nothing mattered except finding his baby girl. A minute later, Keira held the phone to her ear. "Thomas? It's Keira . . . No, everything's not okay. Anabelle's lost . . . A couple of hours . . . Would you mind? . . . Thanks, Thomas . . . I'll tell him."

A breeze kicked up. What had Anabelle been wearing? Was she cold? Hungry? Scared? *God, please don't let her be hurt or—*

"Thomas will search from the air. He should be here in about two hours. The tour place is sending their helicopters up, too. The forests aren't too thick up at this latitude. They'll be able to see her. She'll be okay, Robbie." Her voice had been stripped of all grace. "I'll call your family so they can be praying."

"We need more people on the ground to search." Robbie forced himself into a seated position. He swallowed back a new wave of vomit. "I'm calling the police."

"But if you call them, Vivian, the lawyers, the judge—"

"I know. But I'd rather have Anabelle alive and only see her four days a month than never see her again." Dread washed over him, and he wretched on the grass once more.

T hank God for a midnight sun, eh?" Therese handed Robbie and Keira each a coffee. Although the clock read nine p.m., the sun still flushed the land with light.

Keira thanked her.

Robbie had aged considerably over the last couple of hours. His face ranged from red to purple to green. When he looked at Keira, his eyes wouldn't focus. He was out there in the wilderness, if not in body, then in mind. The Talkeetna sheriff insisted Robbie stay at the lodge to answer questions. Otherwise, he would have climbed Denali with his bare hands if it meant getting to Anabelle.

The crew had all jumped in to help in the search. Isaac took the lead and the rest followed. Only Therese, nursing a bum ankle, stayed back. In one of the lodge's conference rooms, the Denali Rescue Team's leader was formulating a plan while he waited for his volunteers to arrive.

Keira wished they'd get moving. Who knows how Anabelle would fare by the time they got their boots to the ground?

Robbie stepped away from the windows to peruse the map of the area. "I'm telling you that if she got to the Chulitna River, she'd stay by it. We live on a river. She'll feel safer there. And that's where the princess looked for her unicorn on her favorite show."

The sheriff's face sobered even more. "Let's hope she isn't, since that's where the predators are most likely to be."

Keira balled her fists. She stepped closer to the man who stood barely taller than her. "All the more reason to get people along the river. Give me a truck, an ATV, or even a mountain bike, and I'll head out there right now."

"Sorry, miss. We can't risk more people getting lost. We'll find her, but we have to be smart about it."

"What's so smart about sitting around doing nothing for hours?" Her voice was nearly shrill enough to break glass.

Robbie's phone rang from the table near the fireplace. Someone had found a charger for him, since his battery had nearly drained to zero. He raced to it. The cracked screen showed Thomas's name. When Robbie answered, he put it on speakerphone for Keira, the sheriff, and a park ranger to hear.

"Thomas."

"Robbie, I see something neon pink. On the eastern bank of the Chulitna River southwest of the lodge. Maybe three quarters of a mile. Hang on, and I'll send the coordinates."

"Is she okay?"

"I'm not sure. I didn't see any movement, but I'm pretty high up."

The park ranger wrote down the coordinates and checked the map. "There's a dirt road near there. We can take the truck."

"Let's go." Robbie was halfway to the door when the sheriff grabbed him.

"You need to stay here in case something has happened to her."

Robbie lowered his glare on the man.

"Or not," the sheriff conceded.

It took nearly ten minutes until the ranger's truck broke through the trees and a vast riverscape opened wide. Keira panned the scene.

A couple hundred yards north, a ball of hot pink clashed against the blues, greens, and grays.

Robbie flung his door open and screamed, "Anabelle!" He took off at a dead sprint toward the pink.

Keira followed at a snail's pace compared to him. By the time she'd arrived at the scene, he was on the ground cradling his daughter and rocking her forward and back.

Over the crook of his arm, her curls hung. Rounding Robbie, she saw Anabelle's dirty, tearstained face.

"Annie?"

Upon hearing Keira's voice, Anabelle's bright eyes opened, and she turned her face. "Mommy Kat."

Keira's feet disappeared beneath her, and she was down on the rock and sand, kissing Anabelle's cheeks. Her fingers tangled in the mess of curls. "Kitty Kat, you scared us."

"I wanted to find you." Her voice was hoarse.

"I know." Keira looked over Anabelle's arms and legs. Other than a few scratches and a whole lot of dirt and pine needles, she appeared unharmed. *Thank you, Lord.*

Hours later, after the midnight sun finally took its rest, Anabelle was released by a doctor at Talkeetna's health care clinic. Upon returning to the lodge, Robbie and Keira settled Anabelle into her bed. They sat on either side of her with their backs against the headboard while the pink and brown horses from the night-light circled above them. Anabelle slept using Keira's thigh as her pillow and Robbie's arm as an extra blanket.

"I called Cassie, Vivian, and Marie, the social worker. They'd find out sooner or later. I figured it would be better coming from me: All three flipped out, as you can imagine." Robbie sighed. "Vivian let me have it for not calling her as soon as Annie went missing. From the sound of her voice, I think she would have stolen a plane to get here to help. She wants her own doctor to give Anabelle a full medical evaluation as soon as possible."

"You think she's genuinely concerned?"

"I do. Vivian loves Anabelle. I know she does. Which makes this even scarier for me. Thomas is flying us back to Montana tomorrow. I have a lot of damage control to do if I want any shot at all of joint custody. Plus, it will be good for Anabelle to be back home with my family."

Keira swallowed hard. "Montana is where you belong."

"And you belong out there." Robbie nodded to the window, currently draped in heavy curtains to block the early-morning sun, which would rise again shortly. "I never meant to hurt you or betray you, Keira. From the time we were seventeen, I only ever wanted to love you. Failing at that hurts more than any bad grade or insult from a college professor. I should've been honest from the start."

"Yes. You should've." Keira looked into his sorrowful eyes. On the glacier, she was ready to give her life to him. But that was before. She couldn't simply forgive him for his betrayal, could she? Even if she did, how could this work? Either he'd lose his daughter, or Keira would lose herself.

"Robbie, I don't regret any of it. I am who I am because you talked to me in that school hallway. You saved me from my father. You introduced me to my faith. And you pushed me to find myself." Keira swept the curls, still damp from bathwater, off Anabelle's forehead. "And thank you for sharing your daughter with me. Oddly, you kind of gave me a childhood I never had . . . airplane rides, cloud watching, and theme parks. You're a great daddy, and she's lucky to have you."

He blinked several times.

"We leave for Belgium in a few hours. I should go." The headboard creaked as Keira began to shimmy off the bed.

Anabelle stirred. She fisted Keira's shirt and coiled her limbs around Keira's leg.

As if this wasn't hard enough.

No matter if she pried the traumatized little girl from one part of her, Anabelle clung all the tighter to the other. With each second that passed, the burn grew stronger.

Keira felt herself melting from the inside out. "Robbie, please."

He helped loosen Anabelle's limbs, allowing Keira to pull away and stand.

Annie's eyes shot open and searched the room. When she found Keira, she reached her arms to her. "Don't leave, Mommy Kat. Don't leave."

Keira's throat knotted.

Robbie pressed his daughter against his chest.

Turning away didn't silence Anabelle's muffled cries. Curse the guilt threatening to cement her feet to this cheap carpet when her dream was on the other side of the door. Summoning her remaining strength, she lifted her heavy legs, right, left, right, left, until the blessed steel door handle cooled her palm. She froze. "Eleanor."

"Eleanor."

"Eleanor?" Robbie asked from the bed.

"Curley's wife's name in *Of Mice and Men*," Keira said. "I decided it was probably Eleanor. It means 'shining light.' And I've never known an Eleanor that wasn't strong, passionate, and dedicated. Maybe with some different circumstances or different choices, her name would have been Eleanor instead of Curley's wife. Then that story would've ended differently for everyone. She'd have been the hero instead of the victim."

Anabelle was still sobbing softly.

"Kat," Robbie said. "Keira. Whatever your name is, I'll wait for you this time. Forever if I have to. In case there's ever a day that you decide to come home to me."

Keira closed her eyes. "Goodbye, Robbie." Then she opened the door and left.

Chapter Forty-One

❦

On the Moroccan street, Keira looked to the westward sky. For the past two weeks, she'd tried her best to focus on her job. The facts she'd memorized about Belgium, Egypt, and Morocco had come in handy during the couple clips she got to film. Still, it was lonely without Robbie and Anabelle. At least she had Isaac.

"You're adorable. You know that, right?" Isaac held out a spiced coffee to Keira. "Was the 'As Time Goes By' duet your idea?"

Keira accepted the cup with a nod. "I mean, if we're shooting in Casablanca at a restaurant modeled after Rick's in that movie . . ."

"The viewers are going to love it. We're going dancing tonight. Wanna come?"

Could he dance in those painted-on pants of his? Keira bit away a smile. "Not this time. I have a new book."

"You and your books. You know, even Elizabeth Bennet attended balls. One day, I'll get you to come out with us." Isaac called out to Markus, then ran off to meet him.

"You're keeping me on my toes, Kat. Do you realize that?" Margot Jorgensen was standing in front of her, finally acknowledging her existence. Thus far, there hadn't been a single word uttered between them. The woman must hate her.

Keira straightened herself.

Margot was taller in person, but she wasn't as naturally pretty as Keira had expected. *Well preserved* might be the better term. There was a tiredness in her eyes that certain camera angles and lenses didn't capture. And though, in general, she sported an arrogant glower that warned fans and colleagues from approaching her, she was smiling now.

Margot winked. "Walk with me."

The restaurant was a half mile from their hotel. The Moroccan street looked as though it had been stolen from an American city and dropped on a different continent. Businessmen and women, shoppers, and bicyclists casually went about their way. This was not Humphrey Bogart's Casablanca, that was for sure.

"How's the little girl doing?"

Keira's heartbeat kicked up at the memory of Denali. "I'm not sure. I haven't heard from them."

"Not from her father, either? Weren't you and that magnificent specimen an item?"

"We were."

"I bet he was fun while he lasted."

This conversation was as palatable as the snails Isaac had bought her from a street vendor yesterday. Some Arabic music spilled out through the door of a shop selling herbs. Keira considered ducking inside. But brave people don't flee difficult conversations. Robbie taught her that.

"I was married once. Seasons one and two," Margo said. "He was a nice guy, but he wasn't as supportive as I needed him to be. He was like that boyfriend of yours, wanting to hold you back and keep you for himself."

"Robbie wasn't like that at all. He—"

"Don't let him. You've got a big future ahead of you," Margot went on. "Funny. A year ago, if I knew I'd be fighting some pretty, young fawn for my job, I'd have crumbled to pieces. But I've been through it this past year. When you showed up with your innocence, just out of grade school, without wrinkles, it gave me a new purpose. So thank you."

The boiling blood in Keira's veins heated her words the way lava heated a geyser. "Just because I'm young doesn't mean I've had an easy life, Ms. Jorgensen. In fact, it's quite the opposite."

"Call me Margot." The woman reached into her cross-body bag, retrieved what looked like one thousand Moroccan dirham, and slipped it beneath the arm of a man sleeping on the sidewalk. "You've had a hard life? Use that. Your little song back there was cute. But viewers these days want real. If you want to take my job from me, then you need to be willing to show them who you are."

Once they reached their hotel, Margot pulled open the door.

Keira gripped the coffee cup tighter to keep the tremble in her hands from showing. "Why are you giving me advice?"

"Because, Kai Wanderfull, without it, a sweet girl like you will never survive. Cute name, by the way." Then Margot disappeared through the doorway.

August rolled into Montana, bringing with it scorching temperatures and bone-dry conditions. As a result, new pockets of wildfires popped up every day in the region. At River's Edge Resort, Robbie kept busy managing the threats to both the land and his family.

Hand in hand with Anabelle, Robbie walked Marie, the social worker, to her car. Although she was older and played by the book, she was kind to Robbie. In their hour together, Marie had gone over his finances with him. She was dismayed at his lack of savings and explained how much he should expect to spend raising a child. When she learned about his charity repairs for those in his community, she didn't treat him like he was dumb. Rather, she described how he could show generosity within boundaries and still achieve his goals.

Goals he didn't yet have. That was his homework before their next meeting in September. Maybe by then, Marie could stamp *Good Father* on his case. After all, a lot could happen in four weeks. It had been that long since Denali. Since he'd last seen Keira.

Anabelle was sleeping better. Her time in the wilderness was morphing from a near tragedy to a grand "'venture" in her mind.

Robbie, of course, still woke up in a cold sweat from it. Just last night, he'd dreamed Anabelle was lost on an African savannah. But this time, he'd found her too late, after the lions had their fill.

Then Anabelle's red curls, untouched by the predators, morphed into long blond waves, soaked in blood.

The memory of the nightmare unleashed a shudder through his body. Was Keira safe? Happy? In the mail, they'd received postcards from Brussels, Cairo, and just yesterday, Casablanca.

Well, not quite *they*. The postcards had been addressed to Anabelle.

Not him. But he'd hung them on the fridge all the same. On the latest one, Keira stated they were heading to Kenya next. Had the lion dream been a vision of what had happened to her? Or a premonition? How would Robbie even know if Keira was hurt? A phone call from Isaac? Another shudder wracked him.

Marie gave Anabelle a wave and drove off.

"What do you say, Kitty Kat? Want to go bug Ryann in the café? I bet I can drink more chocolate milk than you."

Anabelle's eyes narrowed. "No, me. Race ya." She took off on a sprint, as fast as her sandals could carry her.

After Robbie caught up, he noticed the awkwardness of her shoes.

They were on the wrong feet. Awesome. In front of Marie, too. Ugh.

Once they got to the café, Anabelle ran inside.

Robbie paused when he heard the popping of gravel beneath tires.

A gray Land Rover pulled up next to the building and parked where Keira's leased Jeep had once been. This was not one of the regulars.

Maybe Stuart Ashcroft, his sister's stalker, had upgraded his truck. The car had his income level written all over it. He might be coming to visit Ryann. They'd been spending time together, which made Robbie dry heave. The guy was bad news. Plus, the fact that the bad reviews had stopped as soon as Ryann allowed Stuart back in her life went far beyond coincidence.

Rather than that slimeball, a man in a Carhartt jacket, Wranglers, and boots that probably cost more than Robbie's house rounded the bumper of the car.

Robbie was suddenly right back in the Fifth Summit restaurant. "Teddy Woodward. How are you, man?"

"Hey, Robbie. We're doing well. I told you we'd be down here, checking out property. I needed to come see your family's place and try this breakfast you told me about."

"We've got plenty of room for you." Robbie shook his hand as Angela climbed out of the car. "Welcome, Angela."

She kissed Robbie's cheek and squeezed his hand. "Beautiful country down here, isn't it?"

"Yes, ma'am."

"We didn't expect to see you here. Weren't you supposed to be in Japan or something?"

"It's a long story."

"We've got a cinnamon roll as big as a plate to eat. Why don't you regale us with that tale?"

An hour and three-quarters of a cinnamon roll later, the Woodwards knew the entire ballad of Keira and Robbie.

"What a shame, when life gets in the way of love." Angela sipped her coffee. She gave Robbie a pitying look. "When I told her that she'd have to choose which dream to sacrifice, I didn't realize she only had a few days before that would come to pass."

"How do you feel about the custody battle?" Teddy asked. "I know those can get real ugly."

Robbie shrugged. He drummed on his plate with his last strip of bacon. "I'm trying to be reasonable, but ugly is a possibility for sure." He glanced at Anabelle. Around her, he needed to keep things vague. She'd only just gotten to know Vivian. Pitting her as the enemy would do more harm than good. "We had a visit with the social worker today. She's trying to help me create plans to provide financially for Annie."

"Now that you're no longer working for *Traveling Light*, why don't you start up that luxury-home-building business?"

"I've thought about that. But in these parts, I'm known for fixing busted roofs and sinking porches, not quality construction from scratch."

"Is that your cabin you built a couple of buildings down?" Teddy took a swig of orange juice. "She's a beauty. Would you mind giving us a tour? I'd like to see your work."

CHAPTER FORTY-TWO

***

Keira's stomach churned. She'd already tried to leave the Thai nightclub once but was informed that it wouldn't be safe to head back to the hotel on her own. She'd asked the guys on the crew, one by one, if they'd walk her back. In response, each offered to buy her a drink to help her "loosen up and enjoy herself." Isaac, who had been Mr. Dependable for the past three months, had already swallowed several shots. Evidently, he mistook her request to be an invitation to put his hand on her upper thigh.

Between sips of bottled water, Keira tried to fold herself into the smallest sliver she could until the group was ready to leave. The music was so loud, it reverberated through the couch Keira sat on.

"Let's dance," Isaac said, with a lopsided grin.

"No, thank you. You should lay off the drinks, Isaac."

"I already closed out my tab."

"Good. Can we leave soon?"

There was a twitch in his cheek. He looked over Keira's shoulder and nodded.

Markus was making some kind of hand gesture that Keira didn't recognize. When he saw Keira had caught the motion, he burst into laughter.

"What did that mean?" She focused on Isaac's face.

"You *are* innocent. Some of the crew think it's an act."

She didn't like the way he was looking at her.

"I'll be back in a few. I have to tell Markus something." Isaac pushed himself off the couch. He walked without staggering. If he had, it might have explained the way he was acting.

Whatever he said to Markus earned him a high five.

This isn't where you belong. The voice came from deep inside, loud enough to sound above the wretched music.

She looked around for any kind of light to cut through the dark cloud hovering above her. Seeing none, she closed her eyes and imagined the sound of the Madison River, Anabelle's Princess Patty Cake rambles, and even Robbie's terrible rendition of "Into the Great Wide Open." Montana had never felt so far away.

What time was it? Kat checked her phone. With the time difference, Robbie would likely be starting his workday. Had he gone back to his odd jobs like before? Had Anabelle attended preschool yet? Probably. It was October 1, after all. Which meant the custody hearing was slated for seven days from today. Had it changed? Had Vivian relented, or pushed for an even more extreme parenting plan?

"Ready to head back?" Isaac kneeled in front of her, his hand covering her kneecap.

"Is the group—?"

"No, they're staying a bit longer. Let's get you back to the hotel."

"Thank you, Isaac."

"My pleasure."

On the walk back, Isaac had been quiet. He still said nothing as they stood outside her door while she searched her purse for her key card. Finally, her fingertips closed around the card, and she held it up. "Found it."

Isaac's gaze floated from the card to Keira's eyes then her mouth. His hand slinked around her hip and pressed on her lower back, pulling her toward him.

She stumbled, and he crushed her against his chest. Before she could speak, his mouth was on hers. She withdrew as much as his hold allowed.

"Isaac, no."

"You should invite me inside." He moved to kiss her again, but she turned her head.

His beard felt scratchy against her neck, and it shook chills out of her.

He chuckled, clearly getting the wrong idea even as she pushed against him with her palms.

"I don't want to. Let me go."

Frustration marred his normally kind eyes. As he stepped back, he combed his fingers through the hair at his crown. "I thought this was what you wanted."

Keira wrapped her arms around herself. "Well, I thought we were friends, Isaac."

"Am I a fool for wanting more? Is it because of Robbie?"

Hiding the truth was exhausting. And what good had it done? "Yes, it's because of Robbie. I'm not over him. Not sure I'll ever be."

He dug his hands in his front pockets and rocked back on his heels. "I don't get it. If you love him so much, why aren't you with him?"

Keira released a breath. One she seemed to have held since July. "I don't know anymore."

Anabelle sat in the center of the group of children, her eyes glued to the librarian's big picture book. She loved Thursday morning story time. If she didn't, Robbie wouldn't put himself through the torture of reliving his and Keira's first kiss on repeat every week.

Even now, as he looked to his left by the librarian's desk, he could feel her hands on his chest, her lips on his. He needed out of here.

"Hey, Sylvia," he whispered. "I'm going out to use the computer for a few minutes. Can you keep an eye on Annie?"

Robbie would never again trust a stranger to watch his daughter, but Sylvia had been his girlfriend in junior high, and she was a great mom to Olive. She was the one who invited them to the library in the first place, as they waited in the preschool pickup line.

"You got it," she said.

Back in the main room of the library, he snagged a seat at one of the computers. He browsed one of the big news networks. Not that he followed national news, but he'd do anything to keep his mind off that kiss and each one after. The Dow had dropped four hundred points in a day. Some megachurch pastor from the Midwest got sentenced to jail for attacking one of his congregants. There was a terrorist attack in the Philippines. If his grandma were here, she would say that the world had taken a plunger to its ear and lost its mind.

Robbie's thoughts flickered to all the postcards they'd received from Keira the past three months. Steadily, the crew was moving eastward toward the Philippines. Without wasting another second, he went to Momentso's site and logged into his reactivated account.

Kat Wanderfull's most recent posts were stamped yesterday in Nepal.

But she had promised to delay the postings for safety. He'd have to either text or message her to make sure she was safe.

As if she'd read his mind, the private message icon flashed. All the breath drained from his lungs. Three months without a word. Three months of merely checking in to see pictures of her in exotic locations or with the crew. Many with Isaac.

But now she'd reached out to Robbie. He clicked the mouse. The message read:

DizzyDinosaur has poked you. Wave or poke back.

What on earth was a poke and why was some person named DizzyDinosaur doing it to him? Weird. He returned to Kat's profile.

The message icon lit up again.

That's it. DizzyDinosaur was asking for a strongly worded message. He clicked the envelope.

KAT WANDERFULL: Hey.

Robbie leaned so far forward in his chair that it nearly tipped.

The green dot remained solid on her avatar pic. She was safe. And she was talking to him. Glory, she was talking to him.

MRCUSTOM: Hey. I was worried about you. You aren't in the Philippines, are you?
KAT WANDERFULL: Phuket, Thailand.
MRCUSTOM: Phew! Are you having a good time?

There was a pause.

KAT WANDERFULL: Any news on the hearing?
MRCUSTOM: It's still next Thursday.
KAT WANDERFULL: I wish I could be there, but I won't fly back into Idaho until Friday. Has there been any change in the case?

MRCUSTOM: No change. Viv's still Viv. But Anabelle
    spent the night over there last weekend. She never
    even cried for me.

KAT WANDERFULL: You're a great man, Robbie. Do you
    know that?

He scrubbed his jaw, but his grin remained etched on his
face.

KAT WANDERFULL: Did Annie start preschool?

MRCUSTOM: Yes. She goes on Monday, Wednesday,
    and Friday mornings. She loves it and already has
    fifteen new best friends.

KAT WANDERFULL: Of course she does. She's easy to
    love. I miss her.

MRCUSTOM: She misses you, too. We have all your
    postcards on the fridge. I reread them to her every
    night, and we look up the location on her kid's
    globe.

KAT WANDERFULL: How are you, Robbie?

The truth itched his fingers. *I'm waiting for you. It's as if
the world stopped turning the day we parted. Come home?*

MRCUSTOM: I'm good. I started my business. We broke
    ground on Teddy Woodward's house up the
    mountain above the highway.

KAT WANDERFULL: REALLY?!

MRCUSTOM: Yeah. I said I didn't want his home to be
    my guinea pig. He said they have enough money
    that if I mess it up, they can pay me to fix it later. I'm
    currently in the process of hiring teams for the
    various projects.

KAT WANDERFULL: I'm so proud of you.

MRCUSTOM: Are you serious? We're the ones who are proud of you. The whole Matthews clan.
KAT WANDERFULL: Aww. I miss your family.

So she missed Anabelle. She missed his family. But did—

KAT WANDERFULL: I miss you, too, Robbie.

Robbie sat back in the chair. He placed a hand on his breastbone, trying to contain the swelling of his heart. For three months, he'd imagined those words. He didn't dare hope they'd ever come.

MRCUSTOM: I miss you, Kat. A ton. Now, tell me about the show.

Three dots appeared, then disappeared. That pattern repeated several times.

KAT WANDERFULL: I shouldn't answer that now. I had a bad night.
MRCUSTOM: Did something happen?
KAT WANDERFULL: Nothing happened. We all went out to a club. Wasn't my scene, so Isaac walked me back to my hotel room.

Pain knifed Robbie's left temple. He squeezed his eyes closed.

KAT WANDERFULL: Working on this show . . . It's not what I expected it to be.
MRCUSTOM: How so?
KAT WANDERFULL: Sometimes I miss the simplicity of traveling around the US, understanding the

language, serving the communities, going to
church.

MRCUSTOM: Aren't you almost done with the season?

KAT WANDERFULL: Yeah, we have one more stop. The
Galápagos Islands!

MRCUSTOM: Whoa! Your dream come true.

KAT WANDERFULL: I know, right?! We leave tomorrow. I
wish you could be there with me. My world is much
smaller without you and Anabelle in it.

Robbie's fingers stilled. He could tell her how much he
loved her. How much he wished she'd return to him. But
this was her choice, and he wouldn't try to sway her. No,
this was between her and God.

MRCUSTOM: You need to get some sleep.

KAT WANDERFULL: Don't go. There's something I need
to know.

MRCUSTOM: What's that?

KAT WANDERFULL: What did the unicorn say to his
cousin, the horse? You never told me the punch line
when we were at Royal Village. It's been bugging
me ever since.

MRCUSTOM: I'd tell you, but there's no point.

KAT WANDERFULL: That's terrible. Wait. One more
thing. Back in May, why were you at John's
proposal? I've always wondered but was too
chicken to ask. There's no way you would have
gone if you knew what was happening.

MRCUSTOM: Anabelle and I had gone to see a movie.
And don't laugh, but I've always had this sense
when you're near. I know it sounds like a bunch of
hocus-pocus, but it's true. Maybe it's because
you're my soul mate, if such a thing exists. But I felt

the hair stand up on my arm. Then I saw the crowd.

I decided to check it out. Do you think I'm strange?

KAT WANDERFULL: Yes. But that's nothing new, is it?

MRCUSTOM: Guess not. Sweet dreams, Kat.

Keira stared at the phone screen long after the green dot on his picture disappeared. She felt more centered than she had in weeks. Such was the effect he had on her. She fell back on the bed, and the duvet fluffed up around her like a cloud. Like a turtle-shaped cloud. A stitch of exhilaration niggled her. She sat up and repeated the motion. This time, the tiniest laugh slipped past her lips.

Oh, why not?

Keira pushed herself into a standing position on the bed. The duvet puddled around her feet. She bent her knees and allowed herself to spring up, not quite getting air between her soles and the sheets. She glanced around.

The bed hadn't busted through the floor after all.

She jumped higher this time, feeling a rush surge in her belly. She clapped a hand over her mouth to catch her giggle, while she waited for someone to pound on the door and demand she keep it down.

No one came.

And so she leaped again and again until she was bouncing around the bed in a haphazard circle. Not for Robbie. Not for Anabelle, either.

But for herself.

CHAPTER FORTY-THREE

The rickety stairs from Keira's cabin to Therese's hair-and-makeup tent cut through the lush forest of Isla Santa Cruz. Keira climbed them, holding the itty-bitty bikini on its hanger. She wasn't sure who had decided she should wear these strings to go scuba diving tomorrow, but it wasn't a friend of hers. Sure, she looked good in it. The extra protein, healthy carbohydrates, and regular exercise had added muscle to Keira's skeleton and enough flesh to bring her curves back. More than that, Keira's stomach didn't growl relentlessly anymore, and her thoughts no longer centered around phrases like *calorie deficits*. She felt strong and beautiful in her body, but that didn't mean she wanted to hand it over for others' viewing pleasure.

A canvas curtain had been drawn across the doors.

Keira climbed the last of the steps slowly, feeling the burn in her legs. "Hey, Therese. I'd rather have a one-piece or scuba suit for tomorrow's shoot."

No response.

Keira pulled back the curtain a bit to peer in. "I've got to stand by my convictions and—" Inside, as Keira's pupils adjusted to the dimmed light, she made out a figure in a chair.

The person had short hair, cropped close to the scalp, and a narrow set of shoulders. One hand covered her face. The other fanned over her nape.

"Margot?"

Keira's former idol remained silent.

Only the hoarse whistle of a blue-footed booby outside filled the air. Then footsteps came from the bathroom. Therese appeared, holding a wig—Margot's wig—and a brush.

When Therese saw Keira, the brush dropped and clattered on the teak floor. Her eyes went to Margot next. "Oh no. Margot, I didn't—"

The hand that had been covering her face jutted out, fingers stretched wide, halting Therese's next words. Slowly, both of Margot's hands lowered. She reached over and flicked on the makeup lamps and then swiveled her chair to face the mirror. In the reflection, she blinked several times. Finally, her stare steadied on Keira. "Cancer. Last year."

"I'm s-sorry. I didn't know."

"Not many did. Except my doctors, Therese, and Phil. Everyone else simply thought I was too stubborn to show up to work."

"Would you like me to tell them?"

"No." The word was harsh enough to silence the booby outside.

"Between you and me, I'd rather they all think I'm a witch than weak."

"You aren't weak. You were sick. Are you okay now?"

"I'm in remission. I still get some intravenous supplements once in a while. In Kodiak, Brussels, Johannesburg."

"Oh, Margot. You could've told me."

"And see that look of pity? No, thank you." Margot swept the short dark hair to the side of her forehead. "You think you were brought on because you're better than me?"

Keira steeled herself. Margot's sharp tongue could give

a grand lashing. But that's all it was—her lashing out. In her life, Keira had heard worse.

"Get real, honey." She spit the words at Keira's reflection. Then Margot's eyes fell to her hands. "But, in time, when the big C returns and claims me, you, of all the people that I've seen and met, have the fortitude and faith to carry *Traveling Light* to a new, more transcendent place."

"I don't understand."

Margot scoffed. "Don't you get it? I was the one who hired you. After I'm gone, you will surely keep this show alive. It's my life's work. My baby. I've given everything to this show. If it goes to the grave with me, my life will have meant nothing."

Keira moved closer. After a hesitation, she placed a hand on Margot's shoulder. "Not true. You inspire people to live their best, most adventurous life. For me, when I was trapped in an abusive home as a child, you gave me hope that there was a bigger world out there. That if I could hold on for another day, maybe I could see it for myself. Besides, maybe the cancer won't come back."

"Recurrent epithelial ovarian. Prognosis isn't good."

"Okay. So, if it comes back, you'll fight it off again. You're one of the toughest people I've ever known. Cancer's got nothing on Margot Jorgensen."

Margot tousled her wisps of hair.

"You look beautiful. Like a brunette Mia Farrow." Keira's eyes flickered to the wig in Therese's hand. "Remember what you said about showing the viewers the real me. Perhaps you should follow your own advice. Invite others to share this journey with you. Teach those viewers who are watching from hospital beds and clinics that they can still use each blessed heartbeat well."

Margot rolled her eyes. "You're young. What do you know?"

"I know that the Lord has a purpose for your life. And

the hope and peace he offers lasts longer than momentary adventures and fleeting pleasures."

"Don't you have somewhere to be, 'Kat Wanderfull'?" She snapped her fingers at Therese, who promptly began fitting the wig to Margot's scalp. "I'll see you on set." With a wave of Margot's hand, Keira was dismissed.

Hey, everyone! I'm Keira, and today I'm at the Galápagos Animal Sanctuary, a breeding and rescue organization helping to keep the wildlife of the islands healthy and thriving." Keira focused in on the camera. "I'm going to let you in on a secret. I'm about to fulfill a lifelong dream of mine—meeting a Galápagos tortoise! I make no promises of how I'll act when I do." Keira crossed the dirt yard to where a man in head-to-toe khaki crouched by a giant tortoise. "This is TJ, the director of the sanctuary. Hi, TJ. Thanks for letting us come here today."

"Anytime. I've been a fan of yours for some time now." TJ might have blushed a little bit. He wasn't unattractive, but Keira had learned her lesson about being too friendly with men she worked with.

"Thanks! Who's this guy?"

"This is Mack, a Galápagos tortoise. Now he's only about two hundred pounds, but they can get up to five hundred fifty pounds." TJ continued rambling facts.

Keira only partially heard what he was saying. She ran her hand over Mack's shell.

The tortoise twisted his head to peer at Keira, then returned to his lunch of leaves.

"Watch how far Mack can extend his neck for food." TJ held up the branch as he explained a tortoise's typical diet in the wild and in captivity. "Now, while his neck is extended, you can pet him right under the chin. He'll love that."

Keira obeyed, feeling an Anabelle-esque giggle rise in her throat as she stroked the scales covering Mack's neck. Keira peered closer at the animal's head. "TJ, do tortoises have ears?"

"Actually, tortoises have something that sets them apart from every other class of animal. That is the otic capsule right here." He pointed to a darker spot on either side of the tortoise's head. "The otic capsule is a bony box that holds the eardrum. Vibrations travel up the legs, through the shell . . ."

Keira's chin snapped up to the camera. She stared deep into the lens until her eyes burned. Oh, what she'd give to see Robbie and Anabelle's faces in that black circle. "Kitty Kat," she said. "Turtles do have ears." Her vision blurred.

Something tickled her cheek, then fell. A tiny, dark starburst appeared on Mack's shell. Then another.

Keira grazed the heel of her hand against her jawline, finding it wet with tears.

"Hey, you doin' all right?" TJ asked.

Keira looked up at him, then around at her crew, who stood stone-still watching her make a mess of herself on camera.

Phil did a hand motion, cueing her to move the segment along.

"I'm more than all right. I just realized something." Keira patted Mack's shell gently. "I don't belong here."

"Uh, at the animal sanctuary?" TJ looked confused.

"On this show." Keira sniffled and wiped her cheeks before returning her gaze to the camera. "Adventures like these are great, but they are even better when you get to share the experience with those you love. The Galápagos Islands are a fantastic place for a family vacation. There are many activities perfect for kids of all ages. And when you come, make sure you stop by the Galápagos Animal Sanctuary and say hello to Mack and TJ."

After Phil called cut, he motioned for Keira to join him. "We need to redo that. It was awkward with the tears and rambling to people who aren't even here."

"I think you should call Margot in for the retakes. And she'll have to film the remaining segments on the islands."

"What? Why?"

"Because I'm going home. I thought this was my dream, but I was wrong. This is Margot's dream. She's the star of *Traveling Light*. Not me."

CHAPTER FORTY-FOUR

A few minutes before the final custody hearing was scheduled to begin, Robbie drummed his fingers against his leg. This time he'd dressed to the nines, at least to the extent he could afford to, meaning he'd borrowed Drew's "funeral" suit.

Meanwhile, Vivian's legal team bumped up the sophistication of the courtroom by a good ten points. Lex, the lead counselor, was all business in his fancy suit. The guy probably had more than one. Vivian also looked like a femme fatale in her pin-striped pantsuit and spiffy hairstyle cut in a sharp line at her jaw. But instead of a hard glare, her eyes darted about the room. She grasped her husband's hand. In response, Eric planted a kiss on her forehead.

The seats behind them were empty. Vivian hadn't had a good family life back when they'd been together. Apparently, her friends were as faithful as her family.

A twinge of pity struck him, especially when he compared her support to his.

Behind Robbie, everyone he loved awaited the judge's arrival. His parents, Ryann, and all his friends packed the three rows. The only people missing were Anabelle, who was getting waffles with Sylvia and Olive down the street, and Kat, who was in the Galápagos on her last day of filming. Selfishly, he wished she was here. Either to celebrate his victory or help him figure out how he'd live only seeing Anabelle a few days a month.

Of course, she was not here. And even after filming wrapped, she planned to return to Twin Falls instead of West Yellowstone. What the future held after that was anyone's guess. He hadn't been able to think past this date on his wall calendar.

Allowing his eyelids to shut out the harsh lights of the courtroom, he puffed out his cheeks and let out a mighty breath. *Lord, may your will for Anabelle's life be done. Protect her and don't ever let her doubt how many people love her.*

Suddenly, the air in the room changed. It warmed, and the pressure lessened, like storm clouds dissipating enough to let a beam of heavenly light through. The hair on Robbie's forearms raised.

He lifted his gaze to the door and found Keira, in the flesh.

The rest of the world melted away as he leaped over the bar, darted to the back of the room, then swept Keira up in his arms. Even as he held her, he wondered whether he was caught in a dream. He buried his nose in her hair and inhaled, filling his lungs with the faint melon scent of her shampoo. "You're here."

She drew back her shoulders and placed her palm against his heart. "I'm home."

"For good?"

"My contract was so flimsy in describing my guest-hosting role that I was able to leave a few days early. This morning, Phil called and offered me the full-time hosting job for next season. I said no."

Her words should have made him rejoice. Instead, they caked his insides with dread. He stroked her hair behind her ear. "You shouldn't have given up your dream for us."

Lightly, she pounded her fist against his chest and smiled. "I didn't. I did it for me. That dream served its purpose. It got me through some of the most difficult times of my life. I've realized that I'm strong enough to do anything and go anywhere completely on my own. But, Robbie, I don't want to. It's time for a new dream. One where I don't have to choose between the things I love and the people I love. Whatever that new dream is, I want to make it with you. I love you."

"And I love you, Kat." He tilted his head down, unwilling to let this moment pass without sealing it with a kiss. Gentle. Sweet. Innocent. And lingering. His lips refused to withdraw from hers. Someone poked him in the back.

He waved them off.

"Robbie, it's time," Cassie hissed from behind him.

Finally, he pulled back and met Keira's eyes.

"To be continued," Keira whispered. "Now, go fight for your girl."

"Please rise," the bailiff said.

Robbie hurried back to his seat, this time using the gate. He'd already given Judge Keller enough reason to find him reckless. He stepped behind the table as the judge entered the courtroom.

"You may be seated."

Judge Keller reintroduced the basics of the case. "I have before me the original parenting plan proposed by the petitioner, Vivian Cartwright, the answer to parenting plan by the co-petitioner, Robert Matthews, and the child custody evaluations performed on both the mother of the child and the father of the child. Quite a lot has happened since we last met, hasn't it, Mr. Matthews?"

The flags on either side of Judge Keller seemed to waver, despite the stale air in the room.

"Yes, sir."

"I'd like to hear the position of both petitioners regarding how they believe physical and legal custody of Anabelle Matthews should be divided. We'll start with the counsel representing Vivian Cartwright."

Lex was ruthless in his accusations. Each aspect of Robbie's life was called into question. His impulsivity, finances, lack of intellect, and unsafe living conditions were specifically highlighted. At least they left his family out of it. The most significant charge against him, of course, was his poor decision-making. The missing persons report he'd filed in Alaska was submitted as evidence.

Judge Keller read through the report, occasionally looking down his nose at Robbie. He clicked his tongue. "Counselor for Mr. Matthews, you may present your case."

Cassie rose from her seat with confidence. "Your Honor, the accusations against my client are based on lies and halftruths. Mr. Matthews is a dedicated, capable father. As the sole custodian of Anabelle for over four years, he has cared for her, provided her with a suitable loving and educational environment, and encouraged faith and family values. As you can see in my client's answer to the proposed parenting plan, Mr. Matthews is supportive of Anabelle spending time with her birth mother, even though she had been abandoned by Mrs. Cartwright shortly after birth. The plan he proposes is moderate, while Mrs. Cartwright's plan is extreme. I urge the court to remember that, according to Montana state custody laws, the most important concern is the best interest of the child."

"I don't need to be reminded of that, Counselor."

"Yes, Your Honor."

"Mrs. Cartwright, what was your relationship with Mr. Matthews like?"

"There was no relationship," Vivian said.

"But you shared a residence, did you not?"

"We were roommates. Nothing more."

"Mrs. Cartwright, during the pregnancy, did Mr. Matthews attend any doctor appointments, ultrasounds, or birthing classes with you?"

"Yes, sir."

"What percentage would you say?"

There was silence. Finally, Vivian answered. "Every one."

"Was he present for the delivery of the child?"

"Yes, sir."

"Who would you say covered the majority of the child-care responsibilities after the child was born?"

"Probably him."

"How old was the child when you moved out of the home?"

"Around nine weeks old."

Robbie pinched his eyes shut. *Seven weeks, five days, and about two hours old.*

"What was your reasoning?"

Again, Vivian didn't answer.

Several moments went by.

Lex stepped in. "The child seemed to have colic and acid reflux in her infancy. She had difficulty eating and sleeping and cried most of the day. It is also likely that my client suffered from postpartum depression at the time."

"That's a hard road by all accounts. Was the child under a doctor's care for her medical issues?"

"Yes, sir," Vivian said.

"Mrs. Cartwright, did you seek treatment or counseling for your postpartum depression?"

"No, I did not."

"And tell me, Mrs. Cartwright, between the time your

child was nine weeks old and four years old, how many times did you seek contact with her?"

"Zero times."

"What possible reason kept you away so long?"

"I was waiting until I was in a better position to mother her. As you can see in the child custody evaluation, I can now offer Anabelle a much more secure life than she's ever known."

"Thank you, Mrs. Cartwright. Mr. Matthews, would you please explain to me what occurred on the evening of July 12 in Denali National Park."

Robbie cleared his throat. "I was working as an assistant on a television show. Anabelle was being watched by the show's intern, and she wandered into the forest. She was missing for five hours before she was found, unharmed."

"Did you know, at the time, that by reporting your child missing to the police your parenting rights may be put in jeopardy?"

"Yes, sir. But I would have done anything for her to be safe."

"It's my understanding that on that show, you were an assistant for Keira Knudsen. You and Ms. Knudsen have quite a history, don't you?"

"Yes, sir."

"But still, you quit that job and came back to West Yellowstone after the Denali incident. Interesting. I hear you've recently started a custom home-building business. I have a letter here from Teddy Woodward—"

The crowd murmured.

"—stating that you are building his luxury home, and you have contracts on two others. You're doing pretty well, aren't you?"

"I'd like to think so."

"His isn't the only letter my office has received. We've

been inundated. No less than nineteen letters from folks in the community. Each one paints you as an upstanding man of faith and a good father. Several state you often don't accept payment for the work you've done while fixing up people's homes. That's either extremely dumb . . ." Judge Keller paused to shuffle the letters, allowing for the cheap, familiar insult to burrow into Robbie's head. ". . . or valiant."

One of the wooden benches behind Robbie creaked. The bailiff stifled a cough with his elbow.

All eyes fell on the judge while he scrutinized the paperwork long enough for the sweat to suction Robbie's dress shirt to his chest. After this, he had half a mind to strip off this death suit and plunge into the Madison headfirst.

Keller shifted in his leather chair. The man's laser focus lifted to Robbie, then Keira. Back to Robbie again. He closed the folder and rapped his knuckles on it.

"I've considered the evidence and the testimonies of the co-petitioners. From what I've seen, one of these petitioners has shown a commitment to parenting despite hard times, a dedication to the best interest of the child even if it requires sacrifice, and a history of protecting those he loves. Robert Matthews, I have no doubt that if your child is ever in harm's way, you will risk life and limb to save her." Again, Keller glanced at Keira, then back to Robbie. "Your courage and fortitude are, and always have been, exemplary."

Robbie's breath left him.

"It is my decision that there will be joint legal and physical custody of one Anabelle Matthews by Vivian Cartwright and Robert Matthews. Monday through Friday, she will reside in her primary residence with her father. Saturday and Sunday, she will reside with her mother."

The closing statement by the judge got lost in the whirl of emotions turning Robbie inside out.

Someone hugged his neck from behind.

He didn't know who until the wild red curls of his sister tickled his cheek.

On his right, Cassie nodded with her quaint arrogance.

Once they were dismissed, he hugged his mother and father. Off to the side, Keira waited, with that coy look on her face. Robbie sat on the bar and swung his legs over. Once he stood, she hugged him.

"You did it."

"I'm glad you were here with me." Over the top of Keira's head, Robbie spied her grandparents and her mother standing against the back wall.

Even in the courtroom light, Claire glowed. She looked healthy and happy for the first time since Robbie had known her. The rumor was that Joshua Knudsen had been served divorce papers but immediately tore them to pieces.

"Did your family drive you here?"

"Yeah, they picked me up at the airport and drove me straight over."

"You took the red-eye?"

"Why else would I look this terrible?"

"You'll always be beautiful to me, Kat." He laced his fingers through the hidden section of her hair. "Even with tangles in your hair and bags under your eyes." He lowered his head to hers.

Her lips, like the rest of her face, were bare. And they fit perfectly to his. Forever and always.

"Only you two could make a courtroom romantic. Let's go celebrate." Ryann stood at the end of the row. Everyone else had already filtered out. Almost everyone.

Vivian remained in her seat, alone.

"Kat, why don't you go on out? I'm going to talk to Vivian a minute."

"Sure," Keira said.

Ryann put her arm around Keira's shoulder. Together, they strolled through the door, sisters.

Releasing a silent prayer to the Lord above, Robbie waited until the door closed. What could he say to Vivian after she tried to rip his daughter away?

Grace. Speak grace.

"Anabelle loves you. Do you know that?" he asked.

She folded her hands over her face.

"She's always telling me about the way you brush her hair real carefully. How you paint her nails and take her to get rainbow milk, whatever that is, at the coffee shop."

"That's not love."

"It is to her."

"She's never said it."

Robbie leaned against her table. "Did you know that her first word was *Mama*? Somewhere deep inside, she missed you."

Vivian's scoff echoed off the barren walls. With her shoulders sagging, she leaned back, and the chair creaked a sound of surrender. "I shouldn't have left. But you loved her so much. You'd get this dopey look on your face whenever you'd feel her move inside my belly. You never looked at me that way. Then, even when she was crying and kicking her little legs because her tummy hurt, you'd still hold her against your chest and kind of dance with her. You never once asked me to dance."

Guilt compressed Robbie's lungs. During the hardest time of her life, she'd needed a friend, and he'd failed her. "I'm sorry, Vivian. It couldn't have been easy for you."

"What? To watch you love our daughter and your ex-girlfriend, but not me? No, it wasn't easy. What was so wrong with me?"

"Nothing, Viv," Robbie said. "Nothing was wrong with

you. It's just that Keira and me? We're right together. I look at her the same way Eric looks at you. Man, that guy thinks the world of you."

Vivian's lip twitched. "I don't deserve him. Or Anabelle."

"That's the thing about grace. It's most appreciated by the ones who deserve it the least. I know that more than anyone. My family has plans for a grand feast back at the resort. I want you and Eric there. Anabelle will want her Vivian there."

"After all I've put you through?"

"Absolutely. You aren't my enemy, Viv. And I'm not yours." Robbie stood and held out his hand to her. "Come on. We've got a little girl to raise."

Vivian gave the hand a suspicious glance, as if it might electrocute her on the spot.

He'd have to earn her trust and respect, but he was game for the challenge.

The door opened. Keira peeked in. "Someone wants to see you both."

"You can send her in," Robbie said.

Keira opened the door farther. She held Anabelle in her arms.

The moment the little girl saw Vivian, she beamed.

Keira lowered her feet to the floor, and the courtroom filled with the delightful sound of tiny dress shoes clapping against the tile as Anabelle ran to them.

Robbie lifted her over the gate and handed her to Vivian.

"Oof. You're getting so big!"

"That's because I ate a whole waffle. Guess what." Anabelle cupped her hand by Vivian's ear and began to whisper-shout. "We're going home to have a party. Nana and Papa are going, Grandma, Grandpa, Ryann, Thomas, and Mommy Kat."

Vivian pinched her eyes closed at the sound of Keira's nickname.

"Daddy, can Mama and Eric come to the party, too?" Anabelle pressed her cheek against Vivian's. "Please."

Mama.

Tears filled Vivian's eyes.

For the first time, Robbie could see a bit of Vivian in Anabelle. The shape of the nose and chin maybe. "If they want to," he said.

Vivian took a moment. Finally composed, she looked Anabelle in the eye. "Mama would like that very much."

EPILOGUE

꧁

A nd this one is from Nana and Papa." Keira placed the present in front of Anabelle. Its shimmering pink wrapping paper reflected the colors of the Christmas tree. Keira's grandmother had spent a half hour wrapping it, and yet Anabelle shredded the paper in seconds.

She pulled open the flaps of the white box and lifted a handful of candies like the ones she devoured at their general store that day back in June. The laugh that ricocheted out of Anabelle was equal parts maniacal and victorious.

"The next time I come to visit you, I'm having a word with your grandparents," Robbie said.

"It won't do any good. Anabelle has them wrapped around her pinkie." Keira tucked her feet beneath her as she reclaimed her spot on the couch beneath Robbie's arm. So far, this had been the best Christmas morning ever. After spending the night in Ryann's cabin, she'd snuck into Robbie's early enough to see Anabelle open her first present.

Robbie pulled her tight against him. "I'm surprised they didn't ask you to spend Christmas with them."

"They know what you and Annie mean to me. Plus, they have my mom with them. Robbie, you should see her now.

She's fully alive. She and Papa even crack jokes together. And she's pretty much running their store. She may even get her own place."

"That's awesome. I still can't believe your father signed the divorce papers. Last week I heard that Judge Keller had a talk with him and strongly recommended he not press his luck."

Keira shrugged. "Maybe that means he won't try anything. Against my family, you, or the resort."

"If he does, we'll handle it," Robbie said. "Hey, Kitty Kat, no candy till after brunch, okay?"

"No fair." In a move that could only be described as jellyfishy, Anabelle flopped backward and rolled in a half circle.

"She may have gotten into her stocking before you got here," Robbie said.

"That explains a lot."

"Knock, knock." Ryann let herself into Robbie's cabin. She was balancing three presents in front of her face. "Merry Christmas!"

"Merry Christmas, Ry. Oh, were you expecting a present from us?" Robbie scratched his head.

Kneeling, she placed the stack of presents beneath the tree. "You better have gotten me a present. I'm the best sister you've got. Plus, I've let Keira share my cabin every time she visits your ugly mug."

"Actually, Ry, I did get you a present. It's a mail-order husband from the East. He'll be here on the next wagon train."

"Hardy-har-har. You know how I love the old Ryann-needs-a-new-husband bit."

"New husband? Nah, I got you a used husband. It was way cheaper. But don't worry. His prison guards say he's well trained."

"Aren't you hilarious? I see my actual present right there. We'll open them later. Right now, Annie and I have to go help Dad with brunch."

Keira started to stand. "We can help—"

"No, we aren't quite done yet." With a tug, Robbie pulled her down onto his lap.

Her body melted against his. She breathed him in. A touch of pine, huckleberry, and all-American male.

"That's our cue. Let's go, Annie. I'll get your coat and boots." Ryann and Anabelle dashed to the foyer.

In the minute it took Anabelle to dress for the Montana winter, Robbie's eyes had roved all across Keira's face and down her neck. Every inch of her grew hot under his adoration.

How had they dated for five years during high school and college and kept within the boundaries they'd set? Sometimes, when she lay in her bed at her grandparents' house, thoughts of him drove her mad. Alas, none of the presents remaining beneath the tree were shaped like a ring box. What was he waiting for anyway?

Dora had encouraged Keira to ask Robbie to marry her. After all, running down a dream was the EndeavHerMore— and Tom Petty—way. Keira had considered it. But deep down, she was still traditional at heart.

"I forgot to tell you," she said. "I got a Christmas card from Margot. Apparently, she took off her wig during the Galápagos episode. She got real, right in front of the camera. I cannot wait to watch it when the episode airs."

The blast of cold marked the opening and closing of the front door. Quiet drifted over the cabin. Robbie's lips found the hollow of her neck.

"And get this? She and Phil are dating. Margot blames me. Says I've ruined her life. Next thing you know, she'll be going to church. Are you even listening to me?"

"Yes. It's my lips that are preoccupied, not my ears."

A rumbling noise sounded from outside. "What's that?" she asked.

"I didn't hear anything." He took to her lips.

For several minutes, she allowed herself to relish his kisses, so deep they seemed to touch her soul.

Maybe traditional was overrated. "Um, I was thinking." Breath eluded her, and she gasped between each word. "These past couple of months in Twin Falls have been nice. But my mom's settled now. Maybe it's time I come back here."

Robbie stilled. "And stay at Ryann's?"

"Yes. Actually, no. It's been a while since we've talked about what's ahead for us. Robbie, I want you. And Anabelle. I want us to be—"

"Hold that thought." He jumped up, bucking her onto the couch like a rag doll. On the mantel behind the tree, there was a present wrapped in red that she hadn't noticed until now. He took it and stared at it for the longest time. Finally, he brought it to her.

To Kat Wanderfull, From MRCustom, the tag read.

Willing her hands not to shake, she pulled the wrapping paper off the box.

It wasn't a ring box. No, this box was larger. Like a garment box from a department store.

She lifted the lid and placed it next to her on the sofa. As if turning a page in a book, she unfolded a sheet of white tissue paper, then another. "My atlas? When did you get this?"

"I had Ryann sneak it from your satchel last night while we were watching *It's a Wonderful Life*. She brought it over after you were asleep."

"You two are so mischievous. How did your mother ever handle you?" Her fingertip skimmed the top spine to a bookmark protruding an inch. She cracked the book, careful not to disrupt the pages and their memories. "Arizona?"

Pinned between Arizona's two pages, the bookmark wasn't a bookmark at all, but a ticket for the train she, Robbie, and Anabelle had taken near the Grand Canyon on their way back from California.

"I added some memories from our trips," Robbie said.

She flipped to California. Her eyes landed on the braided leather cord with a silver infinity charm. "My Yosemite bracelet."

Robbie shrugged his shoulders. "I may or may not have broken into the school over the summer to get that back."

"I'm glad you did. Thank you." She slipped her hand through the bracelet. Beneath that, she found a yellow feather and a Royal Village unicorn tea packet. "Okay, I get the tea. What's the feather about?"

"Remember when I destroyed Prince Devin in the push-up contest? The feather on his hat fell on the ground. It was still lying there when we passed by the spot on the way out, so I grabbed it. Now you can always remember who's the best."

"I don't need a feather to remember that, silly." Keira stole a kiss before returning her attention to the gift.

"Go to Montana's page next."

Of all the states, Montana had received more than its fair share of attention. Its stacks of Post-it notes in a variety of colors and shapes created a gap in the fore edge of the book. She flipped to it easily.

She noticed an arrow-shaped marker pointing to West Yellowstone on the map. Along the Madison River, a blue star had been drawn. *A blue star.* Joy flooded Keira's veins, and her cheeks blazed. She focused on the note pinned to the opposite page. After slipping the paper clip off carefully, she handed the paper to him. "Read it to me?"

"Yes, ma'am." He settled back against the couch cushion and lifted his arm.

Happily, she lay against him, her hand on his chest so she could feel the vibrations of the words he spoke.

My dearest Kat, this is not a love letter. I won't tell you how much joy you bring me, or how often I think about you, or how many prayers I've prayed for you. I won't tell you how I wish I could kiss you every day. I won't tell you how I long for the day when I can call you my wife. And I certainly won't tell you how I cannot wait to wake up next to you, fall asleep with you in my arms, and everything that will happen in between.

He quirked his brow, and heat rose in her cheeks.

I will tell you that I'm proud of all you've accomplished. You set a goal, and you achieved it. Although I understand why you aren't willing to chase your dreams to the ends of the earth, I still see that glimmer in your eye when you see an airplane, a train, or a simple road map. What kind of man would I be if I didn't at least try to bring your dreams to you? Your final present from me is waiting outside.

Keira bolted upright on the sofa. "Really?"

At his nod, she climbed up and over the couch.

She flung open the front door to see a recreational vehicle the size of a semi. She turned to Robbie, but he was on the floor holding her boot out to her. She peppered him with questions as she slipped her boots on and waited for him to do the same.

"I'll answer those questions inside." He led her across the crusted snow and held the door as she climbed inside. "Right after the hearing, I was thinking out loud to Teddy Woodward. You know how he has more money and power than, like, all the people in Hollywood combined? He had an idea."

Inside the RV, everything was smooth, shiny, or soft. This was luxury, from the kitchen's countertops to the leather seats in the cab.

"You said you miss your days as Kat Wanderfull, right?"

She nodded.

"I have a proposal for you."

"What's that?"

"This beast goes into storage for a few months, then in April, on the weekends, when Anabelle is with Vivian, you and I will travel around this region." He tapped a small camera above the television. "Our adventures will be captured by cameras like these and a small crew of cameramen. Have you ever heard of Seek?"

"Yeah, it's a small, independently owned multimedia company that focuses on travel."

"Teddy bought it. He wants to record our relationship and our travels and broadcast them to the world. Kind of like a reality show, but we get full say in the content. You know how you've been wanting to tutor students with dyslexia? You can do that during the week while I manage my home-building business. Then we'll hit the road every Friday night. And as Anabelle gets older, or in the summer when Vivian gets her for a couple of weeks, we can take this thing cross-country."

"What you're saying is I get to have my cake and eat it, too?"

"If I'm cake in that metaphor, then yeah, I guess so."

Keira ran her hand over the love seat. She passed by the dinette, refrigerator, and small bathroom, then opened the door to the bedroom and peered in. "There's only one problem with this idea."

"What's that?"

"There's only one bed."

"Funny you should say that." Robbie moved closer and ran his hands from her shoulders to her fingertips.

Keira gathered her next words from behind her pattering heart. "Maybe our first stop should be at a place with a little white chapel."

"Great minds think alike. But why wait till April?" He kissed Keira, long and slow, until she desperately wished they had a pastor on the property right now. To her dismay, he pulled away from her embrace to knock on the next door. It opened to show a full bathroom, with toilet, sink, shower, and Ryann and Anabelle. After Anabelle crossed the threshold, Ryann grinned and closed the door once again, excluding herself from what might happen next.

Anabelle blushed and shrank against Robbie's leg.

"Don't be shy," Robbie said. "Go ahead and say it."

Anabelle held out a fist.

Keira kneeled down to her eye level. She uncurled each of Anabelle's fingers to reveal a platinum ring with intricate designs surrounding the diamond. His great-grandmother's.

"Will you marry Daddy?"

A joy like she'd never experienced surged within her. She clapped a hand over her mouth while her eyes filled with tears.

Then Robbie grasped her hand and lifted her up. He bent his face down to hers. "Ever since I was seventeen, I've only ever had one dream. To love, honor, and cherish you for the rest of my life. Will you make that come true and take me as your husband?"

"Yes. A million times yes!" She laughed and swiped at the tears spilling down her cheeks. Good tears. An overflow of happiness when her body couldn't possibly hold any more.

He slipped the ring on her left hand.

Keira gazed into Robbie's eyes. "Mrs. Keira Matthews. I like the sound of that, don't you?"

"You know you don't have to take my name—"

"I'd be honored to."

Robbie smirked. "It's certainly better than Mr. Robbie Wanderfull."

She cringed. "That might be slightly over-the-top."

"Maybe a bit. But you know I'd do it. For you." He gentled a tendril of her hair between his fingers. "I'm yours, Kat, forever and always."

His lips brushed hers, as soft as the flutter of a butterfly's wings.

A small arm circled her leg. Beneath her, Anabelle's green eyes crinkled. One side of her lips pulled up higher than the other. It was a new smile for her. Yet familiar. And goofy. Keira lifted her chin and caught her own crooked grin in the mirror above the RV's built-in dresser.

"I think she has your smile." Robbie picked up Anabelle, holding her against his side with one arm and tugging Keira close with his other.

"Funny. I was just thinking the same thing."

"My girls." He kissed Anabelle's forehead, then Keira's. "You sure you're up for this happy family gig?"

"Absolutely," Keira said, resting her hand on Anabelle's curls. "Life with the two of you is sure to be my greatest adventure yet."

Ready to find
your next great read?

Let us help.

Visit prh.com/nextread

Penguin
Random
House